The Ghostmaker

The Ghostmaker

Victor Davis

VICTOR GOLLANCZ
LONDON

First published in Great Britain 1996
by Victor Gollancz
An imprint of the Cassell Group
Wellington House, 125 Strand, London WC2R 0BB

© Victor Davis 1996

The right of Victor Davis to be identified as author of this work has been asserted by him in accordance with the Copyright, Designs and Patents Act, 1988.

A catalogue record for this book is available from the British library.

ISBN 0 575 06314 9

Extract from *Zen in the Art of Archery* by Eugen Herrigel, translated by R.F.C. Hull (Arkana 1985). Translation copyright © 1953 by Routledge and Kegan Paul. Reproduced by permission of Penguin Books Ltd.

Typeset by CentraCet Ltd, Cambridge

Printed in Great Britain by St Edmundsbury Press Ltd
Bury St Edmunds, Suffolk

All rights reserved. No part of this publication may be reproduced or transmitted in any form or by any means, electronic or mechanical including photocopying, recording or any information storage or retrieval system, without prior permission in writing from the publishers.

This book is sold subject to the condition that it shall not, by way of trade or otherwise, be lent, resold, hired out, or otherwise circulated without the publisher's prior consent in any form of binding or cover other than that in which it is published and without a similar condition including this condition being imposed on the subsequent purchaser.

96 97 98   5 4 3 2 1

For Janice James

*The wires touch his face: I cry NOW.
Death, like a familiar, hears
And, look, has made a man of dust
Of a man of flesh. This sorcery I do.
. . . How easy it is to make a ghost.*

>From 'How to Kill' by Keith
Douglas (*Complete Poems*, ed.
Desmond Graham, OUP, 1978)

My short experience of the secret world had long ago convinced me that supervision was illusory. The spies weave and duck and cover their traces, which is what people of their calling are paid to do. And their supposed gamekeepers become so enamoured of their charges that they turn poacher overnight.

John Le Carré

Chapter One

He contrived, as usual, to be on the platform at six fifteen, edging through the knots of homegoing City stragglers, the wine-bar happy-hour crowd, and the creeps who never switch off their desk lights until the office gauleiter has left for the day.

She was there, as usual, at the far end. He assumed she aligned herself with the leading coach because it came to a stop opposite the exit at her destination – wherever that was. He deduced that she was not careless with her time.

He had never discovered where she got off because his own route ran only from St Paul's to Shepherd's Bush, eleven stops straight as a thrusting bayonet under West London.

What *was* her destination? Did she go on beyond the Bush? Why could he never remember?

Weaving his way along the platform, he positioned himself behind and slightly to one side, where he could appreciate the rounded half-profile of her left breast. She was wearing the crimson linen suit and the black stockings that gave off a sheen almost intense enough to call a glitter. He experienced a pleasurable flick inside his trousers.

As usual the train came worming out of the tunnel at precisely six twenty and, as usual, he trailed her into the carriage and sat opposite. She crossed her legs. As her stockings came into contact and rubbed together he picked up the tiny screeching sound even above the rumble of the doors closing. Another flick. He remembered she'd done this to him before. She had a half-smile on her face which hovered provocatively in shadows. Had an overhead light gone? He couldn't quite get her into focus.

He looked around the carriage at the usual cast of characters: the cud-chewing dims who only come alive when the music starts to bounce, the counting-house lackeys, resenting every moment of enforced wage-earning, the aggressively suited company men returning to their stuccoed homes in Holland Park . . . They depressed him. He was as trapped in the grey hustle for daily bread as any of them. Nothing unique. It grated that, in this morose company, he was just another bloody trooper.

Only she was special.

All he wanted was to devour the sight of her, but custom and manners always prevailed. As if programmed, he opened his evening paper. He always did that as the train left Chancery Lane. He simply couldn't understand himself being so craven. His battered good looks had always triggered women's curiosity; had drawn them to him.

Holborn ... Tottenham Court Road ... Oxford Circus ... Bond Street. He peeked occasionally. She shifted slightly and recrossed her legs.

The longest uninterrupted section of tunnel ran between Marble Arch and Lancaster Gate. He'd made this journey so often that, even with his eyes closed, he could judge almost to the second the approach to each station.

He glanced up for the arrival at Lancaster Gate but his timing must have been off. Perhaps the train was going slow, although it seemed to be rattling along at a fair speed. Odd. He returned to his newspaper.

A minute went by and suddenly he felt bothered. He looked up to see that other passengers – but not her – were glancing around, ill-at-ease. One of the dims, a rust redhead, whined to her friend, 'Takin' its time, innit?'

But it wasn't. The train ploughed on, the bolted iron ribs of the tunnel flashing by the windows with strobe-like hypnotic effect. Several passengers stood up and shuffled to the doors in anticipation of the Lancaster Gate platform sliding into view.

A tall pin-striper, puzzled, stooped to peer through the window. He was confronted by the grimy tunnel wall and the horizontal power cables still flashing by when he clearly expected to be coming into the station. He turned, a questioning look on his waxy face.

Others were picking up his concern. A woman asked loudly, of no one in particular, 'This is the Central Line, isn't it?' None of the passengers now searching for signs beyond the carriage windows bothered to reply. On rattled the train.

He worked out that ten minutes or so must have elapsed since they'd left Marble Arch. Something was wrong. He folded his paper and laid it beside him on the seat.

As if reading his thoughts, a grey-haired matron said, 'Something's wrong. I don't understand.' She pulled a Selfridge's shopping bag onto her lap and cuddled it.

'Wot she mean?' the dim asked her friend. She stopped her rhythmic gum-chewing.

Two backpacking youths with buttery Scandinavian complexions shrugged at each other. One said, 'Please, Lancaster Gate is next. Yes?'

'Don't ask me, mate,' said a youth. 'I'm going to Notting Hill. But we do seem to have been in this bleeding tunnel a long time.' The train roared on.

Another five minutes elapsed and the scene of ill-suppressed hysteria reminded him of the time he had been on a charter flight to Miami and the plane had flown into clear air turbulence. Only this time there was no pacifying cabin crew and no seat belts.

The interconnecting door with the next carriage opened and a white-faced group pushed forward. 'This can't be right,' said the leader, a bullet-headed authority figure. 'What's the driver playing at?' He shouldered his way down the carriage and pounded on the metal door separating them from the driver's cabin. There was no response.

Bullet Head muttered a curse, then said, 'Christ! He must have had a heart attack.'

A small woman in a hat quavered, 'That may be so, but wouldn't the train have gone through Lancaster Gate anyway? I didn't miss it, did I? We haven't reached it yet, have we?'

The woman with the Selfridge's bag began rocking and crying. This galvanized Bullet Head, who tugged at the red emergency handle and began to attack the driver's door with his feet and fists. Each blow simply bounced back at him. The train ploughed on.

He watched Bullet Head's perspiring efforts and, for the first time, felt the icy douche of fear swilling around his innards. There was something . . . something he should know that was tantalizingly just beyond his ken.

Bullet Head said, 'The bloody fool must have diverted us into a side tunnel.'

'Maybe it's a bomb scare,' said someone.

The tall man, who'd been waiting to alight, abruptly lost his composure and pointed angrily at the tube map. 'What diversionary tunnel? Do you see any damned diversionary tunnel?'

Bullet Head turned puce and roared, 'They don't mark them on the passengers' maps. There has to be some place where they park the trains at night.'

The carriage was becoming oppressively packed as more and more agitated passengers pressed forward from the other carriages. He could no longer see the woman clearly through the bodies. From his seated position, he caught only the occasional glimpse of those mocking crossed knees.

People tugged open the slit windows for ventilation. Curiously, although the iron ribs continued to hurtle by outside, he could feel no incoming blast of air on his face, only the sort of gut-twisting paralysis he'd felt the first time he came under Iraqi shower-and-spray machine pistol fire. Despite an urgent desire to run to the kharsi, he'd stayed long enough to ventilate two of those bastards with neat groups in trunk and head.

The only way he could stand up now was to climb onto his seat. He glanced at his watch. Jesus! They'd left Marble Arch at least twenty-five minutes ago. At this speed they should have gone through a dozen stations and be breaking into daylight and suburban Middlesex.

Women were screaming and several had fainted. An elderly woman in a hat began to pray out loud.

'Oh, do shut up!' said a chic brunette, dressed in lawyer black.

A girl in school uniform began to sob. Through shuddering breath, she cried, 'I know what this is. It's like that book.' Her denimed Neanderthal boyfriend took her by the shoulders and shook her until her head lolled. 'What are you talking about, you silly cow?'

'The one where all these people are on a ship. They think they're trapped in the fog. Only they're not.'

'We're not in a fog. We're in a sodding tunnel, and in a minute we'll be coming into a station,' said the Neanderthal. The girl began to sob again. 'I don't think so,' she said. 'I think we're condemned to be on this train for all eternity.'

'You wicked little girl!' exploded the woman, crushing her Selfridge's bag in her rage and anxiety. 'That's blasphemy!' And then she threw back her head and began a horrifying keening that spread, like a contagion, the length of the suffocating coach and beyond.

He wanted to yell above their heads that it was too absurd, to say give it a bit longer, keep calm. To say . . . pray.

In front of him the press of bodies suddenly divided and he stepped down onto the carriage floor. The muck sweat was sluicing off his cheeks and chin. Somehow he knew exactly what he had to do. He faced the woman calmly. Now he knew how it ended – had always known but, like the goldfish with its two-second memory, had to relearn the scenario each time.

She uncrossed those exquisite legs, smiled up at him and said, in a siren's purr, 'You should listen to that little girl.'

She started to laugh directly into his shocked, uncomprehending face. In her open mouth he could see only darkness. He reeled back, fell into his seat and began to scream.

The train thundered on. Outside, the iron ribs relentlessly followed one upon another, a monster drawing him into its black bowels on the ripples of its iron gullet.

Chapter Two

Jack Boulder's heart leapt in his chest, trying to escape its mountings. He was wide awake in an instant, lying in a sweat puddle, his head throbbing. Grace was already leaning over him, her long, pewter-blonde hair hanging forward over her sleep-dazed face. 'My God, Jack, what is it? Just look at the time – it's not yet five.'

He swung his feet to the floor and rested his damp head in his hands. She touched his bare, hunched shoulders and could feel the heat and moisture coming off his body.

She slithered off the mattress, her nightgown dragging upwards to reveal her elegant legs. It fell back into place as she padded to the bathroom and returned with two towels. She had wetted one and now dabbed it over his brow and the triangular torso that still thrilled her every time she ran her hands over it. As she dried him off, she asked, 'Was it the same dream?'

Jack nodded. 'It's the third time in a week. It's so vivid, so terrifying.'

Grace's brow knitted. Terrifying was an unlikely word for Jack to select. He was fearless – too fearless sometimes.

She looked down at his dishevelled hair. 'Was it the same woman?'

'Yes.'

She hesitated, and then said, 'Is it someone you've met, Jack? Someone you've become... interested in? I mean, you really fancy her, don't you, wanting to get a look at her tits and so on...'

He raised his head to meet her gaze. 'Grace, men are always wanting to look at women's tits. She's just some witch from a dark pit inside my head. A figment. Nothing more.' His arms encircled her thighs and he pulled her close so that his head was against her belly.

She stroked his hair and heard him say, 'I've only ever been in love with one woman and, at the moment, she is rummaging through my hair to see if I've started a bald patch.'

Grace said, 'Oooh!' and yanked at a forelock. She began to giggle. 'I'll start a patch for you if you keeping dreaming about this harpy. Why can't you dream about fancying me?'

His heartbeat had returned to normal and he pulled back his head grinning roguishly. 'Who says I don't?'

'Really?' Grace brightened. 'You never mention it. What do I wear in your imagination?'

'Oh, the usual stuff,' said Jack airily. 'School tunic, blue knickers, thick black stockings . . .'

'Pervert!' said Grace.

As he spoke, Jack's hands slipped under his wife's nightgown and pulled it over her head.

'Do you know what the time is?' she murmured.

'You've already told me,' said Jack.

'We'll have to be quiet or we'll wake the boys.'

'The clap of doom wouldn't get those two out of bed at this hour . . .'

Afterwards Jack, a veteran of early reveilles, said, 'I'll never get back to sleep. I'll go for my run.'

Dawn was not even a suspicion in the sky as he loped from the house to begin his regular three-miler. As he jogged along the empty pavement, there was nothing untoward to draw his attention to the house displaying the for-sale sign. Head down, watching for dog turds, he failed to notice the upstairs curtains shifting minutely as if someone had moved in the room, causing a small displacement of air.

He got back to find that Grace had embarked on her daily act as a female sergeant major, and was shouting up the stairs for the children to stir themselves.

She said to Jack, 'Do you think you ought to see a doctor?'

He shrugged. 'He'd only tell me to stop eating cheese at night.'

The boys clattered in and Grace said no more. They were both fair-headed but after that any similarity between them ceased. Ben was twelve and already a serious boy, a reader who asked questions; Malcolm at eight still had no inkling of the kind of world that awaited him and therefore lived in a state of infant bliss.

Mal headed straight for the cereal box, but Ben stood by the kitchen sink, slapping the back of his head, attempting vainly to make a rebellious tuft on his crown lie down.

'Ben, for goodness sake stop hitting yourself like that. Your eyeballs'll pop out.'

'It keeps sticking up. They call me names at school.'

'What names?'

'Never mind.'

'Mum, they call us both Bog Brush,' piped up Mal.

'Oh, dear! But I'm afraid your father doesn't like you looking like a pair of sheepdogs. You're his little soldiers.'

Grace's flip tone invited a response but Jack held his tongue. She took a comb from her bag and ran it under the tap, then raked it through Ben's recalcitrant locks, flattening them successfully against his skull. Breakfast resumed.

The telephone call came minutes after she'd packed the boys off to the local primary where she herself had taught until Mal arrived. She lifted the receiver. 'Hello?'

A woman's voice, cool and neutral, said, 'Please may I speak to Captain Boulder?' For no logical reason, Jack's word-picture of the woman on the train flashed into her head.

'Whom shall I say?' Her formal tone was a sure sign to Jack that she had a dubious caller on the line. He often teased her about it, saying she sounded like someone who'd taken elocution lessons.

'It's a business matter,' said the measured voice.

Grace opened her mouth to make an acid retort to the dismissive tone, then changed her mind. She held out the receiver and said, 'For you. Sounds like someone selling insurance. You'll be late if you're not out of here in five minutes.' She had made no attempt to cover the mouthpiece.

The voice said to Jack, 'I'm not selling insurance, Captain Boulder. This is a serious matter that I do not wish to discuss with your wife listening in. You have, I believe, made numerous applications recently for jobs a little more rewarding than manager of a gun club. Please just answer yes or no.'

'Yes', said Jack. And added, 'I don't use my rank any more. I'm a civvy now.'

'Very good,' said the woman. 'Thank you for your discretion. Ask me no questions now but, as an expression of my seriousness, you will receive an envelope in tomorrow's mail containing five hundred pounds. Do not show this to your wife. Do not discuss this conversation with her. If you do, you will be squandering a rare opportunity. Your good fortune will come to an abrupt halt with the money that will be in your hands tomorrow.'

'How—' began Jack, mind racing, but the woman spoke over him.

She said, 'If all is satisfactory, I shall arrange a further conversation with you. Goodbye for the moment.' She rang off.

Grace was staring at him. He hung up. 'You didn't have much to say for yourself. Who was she?'

He said carefully, 'You were right. Some insurance pitch. I put the phone down on her.'

'This early in the morning? Strange, isn't it?'

Jack shrugged. 'I think they try to get you before you leave for work.'

In the house across the road, one of the listeners said, 'Good. He hasn't told her. And he thinks on his feet.'

All the same, he was followed on the tube into the City and a daylong check maintained for unusual contacts or any mention of his curious telephone call.

'Nothing,' reported the team.

Chapter Three

The observers watched Jack take his early run and then linger on the corner jogging on the spot.

'Good man,' said one. 'Tough-looking johnnie, isn't he? He's waiting to waylay Postman Pat.'

It was ten minutes before Jack spotted the postman in the distance hauling his trolley, and jogged along to meet him.

They watched Jack being handed his mail, watched him finger the package and slip it into the waistband of his tracksuit trousers under the jacket before trotting back to the house.

They turned to the earphones, listened to the domestic clatter, Grace urging Ben and Mal to hurry, Jack claiming the bathroom, and even caught the sound of ripping as he opened the package. They imagined his stunned look as he fanned out the banknotes, now realizing for the first time that the call had been no hoax.

'Nothing works as well as the old green-backed convincer, does it?' murmured the senior man.

Jack left the house fifteen minutes earlier than usual, leaving Grace still coping with the pre-school pandemonium. At St Paul's he positioned himself at the phone box specified in the typed note that had accompanied the money. He lifted the receiver on the first ring.

'Good morning, Captain Boulder,' said the woman. It was an upper-class accent, with a drawl that spoke of worldliness, the voice of someone easily bored. He wanted once again to correct her salutation but instinct told him to let it go and listen.

'You were your regiment's rifle champion. You shot at Bisley, and were runner-up for the Queen's Prize.'

'Yes,' said Jack. So that was it. He knew that at this point he should ask for an address where he could return the money. He didn't.

'Why didn't you win?'

'Bit of bad luck, really. You need to be in the right frame of mind for shooting at that level. My father had been killed earlier that week in a traffic pile-up. I wanted to pull out altogether but there was pressure from the regiment who were mad keen to have another pot to add to the regimental silver collection. So I played the brave little soldier.'

'Tell me, Captain Boulder, under what circumstances did you leave the Army?'

'Look,' said Jack, 'I like to find five hundred quid in the post as much as the next man. But I don't think you've bought the right to my life story.'

'Oh, but I'm about to,' she said calmly. 'I'm about to offer you a week's work for which you will be paid one hundred thousand pounds.'

'Oh, sure,' said Jack. 'Who do I have to kill?' Even as the words escaped his mouth he knew he had asked the right question.

'Please do not be flippant. This is a matter, as I told you yesterday, of great seriousness. You may correct me if I'm wrong in any detail, but is it not true that you were invited to resign your commission after Sean McGurk, a known IRA leader, came to his front door one morning in the Irish Republic and was shot dead from a great distance by a single shot? The same Sean McGurk whose active service unit had been responsible for the deaths of two of your own men. I'm told the shot was placed so precisely between the eyes that at first the Garda could not believe it had not been fired at close range. A beautiful shot,' she added almost dreamily. 'So neat. So perfectly formed. Just like that little red spot Hindi women sport on their foreheads.'

Jack attempted to butt in, but she gave him no space. She went on, reprovingly, 'Your fine handiwork may have made you a hero to your men and brother officers but the Paddies had to be extremely cross with someone so they picked on the poor old British Government who, in turn, were extremely cross with you – especially as there was talk of a ceasefire in the air.'

'No one ever proved it was me,' grunted Jack, as she drew breath. 'British officers don't go man-hunting without authorization.'

'Don't they now?' She sounded both dry and amused.

'How do you know all this?' said Jack. 'I was allowed to leave the Army without any fuss. They weren't going to give me up to Dublin and cause an even bigger stink. There was nothing in the papers.'

She said, 'I know a great deal about you, Captain Boulder. And be assured you have my respect. I'm only sorry that a man of your talents spends his days in a soundproofed basement among all those stockbrokers nursing fantasies that they, too, could be Sheriff of Tombstone. Rather pathetic, don't you think?'

'It's a living,' said Jack. 'Don't you think it's about time you stopped playing games with me? Who are you?'

'You may call me Mrs Canning.'

'You want me to bump off your husband. Is that it?'

She laughed lightly. 'Nothing so bourgeois. But you really don't believe you can earn a hundred thousand pounds without, shall we say, a considerable tussle with your conscience, do you?'

'I was coming to that,' said Jack.

She cut in, 'You have a forty-thousand pound mortgage, you have two sons aged eight and twelve to educate, you have little money in reserve and you're often unable to clear your monthly credit-card bills. You last took your wife to a restaurant five weeks ago.' Anticipating his reaction she added, 'Don't be alarmed. All that information is readily available to credit agencies and private detectives with access to computer networks.'

Jack glanced at his watch. He was already late. He licked his lips. A hundred thou? Christ! He said, 'Can we meet?'

'Not just yet. Do you wish me to go on?'

Jack said slowly, 'Well, I'm listening. This is all something of a thunderbolt. Okay, I realize this is more than a practical joke. You wouldn't have gone to such lengths to find out so much about me. Although some of what you said is bullshit. You didn't get my Army record from any credit agency.'

She did not reply.

Finally, he said, 'I'd like to hear more.'

'This phone, same time tomorrow,' she snapped, and left him listening to the dialling tone.

Chapter Four

The boys were upstairs, grappling with their homework. Grace swept crumbs from supper off the table into her cupped hand and looked at him curiously.

'All right, Boulder,' she said. 'What's on your mind?'

The listeners paused in their game of pocket chess.

Jack said, 'What do you mean?'

Grace said, 'You've not said a word either to me or the boys all evening. You're somewhere in outer space. What's up?'

'I'm just feeling a bit low,' said Jack. 'I miss the guys, the comradeship. Don't you?'

The listeners resumed their game, cocking half an ear, backed by the reel-to-reel recorder doing its stately eavesdrop.

Grace brushed her hands clean over the swing-bin. 'The Army can get stuffed as far as I'm concerned. I never knew when some embarrassed colonel was going to call on me to say you'd driven over a landmine and ask how I'd like the pieces delivered.'

They had been married fourteen years. Her Jack was no pretty boy but his weatherbeaten face and nose broken in a battalion boxing tournament had left him with the kind of ruggedness that triggered near delirium in some women.

She assumed that from time to time he must have been tempted to stray, even if only in his head, especially when soldiering took him away from home – but his behaviour had never given her any reason to think that he actually had. On home ground he was a model husband. His impetuosity was boyish; it never involved adventures with other women. She knew how much temptation was thrown in his path, had seen the way women reacted to him even when she was within face-slapping distance ... And it had been the same qualities in Jack that attracted other women – his sheer animal masculinity and his blindness to his own sex appeal – that had drawn her to him in the first place.

Grace could see genuine naivety in his face about female predatory instincts and this, she realized with a stab of resignation, was another part of the challenge.

They had met at a wedding: Grace was just out of teacher-training college and was taking infant classes while Jack was a second lieutenant. He was in his dress uniform with his just-earned parachute wings. One of Grace's girlhood friends was marrying a fellow officer from Jack's regiment.

In the marquee, after the toasts and the speeches, when most of the wedding party were tipsy, she had observed no fewer than three bridesmaids and a couple of older women twittering around Jack. He was gazing raptly at his admirers under their wide-brimmed hats and floral circlets.

Grace was sitting in a little gilt chair, watching the group and thinking, idly, that Jack must be the most conceited man on earth, when suddenly he turned and headed straight for her. She stared him in the eye as he advanced towards her, looking so grim that she was already giggling before he reached her. He said, awkwardly, 'You need a refill.' She burst out laughing. He looked like a man going over the parapet in the face of enemy guns.

'Look here,' she said, teasingly, 'isn't your presence required over there?'

He glanced back guiltily at five angry pairs of eyes, then said, 'I couldn't help myself. I needed to meet you,' so simply that it certainly wasn't a practised line.

Four months later they were married and living in Germany. Grace found a job teaching at a school for the children of NATO personnel.

The revenge execution of Sean McGurk – Grace refused to call it murder – and its aftermath had been shattering for both of them. The army and his family had been Jack's life and it had been hard for him to adjust to the civilian jungle. She saw his terrible nightmares as just one symptom of his inner turmoil.

Now, Grace knelt by his chair and laid a hand on his knee. 'Look, Jack, the only thing we can thank the Army for is the cover-up. You must have been insane. If there'd been any advantage in it for the brass and the politicians, you'd be doing life in an Irish prison. And how long do you think it would have taken for the Provos to get to you?'

'Quite right, my girl,' murmured the senior man, taking black's remaining bishop.

Jack said, 'It's just this gun-club job. These people I teach to shoot are clowns from Fantasy Island. What the hell goes on in their heads? I mean, toting .44 Magnums and Browning automatics as a hobby. It's crazy. And in that dungeon I don't see daylight from clock-on to clock-off.'

Grace massaged his knee soothingly. 'You'll just have to keep trying for something better. For God's sake, Jack, don't spoil this one. We're the original beggars who can't be choosers. Think of the boys.'

Jack nodded glumly. Then he brightened and said, 'Oh, by the way, some good news. Some fool paid me extra for giving him fast-draw lessons. I earned every penny – he nearly got me in the foot!'

He was not comfortable with the glibness of the lie but he'd caused Grace enough anxiety with the McGurk affair. He reached into his back pocket and pulled out a wad. 'There's five hundred there,' he said.

'Naughty, naughty,' said the senior man. 'She's not going to go for that.'

But Grace exclaimed, 'Wonderful! That's great timing. It'll almost clear the Visa bill.' Then she climbed into his lap and rubbed herself against his chest, saying mischievously, 'I think the kids are asleep. Let's go upstairs . . .'

'Ah,' said the senior man. 'A spot of slap-and-tickle to brighten the dying hours of the day . . . Pity we couldn't get those stick lenses into the walls.' His queen's knight made a crooked advance. 'Checkmate!' he purred.

Chapter Five

'We're not talking about a job stacking supermarket shelves,' said Jack. 'Why can't we meet?'

'Eventually,' she said, in the same measured tone. 'I still have to be certain that you're the right man. Do you have a bothersome conscience?'

'No more nor less than the next man,' said Jack. 'If you're SIS and have in mind some rat who deserves all he gets, I can do the business.'

'Maybe,' she said. She paused, then said, 'Suppose the object is someone who doesn't deserve a bullet? Could you have stood in Oswald's shoes at the Texas Book Depository window?'

'No,' said Jack.

'And another thing. You assume the object is male. Could you "do the business" to a woman?'

Jack sighed at the complexities. 'Unlikely. Unless she was a proven out-and-out evil bitch.'

'That would be too convenient, wouldn't it? You'd have declined to "do the business" to Helen of Troy but just think of the thousands of lives that would have been saved in the Trojan Wars if you'd put one lovely little vent in the middle of her forehead before she ever set eyes on Paris.'

Jack found this kind of dialogue vaguely irritating, a toying with the outer ring rather than going for the bullseye. He said, 'I don't think Homer would have been too pleased with me. What would he have been left with to write about?'

He hoped the bored note in his voice would encourage her to come to the point. But she went on, 'Ever see a film called *The Third Man?*'

'No,' said Jack. 'I only like Westerns. They don't make 'em any more.'

'There's a scene,' went on Mrs Canning, as if he had not spoken, 'high up in a fairground Ferris wheel. One man points out to another how insignificant people appear at that height, how, if one were to be eliminated, no great harm would have been done. The world would go on turning. That's what's involved here. A speck disappears. The sun rises the next morning just the same.'

'Look,' said Jack, 'my experience is that too much talking and too much thinking make people hesitate and trip over themselves. As you've already delicately pointed out, my life is up Crap Alley and I'm ripe for a proposition. I've forced myself not to think any deeper about it than that. If you start giving me psychological tests, I'm liable to start thinking consequences. So let's get to it. I take it that you're acting on behalf of the Security Services. Is it Five or Six who don't want mud on their doormat? You put up the money, convince me that we can get away with it, and I'll do the business. Fair enough?'

She made no immediate reply. He could hear her making a disapproving tsk-tsk noise. She said, 'Now you worry me. You sound too cocky by half. Listen, once you've been cast, you're bound to a play-or-pay contract.'

'What happens if the play's interrupted by a member of the audience?'

'Well, you obviously know the score. You know what a cut-out is?'

'Yes.'

'For a hundred thousand pounds, the cut-out is you. If the play doesn't reach the final curtain for the target, you're on your own.'

Then she added abruptly, 'There'll be another five hundred in your post on Monday. I shall spend the weekend thinking about you.' She gave him another phone-box location in Cornhill and hung up.

That night Jack had the dream again. But now he fancied he had a name to put to the woman he followed so slavishly onto that coffin train. Mrs Canning.

Chapter Six

They monitored him closely during the weekend. They lived through a tiff with Grace when he backed out of a promise to take the boys to a Fulham home game. They could hear the puzzlement in Grace's voice: Jack was a loving father who enjoyed his Saturday afternoons on the terraces as much as their boys.

There was a second minor clash that weekend when the conversation took a military turn. Grace came into the living room just as Ben was asking, 'Dad, why is it better to wound the enemy rather than kill him?'

Apparently Jack did not regard this as an odd question from a boy of twelve. He said, 'Kill a man, and all it does is make a few hours' work for a burial party and the chaplain. Wound him badly enough, and many people will be involved in saving him – stretcher party, doctors, nurses, surgeons, ambulance drivers, artificial-limb makers ... The enemy is compelled to commit huge resources to an activity that won't help win the battle. Your own wounded are, to tell a truth that no one likes to admit, a darned nuisance.'

Grace broke in, 'Really, Jack! Do you have to fill their heads with blood and guts?'

'Aw, Mum, leave Dad alone,' Ben wailed. 'This is real-life stuff, It's interesting.'

'Quite right,' said Jack, ruffling his hair so that it shot up into the hated spikes. To Grace he said, 'I don't want them falling for that paths-of-glory guff. The military life is what I know and if they want to follow me I want them to be clear in their heads about what they're letting themselves in for.'

After the boys had gone out, he sat brooding over his latest conversation with Mrs Canning. Grace was preparing to go shopping. He said, 'Could you pop into the video club and see if they have a copy of *The Third Man?*'

The listeners registered Grace's curiosity. Jack never watched old movies. And this one was really old. 'I just fancy it,' he said lamely.

They watched from the window as Grace Boulder, in a flimsy summer frock, swung down the road. At the corner, the sun caught her and, in silhouette for a second, they had the illusion that she was naked. 'Oh, to be in Jack's shoes,' said the senior man.

'Oh, to be in Jack's bed,' corrected his colleague.

Two hours later they were listening to the familiar, sinuous dialogue – Orson Welles murmuring into Joseph Cotton's ear, '*Look down there. Would you really feel any pity if one of those dots stopped moving for ever? If I offered twenty thousand pounds for every dot that stops, would you really, old man, tell me to keep my money? . . . It's the only way you save nowadays.*'

Jack shifted uneasily. There was something of Mrs Canning in this scene.

'*In these days, old man, nobody thinks in terms of human beings. Governments don't, so why should we? They talk of the people and the proletariat, and I talk of the mugs. It's the same thing . . .*'

On Monday he met the postman again. And, again, the money was there. This time he did not hand any to Grace. She wasn't going to believe he had more than one fast-draw idiot on his books.

On a noisy phone, Mrs Canning got down to some detailed business. Over what distance did he regard his marksmanship as effective?

'I shoot twelve hundred yards at Bisley. More is possible, especially with a decent scope. Is this an indoor or outdoor shoot?'

'Outdoor.'

'In that case, you have the windage to reckon with. Over a thousand yards, a ten-knot wind can deflect a bullet by as much as eight feet. You wouldn't think it possible with a sharp-nosed metal object travelling at something approaching Mach Three. What about the weather?'

'It won't happen unless it's fine.'

'That could be another headache. Get a heat haze and you may find yourself having a cabby at a mirage.'

'Unlikely,' she said. Jack noticed she didn't query the Army slang for potshot. She knew.

He asked, 'What distance are we talking here?'

'It is difficult to know at this stage but, from what you say, we have to assume that the task will be at the limit of your capabilities. That's why you've been headhunted for this job. You know you're good; we know you're good. That's why you're being offered such a ridiculous sum of money.'

Jack had a further thought. 'Will the object be moving at the time?'

'Yes, but not particularly fast. You will, at least, have one advantage. The object will be in clear view.'

'Which brings us,' said Jack, 'to the object's identity.'

'No, it doesn't,' said Mrs Canning sharply. 'You will not know the identity of our target until after the event. You will not know whether it is man, woman, youth or child. If you want this money, you'd better reconcile yourself to my rules of engagement. This conversation brings us only to one point, where I ask you for your total commitment. Any doubt, and I'd prefer that you back off. You keep the thousand you already have and you never hear from me again. In or out, Captain Boulder?'

Jack pressed his brow against the cool glass of the telephone booth. He could see himself stepping onto the tube train in the woman's wake and the doors rumbling closed behind him.

'Will this person's death be a good thing for our country?' he said at last. He listened to his own uncertain voice and thought he sounded like a schoolboy who'd been force-fed *Boy's Own* yarns of derring-do missions against the Boche.

'It'll be an excellent thing for our country.' Her voice left no room for doubt. 'You'll have performed a significant public service. This particular person has done Britain great harm but cannot be brought to book in any conventional way. By comparison, your Sean McGurk was a minor irritant. So what's it to be, Captain Boulder? In or out?'

'In,' he said finally.

With that moment of his pledge, he mentally boxed away all reservation. He was surprised at how galvanized he felt. He hadn't felt this alive since he had settled himself in a copse on the brow of a hill and waited for Sean McGurk to come to his front door.

'Splendid,' she said in that upper-class way, as if she were complimenting a servant on the shine of the silver. She said, 'I want you to get rid of that regimental haircut. Let it grow long. And cultivate a moustache, a bushy one.'

'How do you know about my hair?' said Jack, but she put him down immediately.

'Don't ask questions. Just do it.'

At Mrs Canning's insistence, Jack returned to open-range shooting to bring his skills up to competition pitch. At weekends he commuted to Pirbright. On one day he scored 373 out of a possible 375 at ranges up to 1,000 yards and at 2,000 he was achieving a consistent two out of three in the bull on a stationary target.

'Christ, Jack,' said the manager, Greg Rankin, 'you've never been better. Pity you can't go back to Ireland to give the Micks another demo.' He laughed. He knew the story.

'What *are* you talking about?' said Jack, well satisfied with his day's work.

As instructed, he put himself on the holiday list for three weeks in May. No, said Mrs Canning, she wouldn't tell him any more at this stage. It was his job to keep hitting those bullseyes and to prepare his equipment so that it was in perfect functioning order by that date. And, oh yes, did he possess clothes of casual sophistication – suitable for a warmish climate? If not, get some with the money he was now receiving every Monday.

'Include a wide-brimmed Panama,' she said, as an afterthought. 'They make a wonderful shield from security cameras in public places.'

He worked out that, by the end of April, he would have received five thousand pounds. Mrs Canning told him he would receive a further fifteen thousand on 1 May, to total a fifth of his promised fee in advance.

He was still taking all his instructions in various telephone boxes around the City and felt somewhat reassured by his mysterious employer's elaborate care. He himself was now observing equally secure routines. He allowed Mrs Canning to open on his behalf an untraceable Sparbuch bank account in Vienna, with his own code word, in which to deposit his growing savings. The account was in a bogus name of his own choosing and he always kept the passbook with him.

The mention of lightweight clothes had alerted him to the difficulties involved in taking his equipment abroad: although he had firearms certificates, he couldn't take his gear out of the country without official sanction.

'It's all arranged,' said Mrs Canning, when he raised the matter. 'Of course, there's no way you can fly with your weaponry going undetected. You'll be driving via the Channel Tunnel, with everything safely stowed.' She refused to elaborate. 'Everything at the right time, Jack,' she said. At least she'd stopped the Captain Boulder routine, which, he reckoned, was intended to plant him firmly among the junior ranks.

He hadn't had the dream for some weeks – not since he'd said yes to Mrs Canning.

He did not know it, but growing confidence was being expressed in his conduct. His household, the watchers and listeners confirmed, had continued along its humdrum domestic way. He had made no suspicious phone calls, had met no unaccountable persons, posted no dubious letters. He was their very good boy.

As a consequence, the bodies were withdrawn – although the voice-activated recorders were still in situ.

On the tapes they heard Grace's growing concern at Jack's edginess. They had lived together too long for him to be able to hide his preoccupation successfully. Once, she lost her temper when he announced he had to go shooting rather than take the family swimming.

Jack's mother-in-law had belatedly told him, an hour after the nuptials were over, 'Our Gracie always did have a bit of a tongue on her,' and now she was haranguing him. 'I thought you'd put that Pirbright rifle-shooting obsession behind you. It's a waste of time that you could be spending with your family, Jack. I've never liked having those guns in the house. I don't want the boys taking them up as a hobby.'

Jack looked at Ben and Mal, who had both assumed exaggerated expressions of innocence. He was relieved that they were both keeping their mouths firmly closed. He had taken them through the routines of small-arms maintenance on a number of occasions and, on Saturday mornings, had allowed them to fire real bullets on the indoor range. They had been thrilled but Jack had warned them, 'If you tell your mother, she'll kill me and take away your Nintendo. This is our secret, so don't drop me in it. Cross your hearts?'

They had both solemnly done so.

Jack fended off Grace as best he could. 'It'd be a shame to let my sharp-shooting skills slip,' he said.

They could hear Grace making sounds of exasperation. 'Jack, for pity's sake, what use is it except in a fairground? The Army is over and done with. You're a civilian now. You only need side-arms skills for those would-be cowboys you instruct.'

Jack tried to mollify her. He said, 'You're right about the influence on the boys. Security is much tighter at the club – I'll keep my stuff there.'

He felt pleased with his low cunning. He still had to find a reason for going away alone in May but at least he wouldn't have to explain why he was taking a rifle, ammo and tools with him.

Jack hummed that old Johnny Cash number about not taking your guns to town.

Then he stopped abruptly, remembering Billy Joe's fate.

Chapter Seven

The postman was beginning to give him questioning looks. Jack had been jogging down to the corner of Hellespont Road to meet him every Monday for the past two months. This time there was more than the five hundred pounds in his package.

He waited until he was in the privacy of his office before examining the other contents. There was a set of Volvo car keys, travel papers and a well-worn blue-and-gold British passport in the name of James Canning who was 6 feet 1 inch tall with brown eyes. Just like Jack. His profession was given as company executive.

The passport had been issued in August 1990. So how come he was gazing down at a passable photograph of himself, head against a neutral background, hair enhanced by an unknown artist and a full moustache skilfully painted in? He experienced a leap of apprehension in his gut: he felt the presence of a ruthlessly efficient organization behind Mrs Canning's honey-for-tea Home Counties accent.

He held up the pages to the light, squinted along the side of the photo where it was overlaid with the official stamp. He could detect no sign of forgery or that his image had been substituted for the original holder's.

Mrs Canning actually laughed. It was so unexpected that it brought home to Jack with a rush just how intense and narrowly focused their conversations had been for all this time.

'You're my husband, James,' she said.

'So why the long separation?' said Jack. 'Does this mean we get to meet at last?'

'Quite soon,' she said.

Jack said, 'I have a worry. I'm keeping my weapons and new travelling clothes at work but I don't know how to break the news to my wife that I'll be disappearing in May for a holiday alone. She's no fool.'

There was a silence on the line. Finally, Mrs Canning said, scornfully, Jack thought, 'You really should have learned to keep your woman in order, Captain Boulder. I'll work something out.' Mrs Canning was evidently not a member of the sisterhood.

The Captain had returned. 'There's no need to be so bloody rude,' he said stonily. 'My wife is her own woman. She doesn't need to be kept in order by me. If anything, I'm the one who sometimes has to be kept in order by her.'

'How very New Man of you. Do you take your turn at the washing up?'

Jack held his tongue. But he was stirred by the idea that he was actually going to come face to face with . . . who? Her name would no more be Canning than he was her husband.

'What do I call you?' he said.

'Well, it says Jane on my passport. And I shall call you James. There! How nice and simple. We've both been christened.'

Mrs Jane Canning was impressively fast to furnish her solution to his problem with Grace. She had evidently latched on to the fact that, although he was out of the Army, he was still a reservist. A seemingly authentic OHMS buff envelope arrived by post. Inside was another envelope stamped Sealed Orders and Secret. Grace watched, curious. The letter was certainly official-looking, with a Ministry of Defence heading, and required Captain Boulder to report to the Ministry, off Whitehall, where he would be transported onward to a secret destination to participate in a weapons appraisal programme. His duties would necessitate his absence from home for the better part of May.

Wordlessly, he held out the movement order to Grace. 'They kick you out,' she said bitterly, 'but they still keep you on their leash. Suppose you refuse to go?'

'Can't do that,' said Jack, endeavouring not to look relieved. 'It's a court-martial offence.'

Chapter Eight

He felt indecently happy as he drove the Volvo estate up the ramp at Folkestone and manoeuvred it into the long, narrow coach of the Tunnel train. Then he remembered his lies to Grace and the moment passed.

All had gone as Mrs Canning had decreed. He'd left his own car at home in Hellespont Road, found the Volvo where she had said – in a car park off Ludgate Hill – and reparked it in the underground bay next to the shooting range. The concealed well under the floor had been expertly cut. His equipment, bubble-wrapped against rattle, fitted snugly. He dropped the lid back into place and threw his innocuous luggage, Panama included, on top, together with the set of golf clubs she'd supplied so that he could carry the rifle in the bag without detection. Jack was not a golfer but he had to admire her foresight.

He had tried not to make too big a meal of leaving home and had taken care not to give the impression that this was any more significant than a hundred other partings necessitated by the military life.

He gave Ben and Mal a hug, kissed the tops of their unruly heads, and uttered the time-honoured words, 'You be good boys for your mother.'

If Grace harboured any suspicions, none showed. Her attitude was one of surrender to the hopeless nature of men who preferred to play boys' games. They embraced and she admonished him the way wives usually do on such occasions: 'Behave yourself,' she said.

Routine. Domestic normality. Nothing untoward.

Grace had approved his longer hair and the moustache. 'Mmmm. That 'tache really suits you.' She briefly pressed her breasts into his chest. 'Just a reminder of what you'll be missing while you're far from home, soldier boy,' she murmured, out of earshot of their sons. 'Try not to have any more dreams of that mystery woman.'

Jack had jumped when Mrs Canning – Jane, as he must get into the habit of calling her – had given him his destination: the Cannes Film Festival in the South of France.

'We're going to do this thing in the middle of a film festival?' He couldn't keep the disbelief from his voice.

'Think about it,' she said. 'The town will be crawling with strangers. All eyes will be on the stars. No one will be paying any attention to us.'

As if to confirm her assessment, *en route* no one had even bothered to open his phoney passport. He'd waved it in the air a couple of times but had barely merited a glance from officialdom.

He had a queasy half-hour as the train plunged into the tunnel and the walls began to slide past his window. In his head the stations of his personal Via Dolorosa unspooled. St Paul's ... Chancery Lane ... Holborn ... Tottenham Court Road ... When the train shot out into sunlight on the French side, Jack was damp from his tousled hair to his new *sportif* moccasins.

It was only as he headed south in the Volvo from Calais that it occurred to him Cannes would be bursting with French security police to ensure that all those heavenly bodies returned to Hollywood intact. He wondered how this would affect Mrs Canning's venture.

He left the Route Nationale once to eat and catnap, but eighteen hours after leaving the Channel, he was easing the Volvo down the Boulevard Carnot into a madhouse. An army of blue-dungareed workmen had descended on the seafront, La Croisette, and were swarming over palm trees and towers of scaffolding, erecting forests of billboards. Posters were being hauled up on cranes to smother the façades of the great hotels that faced the mile-long curve of the beach. The town's elegant frontage was being transformed into a giant advertising hoarding.

Outside the famous Carlton Hotel, which even Jack recognized from television documentaries, lurid film advertisements revolved on a gigantic drum while the *porte-cochère* of this wedding-cake hotel had disappeared under a thirty-foot placard showing a fantasy girl with her legs astride cuddling a ray gun. To enter the building, one had to pass under her barely concealed vulva. The subliminal message was not lost on Jack. He smiled thinly. Most of the posters depicted violence and firearms, which offered ample confirmation of his own view of turbulent human nature. Pity Grace wasn't there to have this pointed out to her.

He located the Hotel Berthier a short distance along La Croisette from the Carlton. He noted with approval its panoramic view of the bay and drove into its underground car park.

The foyer was as chaotic as the scene outside. Handsome marble columns were being utilized as props for yet more placards and the place was jammed with jabbering groups of film-industry pitchmen. Mrs Canning had been right. Who would notice the pair of them in this frenzied atmosphere?

The black-coated receptionist took his passport, gave him a guest form to fill in, and said, 'Welcome to the Berthier, sir. Your wife has already arrived.' The man punched his bell and handed the key to the porter. 'Suite 720 for Monsieur Canning,' he snapped.

Jack felt a tremor, part excitement, part curiosity. In a few minutes he would at last be able to put a face to his employer. He had slung the zipped golf bag over his shoulder. The Panama was firmly jammed on his head. He did not look up to check for security cameras. If he stared at them, they would be staring back at him.

He had to slip the golfbag from his shoulder to ease into the crowded lift. A silver-haired man in a superbly cut jacket eyed the bag with delight. Was he a film star? A Hollywood tycoon? For once Jack wished he knew more about the cinema. The man exposed perfect teeth in a smile and said, 'Hell! I was beginning to think I was the only golf nut in town. Tennis at dawn is more what happens here.'

Jack grinned guardedly.

The man said, 'What do you play off?'

What the hell was he talking about? Jack hazarded a guess. 'Any old club that will admit me,' he said.

The man chuckled. 'There's a decent course up at Valbonne – only a short drive. If you're in need of a partner, give me a call. Let's swap cards.'

Jack said hurriedly, 'I don't have mine at hand. I'm in 915.'

But the porter understood English and corrected him. 'Oh, no, Monsieur. Your suite is 720. The hotel casino is on the ninth floor.'

Jack could have throttled him. He shrugged helplessly. The man – American? Canadian? – chuckled again. He had not taken the error as a snub. With difficulty in the crush, he fished a card from his pocket, scribbled his room number and the word 'Golf?' on the reverse side, and alighted with a friendly wave at the fifth *étage*.

At the seventh, Jack was led to a carved mahogany door marked 720. The porter tapped respectfully with the key tag, and Jack felt like a bridegroom.

Suddenly, she was there. 'James, darling! Here you are at last!'

The sensation was dizzying. He had an impression of a *soignée* woman in heavy horn-rimmed spectacles before she flung her arms around him. He felt a peach-soft pressing of lips against the corner of his mouth and her breasts pushing into his chest. He was reminded, fleetingly and guiltily, of Grace.

'Er, hello, Jane,' he stumbled.

The porter placed his luggage on the slatted ledge in the small foyer of the sunlit suite. Jack studied her back as she pressed a fifty-franc note into the man's hand and said, '*Bien, merci.*' She closed the door and whirled, smiling, to face him.

Mrs Canning was tallish – around five seven – with a lean body and high rounded breasts under wide shoulders. She wore a long, belted shantung dress in dark green and her raven hair was dragged back in a bun. He judged her to be in her mid-thirties, and almost certainly a little older than he was.

The hair gave her a severe look, but when she removed the glasses he could see how magnificently the style emphasized her cheekbones. She was no longer a girl but she was what any clubman would have called a handsome woman. He tried to fix on her eyes but they were dark and somehow elusive, as if the irises had leaked their colour into the eyeballs.

As he stared at her, she examined him. She deployed a brisk, authoritarian air. 'Well, my husband, your home movies don't do you justice,' she said. Could she really have seen them? Jack held his tongue.

She circled him as if she were examining a prize bull, took in his lightweight fawn suit, the plain linen shirt and yellow striped tie. Finally, she said, 'An elegant roughneck.'

'What?' said Jack, genuinely puzzled.

'It is Scott Fitzgerald's description of Gatsby,' she said.

'Is this another movie?'

'Oh dear,' she said.

Jack didn't care for her tone, which was dismissive but at the same time a little mocking.

'I got *The Third Man* on video, but I don't watch movies much.'

'It's from a book, Jack. Do military men read only Clausewitz and Caesar's campaigns in Gaul?'

She locked the door and ushered him from the foyer into the sitting room with its tall french-windowed balcony overlooking the bay. The furniture was hotel classical, the hard-wearing kind, vaguely Louis XV, that travellers encounter from Hong Kong to New York. He peered into the bedroom. Two luxurious beds with painted headboards were separated by a side cabinet. He made no comment.

She said, in that controlled voice he'd come to know so well, 'You'd better let me see what you've brought with you.'

Jack slipped off his jacket, loosened his tie and opened the golfbag, from which he lifted out the clubs one by one. Lastly, out came stock, 'scope, magazine, bipod, bolt and trigger section and barrel of the Super Magnum. She watched as he handled the pieces with something approaching reverence.

He said, 'Assembled, you will be looking at a .338 Super Magnum sniper rifle with Schmidt and Bender sights. If you know what you're doing and using special accuracy ammunition, it's still effective at over two thousand yards. It's a lovely piece of shooter's gear.'

Fascinated, Mrs Canning stroked the barrel. He noticed that her hands, surprisingly, were not of the slender, feminine type that went with the rest of the picture. They looked powerful. Her nails were square-trimmed and businesslike, the lacquer palest pink. The only jewellery was 'their' wedding band.

'You mentioned special ammunition,' she said. 'Does that mean mercury-tipped bullets – the ones that do the most body damage?'

Jack looked at her. Her evident relish was not appealing. 'Christ! No it does not. Give the poor bastard a sporting chance.'

Mrs Canning's bonhomie vanished and she erupted in fury. 'This isn't a gentleman's sporting event. We are here to kill someone,' she hissed. 'The fact that neither you nor I has ever met the target doesn't make it a game. This is a business transaction. You do your job efficiently and you get paid. Let's hear no more rubbish about sporting chances.'

She subsided abruptly, as if she had prematurely revealed too much of herself to him. She nodded at the weapon. 'Get it fitted together,' she said curtly. 'Then we'll talk.'

A strained silence hovered between them as she watched him open his toolkit and wipe each segment before clipping or screwing it to the preceding piece. The bipod to the body; the elevation and windage turrets to the twelve-power sight; the finely-oiled bolt to the chamber, the box magazine, with its match-grade Lapua Magnum rounds, clipped beneath; the customised leather cheek pad to the butt. He was a study in quiet concentration.

He took a soft cloth and polished each deadly round as if it were Georgian silver. 'The rounds are the first of a new batch off the machine, taken before the minor distortions of mass production set in.'

Still watching, she sat and crossed her legs. Jack shuddered: someone had passed over his grave. Her elegant tan stockings had made the same screeching noise as those of the woman on the train. He shivered again, dropped a tiny club screw onto the carpet and had to kneel in search of it. Out of the corner of his eye he saw her smooth knees shimmer in their nylon.

'A formidable-looking weapon,' she murmured, as Jack stepped back from the slanting rifle, its muzzle pointed towards the room's elaborate cornice. The sight of it glinting dully under the crystal chandelier, seemed to have restored her good temper.

'Before we talk,' he said, 'I have some preliminaries of my own.' He began a careful examination of the suite. Apart from the foyer, it consisted of two high-ceilinged rooms, a marble bathroom of considerable splendour and a tiny kitchen that also served as a bar. Alongside the bar stood an aluminium cube, the size of a packing case, marked FRAGILE, CAMERA EQUIPMENT. Jack unclipped its fasteners and raised the lid. Apart from the sponge rubber lining, the cube was empty. Its red-letter labels marked it for return to a furniture repository in Battersea, south-east London.

'It's a prop for the business we're supposed to be in – movie camera supplies,' she volunteered. 'Scores of these cases go back to London in a juggernaut after the festival. It will be useful if there's anything awkward we need to ship out – your rifle, for instance.'

Jack nodded. He worked his way through the two wardrobes and the drawers, most of which were empty. Touch alone told him that her clothes were expensive. He recognized some of the labels from Grace's fashion magazines: Jil Sander, Donna Karan, Emporio Armani, Calvin Klein. He even went through her underwear.

'What are you looking for?' she said.

'I just want to be certain,' said Jack, running his hands down a blue dress on its hanger, 'that the only firearm in this suite belongs to me.'

'And why do you need to know that?' she said coolly.

He turned to face her. 'I've been sacrificed before for what others saw as a wider interest. I just want to be sure it won't happen again. Once this job is completed, I'll be expendable, and I'd hate the chambermaid to find that poor Monsieur Canning requires an undertaker from room service.'

She returned his level gaze. Her eyes seemed wreathed in a dark mist. 'You should trust me, Jack. I'm making you rich.'

He stepped up to her and said shortly, 'So you say. You'll excuse me for a moment.'

She could not suppress a blink of surprise as his hands travelled at waist level round the soft fold of her dress where it overlapped a gold belt – the only place on her torso where a small sidearm might be concealed.

Then, without apology, he went down on one knee and slid his hands up the inside of her legs, under the hem of her skirt to the warm, bare flesh above her stocking tops.

Recovering her poise, Mrs Canning surprised him by shifting her feet so that she was standing legs apart to facilitate the passage of his hands. She gazed down at him and laughed. 'My, my. We are a bold bad fellow, aren't we?'

Jack stood up and said impassivly, 'Show me the money.'

'It's in the hotel's safe deposit. We'll have to go down.' She watched him place the weapon and his tools in a wardrobe, run a thin steel chain through the double handles and secure it with a brass padlock. He pocketed the key.

She said, 'First, some ground rules. We'll go downstairs separately and meet up at the cashier's desk. While we're here we should be seen together as rarely as possible. We will give the hotel staff little reason to remember us and therefore we will be sparing with room service. When the maid comes in to clean, we will move to the room in which she is not working. When we go out to eat, we'll leave separately, meet up and drive out of town. We'll not make phone calls to the outside. They'll be logged.'

'Sounds wise,' said Jack. 'Now. The money.'

At the cashier's desk, he watched her sign the keyholder's card 'J. Canning'. He was reassured that the young male clerk, harassed by a line of clamouring guests, barely glanced at them as he pressed the button to buzz them into the vault. When they got there Mrs Canning handed Jack her box and said, 'Go ahead. Count it.'

Jack lifted the lid. Inside was a holdall. The eighty thousand pounds was stacked in tight bundles of twenties and fifties. The bank wrappers had been removed and rubber bands substituted. His lips felt powdery. It took all his self-control to stop his hand trembling. He'd never seen so much cash in one place. He selected a sample bundle, riffled through it, took out a twenty and scrutinized it alongside a note from his own wallet.

'Neither my talents nor those of my service run to counterfeiting,' she said, drily.

'That surprises me,' said Jack. 'I would have thought any organization that can arrange an assassination would find printing dodgy banknotes a bit of light relief.' He fingered the bundles but made no attempt at a careful tally. 'It looks okay to me,' he said. 'You'd be crazy to short-change me.'

'Very crazy, Jack. After all, you're the man with the gun.' She returned his gaze coolly.

Chapter Nine

By nightfall Mrs Canning had still not revealed the target. 'Tomorrow will be time enough,' she said. In the bathroom she changed into a discreet, charcoal-grey wool suit, with an emerald green cravat at the throat. They made their separate ways to the hotel garage and met up at his car.

'Which is yours?' Jack asked.

'I flew into Nice and took a cab. I have no car.'

The answer worried Jack. 'You didn't travel with that bloody great camera case?' he said.

She was unperturbed. 'Quite correct. Hauliers bring those things from London by the truck-load. As I told you, it will return the same way.'

Considering the extraordinary nature of their partnership, Mr and Mrs Canning spent a prosaic evening. She evidently knew the Riviera well and directed him along the coast road to the old quarter of Antibes. There, by the canopy over the marketplace, she introduced him to a tiny restaurant, the back of which burrowed into the rockface.

Her French was excellent. In her dealings with the enthusiastic young couple running the place, she revealed herself as something of a milady, accustomed to command – and to being obeyed. Jack chided her, 'Ease up. I thought you didn't want to be remembered.'

She blinked and visibly turned down her imperious manner a few notches. 'Thank you, Jack.' She actually smiled warmly at him, as if he were a fast-learning pupil.

'I'm James now, remember?' he said.

Their conversation across their shellfish platters was necessarily guarded. The tables were tightly pushed together and soon packed with townspeople talking across each other and passing dishes over each other's heads.

At one point his desultory conversation drifted towards his sons and their schooling. 'Shut up!' she said abruptly, dropping an oyster shell onto the cork platter. 'I don't want to know the heartwarming details of your family life. And you certainly won't get to know about mine.'

For a few minutes, Jack was thoughtful. She must already know a great deal about his life, but she had drawn back abruptly when he had tried to put flesh on the bones of her dossier. She wanted to keep his family as an abstract entity and he asked himself why.

Despite all that he already knew or had deduced about Mrs Canning, he found himself becoming attracted to her. The cravat was tucked into her neckline but, when she twisted sideways to speak to the proprietress or engage in the pass-the-plate game he could see an area of soft, tanned breast swelling from a beige lace half-cup under the lining of her jacket.

She was a sexy matron, made the more desirable by her – Jack fumbled for the right word – masterful air. There wasn't a simpering molecule in her body. She had to be someone born to dish out the orders. If she had been a man, he'd have thought Brigade of Guards.

Back in Suite 720, Jack examined the padlocked wardrobe for signs of tampering and was satisfied that nothing had been disturbed.

Mrs Canning opened the mini-bar and offered him a nightcap. Jack had drunk only a single glass of wine at dinner. 'Best not,' he said. 'Booze and marksmanship don't sit well together.' She nodded approval and poured herself some mineral water.

At home, Jack slept naked. Here he wrapped himself in a towel. When he emerged from the bathroom, Mrs Canning had already changed into a pair of men's pyjamas.

He wondered what would happen next. Mrs Canning cleared away the breakfast order form and the gold-wrapped chocolate left by the maid on her pillow, slipped between her sheets, said briefly, 'Don't forget the lights,' and snuggled down.

Jack sat for a long time, back against the headboard, staring into the dark and thinking of the next day. He fell asleep only reluctantly. He was afraid that the dream would recur. It didn't.

Even so, he was up before Mrs Canning. He put on his jogging kit and trainers and was tiptoeing from the bedroom when, from her bed, she said, 'Where on earth do you think you're going?'

Jack turned. She was sitting up, rumpled and sleep-dazed, her top two buttons undone. He said, 'Just for a jog before the carnival gets going again.'

'No, no, no!' Exasperated, she thumped the bed. 'Our best protection is to move only in a crowd. A lone jogger on the Croisette will draw attention and be remembered.'

'You're the boss,' said Jack, abashed at not having thought of that for himself. He slipped off his top and performed a series of calisthenics on the carpet. She watched the sweat course down him. Her gaze and interest were direct and undisguised.

Afterwards, Jack asked, 'Do you have a fitness regime?'

'Too boring,' she said.

When the floor waiter delivered breakfast on a trolley and set it up in the sitting room, they both contrived to be in the bedroom. The man did not see their faces.

After Jack had dressed he found Mrs Canning at the open balcony doors. 'Come here, Jack. Now's the moment for your enlightenment.'

The day was springlike and radiant. Across the road, through the palms, he looked down on the beachboys raking the sand and setting out the parasols and mattresses. The sea was so calm that the white yachts were anchored over their own reflections.

She pointed to the centre of the bay. 'At around noon a rather large yacht will appear and drop anchor. It will remain on station for the period of the Festival. The owner is the international financier and industrialist Sir Gilbert Metzhagen of the MetzCorp conglomerate. Among other things he deals in arms and is a major shareholder of film studios in Los Angeles and Florida. That is the reason for his presence here.

'For him the movies are a pastime, a source of supply of beautiful young women, and a relief from the tedium of making money. Everyone at the Festival who is of any importance will come to pay their respects because he has it within his power to give the green-light to new movie projects without the need to consult either bankers or shareholders.'

'What has he done to upset the British powers-that-be? Why am I having a go at him?'

'You're not having a go at him. Just listen. Sir Gilbert has twelve guests aboard his floating gin palace. At various times, all will come ashore except three. One of those three is the target.'

'The other two?' asked Jack, staring out at the turquoise expanse.

'They are the target's bodyguards.'

Jack raised an eyebrow.

'No,' she said, reading his thoughts. 'They have no reason to suspect imminent trouble. The target – all right, if it eases your concern, it's an adult male – has been under guard for a long time. He's heavily protected on land but has one foible that makes him vulnerable at sea. He adores parascending.' Mrs Canning smiled thinly. 'He says he gets a high from it – whatever that might be. Parascending is one of the few sports he can follow where he does not feel under threat. Drifting along, a couple of hundred feet above the waves, is his cocaine. If the weather holds, he'll be going up every day.'

'I'm to pop him in mid-air from this balcony?' Jack shook his head. 'If that yacht stays way out, it'll be a miracle shot. Are you expecting me to do it from this room? Is that your idea of an open-air operation?'

'All right. Let's take the problems one at a time,' she said briskly. There appeared to be neither doubt nor fear in her. 'He'll take off from an inflatable pontoon. He'll be towed by a powerboat containing his minders. You can't get him while he's waiting on the pontoon for the towboat to position itself because they'll know instantly that he's been shot and have a good idea of the direction from which the shot came. But get him on one of his mid-air circuits, when he comes closest to the shore, and they won't know anything's wrong until he's dropped back onto the pontoon.'

She took his elbow and steered him onto the balcony. 'Just look at this panorama. There must be thirty thousand windows and vantage points overlooking the water. Where could they start to look? Did the bullet come from landward or from another vessel? How could they tell?'

She steered him back into the room. She tapped a wall. 'Solid. Built eighteen ninety. Your rifle makes a sharp cracking noise? Right?'

'Right,' agreed Jack.

'And, as I understand these things, you're unable to use a silencer because it would detract from accuracy.'

'Right again.'

'Very well,' said Mrs Canning. 'The sound will be muffled by the walls and by the existence of the foyer as a sound baffle between us and the corridor.'

'Are you handing out earplugs to the passers-by on the pavement beneath the balcony? You're crazy.'

She gripped his arm. 'You shoot from within the room. They can't see you. Seventy feet below, they'll hear a distant crack mingling with the other street noises. They'll look round, see nothing and assume they heard a car backfiring.'

Jack stepped back ten paces into the room. He pictured a toytown figure at the end of a parachute floating across the patch of sky now framed by the balcony doors.

She could be right. He warmed to the possibilities – and to the challenge. 'The shot would have to be above the parapet. Shooting through the balustrading would give me almost no vision at all. Even aiming above, our mystery man would cross the airspace framed by the window and disappear from view within a few seconds.'

For the first time Mrs Canning's unreadable eyes displayed an emotion: excitement. They were glittering. She said, 'It's the reason we selected you, Jack. We couldn't turn up anybody better qualified to do this. You can do it. I know it! It'll be an incredible shot.'

Jack stared at her then at the oblong of blue sky again. The killing field. 'Sure,' he said drily. 'One for the *Guinness Book of Records*.'

He nodded at the polished sideboard with its marquetry top. 'Help me line this up at right angles to the balcony. Then I can shoot over the parapet from a fixed position.'

'Good!' she said.

Jack saw how easily she lifted her end of the sideboard as they hauled it into the centre of the room. She was no frail female despite her alleged antipathy for physical training.

He took the Super Magnum from the wardrobe, set it on the sideboard and practised a few swings. 'Will he be coming into view left-to-right or right-to-left?' he said, squinting down his 'scope.

For once, Mrs Canning did not have an answer. 'I'm better with movement from right-to-left,' he said. 'It suits both me and the barrel rifling best.' And, to josh her, he added, 'I thought you knew everything there was to know. Like, for instance, the name of this villain I'm to dispatch. What name do I put on the bullet?'

'Cut it out, Jack,' she said. 'All will become clear in due course.'

The sideboard was of sufficient height but his bipod skidded on the shiny surface. They drove to Cap 3000, the giant shopping mall outside Nice, where Jack paid cash for steel clips, a length of cable and some cable tension bolts.

They arrived back at the Berthier in time to watch Sir Gilbert Metzhagen's West German-built white-hulled, black-glass vessel nose slowly to the most prominent position in the bay, the spot once reserved at festival-time for the late Sam Spiegel, producer of *Lawrence of Arabia* and *Bridge on the River Kwai*. From that distance they could not hear the rattle of the anchor as it snaked down into the water.

'"*Die Tat ist alles, nichts der Ruhm*"' Mrs Canning murmured, almost to herself.

Jack waited for her to translate, but he had to ask.

'Goethe,' she said. '"The deed is all, and not the glory."'

'Yes,' agreed Jack. 'Let's hope that's the way this show turns out for us. "Paths of glory lead but to the grave." Thomas Gray,' he riposted, straight-faced.

Mrs Canning threw back her head and laughed, exposing fine white teeth.

'There's hope for you yet, Jack. Even if you only like Westerns.'

Chapter Ten

Jack rigged his weapon for maximum stability and they kept watch for the remainder of the afternoon. There were some comings and goings to the beach jetties that Mrs Canning studied carefully through her binoculars but each time all she said softly was 'No.'

After they had restored the sideboard to its place and stowed Jack's equipment in the secure wardrobe she allowed a maid into the suite to turn down the beds.

That evening they found an obscure inland restaurant beyond La Napoule. Their table-talk was as anodyne as before, which added to Jack's frustration, He knew he was becoming seriously intrigued by this woman, so unlike any other woman he'd ever known. After they had eaten, she agreed to a stroll round a marina to get some fresh air, after their hours cooped up in suite 720. They were just leaving when, as they passed through a pool of sodium light from overhead, they heard a male voice shout something. It sounded like 'Hey, Tinny!'

Mrs Canning froze and said, 'Fuck!'

She did not look round to locate the shouter, which must have taken a high measure of her seemingly infinite self-control. She grabbed Jack's arm and ran with him to the car.

He said, 'What was that about?'

She waved his curiosity aside. 'I don't know and I had no desire to stay and find out,' she said, dismissively.

It must have been around three a.m. when Jack had the dream. It was as terrifying as ever. He woke, shouting and fighting, to find the shadowy shape of Mrs Canning in her pyjamas looming over him.

'Sssssh!' she murmured. She reached towards a bottle on the bedside table and he felt cologne being massaged into his temples. He would never have taken her for a ministering angel but the relief was immediate.

'Just lie back. You've had a nightmare,' she said. He closed his eyes and felt the liquid trickling down the centre of his chest. Her hands moved across him, spreading the moisture to his flanks. Then he felt a sharp tug at his waist as she pulled open his towel, leaving him naked, face up and submitting to the cologne and her knowing fingers. Her hands slid downward over the hard abdomen, of which he was so proud and which Grace said always turned her on, then slid to his feet. She began to dribble the cologne upwards, massaging his legs and parting them as she explored him. His erection was huge even before she arrived at his crotch.

In the gloom he looked up and waited as she threw off her pyjamas and straddled him.

'Don't you dare come,' she said and, without further preliminaries, began riding him with fierce abandon. This was the first time he'd seen her lose control. So she, too, had her hidden tensions. He was not alone. He moved to take over. 'Lie still,' she panted. 'Leave it all to me.'

Jack struggled to hold back. His usual trick with Grace was to concentrate on a picture of a plain brick wall and that is what he now conjured up to block out the erotic vision of Mrs Canning, dark hair tumbled forward over her perspiring face, lips wet and parted. Her hip movement was frantic, backwards and forwards.

'Good boy!' she urged, as if he were a gymkhana horse taking the fences. 'Good boy!'

She suddenly sat upright and leaned backwards. In the low light, her breasts stood out, capped by dark, engorged nipples. She stretched up like a ship's figurehead as she reached behind and under herself and captured his scrotum.

'Now, you bastard, *now!*' she shouted.

Jack's brick wall disintegrated. '*Yes!*' he cried as she writhed on the summit of his arched body.

She rode him for every last drop and finally rolled off replete. She lay beside him, making little mews of pleasure, her hands now massaging herself.

After five minutes, Jack, organ erect, moved across her body. But she put a firm palm to his chest and said in a matter-of-fact tone that dumbfounded Jack, 'No. I was just making use of the facilities the hotel has to offer. For which I thank you.'

For a moment Jack was speechless. 'Then fuck you,' he said finally. 'You're really a cold bitch, aren't you?'

'Most probably,' she said airily, heading naked for the bathroom. She turned back. 'Just to ease your conscience, adultery in hotel rooms is not supposed to count. In any case, don't think you can award yourself a medal for fucking me. It was *I* who fucked *you*.'

She slammed the bathroom door, leaving Jack nonplussed.

When she returned, in her pyjamas, she was her usual composed self. For a moment she stood listening to the silence. She said, 'Well, our screaming and shouting proved one thing: the walls are solid. There's not been a peep from the neighbours.'

She got into her bed, turned her back on him and, as far as he could tell, fell immediately asleep. Jack lay staring up into the dark. He could still feel her wetness. He continued to pulse.

Chapter Eleven

They breakfasted early in near silence, pushed the waiter's trolley out into the corridor so that he would have no need to re-enter the suite, took in the film magazines, *Daily Variety, Hollywood Reporter, Screen International*, a set of which had been dumped outside each door along the seventh floor, rehung the don't-disturb sign, and got to work.

Mrs Canning helped Jack lift the sideboard into position. While they had been copulating a few hours earlier he had felt the athletic quality of her muscle tone, which did not suggest a passive woman who found exercise boring. How many other lies had he been told?

Assembling and anchoring the Super Magnum to the makeshift platform took thirty minutes. Mrs Canning, three paces back from the balcony doors, already had her binoculars trained on the yacht.

The weather was all that Riviera weather can be. Jack studied the desultory flutter of the flags above the beach restaurants and, through his 'scope, the movement of the yacht's pennants. There was no variation. 'It's very important in long-range shooting,' he said. 'If there are differing wind speeds along the trajectory, it can play hell with the calculations.' He inserted the box magazine.

He felt jumpy. He circled the room, shaking his arms, loosening his wrists and fingers, and at last felt calm enough for his mental exercises. He had warned Mrs Canning of the spiritual process and self-effacement involved in fitting himself to the purpose. She had known better than to mock. He squatted on the sofa and closed his eyes.

The words of Zen master Suzuki flowed through him: '*Man is a thinking reed, but his great works are done when he is not calculating and thinking. Childlikeness has to be restored after long years of training in the art of self-forgetfulness.*'

Jack began to breathe deeply and steadily. '*The arrow is off the string but does not fly straight to the target, nor does the target stand where it is. Calculation which is miscalculation sets in.*'

He listened to the ancient wisdom and, for a while, the room receded.

Mrs Canning remained composed until at ten a.m. she made a sharp motion with her left hand and hissed, 'There's activity.' Jack opened his eyes and went to work.

They watched the Sunseeker towboat being lowered from its davits and six figures clamber aboard. Metzhagen's other guests were watching from the ship's rails. Mrs Canning counted, 'Driver, two minders, two crew – and our man. Jack, you're on!'

He handed her some cottonwool and they rolled their own earplugs. He massaged chalk powder into his hands and handed her two leather elbow cups to buckle to his arms.

The target, handily dressed in a distinctive orange lifejacket, took off from an inflated rubber pontoon some thirty feet in length anchored two hundred yards from the yacht. Two seamen held open the 'chute to capture the wind as the towboat took up the cable slack and the target took off, his feet briefly skimming the waves as he went off the pontoon.

The bulky protective clothing and harness made it impossible for Jack to gain any clear picture of the man's age, size or looks. It could have been a robot under the webbing and the inflated rubber. Jack felt comforted by the thought.

The green and yellow 'chute climbed rapidly at the end of the tow-cable. The target's legs swung violently before his body adjusted to the forward motion.

Jack said, 'Oh, balls!' The tow was taking the target out to sea, beyond Metzhagen's yacht.

Mrs Canning said, 'No good?'

'No bloody good at all,' said Jack. 'You'd have as much chance of hitting him if you were aiming from North Africa.' They both watched the parachute gliding lazily in oval circuits, the tiny figure dangling immune beneath.

After a nail-biting twenty minutes, the Sunseeker suddenly tilted to port and began to tow the 'chute closer inshore. The craft was now between the beach and the yacht. Mrs Canning said urgently, 'Go for it!'

Jack pulled the rifle's short butt tight into his shoulder and put one in the breech. At this distance the slightest body tremor would throw his aim right over the rainbow. This would be a shot that could only be made between heartbeats. He took up a firing position, elbow pads resting on the marquetry, facing the rectangle of azure sky. He said, 'Stand back but give me a directional warning a couple of seconds before you judge he'll come into my view.'

He blinked to clear his eyes and waited. His throat felt constricted but his grip, as ever, was nerveless.

Mrs Canning said rapidly, 'Coming now! Right to left!'

And there he was, hanging blissfully in the sunlight, rocking gently. Jack, lying forward over the end of the sideboard, got him into focus on the 'scope. Christ, the distance was not far short of two and a half thousand yards. The outcome rested now on Jack's co-ordination and gut instincts as much as the excellence of his weaponry.

He shifted his long muzzle minutely, leading the swaying figure across the blue patch. Mrs Canning, the room, the reasons that had brought him there, were forgotten. His concentration on the target was total. He judged that he had some twelve seconds before the figure exited to his left.

Jack waited for the heartbeat and, in that following moment of bodily calm, he squeezed the trigger.

Even with the earplugs, the crack-pop was shattering in the confined space. He and Mrs Canning held their breath and stared at each other. She recovered herself and said, 'Stay away from the balcony. People down below will be looking around.'

They stood back for five minutes, then Mrs Canning lazily sauntered outside and leaned on the balustrade. 'Everything's normal,' she murmured over her shoulder. Jack joined her. The clusters of film fans at the various hotel entrances had eyes only for the comings and goings of the Festival delegates. On the terraces, late risers were taking their coffee and croissants. There were no signs of alarm or agitation.

They watched the Sunseeker cut a bone-white path through the turquoise water, but now the driver had progressed to figures of eight. The target dangled, enigmatic, two hundred feet above.

'What do you think? Did you get him?' she said.

Jack shrugged. 'It felt right. But it was a bitch of a distance.' He took her binoculars and studied the tiny figure. 'Well, he's not walking wounded or he'd be making frantic signals to the boatmen. And he can't have sensed anything amiss, such as a round whizzing past his ear, for the same reason. So he's either dead or so gravely wounded that he can't signal. Or,' said Jack, gazing steadily at her, 'he's alive and unaware of dirty work afoot at the crossroads.'

Mrs Canning seemed not to appreciate his attempt at humour. She returned inside and switched up the air conditioning to disperse the smell of cordite.

They had their answer twenty minutes later when the Sunseeker slowed, allowing the parachute to descend gently onto the inflated pontoon. The target toppled forward onto his face, his 'chute draped over the pontoon's edge touching the water. A helper rushed forward to drag the lines clear.

Neither Jack nor Mrs Canning showed any signs of breathing. Their gaze was fixed on the toppled figure.

They both saw his arms move. Then he pushed himself to his feet and began freeing himself from his harness.

Mrs Canning blazed. 'You cunt!' she said. 'You missed him.'

'There were no guarantees,' said Jack, watching the target supervising the hauling in of his 'chute. 'And I don't like that sort of language coming from a woman.'

'You bourgeois prick,' she fumed. 'We're going to have to go through this all over again.' She didn't try to hide her contempt and could barely bring herself to speak to him as they began to restore the room to its normal state.

Her attitude, however, worked on Jack like icy sleet driving into his face. Hauling the sideboard to the wall, he felt himself somehow awakening, as if from a trance. He rubbed his eyes. What could he have been thinking of when he took on this assignment? He had no official standing. He wasn't a duly appointed state executioner. What gave him the right . . .?

The full realization of the lunacy upon which he had embarked and of the likely consequences for his family if anything should go wrong, crashed in upon him. He shook his head, like a punch-drunk boxer attempting to get his opponent into focus. He choked out, 'I can't go through with this.'

Mrs Canning said, 'What?'

'I must have been mad even to listen to you. I don't know who that poor bugger is out there, but he's not my enemy and I've got no reason to kill him.'

Mrs Canning was standing stock still, her stare ominous. She finally found her tongue. 'The deal was play-or-pay, Captain Boulder,' she grated.

Jack waved a hand, brushing aside a minor problem. 'I'll return all the money. Don't worry.'

'I'm not worrying. You don't understand. The pay exacted if you fail to carry out your obligations will not be in cash.' She faced him squarely.

'There won't be much point in taking it out on my hide,' said Jack. 'You'll get your money back and we'll call it quits.' He began to dismantle the gun.

'This operation has been a long time in the planning and an opportunity may not come again for many months, if ever. This man has to be destroyed. If he isn't, it's not you that will be in jeopardy. Think of your family, Captain Boulder.'

Jack froze. 'What about my family?'

She hesitated, then said reluctantly, 'They've been taken to a safe house. They're in the hands of my colleagues.' She took two steps back, anticipating his reaction — and had not misread him.

Jack roared with rage and lunged at her. He slammed her against a wall, one hand holding her throat. He hissed, 'If a single hair of one of their heads is as much as ruffled, I'll hunt down every last one of you as I hunted down Sean McGurk.'

She gurgled and tried to speak. He eased his grip, and she gasped, 'Kill me and they'll kill one of yours. You're being asked to dispose of a piece of scum, not Mother Teresa. You're a soldier. Where's your training? Get a grip on yourself.'

Jack shoved her to one side and headed for the telephone. 'No! No!' she shouted. 'You mustn't use the hotel phones.'

Cursing, Jack said, 'You're a lying bitch. My family is still at home and I'm going to ring them.'

Mrs Canning made a rush at him but Jack fended her off with his forearm. He raised the receiver and realized he did not know the code for London. He called the hotel operator. She came on almost instantly but as she said, '*Oui?*' the line went dead. 'Wha—?' Jack whirled round.

Mrs Canning, panting, had the wallplug in her hand. She put the table between them. 'Listen to me, Jack. I'll put your wife and children on the phone for you — but not from this phone in this room.'

He put down the handset and started to circle the table but she moved as he moved, watching his hands clench and unclench. 'Jack, stop being stupid. Your family is simply on holiday. Your wife has been told you're on an important mission and that taking them to the country for a few days is merely a precaution. They have no sense of personal danger. They believe they're in the warm embrace of your colleagues. It's spring. They're having a good time.'

'So that makes it all right, does it? They can dance round the maypole but the pole accidentally falls on them unless I go ahead and pot this guy? I can't believe you'd murder three innocent people. You're bluffing.'

Mrs Canning dropped the plug on the table from where the cable dragged it to the floor. She watched it snake out of sight and then said, 'You're seeing this through the eyes of a British Army officer – with all that means in terms of honour and courage. But some of the people you and I are dealing with don't have that background. They'd kill for much less than a hundred thousand and with much less justification. If you kill that man out there on Metzhagen's yacht, you'll ultimately be saving thousands of lives. It's a trade-off, Jack. One miserable life for a multitude.'

'And what if I miss?'

'If you've made a genuine attempt and I'm convinced, we'll abort the operation. No recriminations – but no more money, either. And, be warned, you won't be able to fake it. I'll know.'

'If I get him, will you immediately make the call to have my wife and children returned home unharmed?'

She looked relieved. 'You have my word, Jack.' The tension started to leave her and she relaxed visibly. She could see him wavering and the crisis evaporating.

His rage had gone cold. He said quietly, 'I want to speak to my family.'

She nodded. 'We'll go separately to the public phones at the railway station. You go first.'

It was nearly six in the evening in London. Grace and the boys should all have been home. Mrs Canning stood by while he got only the answering machine. Wordlessly, she took the phone, dialled another number and murmured something. She waited a full two minutes, then stepped out of the booth and handed him the phone, saying, 'Don't frighten her.'

Mrs Canning had not lied. Grace obviously thought she was among friends but the anxieties of the Army days had returned. Was he risking his neck? Why hadn't he said his mission was more than weapons evaluation?

Jack placated her with platitudes. She and the boys had been taken to the country as a precaution against a most unlikely eventuality ... They'd be home in a week ... He was helped in that during his service days she had been used to the daily routines of checking under the family car, keeping an eye open for strangers, being wary of unexpected packages. Grace understood the need for security and, although anxious, did not sound panicked by the unexpected return of such tense living conditions.

The boys were out in an orchard playing, but Grace chattered on without anyone trying to cut her off. No, she didn't know exactly where they were. For security reasons, they'd been collected in a windowless van. They were staying in some sort of dower house of a large country estate. The garden was lovely. She had been advised they should not wander from the grounds. They were under twenty-four-hour guard ...

It was Jack, a tennis ball in his throat, who brought the conversation to a close. 'Just remember, I love you and the boys.'

'Take care. We love you, too,' said Grace.

He felt Mrs Canning's hand on his shoulder and he replaced the receiver. 'You bastards,' he said grimly.

On his way back to Suite 720, Jack's brain whirred furiously as he tried to think his way out of his dilemma. He barely noticed, and then only with resentment, the jollity of the Festival crowds and the elegance of the shoppers along the rue d'Antibes. That evening the weather changed: there would be no parascending next day for Mr X – or for some days after.

Since the phone conversation, the atmosphere in the suite was frigid. At night Mrs Canning kept to her own bed. If she crept up on him again he had resolved to throw her off. However, she made no attempt – and the same excuse did not present itself again. The dream stayed away.

During the day they suffered cabin fever, and in the evenings when they drove through noisy crowds to find obscure out-of-town restaurants, they were hardly able to exchange a civil word. On the second day the rain had been torrential, hitting the open-sided beach restaurants horizontally and driving the lunch crowds up into the hotels. At one point, Mrs Canning spat, 'This thing has been in the planning for nine months and it has all the hallmarks of going pear-shaped.' Apparently, the idea that there could be poor weather in May in the South of France had not occurred either to her or to her co-conspirators.

She was jumpy, and Jack drew satisfaction from the thought that, despite the pose of effortless superiority, her nuts were in the crusher too. Mischievously, he said, 'I suppose it's possible this rain will hold. The poor bastard may not go up at all.'

She shot him a withering look. 'Most amusing, Jack.'

He began to pray for the storm to continue – it could be the penalty-free way out for him – but on the fifth day the clouds began to drift south-easterly and on the following morning the sun came up on full power into a clear sky. The wind was barely perceptible and the drying flags hung limp against their poles.

Jack's heart slumped but Mrs Canning's cheeks were flushed and excitement glinted in those elusive eyes. 'Play or pay, Jack,' she reminded him pointedly.

He nodded glumly. 'If he comes out, we'll follow the procedure as before except that when I've got a bead on him I'll lay two shots in his path. There'll be two rounds – all I'll have time for – that'll arrive in his air space at minutely differing moments. He'll be literally advancing to meet them. And I'm relying on one of them to make contact.'

'Two chances instead of one?'

'Right,' said Jack. He squatted on the sofa, closed his eyes and began to empty his mind of his despair. *'The hitter and the hit are no longer two opposing objects, but are one reality . . . he becomes one with the perfecting of his technical skills.'*

He returned, serene, to an awareness of the room and was almost relieved when he saw the Sunseeker being lowered and the rubber pontoon inflated from compressed air cylinders. There was to be no reprieve. He'd get it over with. He made an effort of will, and pride in his own marksmanship overrode the helplessness he felt in the company of this iron-willed woman. He knew, without a scintilla of doubt, that, should he miss, she would never believe it had not been deliberate. Like a mantra, he silently repeated to himself, 'This man is scum. This man is scum.'

The target soared aloft once again. And, once again, Jack crouched patiently behind his Super Magnum through a dozen or more circuits before the Sunseeker towed the target nearer the shore.

Jack prepared himself, tuning into his own heartbeats. The cold feel of the butt leather against his cheek always calmed him to a state approaching tranquillity. Today he felt omnipotent. Suddenly, Mrs Canning snapped, 'Coming in, left to right!'

It was not an ideal set-up but Jack was ready. Despite the magnification of the 'scope, the dangling figure seemed impossibly small – like one of

Harry Lime's dots, far below him in the Prater Garten. The distance was an awesome two thousand yards, at least.

The rapid repeat of the two rounds was skull-slamming. He could only imagine the reaction out on the Croisette. People would be looking round, mouths open, 'What? . . . Where?' But there would be nothing to see.

Jack said immediately, 'I've got him.'

Mrs Canning said through her binoculars. 'How do you know? There's no sign of it. He's still going round.'

'I just know,' said Jack doggedly. 'I can feel it. In competition shooting, it's a feeling you get even before the butts people signal the score.'

Mrs Canning continued to peer through the binoculars. 'His head's lolling. Or is that wishful thinking?'

Twenty minutes later they witnessed the drama unfold. The Sunseeker slowed to a halt and the billowing 'chute expelled its air and collapsed. The target had not manoeuvred his lines. He failed to land on the tip of the pontoon and, instead, sank softly into the water. The two crewmen peered over the pontoon's edge and the boat circled to pick up Mr X who was bobbing on the surface in his lifejacket.

The Sunseeker's occupants were ten yards away when they realized something was wrong. One minder jumped into the water and braced the man they had been employed to protect. He was face down until he was heaved upwards and dragged onto the diving platform.

From the Berthier, Jack and Mrs Canning watched the resuscitation attempts as the Sunseeker, dragging the 'chute, which was still half in the water, sped back to Metzhagen's yacht. They could see figures running along the deck, gesticulating and indecisive in the face of the shouted messages coming over the two-way radio.

The target was clearly slumped without movement on the deck. 'It looks like a kill, Jack. Bloody marvellous. A miraculous shot.' Mrs Canning's voice was warmer than it had been for days.

They dismantled the Magnum and restored the room to normal.

When the police boats began to appear, Mrs Canning said, 'We may not get a confirmation for some time.'

'Dead or winged, I've kept my end of the deal. We're going to a phone now to have my family returned home.'

'Why don't we wait to see if it's a kill?'

'No!' said Jack. 'We're going to do it now.' She looked into his set face and nodded.

They followed the same procedure as before and he stood close to her as she said into the mouthpiece, 'It's a definite hit. Terminal? We don't yet know. The hired hand wants his family driven home right away.' She listened for a few seconds, said, 'Good,' replaced the receiver and turned to Jack. 'There, it's done. Satisfied?'

Before they split up to go back to the hotel, she said, 'Why don't you take a stroll along the Croisette and check for any unusual activity that the shots might have triggered?'

Apart from the short walks between hotel and telephones, it was the first time Jack had been permitted to mingle alone with the Festival crowd. Everything seemed normal. Back at the Berthier, the huge foyer was lined with booths advertising, and video machines screening, the movies of many nations. Most, judging by the lurid posters, were pornographic, not his sort of thing, and Jack stepped out onto the terrace where he found a canvas-backed director's chair. Stencilled on it was the name William Wyler. He wondered briefly who that might be. He sat down and ordered a much-needed Scotch and soda. Could he trust those bastards back in England to take their hooks out of Grace and the boys?

Around him, people were chatting normally. Nothing untoward was happening. All the excitement was taking place out of sight, across the road and beyond the beach.

He was sipping his drink quietly and assembling his thoughts on the events of the morning when a hand gripped his shoulder. Jack twisted in his chair and found himself gazing up at the impossibly perfect teeth of the man he'd encountered in the lift on the day of his arrival at the Berthier.

'Hi there!' said the stranger. 'Mind if I join you?'

'No – I mean, yes,' Jack blurted, startled.

The stranger's tanned face dropped from smile to frown and Jack silently cursed himself for his clumsiness. 'Look, I'm sorry,' he said, 'but I'm waiting for someone to join me for a business meeting.'

The man said coldly, 'Sure, don't give it another thought. Just checking you out for that game of golf.' He moved away between the tables without waiting for an answer.

Twenty minutes later Jack paid cash for his drink and stood up to go back into the hotel. The golf man was sitting with a slim, raven-haired girl at a table in the back row. He eyed Jack accusingly. He had been well placed to know that no one had joined Jack. He and the woman, face largely concealed by shades the size of saucers, wordlessly observed Jack's shame-faced retreat through the hotel bar and into the lobby.

Chapter Twelve

Mrs Canning was leaning against a wall, watching CNN with the sound muted. She was dragging on a long cigarette. He had not seen her smoke before, although he had noted a packet when he had checked her handbag on his arrival. Good. He liked the idea of the ice matron being unsettled.

She had opened the massive camera case and tossed in the overalls he had worn for the shoot. She had needed no lecture from him about the gases and sooty residue that spew from a fired weapon onto the user's unprotected skin and clothes, leaving their traces for the forensic scientist to scrape up.

For once, there was something hesitant in her manner. She seemed preoccupied, then said, 'You'd better get into a hot bath, scrub up and wash your hair. You must have traces on you. No point in leaving anything to chance.'

Jack gazed steadily at her. Her voice was unusually brittle. She turned her back, waving aside her smoke and staring out at Metzhagen's yacht the deck of which was now black with purposeful figures.

Jack used the hotel's shampoo and body gel, scrubbing his face and hands until they were red. He was lying back in the handsome marble bath, allowing unexpected fatigue to ooze from his pores, when the door opened quietly and she took one step into the steamy room. She was stark naked, and in her right hand she carried a 9mm Browning automatic, complete with sound suppressor.

Jack stretched, luxuriating under the foam. His arms came dripping out of the water and he placed his hands behind his head.

He nodded at the silencer and said, 'There was no need to pack that, you know. A condom stretched over the hole in the front does almost as well. In any case, aren't you being over-cautious? I thought we'd established that this suite is soundproof.'

He gave an elaborate sigh. 'I guess I always knew that bumping off some poor sod wasn't going to be enough to earn me a hundred thou. But does the Secret Intelligence Service need to play it this dirty?'

A wary look crossed her face. She hadn't expected jokes. She said,

'I'm sorry, Jack. It's the way it's got to be. Ruby took out Oswald; I have to take out you.'

To her surprise, Jack said, 'Ruby at least kept his clothes on. Why the striptease?'

She shrugged, looking uncomfortable. 'The Lizzie Borden theory,' she said shortly.

'The one who gave her mother forty whacks?'

Mrs Canning nodded. 'She got off because there was no evidence, no blood – nothing – to link her to the killing. The theory is she stripped before doing it and had a good scrub-up afterwards.' She took another step into the room.

'Careful,' teased Jack, 'I might splash water in your eyes.'

She looked genuinely ill at ease. 'Don't make this worse than it already is. I argued for letting you have the money and sending you on your way. But they said you were a flake. They said only a bloody fool would have let himself get fingered for the McGurk job. They said you might just as well have placed an ad in the *Irish Times*. They said that sooner or later you'd get careless or tell wifey or somebody.'

'They, whoever "they" are,' said Jack, contemptuously, 'are a bunch of creeps. Is MI6 now skulking behind women's skirts? Or, in your case,' he added drily, 'lack of 'em.'

The water was growing cold and she still hadn't fired. She was struggling with herself, he noted with satisfaction, and he wanted to see just how far she would go.

In the steamy atmosphere, her dark hair was becoming plastered to her forehead and her jaw was working as if she were trying to stiffen her resolve. She said, 'Jack, everything is not quite what you think. But there's no point arguing. The stewards' decision is final.'

She brought out her left hand from behind her back and proffered a small plastic object that Jack at first thought was an open powder compact. She lowered it so that he could see the red capsule inside. She said, 'Take it, Jack. It's the painless way. It'll all be over in a moment. Don't make me use this.' She levelled the weapon at his midriff.

Jack said, 'Aren't you even going to tell the condemned man the identity of the guy on the parachute?' She shook her head. He said, 'Jane, or whatever your real name is, you and your colleagues have been very clever but you personally have made one big error.'

She raised her eyes from sighting the Browning. He said, 'You shouldn't have hidden the gun in that tissue-box fixture on the wall behind you. This is the one room where we've each spent time alone. So you couldn't know that I'd found it. Nor,' he added deliberately, 'that I've spiked the silencer.'

'Nice try, Jack,' she said. 'I checked the gun and magazine while you were downstairs.'

'I'm sure you did,' said Jack evenly. 'That's why I was let out on my own, wasn't it? But I'm betting you just screwed in the silencer because there are no working parts to jam or check out.'

'You're lying,' she said, wiping beads of sweat from her upper lip with the back of her gun hand. 'But I admire you for it. I really do. Grace under pressure. And I'm not making a pun at the expense of your wife.'

'About my wife – and my children. Would you tell me the truth? Have they really been taken home or is that just another lie?'

'They're safe, Jack. I wouldn't lie to you now. They'll be back in Shepherd's Bush this evening.'

'Thank you for that,' said Jack politely. He settled himself comfortably in the water and added, 'Jane, you have a dilemma. If I'm telling the truth and you discharge that thing, you will lose fingers – or worse. If you try to remove the silencer before firing, I will be out of this bath and at your throat the moment you start to unscrew it. The only sensible course is for you to put down the weapon and negotiate.'

'Please, Jack,' she said. 'Take the pill.'

'Fuck the pill,' said Jack.

And Mrs Canning fired.

Chapter Thirteen

Instinctively Jack slid flat, sending a wave of perfumed water over the side and surging across the tiled floor towards Mrs Canning's bare feet. He came up blowing water from his mouth. The sound of rending metal in the confined space drilled into his eardrums as painfully as chalk screeching across a blackboard.

Jack shook his head to clear his stinging eyes. The sight that confronted him was appalling. Mrs Canning was sliding down the tiled wall, leaving a wide track in the condensation. Her legs were obscenely splayed and she had not escaped with the mere loss of fingers. The suppressor had splintered, sending a shard up into the underside of her chin and the soft tissue behind her face.

'Jesus Christ!' said Jack. He hadn't seen such a severe wound since the Enniskillen bombing. He jumped from the bath and took her by the shoulders. 'You stupid, stupid woman!' he said.

He could see quite clearly that she was already past hearing. Bright crimson blood was pumping from her mouth and nostrils. Those mysterious dark eyes were already losing their focus. She would not have had time to feel pain.

Jack tilted her forward to examine her back and head for an exit wound. There was none. The metal fragment was still lodged in her skull. Jack had not anticipated such a cataclysmic outcome.

He gazed around, momentarily dazed by the extent of the disaster. Her blood was diluting in the pool of bath water, spreading like pink champagne across the mosaic floor and glugging into the tiny brass drain. Jack swore, picked up the limp body and laid her in his now-cold bathwater where her blood continued to flow.

He had to think. A doctor was no use – she was past any hope of resuscitation. He looked down at his own bloodied body, then took the handspray from the shower unit, hosed himself down, snatched a clean towel from the shelf and stepped gingerly between the red puddles into the bedroom.

His mind went into overdrive as he dried himself. In the living room he discovered that she had opened the camera container. He had suspected, but knew now for sure, the true function of this object. It was to have been his coffin. The sticky-backed destination labels, bearing the address of a storage warehouse in Battersea, south-west London, were lined up neatly on the sideboard from which he had taken his pot at Mr X.

Mr X. Jack had forgotten Mr X. Was he dead? Wounded? He still didn't know. He wrapped the damp towel around his middle and moved towards the balcony doors.

There was intense activity in the bay. Through the palm trees in the foreground, he could see uniformed men clustered on a number of yachts, with small official-looking craft scuttling between them. The floating gin palaces of Hollyhood were being combed for the marksman. The sight afforded him a passing moment of grim satisfaction. Good. The police obviously could not believe the shot had come from land.

Jack padded back to the bathroom door. Mrs Canning's heart had made its last beat, her blood was no longer flowing and the water in which she slumped was now bright red. There was something erotic at the way her fine breasts and thoroughbred legs were thrust upward, clear of the water's surface. His mind raced back involuntarily to the nightmare and his sexual encounter with this bizarre woman and he felt a pang of guilt.

He pulled the bathplug and watched her blood swirl away. He winced, reminded of the embalming job an Irish undertaker had performed on one of his men. The man had drained the corpse's blood into a jug and flushed it down the lavatory.

Jack was in no state yet to think ahead beyond knowing that, if he was to survive this mess, he had to clean up. He took the shower handset again and worked his way across the floor, swilling the blood stains into the drain. He retrieved Mrs Canning's pill case with its glass capsule and slipped it into one of his jackets. He dried off her shattered automatic. The silencer had split open like a blossoming metallic flower. He dried the bathroom floor with a towel and then turned to the gruesome task of washing down Mrs Canning and cleaning the bath. He pressed her eyelids closed. She lay there, he thought, ivory pale like an odalisque painted by that Viennese chap whose stuff he'd seen on calendars.

He dabbed her gently, somehow unable to feel angry that she had intended to murder him. He'd long accepted the possibility of his own death as a legitimate transaction of the professional soldier. Certainly, he did not feel the hunger for revenge that had moved him to stalk Sean McGurk on behalf of his dead men. But the rage he felt over their using his family remained.

Then he began to clear out the dead woman's wardrobe, laying some of her clothes in the bottom of the camera packing case. He had been around enough death to know that he had, perhaps three hours before rigor mortis set in, transforming the body into an unbending mannequin. He hauled her from the bath, dragged her to the case, folded her into the foetal position, and lowered her in. Around her, he wedged the remainder of her clothes. He removed the magazine and placed the Browning automatic beside her.

Jack was about to close and seal the lid when he had a thought. He tore the letterhead from a sheet of hotel stationery and wrote on the blank: SHE BROUGHT THIS ON HERSELF. SHE FIRED THE WEAPON. He covered her matted hair with the bloodstained towels, placed the note on top and clipped the lid into place. The relief at no longer having the body in view was immediate.

As if recovering from a trance, Jack was surprised to find he was still naked. He dressed rapidly and poured himself a steadying Scotch from the minibar.

He surveyed the bathroom and offered up a silent prayer of gratitude for floor and walls that could be wiped clean. He opened the suite door and peered out, waited until he saw the chambermaid enter a room then strode swiftly down the corridor and purloined a fresh set of towels from her trolley.

His head was pounding when he got back into his room. What else? What had he missed? He'd emptied her pockets and bag. He studied the contents: cash, the phoney passport, phoney driver's licence, cigarettes, a minimal selection of cosmetics, dark glasses – and the safe deposit key. He took the cash and the key and placed the other items alongside her body.

One thing caused the fine hairs on his back to stand on end. When he'd first arrived and peered into her handbag, he'd noted what he thought was a lipstick in a neat gold tube attached to a carrying ring. Now a tug on the ring unreeled a spring-loaded wire cheesecutter similar to those used by wartime commandos on the throats of dozing enemy sentries. Browning automatic, cyanide pill, cheesecutter. Mrs Canning came well equipped as a bringer of death.

There was nothing to indicate her true identity, not even a set of domestic house keys. The cheesecutter made him feel better about her demise.

He telephoned the *concierge*. What arrangement had Mrs Canning made for returning the camera equipment to London? It would be transported by road with other business guests' heavy luggage.

When? On the day following the end of the festival.

Could the case be taken to the hotel's luggage room now? But certainly, Monsieur.

Jack stuck on the labels. It took two porters to manoeuvre the metal case onto the trolley. Jack watched, grim-faced, as Mrs Canning was trundled away to the service lift.

Chapter Fourteen

Jack remembered the rifle. Christ, how could he have forgotten? Was he going mad? He unlocked the wardrobe and hauled the golfbag down to the garage. He had to sit in the Volvo for fifteen minutes before he was sure that no curious eyes would witness him stow the dismantled weapon in the concealed compartment.

He was in serious need of another drink. With the bag – now containing nothing more lethal than the golfclubs – slung over his shoulder, Jack stepped out onto the busy terrace. He selected a chair with Rita Hayworth's name stencilled on the back. Even Jack knew who *she* was.

'Hello!' said a voice. Coolly looking down at him was the ravenhead in the outsize sunglasses, the companion of the golfing nut who had pestered him. She said, 'You've taken the last table. May I join you?'

Jack's hesitation brought a grin to a pert face. 'Now, don't tell me you're waiting for Sharon Stone.' She nodded at his golfbag. 'Going for a game?'

'Just been,' said Jack.

She looked oddly at him and said, 'Sure.'

She settled herself and added, 'You know, you really pissed Sidney with that brush-off this morning. You're not exactly Mr Tactful, are you? A great many men here would pay money for a chance to play golf with Sidney.'

As the waiter approached, she said, 'Mine's a whisky sour.'

Jack noticed that there were a few empty tables. She'd ignored them to reach him. He said, 'Who is Sidney and who is Sharon Stone?'

She threw her head back and let out a loud guffaw. 'Oh, boy! Do you mean you aren't connected to the movie business? I think I'm in love!' She took off the ridiculous shades. 'And I had you down as an actor on the hustle. Forgive me.'

The drinks arrived and Jack again paid cash – which made her curious. 'No hotel tab?'

He shrugged. 'I like to pay my way.'

She looked over her shoulder conspiratorially. 'For God's sake don't tell anybody or you'll have ten thousand instant friends. You must be the only living creature at this benighted wing-ding not living on an expense account.'

She put out a hand. 'By the way, I'm Betty Bentinck. If you've never heard of Sharon Stone, you've certainly not heard of me. I'm also an actress. I've just made my first motion picture for Sidney – Sidney Zuckerman, that is. He's an independent producer who dreams the impossible dream of becoming a Selznick. I'm what they call his squeeze of the moment.' The side of her delectable mouth stretched into a wry expression. 'Yeah, go ahead and jump to conclusions. You won't be wrong. I'm a trained and good actress, but without Sidney's juice in Tinseltown I might as well have trained to catch fish at Marineland.'

Jack nodded sympathetically. This American girl's lively candour was a refreshing diversion from his anxieties. He said, 'I'm James Canning. Where's Sidney?'

She craned upward in her seat. 'I think I can see him at the end of the jetty. He was supposed to go out to the Metzhagen boat to pay his respects but he came back a few minutes ago to say something peculiar was going down.'

'Peculiar?'

'Yeah, the French gendarmes were on some kind of a security alert and preventing anybody going out to the boats. Sidney's down there again giving them the benefit of his don't-you-know-who-I-am? routine.'

Jack, fighting to keep his tone casual, said, 'Is he a good friend of Metzhagen?'

'They have business dealings,' said Betty. She leaned forward. 'Wanna know something? I've got a secret. It's not Metzhagen Sidney's going out to do kiss-kiss with.' She stopped abruptly, then said, 'Cross your heart and hope to die if you tell?' Jack traced a finger across his chest. Her voice fell to a whisper. 'There's a reception on board for that crazy Limey, Conrad Niven. I'm only telling you because you're a fellow Englishman and I trust you.'

Jack's mind whirled. Niven's notoriety stretched further than the world of film buffs. In a reckless gesture of defiance in the outraged face of the Islamic world, Niven, working out of Hollywood, had gathered together a cast of unknown actors and anonymous financial backers and had directed a lightly disguised account of the agony of Salman Rushdie, the British author condemned to death in a *fatwah* issued in Tehran by the Ayatollah Khomeini. The alleged sullying of the Prophet's name in Rushdie's book, *The Satanic Verses*, had prompted the Iranians to place a million-pound price on the author's head. The bounty hunters had yet to collect.

Despite the film industry being hailed by commentators for a rare act of foolhardy courage, the movie, *Satanic Times*, had the shortest credit 'crawl' in cinema history – just the name of Conrad Niven. For once, neither cast nor crew desired their customary screen acknowledgements.

The film had a brief run to packed houses but after three cinemas had been bombed, the exhibitors had withdrawn the picture and run for cover.

Worse followed. Despite the precaution of disguising the entire cast in heavy make-up, the Iranians had identified the Indian actor portraying the fictionalized author. He had been found in his Bombay home with his throat cut and the ayatollahs had issued a second *fatwah*, putting a price of another million pounds on the head of Conrad Niven. Few in Hollywood disputed that the crazy schmuck had brought it on himself.

Jack Boulder gulped the remainder of his whisky and attempted to sort through the bedlam of his thoughts. Finally, he said, 'It must be a dangerous business, hanging around someone like Conrad Niven. If the Iranians throw a bomb at him there's no telling how many people could get caught in the blast.'

Betty shook her dark curls. 'Nah. They'd never get near enough. Sidney says he has armed bodyguards from your Special Branch when he's in Europe and FBI agents when he's in America. The poor slob isn't even allowed to come ashore to see his own movie.'

Jack gagged. Surely Niven couldn't possibly have been his target. It made no sense. MI6 assassinating a man under the protection of Special Branch? Comrade set against comrade? No, his target must have been someone else.

'Uh-oh,' said Betty, gazing over his shoulder towards the beach. 'Sidney's on the way back. Looks as if the cops have put him in turnaround. Either that or his opening weekend grosses have headed south.'

But Jack wasn't listening. He realized suddenly that she was staring at him. She said, 'Are you all right?'

He stood up abruptly, toppling Rita Hayworth's chair, said, 'I've just remembered a call I have to make,' and was gone before she could say another word.

Puzzled, Betty followed his progress as he wove swiftly between the tables. 'Now there is one strange dude,' she murmured to herself. 'He says he's been for a game of golf yet those clubs are brand new. The heads have never so much as said hello to a ball. Plus he doesn't know his Emily Post. Here's one English gentleman who doesn't raise his hat to a lady. He never takes the damn thing off. And what the hell is he doing here if he has no connection with the movies? These are deep waters, Watson.'

Chapter Fifteen

Jack did not have long to wait for confirmation of his fears. The BBC World Television Service broke into a programme first: 'Reports are coming in of a shooting incident at the Cannes Film Festival involving the Hollywood-based British director Conrad Niven.' There followed a rushed résumé of the dangerous life Niven had led since making his film. In ninety minutes the news flashes went from 'shooting incident' to 'attempt on the life of' to 'has been murdered'.

Jack watched from his balcony, stunned, as the increasingly hysterical television reports drew people from their homes and hotel rooms. They began to gather along the sand, many with binoculars trained on Metzhagen's yacht which now seemed in danger of capsizing under the weight of the numbers on board.

Press and TV helicopters whup-whupped overhead and Jack could see that the police were having difficulty in fending off the media speed launches attempting to get within hailing distance of the yacht – and the first interviews with anyone who might have witnessed the event.

He paced the room, cursing his own stupidity. Three times the telephone rang – the first calls of any kind that had come through since he and Mrs Canning moved into the suite. Three times Jack picked up the phone and three times, as he said, 'Yes?', the callers replaced the handset.

Whoever they were, they had expected Mrs Canning to answer. To congratulate her on a mission accomplished? And on his extermination? He was paralysed. Should he sit tight or make a run for it?

This question, at least, was answered for the moment when his eyes once again fell on the television screen as a CNN reporter pinned down an official of the Sûreté in Paris. The Frenchman pointed out that Monsieur Niven had been under the protection of the British. A delicate shrug, suggesting their incompetence. Of course, the French authorities had offered additional officers but had relied on British Embassy assurances that they would not be needed ... Such a pity. Perhaps a failure of Intelligence on the part of the British?

It was a deft performance, the opening skirmish in the political row that was bound to follow.

Of more interest to Jack than the pass-the-buck manoeuvres was what the man said next. First inquiries indicated that Conrad Niven had been shot by a gunman concealed on another vessel in the bay. French naval patrols were being brought in to assist in the searches. The nearby islands of Saint Honorat and Sainte Marguerite were being combed. Road blocks had been set up throughout the Alpes Maritimes. Iranians were being rounded up for questioning.

The CNN reporter got down to details. What was the nature of the wounds? 'He was fatally hit in the chest.' Jack buried his head in his hands.

'Good marksmanship?'

'Extraordinary marksmanship,' corrected the policeman.

The CNN man then asked the question that created the headlines next morning. Where had Monsieur Niven been standing on Sir Gilbert Metzhagen's yacht when the assassin struck?

'Oh, he wasn't on the yacht,' said the Sûreté spokesman, quite relishing the revelation he was about to make. 'He was airborne.' He paused to let the reporter's face register surprise.

'I don't understand.'

'Monsieur Niven was parascending at a height of some seventy metres across the bay of La Napoule. Even his own bodyguards did not realize he had been harmed until he came down in the water at the end of his run. They heard no shots above the roar of the towboat's motor.'

'He was a moving target, then?'

'Oh, most certainly. To hit him at all was an evil but most accomplished piece of work.'

Jack put the TV on mute. He turned away his head as the camera caught the arrival of an ambulance at the central hospital Pierre Nouveau in the avenue des Broussailles. A shrouded body was wheeled inside on a gurney.

He had to think this thing through. Road checkpoints manned by the ruthless security police, the CRS, probably meant he was better off staying put. While he had been monitoring the screen, no one had as much as hinted that the shots might have originated from a point on shore. Once again, he checked the view from the balcony. All the frantic activity of the investigating authorities was safely at sea and the ink-bright waters of the bay were churned white by the wakes of the official-looking boats carrying investigators.

Jack had to concede that Mrs Canning and her associates had devised a brilliant plan to keep themselves at arm's length from discovery. Theirs had been the achievement – if achievement it had been – while he had been merely the mechanic, the hired hand, as she had described him so dismissively on the phone, sent to carry out the single act for which he was so eminently qualified. He felt demeaned and stricken.

He was sickened when, later in the evening, CNN relayed scenes of the street celebrations that had greeted the news in Tehran. The mob acted up for the benefit of the cameras, men frenziedly jumping up and down, jellabas billowing out from sandalled feet, while the veiled women made shrill, ululating sounds of ecstasy.

Jack felt the elegant walls of the room closing in on him. Once, he picked up the telephone to check that Grace and the boys had reached home but changed his mind. The hotel would log the call.

Once again, he walked round to the railway station, shouldering his way through the Festival crowds who now had two sources of excitement to titillate them: the hope of a glimpse of a film star and the frisson of being at an event that had made global headlines.

Jack fed francs into the box. Grace answered on the second ring.

'Thank God!'

'Jack?' Grace was puzzled at his evident relief.

'Are you and the kids all right? Did those bastards do anything?'

'Bastards? Do anything? Jack, what are you blathering about? They've been protecting us. We could have done with some early warning that you were up to your old tricks but, otherwise, we've had quite a pleasant time.'

He started to blurt out the truth but suddenly changed his mind. She'd have to know soon enough – and before Mrs Canning's friends took delivery of a certain movie camera case.

Grace broke into his thoughts. 'Where have you been?'

Where *had* he been? Oh, yes, weapons evaluation.

'Sorry, love, I've been on the range.' He realized she had no idea he was out of the country.

'Yes, and I've been to Buckingham Palace to see the Queen. I don't know why I bother to ask.' Grace sounded as dry as the Kalahari. 'Where are you now?'

Jack floundered. 'Er, I'm not sure. There's no number on this phone.' He fed in more coins.

There was no satisfactory way to say what had to come next. 'Grace,' he said sweating, 'I've run into a spot of real bother.'

She was silent for a moment, and then said calmly, 'Tell me, Jack.'

He said miserably, 'It's a bit like the Irish business. Can't say more.'

Grace held the silence even longer. Then he heard her order the boys out of the room.

He said, 'It's serious stuff and I can't go into it on the phone.'

For the first time Grace sounded apprehensive. 'Why not? Are you telling me someone's listening in?'

'I can't rule it out,' said Jack.

'I thought the Irish business was the reason we've just had a holiday.'

'No, it's something different.' He hesitated, then added, 'Look, I don't want to frighten you, but I think it best if you lock up the house right away and take the boys to the place we went last August for the holiday.'

Grace said quietly, 'Jack, we've just arrived home. Why should I drag the boys out of school yet again and take them all the way to—'

'DON'T SAY IT OVER THE PHONE!' yelled Jack. 'Please, please, Grace, I love you. Do what I ask.'

He was weeping, which was the worst thing Grace could have heard. 'Oh my God!' she whispered. Nothing Jack said could have conveyed more urgently what he was trying to tell her. 'We're on our way,' she said abruptly, and hung up.

Chapter Sixteen

The senior man said, 'It's a wild success. They seek him here, they seek him there, those bloody Frenchies seek the shooter everywhere. They're running around like headless *poulets*. They're going to take stick galore for this.' He rubbed his hands with unalloyed anticipation.

Then he added, 'So far there's only one blip on the screen. Our girl doesn't yet seem to have completed the business. I daresay it's proving awkward to manoeuvre our wondrous boy into the right mode for the quietus. At any rate, he's answered the phone each time I've called. We'll just have to be patient until she has something to report.'

The mood of euphoria blunted a sharper judgement. It was three days before the courier went to collect the voice-activated tape and they listened to the anguished phone-booth conversation between Jack Boulder and his wife. The brief exchange confirmed that their growing concern at Mrs Canning's continued silence was not misplaced.

'Shit!' said the senior man. 'The family's done a bunk – and what's happened to our girl?'

In Cannes the weary French police, after a rigorous search of the yachts at anchor, had achieved nothing more than the arrest of a number of Hollywood notables for possession of cocaine. Of the assassin, there was no trace.

On shore, the usual crowd of narks, astrologers, psychics, the mentally ill and concerned citizens had volunteered their services or had supplied information that they deemed might have a bearing on a crime that had now shouldered the world's most famous film festival from the headlines.

In his tiny office beside the Vieux Port, an inspector of the Municipal Police, Raoul Diot, was leafing moodily through a tangle of these reports. The big boys from Paris had taken charge of the glamour end of the investigation – they were the ones flying around in flash cars, hogging the limelight.

Here was one theory that Conrad Niven had been shot from a passing biplane – one of those used at each Festival to haul movie publicity streamers across the sky. Far-fetched but not impossible, he thought. Inspector Diot sighed and placed a call to the control tower at the nearby airfield of Mandalieu where the biplane collection was hangared. He couldn't risk neglecting any potential lead.

'What times are you talking?' asked the airport manager.

'It's a little uncertain,' said Diot. 'Say, between eleven thirty and one p.m.' He rested his chin on his fist while the manager sorted through the logs.

'No,' he said finally. 'We had nothing local in the air between those times. We put the squadron up at one thirty to catch the lunch crowd in the beach restaurants. Advertising *E.T. – The Return*. Your poor bastard was dead by then.'

'Yes.' Inspector Diot sighed again and returned to the rubbish pile. He was beginning to think of his own lunch when he came across the report on one Henri Traverso. The man had walked into the police post on the day following the shooting, after the possible time of death had been published in the newspapers and while the prevailing police theory had been that everything had happened at sea.

Traverso said he was a translator who assisted monolingual stars at their press conferences. He wondered if the authorities were mistaken in the direction their investigation was taking and that perhaps Conrad Niven had been hit not by a marksman on a boat but from a building along La Croisette.

'Why would you think that?' the gendarme conducting the interview had asked.

'Because I heard rifle shots on La Croisette at around midday,' said Traverso.

'Oh, yes? You're an expert on rifle shots, are you?'

'Well, I've heard enough of them in the movies.'

'This is real life, Monsieur Traverso.'

'So what? Do you think film-makers fake the sound of gunfire? They spend millions of francs to obtain authenticity.'

'All right. So where did you hear these shots?'

'I was walking on the pavement between the Martinez and Carlton Hotels.'

'Were you the only one?'

'Absolutely not. The pavements were crowded. Lots of people looked up.'

'And what did you and they see?'

'Nothing.'

'Nothing? No bright flash or flame? No smoke?'

'Nothing like that. Just the sound of two shots.'

Inspector Diot sat up. The information that Niven had been hit by two bullets had been withheld.

'What did everyone do? Dive for cover? Look for a gendarme?' The interviewer's scepticism came off the page of the transcribed interview. Inspector Diot made a mental note to kick his arse.

'Went on with their business, I suppose,' continued Traverso, unfazed. 'There was the noise of people and traffic. It wasn't possible to pinpoint the source. I suppose a lot of people thought it was something backfiring. There were a lot of motorbikes about.'

'Is that it, then?'

'Yes, that's it. You must admit, it was very odd to hear those sounds on the same day and around the same time as Monsieur Niven died.'

Inspector Diot swore. 'Very odd indeed.' He reached for the phone and got the festival administration office. A jobsworth answered. 'Henri

Traverso? If you turn on your television, you'll see he's busy translating at a Clint Eastwood press conference,' he was told.

The inspector flicked channels and there was Traverso, an animated, cherubic-faced man, with floppy, greying hair and an air of competence, sitting alongside a grizzled Eastwood.

Inspector Diot liked the look of the translator. Traverso did not give an impression of living in Cloud Cuckoo Land, like so many people connected with the film industry.

'Get him out of there and get him to the phone,' yelled the Inspector. 'Clint Eastwood is big enough to fend for himself.'

Twenty minutes later, he was asking, 'Monsieur Traverso, what is your best guess at the direction of those sounds you heard?'

Traverso pondered and said, 'The best bet has to be from a hotel window or from one of the apartments overlooking the Croisette. Or perhaps from a rooftop, although I think this less likely. The shots did not make the sharp crack sound that you get when a gun is fired in the open air. They were more muffled or hollow – as if coming from inside a building.'

At dawn next morning the police – whole battalions of them – began working the buildings facing the sea. Rooftops were scoured for signs of forced access or ejected cartridge shells. An alarming number of people had now been found to back Traverso's account of two shots being heard. Confusingly, there were accounts of a similar incident involving a single shot from a few days earlier.

The man in charge of the investigation, Commissaire Victor Massillon sent down from Paris, was reluctant to believe that any of this could be linked to the killing of Conrad Niven. He had exhaustively questioned the dead man's downcast minders, who had insisted they had not towed him within range of the shore. His own firearms expert had hesitated. 'If it happened like that, sir, the marksman has the kind of skill to make the so-called Jackal seem like a fairground duck-shooter. It's the longest of long shots, Commissaire.'

The object of their speculation, in defiance of Mrs Canning's strictures, was up and ready for a jog at seven. He changed his mind when he looked out and saw the array of police vehicles stretching along the front.

Downstairs, in the manager's office behind the reception desk, he could see uniformed men making notes from the guests' registration cards. Others were tapping on the first-floor doors of the rooms facing the sea.

Jack made a fast decision. There was nothing in the suite to excite the police. And it would not be remarkable if he were out when they came calling to conduct a room search. He slipped down to the garage. Driving up the incline onto the side-street, he was briefly waved down by two CRS men with machine pistols strapped across their chests. They peered in, saw that the back of the Volvo was empty, and languidly waved him on. They had no confidence in the new theory either.

Jack studied his map, drove to Antibes, bought himself a pair of swimming trunks and drove on to the Cap. He spent the day on the secluded Garoupe beach, sunning himself, eating and thinking. He kept off the alcohol.

The hotel search had been completed by the time he returned at sundown.

The phone rang. For once there was a voice at the other end. An assistant manager said, 'We've had the police in while you've been at work, sir. They've been interviewing the guests and having a look at the rooms.'

'Because of the shooting?' said Jack.

'That is correct, sir. They will need to eliminate you and Mrs Canning from their inquiries. It is purely a formality. All the guests in the rooms at the front of the Berthier are required to co-operate. Therefore would you and your wife kindly take your passports along to the police tomorrow? You'll find that they have set up a special headquarters in the *mairie* at the foot of the Old Town.'

That night the dream came back to him in all its terror. The dark lady's face was now clear – a laughing Mrs Canning, tantalizing and luring him towards oblivion.

Jack showered and stood under cold water to clear the muzziness from his head. He had to produce a wife or take flight. There was only one possibility: Betty Bentinck.

He fished out Mrs Canning's passport. The photograph was an old one, usefully closing the age gap with the present-day Betty. The two women were both dark-haired and not markedly dissimilar in features.

He went through his pockets until he found the visiting card that Sidney Zuckerman had pressed on him after scrawling 'Ch. 539' on the back, alongside the invitation to a game of golf.

Jack poked his head out into the corridor. Good. The odd-numbered rooms were on the town side of the building. Neither the film producer nor Betty would have been of interest to the police during yesterday's raid. He was forced to linger around the lobby until ten forty-five before he spotted Sidney striding out onto the Croisette. Jack went straight up to 539.

A tousled Betty answered the door in her peignoir. She was only just eating breakfast. She adopted an exaggerated pose, hand on hip. Very Mae West. 'Well, helloooo there, big boy,' she drawled. 'Is that a room key in your pocket or are you just pleased to see me? Come in, James.' She'd remembered his name but he experienced a moment of shock when she used it – he'd almost forgotten it under the strain of the last few days. She poured him a cup of coffee and told him, 'Sidney's out a-hustling for the day.'

Jack nodded and said nothing. How was he going to put his plan to her? She said softly, 'Something's on your mind. I just hope it's me, is all.'

Her robe was in disconcerting disarray and he caught glimpses of her creamy flesh every time she shifted in her chair.

He said, groping for the least alarming words, 'Betty, I realize I'm a total stranger, but I wonder if you could help me with a little problem?'

'I've no money of my own,' she murmured. 'Sidney's the paymaster hereabouts.'

Jack shook his head. 'Sorry, I'm giving out the wrong signals. I want you to do a little acting job for me.'

She laughed. 'Now you've disappointed me, James. You told me you had nothing to do with movies.'

'I haven't,' said Jack, plunging in. 'I want you to impersonate my wife.'

Betty laughed again, happily, with her head thrown back. 'Do we start now?' she said, starting to slip the peignoir from her shoulders.

Jack groaned. 'I'm sorry, Betty. I'm not putting this too well.'

'It sounds all right to me, kiddo.'

'It's quite serious. I have to produce my wife to the French police and she's not here. They're checking out all the hotel guests occupying the front rooms. It's because of the Conrad Niven killing, you know. And we weren't here yesterday when they went through the building.'

Betty looked at him steadily. 'James, are you a scam artist? It's already crossed my mind that you are. Those brand new golf clubs without a scratch on them are just props, aren't they? I bet you don't even play the stupid game.'

What was he to say to that? How far could he go?

She went on, 'Why don't you tell me your story and I'll decide how much to believe? First of all, are you involved in the Niven business?'

'No way,' said Jack, attempting an expression of sincerity. 'Nothing like that. It's just that our business has been caught up in *that* business and we simply can't afford to let ourselves become conspicuous to the police. We have to check in with them not because we're under suspicion but simply because we occupy front rooms. It's only routine. If we don't comply they'll come searching for us. They might start asking awkward questions that I'd rather not answer.'

Betty looked him up and down with pursed lips. 'Three things,' she said. 'Why can't your wife go herself? Is she really your wife? What is your game?'

Inwardly Jack quailed, his brain in overdrive. 'I have no money of my own,' she had said. Perhaps that was the way . . .

He said, 'She's not my wife. Like me, she's travelling on a false passport. We weren't here working. We were here to spend money – to enjoy ourselves and see the festival.'

Jack astounded himself at his newly found powers of invention. Warming to his theme, he added, 'Then she spotted someone in the crowd she couldn't afford to let recognize her and she skipped the country using another identity.'

Then what? Jack asked himself. He thought for a moment and went on. 'She was in such a hurry she forgot to open her safe deposit box downstairs and transfer the money to me, but if you'll spend a couple of hours being her, you can sign for the box and help yourself to ten thousand pounds sterling from it. That makes a lot of dollars.' He stopped and studied her querying face. 'Of course, I take the rest,' he added.

'Two more things,' said Betty, ignoring his discomfort. 'How much is in the box and how do I know you haven't iced her to have all the money for yourself?'

Jack said evenly, 'The box contains eighty thousand pounds. The money is not hot. It's the proceeds of an insurance fraud that has not been detected. No one is on my tail. Come up to my suite and see for yourself that there's no body under the bed for the chambermaid to find. You'll see Jane just packed her things and left.'

'Bullshit!' said Betty, draining a cup of coffee. 'My, my. You are a glib one, aren't you, Mr Canning – or whatever your real name is? That's the most confusing plot since *The Big Sleep*. Are there really eighty big ones in a box downstairs?'

'Yes,' said Jack.

Betty sighed and said, 'I just know I'm going to hate myself later. But, okay, I'll do it. In case you think I'm in the habit of breaking the law, let me put you straight. I'll do it for the money of which I'm in dire need. Sidney's charms are beginning to wear a trifle thin. And puh-lease don't ask me to believe a word you've told me. I'm not from Oshkosh, Illinois.' She gave him a sideways look. 'I'd say you were just chiselling your partner out of her end while her back's turned. Jesus! Why are all you great-looking guys such bastards? Hollywood's wised me up to men like you, James, and you're giving a convincing impersonation of Mr Trouble from Griefville.'

Jack thought it best not to answer that.

She stalked towards the bathroom, saying, 'Lemme take a shower while I think about it.' Before she reached the door she had already tossed her peignoir onto a couch. Naked, she wiggled her tight little buttocks as she disappeared, saying, 'Look what was on offer – until ten minutes ago!' and slammed shut the door.

Chapter Seventeen

Betty Bentinck crisply took charge. 'You're a worse actor than Arnie Schwarzenegger. If you're going to lie, you'd better learn how to look people in the eye. As they say in Hollywood, when you've learned to fake sincerity, you've cracked it.'

She immediately vetoed Jack's proposal that they first make the call on the police. 'No way,' she said, briskly. 'First, this mercenary wants to see the colour of your money.'

She nosed around Jack's suite, peering in wardrobes and pulling back the sheets on the bed. There was nothing, apparently, to alarm her.

'Do you have one of the passports your "wife" didn't use?' she said, sarcastically. Jack produced the British passport with Mrs Canning's – deliberately? – fuzzy photograph and her signature.

Betty studied it for a minute. 'She's a deal older than me, but I guess I can fix that. The poor quality of the picture helps.' She practised the signature and achieved an approximation with which she was not entirely satisfied. 'It will be even more difficult when I come to sign the keyholder's card to get into the vault. I won't have the genuine specimen in front of me.'

'Yes, you will,' said Jack. 'Her signature's already on the card twice – once when she rented the box and a second time when I went with her to the vault.'

All the same, she sent him to the pharmacy on the rue d'Antibes to buy surgical plasters and a bandage. When he returned, she was seated at the dressing table with her make-up box open and Mrs Canning's passport photograph propped up in front of her. He watched as Betty the Actress went purposefully to work.

She subtly changed the curve of her eyebrows, pulled back her hair with grips, reshaped her lips to Mrs Canning's contours, and aged herself with a modicum of shading to the cheeks, and a harder eyeliner. At the end, the effect was not Mrs Canning but it was close enough to the woman who stared impassively from the passport. She stuck two plasters on her fingers and then wrapped the hand in the bandage. Her Hermès scarf substituted for an arm sling.

In the foyer they both studied the harassed cashier who was relaying hotel guests into the vault. 'Are you sure that's not the one you dealt with last time? These hotel guys usually have good memories for faces,' whispered Betty.

'Positive,' said Jack. 'Let's go.'

The young cashier displayed proper concern for Betty's injury – or perhaps a more wary concern for the legal vulnerability of the hotel. 'Madame has had an accident?'

'I shut the minibar door on my hand,' she said and shrugged. Jack was impressed at the fluency of her French. Later, she said, 'I saw your surprise, buster. I told you I wasn't from Oshkosh. Why do you snotty Brits always assume Americans are dumb?'

She showed the cashier the deposit box key and made a performance of taking the cashier's pen between her injured fingers and slowly scrawling a shaky 'J. Canning' on the keyholder's card.

The man barely glanced at it before pressing the button to admit them to the vault. Jack lifted the holdall from the box and said, 'Not here,' as Betty began to look excited.

Upstairs in the suite, he said, 'Go ahead. Open it.'

Betty slowly pulled on the zip and whistled at the sight of the bundles. 'Who's the jerk who says crime doesn't pay? You've been a very wicked boy, James.'

'I know.' He endeavoured to look contrite and boyishly delinquent at the same time. He said, 'Help yourself. Ten thousand.'

He watched her sort enthusiastically through the unfamiliar Bank of

England notes and take her share, which she stuffed into her quilted shoulder-bag. 'Have you every heard of fuck-you money?' Jack shook his head. 'Well, that's what this will represent to me when I kiss off Sidney.' She slapped the bulging leather happily.

With Betty still wearing the sling, they set off for the magnificent baroque *mairie* where the police had set up their incident centre. Betty had said shrewdly, 'Let's aim to arrive just before one o'clock. You know what the French are like about food. They'll all be desperate to get away for *déjeuner*.'

They found themselves in a line of people being processed by a battery of police clerks, each seated at a computer terminal. Betty muttered, 'Let's go for the fat one. I'll bet his stomach's rumbling right now.' Jack was sweating but she was almost gay.

The fat one, his uniform straining at the buttons, studied their passports with his dead fish eyes, and fed their personal details into the system. 'What is your business in Cannes?'

'We are here to enjoy the Festival and do a little business,' said Betty.

'Let me see your accreditations.'

Jack looked at Betty for help. She didn't miss a beat. 'Oh, I'm so sorry. No one told us they would be needed here.'

The fat one's lips blew outward in exasperation. He glanced back at the screen. 'According to the hotel management, you are in the movie camera sales business? May I see your business card?'

It was Betty's turn to stare at Jack. But Mrs Canning's preparations had been thorough. Jack hastily produced a card holder and extracted an embossed card that gave an address for Canning Cameras in Tilney Street, Mayfair, London, England. Betty smiled the sweetest smile, nodding in approval.

'Okay,' said the fat one, listlessly tapping in the details. 'Do you have any information that might assist the investigation? Did you notice any strange happenings, mysterious activity?'

Betty gave him her widest-eyed look. Jack wondered for a moment whether or not she was overdoing the saccharine. 'We were shopping in Nice the morning that poor man was shot.'

The fat one lost interest. He finished feeding their statement into the terminal and handed them back their passports.

Jack had to grip Betty's arm to stop her laughing as they were dismissed and turned to leave. They could actually hear the police clerk's stomach rumbling.

On their way back along the Croisette, Jack stopped at the newspaper kiosk opposite the Noga Hilton Hotel and bought all the English-language newspapers that had just arrived on the morning plane.

Back in suite 720, he greedily absorbed every word. The police were still seeking non-existent Iranian killer squads. More importantly, no one had been able to position the marksman. He was surprised to see that the hunt had spread to Corsica, where an Iranian hit team had supposedly headed in a high-powered launch after their successful mission. There were even 'witnesses' to this event.

The newspapers were putting their most imaginative writers to work and Jack felt some relief in their outlandish outpourings.

Chapter Eighteen

Jack hated to see Betty go. He had come to realize quickly that she possessed the enviable gift of making a grim circumstance hum with life. He made a silent wish that her sunniness was a quality that the movie camera would capture and perhaps make her adored and famous – like Rita Hayworth of the terrace chair.

In Betty's company, his own burden of anxiety, distress and paranoia had somehow seemed lighter, hinting even at a hope of containment. In another world, she would have been easy to love. He fervently hoped she wouldn't squander herself on slick Sidney.

'I'd have liked to stick around to see how your little scam works out,' she said, looking sad. 'But something tells me you've landed the Jack Palance part. He never makes it to the last reel.' She pecked his cheek and he wanted badly to hold her close for a comforting moment, but she stepped smartly back and said, 'So long, you big hunk. I wish you long life.'

She made to step out into the corridor, but turned with a final thought. 'James, I take it you realize that our visit to the police won't be the end of the matter?'

Jack looked blank.

She shook her head wearily. 'You ought not to be allowed out on your own – especially with all that dough.' She went on patiently, 'Listen to me. I didn't do thirteen episodes of *Girl Agents of the FBI* for nothing. Just because the human balloon who took our statements was dreaming only of his bouillabaisse, don't think you can just stay here soaking up the rays and the rotten movies. The information on those lovely people the Cannings is now tucked safely in the computer system. Soon, somebody above Fats and smarter than Fats is going to scan the stuff. And it's going to occur to that someone to ask Interpol to ask your Scotland Yard to check that Mayfair address you gave. Strictly routine, you understand. But when Holmes of the Yard reports that there ain't no such camera company at that address, and nobody has ever heard of the charismatic Cannings, he's going to fax Interpol who are going to fax Inspector Clouseau in Cannes with the bad news.'

Betty now had the door open. 'This'll be the very door that'll get knocked off its hinges in the rush of *les flics*. I wouldn't hang around for showtime, if I were you, James.'

And she was gone.

The now familiar sense of desolation returned. Jack knew she was right. He had to run. He kept the TV set tuned to CNN, hoping for a report on the progress of the investigation. Were the roadblocks still in place? CNN failed to cover this point, which increased his anxiety.

While he monitored, he took a towel and began wiping every smooth surface he could remember touching.

When he called reception to announce that he and Mrs Canning would be checking out first thing next morning, he was met with perplexity. 'But you are booked and paid for another two days, Monsieur Canning.'

'I know,' said Jack, trying to emulate Betty Bentinck's insouciance. 'But we've completed our deals and other opportunities call.'

'You realize, sir, that the extra two days are not refundable?'

Greedy fucking French, thought Jack. But he wanted no scenes to make his presence easy to recall. He said, 'Oh, that's quite understood. We booked for the duration of the Festival so we expect to pay the full amount.' He had an afterthought. 'That container of camera equipment you have in your baggage room – when does it get to London?'

'On 23 May, three days after the Festival ends,' said the assistant manager.

That night the dream came, vivid and terrifying. He slept badly and was on the road by eight, with the money concealed alongside the weaponry in the under-floor compartment. He hit the first roadblock on the Route Napoleon, south of Grasse.

The patrol, who had placed a tyre-puncturing chain of spikes across the northbound traffic lanes, made him step from the car. They removed the golf clubs from the bag, which they examined closely. He prayed they didn't share Betty's sharp eye for an unused head.

They rummaged through his luggage and fed his passport and vehicle particulars into a handheld computer. He waited in the thin sunlight, feeling suspended in space and time, praying fervently that Scotland Yard had not yet got round to Tilney Street, Mayfair.

An agonizing ten minutes passed before the computer beeped and the patrolman read his clearance on the tiny screen, rolled back the spikes and beckoned him on.

En route, fatigue forced him to pull over and sleep for four hours. He was tempted to telephone Grace but a growing paranoia about bugged lines stopped him.

Was there a ports alert already out on the Volvo? His senses heightened as he joined the pre-dawn queue to drive aboard the Channel Tunnel train. His eyes began to scan. He was a dozen cars behind the leading one when he stiffened in his seat. In his rear-view mirror he could see the line being held back by a uniformed attendant. An Audi inserted itself immediately behind him. The overhead lamps glinted malevolently off its black surface.

Jack could see two men occupying the front seats. The number plate was British. He edged the Volvo up into the shiny coach and parked alongside one of the small windows that gave a limited view of the passing tunnel walls. The Audi came up behind. The two cars were almost bumper to bumper. Jack closed his window and pressed the central locking switch.

As they took off for the undersea ride, he watched other drivers stepping out to stretch their legs. There was no buffet so most remained alongside their cars. Jack stayed put, eyes glued to his rear-view mirror.

If the duo were who he thought they were, he couldn't see that they would try anything drastic while they were in the tunnel. Cameras monitored every coach and they could not drive their Audi off unless he moved first.

He briefly considered the possibility of one of the pair strolling up alongside the Volvo, plugging him through the window and usurping his driving seat. With his only weapon stowed and, in any case, far too big for this confined space, Jack felt naked. He comforted himself with the thought that they would have some difficulty explaining a corpse to British Customs. Or would they? Could they merely flash some magic

ID card and cart him off to an unmarked grave? Jack's paranoia at the extent of the forces ranged against him took an upward turn.

The man behind the Audi's wheel was older than his companion. He was thickset, with a heavy round head that sank into his shoulders. He lit a cigarette, ignoring the no-smoking signs that shouted at him at every turn. Jack watched the passenger point this out to him but the driver shrugged and continued puffing.

The passenger was a fair-haired man, almost a youth. He would be the first to climb out if they intended any funny business under the Channel. But he made no move and the Audi doors remained shut.

Perhaps their orders were simply to tail him.

The formalities on the Kent side were brief and Jack took off in heavy London-bound traffic. The Audi dropped back and put two cars between them and him.

Jack nursed a niggling doubt. It was still possible that the Audi pair were just a couple of champagne salesmen. He had to put them to the test.

He came off the motorway and turned towards Faversham. No doubt now. They followed him off the exit ramp and eased well back so as not to be prominent in his mirrors. Jack felt gratified. This was enemy action and he would be ready.

On the edge of a one-shop hamlet Jack found the battlefield he was looking for: a red tile-hung pub, not yet open, with an outside lean-to that served as a lavatory.

Jack drove into the forecourt, leaped insouciantly from the Volvo and did not look back as he headed for the timber door, drooping on its hinges. He prayed that it was not locked during non-drinking hours. In the open forecourt they would not even have to step out of their car to nail him. He gave it a push. It screeched open on ancient hinges and he breathed easy – until the smell of stale urine assaulted his nostrils.

He let the door bang closed behind him and swiftly surveyed his redoubt. There was a stand-up urinal, a vandalised condom machine and a foul cubicle. The lid of the pan was missing.

Jack applied an eye to the crack alongside the door-jamb. The nose of the Audi crept into view almost immediately. He could see them conferring. Then the car eased alongside the Volvo and both men got out. 'Shit!' said Jack. The duo closed their doors so carefully that even at that short distance he couldn't hear the locks click.

Silently they advanced on him. The young blond unbuttoned his lightweight jacket and plucked a snub-nosed, nickel-plated automatic from a hip holster. Bullneck, who appeared to be serving only as chauffeur, handed him a sound suppressor. He appeared otherwise unarmed.

At the rear of the lean-to was a small, high window. They could only come at him through the door. He stepped into the cubicle and unhooked the old-fashioned pull-chain from the cistern. He had a weapon of sorts – and surprise on his side. He was convinced they believed they had not been rumbled. The logic must be that the man with the gun would come in first and shoot him before he had a chance to react. Jack stepped to the side of the door and waited. The automatic flush for the urinal came on, accompanied by the loud swish of gushing water.

It was a lucky moment of happenstance for Jack. The familiar sound reassured Blondie that his quarry was preoccupied and he hurtled in with a rush that sent the door crashing open. Just as violently, Jack sent it crashing back just as the man's gun hand came into view.

Under the impact Blondie fell sideways, wildly spraying shots into the walls and condom machine. Jack took just one step forward, grabbed his head and smashed it against the far wall. The gun dropped from his hand and Jack hurled the body back at Bullneck who had been on his companion's heels.

Jack gave Blondie a hard kick in the guts as he jumped over the slumped body and rushed full tilt at Bullneck. The thug landed one winding blow to Jack's rib before Jack had the lavatory chain round his opponent's formidable size eighteen neck. He twisted the two ends together and the rusting metal links sank deeply into Bullneck's rolls of fat. The man continued to lash out but now Jack had leverage and dragged him off balance and into the lavatory. The battered door closed and the three now occupied their own small, violent world.

Bullneck was on his knees, gurgling and clawing at the chain. Blondie was dazed but recovering. Blood trickled from his temple. He groped around for the gun.

Jack stretched out a leg and hooked the weapon towards himself. Savagely, he thrust it into Blondie's face. 'Is this what you're looking for, you bastard?' he shouted, while his other hand twisted the chain viciously, forcing Bullneck face forwards onto the evil-smelling cement floor.

Blondie sat up slowly, his blue eyes darkening with hatred. He looked at Bullneck, whose face was turning puce, 'You're killing him,' he said.

'Well, isn't that too bad?' said Jack. 'And what had you intended for me with this little toy?' The automatic was a Czech-made .32, effective at close range.

Blood was clotting in Blondie's floppy forelock. 'Oh, very clever,' he said bitterly.

Jack looked down at Bullneck, who was gurgling. Satisfied that his adversary had lost consciousness, he unwound the chain. Blondie pulled himself up into a sitting position against the wall. He was not prepared for what happened next.

In a single movement, Jack looped the chain around his more elegant neck and twisted the links just enough to force the man's mouth open to gasp for air. Just as swiftly, he clapped a hand over it, released the chain, clamped the man's mouth shut, then dragged him by the head away from the wall. He said, 'I wouldn't swallow, if I were you. And I certainly wouldn't chew on that little glass capsule I've just popped into your mouth.'

Blondie's eyes bulged and he began to struggle frantically. 'Yes, you bastard, you know what I'm talking about. That capsule was meant for me.'

Jack suddenly withdrew his hands and released Blondie, who instantly spat furiously, spittle dribbling down his dimpled chin. The cyanide capsule ricocheted off the wall and onto the floor. Jack crushed it with his foot. There was a fleeting aroma of bitter almonds.

Blondie bent double, still gagging. His partner was beginning to stir and groan. Before he became any livelier, Jack dipped into his jacket pockets and found the Audi's keys.

He bent over Blondie, who was weakly mopping himself with a handkerchief. Jack whispered, 'I'll kill the next one of you who comes after me. I've done your dirty work. Now leave me and my family alone.'

Blondie found his voice. 'Captain Boulder, where is Mrs Canning? We have to know,' he croaked.

'You'll know soon enough,' said Jack grimly. 'You go back and give your masters my message. It seems to me I've unwittingly made them the best part of a million pounds. My advice is: be satisfied. Take the dirty money, bury your dead, and leave me and mine in peace.'

'Dead?' Blondie's bloodied face tightened. 'Do I take that to mean you have,' he hesitated, choosing his words carefully, 'disposed of Mrs Canning?'

'She disposed of herself,' said Jack. 'You'll understand when you collect the body.'

At the door, Jack turned and watched the two men slowly getting to their feet and propping themselves against the scabrous walls. 'Just remember this,' he said. 'Nothing would be easier for me right now than to put a bullet into your heads. But I don't want to be forced to kill you and I don't want you to kill me. When you find your feet and walk out of here, think about it – and be grateful. You owe me.'

The urinal smell had been unpleasantly pungent and Jack was glad to step out into the crisp morning air. He gazed around. All was silent, apart from the sounds of birds nest-building. He tightened the silencer in the .32's muzzle and walked round the Audi, shooting out all four tyres. Let those bastards explain that to the AA man.

In a service station lavatory, Jack shaved off the moustache. At Rochester, a barber gave him his customary short-back-and-sides. He also broke down his assailants' gun into its component parts and scattered the pieces and cartridges in streams and culverts across two English counties.

He did not arrive in Southwold until the late evening. It was the bracing Suffolk coastal town where the family had spent their last summer holiday, in a clapboard cottage hunkered down amid windbreaks between the grey North Sea and a bird sanctuary. He spotted the boys first. They had acquired two decrepit bikes and were endlessly circling a stone birdbath when they spotted him and raced down the gravel track to pedal alongside the Volvo.

Jack wound down the window. 'Afternoon, guys. Would one of you open the garage door?' He was trying to sound casual but he wanted to get the Volvo out of sight fast.

Malcolm pedalled ahead to do as he asked, but Ben was curious. He peered in at the luggage. 'Dad, since when have you played golf? And where did you get this car?'

All at once Jack felt heavy and dispirited. Christ, these were just the easy questions. There were more painful ones to come. 'The car's borrowed. I'm just giving golf a try,' he grunted, scanning the cottage for signs of Grace.

He could hear Malcolm shouting, 'Mum, Dad's shaved off his moustache!'

A door, coated in pitch against the harsh winter weather, opened and she stood there, looking heartbreakingly lovely – and strained. She was wiping her hands on a tea towel. The simple act brought a lump to his throat: it encapsulated everything that was normal and reassuringly domestic in his life – a comforting world that had continued to meander along while he had been engaged in the bizarre and dangerous events that now threatened to destroy them all.

He hugged the boys and held Grace tightly in his arms for a full minute. Against her soft, welcoming flesh he felt the tension dropping away from him.

Grace kissed his ear and he could feel her patting his back. 'It's all right, Jack,' she whispered. 'It's all right.'

She pushed back from his embrace and gazed intently into his face. She said softly, 'Ben, Malcolm, go for a ride on your bikes. Daddy and I want to have a talk.'

'Aw, Mum, can't we see Dad for a bit?' Malcolm pleaded. 'He's only just got here.'

'You can see him all you want later.'

'C'mon,' said Ben. 'They want to get lovey-dovey.'

'Yuck!' said Malcolm. They giggled and rode away.

Grace and Jack faced each other across the kitchen table. 'Well?' she said. She could see that what was coming was bad and reached across to grasp both his hands. He had not yet taken off his jacket.

On the long drive, Jack had been rehearsing various innocuous scenarios in his head but suddenly he felt sickened by his own deceit. The burden of it was now a gross thing in his gut that threatened to choke him. No matter how shocking and no matter what the consequences, he saw with sobering clarity that he had to tell Grace the truth.

She sat stiffly as he began with the first phone call from Mrs Canning. She slumped as he reached the moment where he had accepted her proposition and she was weeping by the time he reached in his broken-voiced recital the moment when he loosed off the two fatal shots. He held back only the shaming incident in the night.

Jack watched his wife's distress helplessly. He wanted to vomit. He moved hesitantly round the table to take her hunched shoulders in a hug but she shook him off. Suddenly she leaped up and began to hammer his chest. Jack fell back but made no attempt to ward off the blows. If Grace had taken a knife to him, he would have faced the blade without flinching and without defending himself.

Tears glinted on his cheeks as she continued to scream and pound at him in an uncontrollable fury. Then, exhausted, she collapsed against his chest and he wrapped his arms around her. Her sobs vibrated through his body and he let them run their course. Finally she said, in a choked voice, 'That is the most terrible thing I've ever heard.'

Jack said awkwardly, 'Yes.' But he'd come to a decision. 'I think it's time to put the whole bloody business in the hands of the police.'

Grace brushed back her hair. 'No!' she said, with sudden resolution. 'Jack, you're breaking my heart. Do you think the police are going to pat you on the head for a job well done, give you a medal and send you home?'

Jack made a futile gesture with his hands. 'Grace, I thought it was an official mission. You know the way the Security Services work. They like to employ mercenaries so that they can disown you if you're caught. It's what they call the cut-out system. But I think I've been used by bounty hunters.' He was disgusted at the bleating in his voice.

Grace said firmly, 'You can't go to the police. This family will be devastated. They'll send you back to France where I'm not so sure they don't keep a guillotine for this kind of offence. My God, your name will go down in history in a roll-call of assassins alongside Lee Harvey Oswald, Mark Chapman and that evil bastard who shot Martin Luther King. Oh, Jack, how could you?' She began to cry again.

When the boys returned, the family sat down to a fraught meal of cold meat and salad. Ben caught the mood immediately. 'What's wrong?' he said.

'Just eat your supper like a good boy,' said his mother. 'Daddy and I have had some bad news about – a friend.'

'Who?'

Grace absently rubbed Ben's neck. 'No one you know. Just someone Daddy met.'

Across the table Malcolm made a face at Ben and shrugged. Grown-ups' secrets.

Afterwards, Jack and Grace went for a walk on the dunes. He needed some air and they both had to come to terms with what he'd told her. Huddled in a Barbour against the cutting wind, Grace asked, 'Is there any way you can get to the bottom of this? If you could find these people and turn them in, or just shut them up, you might get yourself off the hook.'

Jack pondered. 'There's one possibility. In four days' time, Mrs Canning's body' – Grace shuddered and not from the cold – 'will be delivered to the warehouse. Her partners will collect it – now they know for certain they won't be collecting me. They must be seriously rattled even though they know the objective of the operation has been achieved. But after chasing me from the Channel Tunnel, they also know it hasn't all happened as they planned.' He stopped, not sure that he should reveal his deepest worry.

Grace caught his hesitation. 'Come on, Jack. We're all in this together now. What else?'

He said slowly, 'Despite my putting the frighteners on their thugs, I don't think they can leave me as a loose cannon. I'm the man who knows too much. They may want to believe what I told those two jokers: leave me alone and I'll leave them alone. But it's not what they can afford to believe. Maybe I'll keep my mouth shut for now, but what about later? Maybe I'll crack, have a breakdown, go to the police, go to the papers.'

'So what are you suggesting?' They watched a tug laboriously towing a letterbox-red lightship through a choppy slate sea.

'I could try to follow whoever collects the body. They may lead me to the truth. It's my only hope – to learn enough about them to have some really damaging bargaining muscle.'

Grace thought about this for a while, then said, 'Why did you make us leave London? What danger are we in?'

'I don't know.' Jack kicked sand in frustration. 'But at some point I guessed they were watching you or tapping our phone. They knew too much about me. They even had photographs.'

Grace said, 'I didn't suspect anything – not even when they took us to the safe house. I cursed you a bit under my breath for playing silly buggers again but . . .' She shivered. 'I thought they were friends, not the enemy.'

He took her shoulders and this time she did not resist him. 'They are amazingly well organized and totally ruthless. The only clever thing I've done in this whole mess was to insist you and the boys be driven home once they had confirmation that I'd done what they asked. If they'd held you until Mrs Canning had also confirmed she'd killed me, I dread to think what might have happened – although it's more likely they'd have spun you some bullshit that I'd bought it on a secret assignment, laid the Official Secrets Act on you, and given you my blood money as compensation. They're going to go ape when they take delivery of the body. It's best to keep the boys here until this thing is sorted out. Maybe you could do some schoolwork with them so they don't fall too far behind. At least we'll have no money worries.'

On the way back to the cottage, he took Grace into the garage, lifted the trap and opened the holdall. Wordlessly, she gazed down at the rifle in its bubble wrappings and the mound of cash.

Jack grabbed a bundle of fifty-pound notes and thrust it at her but Grace put her hands behind her back as if the banknotes were diseased. 'There's no point in being silly about the money,' he urged. 'For us, it's a life-saver. We can't use our credit cards. They have access to the computers that register the transactions – that's how they trace people's movements. It's cash only, if we're to avoid discovery.'

'Give it here,' she said, her face set.

Replacing the false floor, Jack said, 'I won't be able to take the Volvo out onto the road again. They have the number. But it would be useful if I could drive it.' He pondered and said, 'This is Volvo country. See if you can spot a similar one to this, make a note of its registration number and have plates made up at the local garage. But, until I can safely drive it away, this car will be your bank. I'll be happier knowing that if anything happens to me at least you'll have money.'

Grace digested this in silence, then fell against his shoulder, once again in tears.

Chapter Nineteen

He holed up at Southwold for two days and lost count of his grovelling apologies. At night he clung to Grace.

She softened slowly. 'Jack, why do you always act before you think?' she said. And added, 'I'm sure the Army was happy to get rid of you. You were a disaster waiting to happen. This time you've brought the disaster home with you.'

One night, lying in bed, lulled by the distant susurration of the sea, she said, out of the dark, 'Did you fuck those women?' She switched on the bedside-light and studied his face intently for signs of deception.

Jack groaned inwardly. Here comes another. What had Mrs Canning said? Adultery in hotels doesn't count? 'For God's sake, Grace. Don't you think I had enough on my mind without that?'

'I don't know.' She was dubious. 'You were staying as man and wife with one and you said you liked the American girl.'

He had a momentary flash of Betty's delightful little bum wiggling into the bathroom, and a darker vision of Mrs Canning astride him.

'Well, the answer is I didn't,' he said, despising himself anew. 'We had twin beds and the girl was with some American producer. She only helped me because I paid her.' At least that was true.

He reached for her, and laid his head between her breasts. 'Please love me,' he said humbly. 'I feel so lost. Without you, I'd just as soon turn myself in.'

Grace kissed his rumpled hair. 'Whatever happens, never forget we love you too. Desperately,' she added.

And that's how they made love. Desperately, frantically, almost hysterically – as if there might not be a next time.

Later, the dream came again but stopped abruptly just as Bullet Head began to attack the driver's door. Grace was shaking him awake. 'No, Jack! No!' she said, and clasped him tightly to her.

Jack drove to London in the family's old Saab and checked in with his under-manager, Joe Carsby, at the gun-club. 'Anyone been asking for me?'

'Two or three phone calls, but no one left a message,' Joe looked at him quizzically. 'Don't think much of your suntan, Jack. You look paler than when you went away.'

Jack shrugged. 'They had me on bloody night exercises most of the time. But it's all hush-hush, Joe. Not a word to anyone.'

A couple of members made a boisterous entrance and Joe went off to attend to them, leaving Jack to unlock his personal arms cabinet and help himself to a 17-shot Glock that he tucked into his belt. Two clips of ammunition went into his pocket.

At Shepherd's Bush everything appeared normal. Among the letters on the doormat was a handwritten note from the boys' headmaster. Where were they? He'd have to concoct a convincing yarn – something he was becoming adept at.

He took off his jacket, selected a screwdriver from his toolbox and combed the house. He ended up dizzy with disbelief. He had uncovered two tiny transmitters in each main room – on pelmets, under console tables, in a light fitting, behind picture frames. Some were no larger than a thumbnail.

He deduced – correctly – that the only reason he did not find any in the bases of the two telephone sets was because the Boulder family's lines had been tapped. Chilled, Jack was beginning to understand the extent of the surveillance to which they had been subjected. In a black rage, he took the bugs out to the garden path and hammered them to smithereens.

Then he went back into the house and sat with his head in his hands. Suddenly he had an idea and went in search of Grace's sewing scissors, the boys' modelling glue and a mound of newspapers.

Chapter Twenty

Gatti's Repository was a hulking Victorian blockhouse whose lower floors presented a blank face to the dingy street: the windows had been bricked up. Strolling past, Jack saw with frustration that the two loading bays were within a courtyard. He had intended parking the Saab at a vantage point along the street and monitoring the vehicles that arrived to make collections and deliveries. The problem was that, from his car, he would be unable to see Mrs Canning's aluminium coffin either arriving or being picked up.

From the corner, he studied the depressing vista. Opposite the Repository was a pre-war London County Council block of flats with the grubby shield emblem of the long-abolished authority still displayed above the entrance – a solid, brick structure that had outlasted the gimcrack system-built municipal hutches of the sixties. The staircase windows and the long, open landings overlooked the warehouse.

Jack took the stone stairs two at a time. From the fourth-floor window he had a perfect view over the Repository's wall. He stood patiently, watching the comings and goings below of furniture and cardboard containers.

He was three hours into his vigil before he saw a pantechnicon, its sides advertising that it had come from Nice, France, backing into the gate and aligning itself with the first bay. A forklift truck trundled forward and began to shift cases into the building. The seventh item of the consignment was a gleaming cube of metal. 'Yes!' breathed Jack.

He was still lurking by the cracked window an hour after the Nice truck had departed when he heard a soft sound behind him. Jack wheeled round. Confronting him were two Afro-Caribbeans, dread-locked, earringed, hip-loose – and menacing. One, with a week's growth of beard filling his pock-marks, said, 'You don't live here, man.'

'No,' said Jack, eyeing them carefully.

'We don't like whitebread boys who ain't got no business here being here,' said the smaller one, whose skin was sallow and whose eyeballs bulged.

'But I do have business here,' said Jack politely.

'What business is that, white man?'

'That's my business,' said Jack.

'How do we know that your business ain't poking your dumb nose into our business?' asked Pock Mark.

'What business would that be?' asked Jack, fencing.

Pock Mark stepped forward threateningly. 'You've got a smart mouth, white man. Someone gonna take your tongue and show you how to lick your own ass with it.'

'Now, who would that someone be?' asked Jack pleasantly.

The two glanced at each other. They were not at ease with Jack's composure.

Sallow said, 'Are you The Man?'

'The Man?' queried Jack. 'Which Man is that?'

'Don't fuck with us. The po-lice is who,' said Pock Mark.

Jack said, 'Relax. I'm not a policeman. Whatever you two characters are up to is no concern of mine. Now, why don't you go away and leave me to get on with my business?'

'You ain't told us what that business is yet,' pointed out Pock Mark, leering nastily and revealing purple gums.

'I thought I'd made myself clear,' said Jack. 'My business is my business. Now go away and leave me alone.'

They reacted in unison. Sallow drew a switchblade from the sleeve of his embroidered jacket and Pock Mark, to Jack's alarm, magically produced what appeared to be an American-made Cobray M-11 semi-automatic from an underarm sling.

'Semi-automatics in Battersea? What the hell is going on?' asked Jack. As he spoke he slid his hands up to his hips, arms akimbo, which lifted the bottom edge of his leather jacket. His fingers were now underneath the elasticated band within inches of the Glock that nestled against his spine.

'What's going on,' said Pock Mark, 'is that you are gonna give us your money and credit cards and then get the fuck outa here.'

Jack nodded at the Cobray. 'You think you can use that thing here in broad daylight and get away with it?'

'We is the law here, you cocksucker,' said Pock Mark. 'We say who lives. We say who dies.'

'I don't think so,' said Jack.

'Huh?' said Pock Mark.

Neither man could believe his effrontery. Sallow was making preliminary slashing motions with his long, thin blade.

Jack decided it was time to bring this charade to an end. 'As a matter of fact, gentlemen,' said Jack, 'I'm the one who says who lives or dies. Before you pointed that thing at me,' he added for the benefit of Pock Mark, 'you should have fitted the magazine. But they're rather long and awkward, aren't they? If memory serves, they take thirty-two rounds. In your pocket, is it?'

Jack's Glock came smoothly out of his waistband. Now Pock Mark's eyes were bulging too.

Calmly, Jack said, 'On the floor, you bastards, before I take your ugly heads off.'

But Sallow had to try his luck. He lunged forward. Jack instinctively took a step backward to give himself room, took precise aim and shot Sallow through the upper thigh. He screamed and toppled sideways. Pock Mark fell to his knees and raised his arms in the air. 'Don't do it, man. Okay, your business is your business.' He stared, hypnotized, at the Glock's muzzle. Sallow was clutching at his leg and whimpering.

Jack said to Pock Mark, 'Take off your jacket and belt.'

The man hastened to comply. 'Now take the belt and make a tourniquet above his wound.' Pock Mark shuffled on his knees over to his companion, eyeing the dropped knife as he went. 'Don't even think it,' said Jack softly. 'Just push it this way.'

He scooped up the blade with his spare hand and tossed it in the refuse chute that ran parallel to the staircase.

He patted down Pock Mark's jacket and discovered two loaded magazines for the Cobray. When he thrust his hand into an inside pocket, these two jokers' business became clear. Out came a pouch containing a large cache of white powder made up in small glassine bags.

Jack glanced out of the window. Nothing untoward. It astonished him how pistol shots could go unremarked in an urban setting. This was a repeat, more or less, of Cannes.

The thugs were looking at him resentfully. He said to Sallow, 'You're lucky. I deliberately avoided the bone so you should be able to stand.'

They looked at him for the first time with something approaching respect.

'Shit, man. You can do that?' Pock Mark was awed.

'Yes.' Jack hefted the cocaine thoughtfully in his hand. If it followed the knife into the refuse chute, they'd have to come after him again – if only for revenge.

Pock Mark looked alarmed as he saw Jack's eyes wander briefly to the metal door on the chute. 'You gonna give me back my stuff, man? If you do what I think you're thinking, I'm dead.'

Jack said, 'Here's the deal. You get back the stuff. I keep your weapon. You take your friend to hospital before that wound turns septic. You don't come back to bother me any more.'

'Yeah, yeah,' said Pock Mark eagerly. 'You gimme the stuff, you don't see my black ass again. Man, you is a fucking star with that piece. I wouldn't come looking for you with a tank.'

'You've made a wise decision,' said Jack. 'I'm glad you're seeing sense.' He placed the coke on the floor and pushed it with his toe towards Pock Mark. 'Now throw me the shoulder sling for the Cobray' – Pock Mark's eyes widened at the accurate identification of his armament – 'and split.'

He watched them slowly descend the urine-smelling stairs, Sallow leaning painfully on Pock Mark's shoulder.

Jack turned away, pleased with himself and spotted an old lady peering from her front door. Her eyes were bird-bright in her wizened face.

'Son,' she said, 'that was bleedin' marvellous. If we had a few more coppers like you, we'd soon chase those bloody Yardies back to Jamaica where they came from.'

He grinned at her. She watched him as he slung the Cobray under his jacket and stowed the Glock where it had come from. 'You've earned a cup of tea, son. Come on in.'

Jack was taken aback by her *sangfroid*. Was this an everyday occurrence for little old ladies? 'Weren't you scared?' he asked.

She looked disgusted. 'I was in the Blitz. Since then I was only ever scared of my old man, Gawd rest him!'

Jack chuckled. She'd obviously decided he was the police. Then she proved it by asking, 'Why didn't you run them in?'

Jack said carefully, 'I should have done. But that would have been piling up trouble for myself – I shouldn't have shot him. There'd be an inquiry so I just frightened the life out of them and let them go.'

She nodded, satisfied. Jack looked around and registered that her living-room window overlooked a railed break in the outside brick parapet. He said, 'I'll take the offer of that cup of tea if you'll let me keep observation from your window.' He winked. 'I'm on special assignment.'

'Mum's the word,' said the old girl. 'Take a seat.'

Her name, she told him, was Jessie Pocock and, behind her front door with its two locks and two dead bolts, her flat smelled of furniture polish and baking cakes. 'Home cooking,' she said. 'That's the secret of a long life.'

Jack's eyes took in the worn couch covers, the knitting bag and the book of crossword puzzles. She was so excited by his presence that he judged she did not have many visitors.

She caught him examining the framed photograph of a corporal of the military police directing traffic – a column of Churchill tanks – with a tommygun slung over his shoulder. Behind him, the road sign pointed to Schleswig-Holstein. 'That was my Arthur,' she said. 'Went all the way from Normandy to Denmark without a scratch. Came home and was dead three years later. Cancer of the liver.' It was her only photograph.

'No children?' queried Jack.

'Couldn't have 'em. Not after they dug me out of the mud at Balham tube station. Direct hit,' she said, without self-pity.

Something clutched at Jack's heart. Here was this indomitable little woman in her tiny redoubt of civilization, a surviving remnant of the vanished England of Arthur Pocock while, outside, animals with semi-automatic weapons ruled. He thought of his own mother with her turned-down mouth, her idle life and preoccupation with her looks. Her idea of tragedy was a broken fingernail. She'd disapproved of Grace because Grace's father was what she termed a 'municipal worker', and had greeted with disdain the news of his lowly gun club job. Shepherd's Bush, in her books, equated with Calcutta.

Jack settled himself by Jessie Pocock's window. Vans and trucks came and went but no one collected the silver coffin. His bustling hostess brought him tea and slices of seed cake and let him use her lavatory. She was loving the drama.

'Of course, you must never breathe a word of this,' Jack cautioned.

'Don't worry, son,' said Jessie. 'The only human being I see, and only once a week at that, is my home-help. I send her out for the shopping. She's bloody useless for anything else. I once showed her a bucket and scrubbing brush and she had kittens on the spot.'

Jessie's chatter kept Jack going through the long day. At six o'clock his heart sank as employees streamed out of the repository. The steel shutters came down over the loading bays and, soon afterwards, a man in overalls – the night watchman – stepped out to close the main gates.

'Jessie,' said Jack, 'how would you feel about me coming back tomorrow?'

'You're more than welcome, Jimmy,' she said. He'd told her his name was James Canning.

She pressed another cup of tea on him, and unwittingly created a crucial delay in his departure.

Jack took two fifty-pound notes from his wad and said, 'We have a fund for civilians who aid the police in their stake-outs.'

He had difficulty in getting her to accept them. 'That's the best part of two weeks' pension,' she protested.

'You've earned it,' Jack insisted.

He was at the open front door when he saw renewed activity below. A Transit van and a black Daimler had pulled up. A tall, lean man in a well-cut double-breasted suit was standing at the gate pressing the bell.

Jack bent down hastily and kissed the top of the old lady's head. 'Thanks for everything, Jessie. But it looks as if you'll be on your own tomorrow, after all.'

He took the stairs three at a time and reached the bottom in time to see the suit showing the night-watchman a sheaf of papers and an identity card. With ill grace, the watchman began to haul on the gates.

Another man was sitting in the Daimler, sartorially a twin of the first, but younger. His blond hair flopped over his high, pink forehead. Now he climbed out and stood silently watching the Transit, driven by a third man, being backed into the yard.

Jack drew breath sharply. The blond was the man he had roughed up in the pub lavatory – as he turned his head, to glance at each end of the street, Jack could see the plaster stuck to his left temple where he had made hard contact with the wall.

The suits were not exactly furtive but they gave the impression of purposeful discretion; men whose habit was to tread softly.

Jack raced back upstairs to observe the loading bay. He experienced a thrill when the silver cube containing the earthly remains of Mrs Canning made the short, and appropriately stately, journey into the back of the Transit, where solemnity ended abruptly as the van driver vigorously seized Mrs Canning's coffin and rocked it inside. Jack winced.

He was in his Saab and ready to roll as the Daimler fell in behind the Transit and the convoy set off.

All three vehicles were carried along in the flow of homebound rush-hour traffic, south-east into Kent, which, at least, gave Jack cover. Ninety minutes later, they passed through Tunbridge Wells and turned onto the Frant road, crossing into East Sussex.

The traffic was thinning now and Jack was laid well back as they drove past the Frant village green on their near side and headed for Wadhurst.

Jack almost missed the turn-off, just glimpsing the Daimler's right tail-light before it vanished. He stopped at the roadside for a minute and then drove on slowly. He was in time to see a heavy iron gate, entrance to a large estate, sliding shut automatically and caught sight of a long drive disappearing into the greenery and dusk.

A man entering a grey stone gatehouse was framed by the lighted doorway. He glanced towards the road as he heard Jack's engine but Jack stared straight ahead and drove past, though not before he had seen the shotgun slung over the gateman's shoulder. Once upon a time in Britain you wouldn't have seen a civilian packing a gun in ten years. He'd now seen two in one day. Jack shook his head at the implication.

He peered ahead for a place to park and spotted a grassy apron in front of a five-bar gate leading into a field. He pulled over, switched off and got out.

He jogged back to the estate, the Cobray banging reassuringly against his ribs: a weapon that could spray thirty-two rounds of 9mm ammunition in one long burst was a great boost to confidence.

The estate wall was in excellent repair and topped by razor wire. Jack had no doubt that there would also be intruder alarms. He scrambled into the undergrowth opposite the gate and waited – for what he did not know. But he was exultant. They – whoever they were – had manipulated him by remote control, almost as if he were a puppet, yet, despite all their security measures and attempts to kill him, here he was, literally at their gate.

He hunkered down in the growing chill of night. A blue Ford Mondeo entered at ten o'clock and left forty minutes later. This time the gateman wore his jacket and stepped out into the lane to wave the car forward. Jack ducked. He could see the man's legs just five yards away and cursed silently – they were obscuring the car's number-plate.

By midnight, Jack felt in need of another chunk of Jessie Pocock's seed cake and was beginning to think he should find an hotel for the remainder of the night when suddenly a light came on above the gatehouse, flooding the area with deep contrasts of light and shadow, and the younger Battersea suit loped down the drive.

He moved like an athlete and, despite the Savile Row outfit, Jack decided he was muscle. He had a hand to his ear, as if in pain, but was listening to his radio earpiece. He said something to the gateman who went back inside and moments later the gate slid open. The muscle positioned himself to receive visitors. Jack felt rising excitement. Somebody of importance must be on the way. Muscle was standing almost at attention.

Jack saw headlamps sweeping the trunks of the trees that shrouded the road. Then into view came a late-model Bentley. It turned into the entrance and halted. Jack could see a lone occupant in silhouette at the wheel. The muscle stooped deferentially, exchanging a few words with the driver, then slipped into the front passenger seat. The Bentley proceeded down the drive. The gate slid closed behind them as Jack scribbled the number on his wrist.

The sight of Mrs Canning's corpse had triggered an emergency, Jack realized. Why else would there have been this early-morning activity in the heart of the countryside? He could imagine the uproar, the recriminations, their anger at the dupe who had not played the game.

An hour passed. Jack was beginning to droop. He pressed a cool broadleaf to his forehead. He had to stay alert and think. He had located one operations centre of his mysterious enemy inside of which was the driver of the Bentley, who must be a key figure in the organization. Conclusion: establish his identity. Method: follow him when he emerged – if he emerged.

Jack retreated down the road and brought the Saab to a point where he would see the Bentley's lights when it drove out.

He had a long wait during which he struggled against his fatigue. He was standing outside in the bracing early-morning air, exercising to keep awake, when he saw headlights and dived back behind the wheel. He prayed it would be the Bentley.

It was. Jack had the good sense to hold back until he could be sure the gateman had returned to his lodge. He had remembered the suspicious stare as he drove past the first time and did not want his target alerted by car telephone.

The tail was easy. The Bentley took the conventional ring-road and M4 route into west London and Jack was able to stay well back until they reached the streets of the suburbs.

The Bentley rolled smoothly through the slumbering streets of Kensington, at last nosing into a square off Holland Park Avenue. From the far side of the grounds of a Victorian church that occupied the centre, Jack watched his quarry activate a shutter door and drive into his own garage. The attached house was commodious, with arched windows and a front garden. To be sure this was really the home of his quarry, Jack waited until a downstairs light went on.

He then drove home, hugely satisfied with his long day's work.

Chapter Twenty-One

Commissaire Victor Massillon of the *Police Judiciaire* sat down heavily. He was a big man with a splendid, patrician profile and wavy silver hair of which he was inordinately proud. The sight of much younger subordinates already balding gave him a secret pleasure.

'It's a bastard,' he announced, without preamble. 'I've rounded up so many Iranians I could start my own carpet factory. And I can't make anything stick to any of them.'

The investigating magistrate, Hilaire LeConte, allowed his tongue a brief sympathetic cluck. He was not a man to commit himself to what was shaping up as an inquiry on the bitter road to nowhere.

'There's not a shred of evidence that the shots were fired from a boat,' grumbled the policeman. 'Those English idiots who were supposed to be nursemaiding the poor sod both insist they heard no gunfire. If the marksman had been on another craft, I think they must have heard – even above the noise of their own engine. Sound carries well across water.'

He slumped further into his chair. 'We are left with the impossible – that someone did Niven from the shore. It couldn't have come from a crowded beach in broad daylight. So we are left with a remarkable sharpshooter in a window or on a roof somewhere along La Croisette. The possibilities run into thousands. I have practically the entire force of the Alpes Maritimes, plus my mob from Paris, rummaging around. Those Film Festival people are appalling. We've pulled in tricksters raising money for non-existent movies. There's hardly a man whose female companion is his wife. In the Berthier we discovered four Australian girls operating a makeshift brothel. All our own whores we shooed home to Paris and Marseilles. We encountered seven men living as women, and confiscated cocaine, cannabis and happy pills from half the Hollywood contingent...

'The one certainty is that our man – or woman – is no longer here.

'Forty thousand people from every country boasting a cinema have left town since the Festival ended. There was no adequate way to stop and search such an exodus. The bastards who planned this little number planned it well.'

LeConte listened to the threnody in silence. Then, as the Commissaire ground to a morose halt, he said, 'Don't you have even a sniff?'

'Maybe,' said Massillon. 'A number of people we accept as sensible citizens – not the usual nutters who emerge from the woodwork in a case like this – have come forward to say they heard shots. Most swear to two at around the time Conrad Niven was floating through the air – the bloody fool – although we have others who testify to a single shot some days previously. The day Niven died also happened to be a day of good weather and he might as well have been displaying a please-shoot-me sign.'

'A first attempt that missed? A ranging shot?'

'It figures, doesn't it?' said the Commissaire.

He turned to the town map on the wall. 'All our witnesses were going about their business in this section of La Croisette, between the Carlton and the Martinez hotels. That embraces more than a thousand rooms and private apartments.'

The magistrate's eyes travelled from the building line on the map to the blue-inked bay and a series of ovals and loops that showed where the Special Branch men had attempted to reproduce their course through the water. The nearest pass was at least two thousand metres from the façades of the buildings.

'It's still hard to credit,' he murmured.

'Well, you'd better believe it because we have nothing else to believe,' said Massillon bluntly. 'We have interviewed every room occupant we could find but, of course, authenticating what they have told us depends on umpteen other police and security services. We just have to sit waiting for the feedback and hope to God there is some.' He shrugged. 'It's not very dynamic, I know, but this may prove to be the one time when sitting on our arses is the right thing to do.'

'*Merde*,' said LeConte.

French detectives do not need the testimony of Simenon. They are celebrated throughout the world of law enforcement for their brilliance and ruthlessness. And now they began to live up to their reputation – with a little assistance from their arch-rivals, Scotland Yard.

When over three hundred French requests for follow-up inquiries flooded into London, covering actors, film-company executives, cinema exhibitors, publicists, photographers, journalists, freelance tarts and assorted filmland groupies, the Metropolitan Commissioner set up a task force under Commander Tom Ringrose, who had worked with Victor Massillon before, on the notorious Queen of the Earth kidnappings. Ringrose's team plodded painstakingly through the well-tested routines.

The general idea is that when the foot soldiers of the task force encounter anomalies, suspicious circumstances, absence of checkable data or any other worrisome feature, they pass the details up the chain of command. The more puzzling the anomaly, the higher it rises to receive more intensive examination by senior officers, and only the most egregious and intractable cases appear on the desk of the officer in charge.

So it was – as Betty Bentinck had accurately predicted – that the case of the non-existent Mr and Mrs Canning reached the attention of Ringrose.

Tom Ringrose, at the age of forty-nine, stood at the height of his powers. Given the current preference for university graduates on the fast-track rise to senior command, Ringrose's had been a remarkable ascent from the pavement beat of the uniformed bobby to criminal investigator of exceptional instinct and sure perception. He'd always thought himself unambitious and his outward aspect was courteous and diffident – the theatricals of some of his peers only embarrassed him. He was a tall, lean man with a distinctive white streak running through his greying hair.

His wife had once dragged him along 'for fun' to a medium and fortune-teller. The old woman, surrounded by her ludicrous paraphernalia, had said to him, 'Oooooh! What a lucky man you are, my dear. I've never seen such an aura. It's the colour of pearls. You ought to be sitting here doing my job. You're wonderfully sensitive. Have you ever considered helping the bereaved get in touch with the Other Side?'

After that, whenever he was asked about his successes, Tom Ringrose would say, 'I've got a pearl-coloured aura, you know. It helps me contact people on the Other Side.' He meant, of course, on the other side of the Law.

He had been personally in charge of forty-three murder inquiries, all of which he had brought to a satisfactory conclusion. For one result he had had to wait nine years. A kindergarten teacher had been found raped and strangled; the only forensic evidence of any worth had been a left thumb-print that had no equivalent in police records. A mass fingerprinting of more than twenty thousand local men had failed to uncover a match and for nine years Ringrose ran national computer checks. Then, on one exhilarating day, he received a positive print-out. The thumb-print matched one recently taken from a Wolverhampton travelling salesman with no previous convictions who was now serving six months for stealing his firm's products.

In the prison interview room, Tom Ringrose sat across from the man and silently placed in front of him some of the children's finger paintings that the teacher had been carrying home from school on the day of her death. The man began to sob. The new science of matching the DNA genetic code with semen traces confirmed that Ringrose's record for murder clear-ups was once again intact.

Now, his assistant, Detective Inspector Lionel Firth, a dark whippet who had barely made the police service height requirement, ticked off on his fingers the facts about the mysterious Cannings that were bothering the task force. 'One, they are not known at the address they provided. Two, the film industry has never heard of their company. Three, their passports were stolen from a married couple named Canning in 1991. Four, the genuine Cannings were confirmed as being at home in Bournemouth during the entire period of the Cannes Film Festival. Five, the British car registration number on the Cannings' Volvo, as noted in the parking attendant's register at the Berthier Hotel, had never been issued by the vehicle licensing authority at Swansea.'

'Is there a six?' asked Ringrose.

'Yes, they never used credit cards. Cash was paid to a London travel company in advance to reserve their suite.'

'Could be a couple of con artists setting up some kind of a sting,' mused Ringrose.

'Could be,' said Firth. 'But I think we have to put them in the list of runners, guv'nor. Don't you?'

'Without question,' said Ringrose. He reached for the telephone. 'Get me Victor Massillon in Cannes,' he ordered.

Chapter Twenty-Two

Commissaire Massillon put down the handset and came alive. He burst into LeConte's office and said dramatically, 'The sniff has become a stink,' and charged down the hall into the incident room bellowing commands.

He led a forensic team down to the Berthier and seized the hotel register, the garage log and the safe deposit keyholder's cards.

The new occupants of suite 720, a blameless couple who had just checked in from Grenoble, were tipped out and transferred to other accommodation. Their fingerprints were taken for elimination purposes and suite 720 was sealed *pro tem*.

Over the protests of the management, Massillon commandeered the hotel restaurant and the staff fell in line to have every detail that they could recall of the Cannings squeezed from them. Off-duty staff were brought in from their homes to assist.

'Where would the trash from the Cannings' occupation of 720 be now?' Massillon despatched a disconsolate team to recover it from the municipal hellhole to which it had been consigned. 'Don't come back and tell me it has been dumped at sea,' he roared. He was in his element with this kind of operation.

Four floor waiters and six chambermaids who had worked the seventh floor during the Festival were isolated from the rest of the staff. Each was taken separately into a room and interrogated. Studying the hastily typed reports ninety minutes later, Massillon's antennae started to quiver. Two of the waiters and three of the chambermaids had no memory of the Cannings, which is exactly what Massillon would have expected if he were on the scent of the right parties.

A chambermaid said, 'For several days, at the end of their stay, one of the beds was not slept in.' She, with the other two still being questioned, agreed that whenever they had gone to clean the room or turn down the beds, the Cannings had been either out or in the bathroom. However, they each remembered the huge movie camera case in the living room. Certainly, one could get a big gun inside it.

Massillon cursed. Had the Cannings taken the case with them? And, if so, how had it escaped the attention of the road blocks?

'No,' said the manager, consulting his files. 'It went to London by carrier after the road blocks were lifted. I have the delivery address. Would that be of any use to you?'

Massillon held tightly to his temper. 'That would be most kind.' He smiled icily.

The floor waiters had both seen Mrs Canning because she had signed the room-service chits. Yet she, too, eluded description. She had always been washing her hair, had invariably greeted them with a towel draped across her head, partly concealing her face. It had not seemed significant at the time . . .

Massillon ended up with descriptions and an artist's impression that depicted a mature woman with a voluptuous figure and a tall man of good physique. Their faces were tantalizingly vague.

'They carried British passports but can we be sure of their nationality?' asked Massillon.

'From their accents, they could be American. Or Canadian. Or Australian. Or—' ruminated the manager.

'Yes, yes, I get the picture,' interrupted the exasperated Commissaire.

'I'd put my money on British,' broke in the under-manager.

'Oh, why?'

'His tie,' said the functionary.

'His tie?' repeated the Commissaire patiently.

'Yes. The stripes descended diagonally from left to right.'

'I don't get it.'

'North American ties more usually have their diagonals dropping from right to left. You watch, the next time you see an American movie.'

'I never get time for the movies,' sniffed the Commissaire.

All members of staff who, however remotely, could have come into contact with the Cannings were herded into a darkened lounge for a run-through of the hotel's video tapes from the security cameras, which were of the usual quality that frustrate police the world over: badly lit and lacking depth of focus. Yet there was some agreement about a man in a straw hat, face shaded, in the milling crowd, but disagreement over the woman. Several staff identified a female guest who kept her head down, but a cashier was vehement that a woman with her right arm in a sling was the one. Yet her body was slimmer, less rounded, younger than that of the woman pointed out in the earlier tapes.

Still, this was the only picture that gave a facial view. Massillon had the tapes put on a plane for Paris where they would be electronically enhanced.

It was time to tackle suite 720. A gendarme saluted and opened the door. Massillon entered alone. He stood silently in the centre of the living room, willing himself to be receptive to the vibrations, to the spoor of the recent occupants. He squinted at the clear sightline over the terrace parapet and the palms to the open sea beyond. He noticed immediately the fresh scratches on the otherwise unscored surface of the sideboard. He was becoming convinced by the minute.

He stepped back to the door. The corridor was crowded with his specialists. He said, 'Scientific team first, fingerprints to follow.'

The white-overalled quintet from the Paris laboratory trooped in with their bags of chemicals, ultra-violet lamps and microscopes.

Then, satisfied, for the moment, that everything was under control, Massillon announced, 'You'll find me at Felix having lunch.'

He was about to cut into his steak Diane, seated alfresco at the Croisette restaurant, when his portable telephone trilled. 'There are traces of cordite on the walls and in the curtains,' said a triumphant voice. Commissaire Massillon charged his glass with a robust Gevrey-Chambertin and raised it in a toast to himself.

More puzzling news was to follow. Back in the suite, one of the boffins conducted him into the bathroom. His boys had been gouging the grouting from between the azure tiles. 'This is all very odd,' said the expert. 'We dug out a sample, more as a matter of routine than anything else. The place has been thoroughly cleaned by a maid since the Cannings left so we were not expecting a result.'

'So what came up?' said the Commissaire.

'Blood,' said the boffin.

'Yes, that is a surprise,' said Massillon thoughtfully. 'Someone cut themself shaving?'

The boffin shook his head. 'Improbable. The traces are minute but they're spread over a considerable surface. The shaver would have had to walk around dripping quite copiously.' The boffin showed Massillon a selection of filter papers that had all turned pink in an on-the-spot Kastle-Meyer test.

'I hate mysteries,' said Massillon, who had spent his adult life tormented by them. 'Conrad Niven could not have flown through the window and been shot here.' He groaned. 'I've just had a terrible thought. Suppose we are putting all this effort into a different crime entirely. It hardly bears thinking about.'

Massillon had the sideboard lifted into the middle of the room and his technicians encircled it. 'Any suggestions about those marks?' he asked.

One dropped to his knees and eyed the bottom edges, waddling around the piece of furniture like a crippled duck. He said, in his lecturer's voice, 'Please observe that the scratches on the lower edges are replicated by the scratches on the upper edges. A loop has been wound round this item, either to secure something to the flat top or to act as a lifting handle.'

'What about the two surface impressions at the front end nearest the terrace?'

The group studied the two shallow indentations in the marquetry.

Finally, Massillon said, 'If we accept that the murder was committed from this room, then it was done with a sniper's rifle. If it was done with a sniper's rifle, the criminals needed a platform for the weapon. Does this sideboard fit the theory?'

One exclaimed, 'Of course! A bipod, secured tightly to the surface would make those double dents, giving a powerful weapon additional stability.'

'Well done, I buy that. That's precisely what I was thinking myself,' Massillon lied genially. He had his legendary reputation for infallibility to foster.

He stepped to the door and bellowed into the corridor, 'Has the sniper expert arrived yet?' An Army colonel in khaki drill stepped forward. Massillon modified his tone at sight of the man's rank. 'Please come this way, sir, and give us the benefit of your knowledge.'

He showed the colonel the sideboard and explained the theory. The man crouched at the end of the sideboard and assumed a firing position with an invisible rifle. The policemen watched him as he murmured sounds of incredulity. At last, he straightened, tugging down his jacket to show its ironed creases to advantage. 'You are dealing here with an exceptional man,' he began. Massillon rolled his eyes to heaven. He was getting tired of hearing this.

The colonel raised his arm in invitation. 'Be so kind as to come here, Commissaire, and take up the man's position.' Massillon did not like taking orders, no matter how delicately expressed. He frowned but complied. 'You see before you a width of terrace window, flanked by inner walls of equal width. Yes?'

'Of course,' said Massillon, unable to keep the irritation from his voice.

The colonel went on unconcerned. 'Is your eyesight good?'

'Good for a man of my age,' grunted Massillon, squinting with one eye closed. He knew his underlings were beginning to enjoy this.

'Would it be accurate to say your peripheral vision extends to both corners of the front wall of this room?'

'It does,' said Massillon heavily.

'Therefore,' said the colonel, 'you would agree that, from the position you are now holding, your sniper has to make do with only a third of his horizon in which to frame his target?'

'That would appear to be the case.'

'When a man is looking straight ahead, his field of vision extends to a hundred and four degrees. But this fellow was able to utilize only a field of vision of some thirty-five degrees. Shooting at the distances you posit, at a moving target, requires a considerable amount of what we call 'aiming off' – shooting, in fact, at the spot where you anticipate the target will be when the bullet arrives. With his restricted horizon, your fellow would have had almost no time to adjust his sniperscope. If indeed the firing did occur from this room, he must have relied largely on an instinct that was no less than uncanny. I intend no disrespect, sir, but are you certain you are on the right track?'

Massillon returned to his temporary headquarters in the *mairie*, his earlier elation turned to gloom and foreboding. Listlessly, he had the details of the silver box's journey to London faxed directly to his old friend Tom Ringrose. Their joint efforts in the beauty queens case had made them, for one shining hour, world famous, with an artist's study of their keen profiles on the cover of *Time* magazine under the headline 'The Mancatchers'. Those were the glory days!

The French police chief had to wait a further twenty-four hours for his team to produce further puzzles to add to his woes. The bath in suite 720 had been dismantled and further blood traces found in the S-bend water trap. The blood on the floor and the blood in the drain were of the same type – B positive – shared by 9 per cent of the population, whereas Niven was a group A, shared by a massive 42 per cent of Westerners.

Had one of the assassins injured himself? Perhaps the victim of an accidental discharge of the weapon. Then he remembered the video of the woman at the cashier's desk with her arm in a sling. Had she been the injured party?

'Damn mysterious,' grumbled Massillon.

The men he had dubbed the Shit Legionnaires had returned from the municipal dump with what appeared to be half the detritus of the Berthier Hotel. To the fury of the Festival authorities, the police had insisted on spreading it thinly over trestle tables set up in the vast conference room on the fourth floor of the Palais des Festivals, the only arena that was both available and large enough.

The smell of decay polluted the air because Massillon had decreed that the remains of food served to seventh-floor guests should be examined. 'Oh, for a set of toothmarks in an apple,' he had rhapsodized to the amusement of his staff.

They led him directly to their successes: the duplicate copies of guests' laundry lists, which contained the carbon facsimile of Mrs Canning's signature. The items sent for cleaning were as one would have expected: the suspects had sent out in the morning, had their *blanchissage* expressed and returned in the evening of the same day, as if ever ready to pack and run.

Massillon spotted that after the sixth day, the lists had been signed by Mr Canning and only items of male apparel sent for cleaning. He took a pencil and began to probe fastidiously among the items around the laundry lists. He flicked over a dripping fruit-juice carton and revealed a crumpled business card. He held up his hand for a pair of tweezers and lifted it out of the stinking mess. On the reverse side was scrawled in ink: 'Ch. 539. Golf?' The front bore the name of Sidney Zuckerman, film producer, with the address of an office in Century City, Los Angeles, California.

'I have seen this name before,' said Massillon. His aide peered over his shoulder. 'The British okayed him. He was on Conrad Niven's list of guests for the boat reception that was due to take place on the day of the hit.'

'So what was his card doing on the seventh floor and in the same garbage bag with 720's crap?'

Massillon stood brooding, waving the card back and forth like a fan. 'Let's ask the Americans to red-flag Mr Zuckerman. At the moment he is merely on the low-priority check-list. Get to it!'

Massillon rubbed his hands together. 'Momentum! Momentum!' he urged.

Chapter Twenty-Three

Commander Ringrose put down the telephone and said, 'The Ministry of Defence know nothing about it. The Security Services know nothing about it. Or, at least they *say* they know nothing about it.'

'Are they playing silly buggers?' asked Lionel Firth.

Ringrose glinted dangerously. 'If they are, I'll play merry hell. The Home Secretary is feeding the Prime Minister a daily progress report on this one and I'll see my protest goes right to the top if I think our investigation is being shafted.'

On Ringrose's desk was a Battersea detective's account of an interview with one Alfred Tickner, night guard at Gatti's Repository. It read, in part: 'The gate bell went just after six when I'd started my first round of security checks – buttoning the building up for the night. Outside were a couple of posh-looking blokes with a black car and a driver in a Ford Transit. They showed me collection papers from a film company. I don't remember the name but the office will have it. I told them they were too late, they'd have to come back tomorrow. The one with the documents said it was a matter of supreme importance to the State. They were his exact words but I wasn't going to fall for that old malarkey. I told him so but he produced some sort of red pass and said, "Ministry of Defence." I tried to take it from him to have a good look but he said he was not allowed to let it out of his possession. He held it up for me to read. The trouble was, his hand kept moving and I couldn't read it properly. But it definitely had a little crown printed in one corner and a picture of the bloke. It looked very official and they did have the correct documentation for the goods, so I opened up and let them collect. It was a single item – one of those lightweight aluminium camera cases that the film people use. It was heavy. I needed the forklift to transfer it to the van.'

Lionel Firth said, 'He must have been going around with Play-doh in his eyes. His descriptions are pathetic – and he didn't make a note of either vehicle's number. It's a bummer.'

Ringrose was troubled. He shared a distaste for the serpentine, unaccountable ways of the Security and Secret Intelligence Services with most officers in the police force. Too often, they acted outside the law and were allowed to get away with it. Too often, their high-handed methods had upset colleagues.

Ringrose had an interview with the Commissioner. Up in the eighth-floor corner office, he said, 'This has to be resolved, sir. If those men were Five or Six I want to know, and I want to see the box and its contents.'

Three hours later, the Commissioner summoned him back to his office. 'Tom, I passed it up to the Home Secretary who took it to the Cabinet Office who dumped it on the Co-ordinator of Security Services – the usual channels. The Co-ordinator has received verbal assurances from both director-generals that their staffs were not involved in the Battersea affair. They do not have the box. The men were impostors. Everyone passes to you their assurances of complete, open-book co-operation. Ask for anything you want.'

Ringrose stood to go, but the Commissioner went on, 'One final thing. The Home Secretary took me aside for a quiet word.' The Commissioner turned to his window and the view across Broadway to the London Transport headquarters. He did not seem to want to meet Ringrose's eyes. He said, 'He and the Prime Minister are fervently hoping that you can prove the killers were not British. The Government is taking enough flak for the cock-up by the Special Branch protection squad. And I've taken my share, too. If you can dig up some Iranians or, better still, toss it back to the bloody French as a hit by a French team – some of those Algerian tearaways or hired French Foreign Legionnaires, perhaps – the PM would be over the moon. The French will take great delight in leaking the British passport angle. When they do, our official line will be that the passports prove nothing. They could have been stolen by anyone and not necessarily Brits.'

The Commissioner was in his blue uniform with silver accoutrements and a regulation plain necktie. Ringrose said, 'Sir, do you own any striped ties?'

He turned back to face Ringrose, eyebrows rising. His most celebrated detective did not usually stray from the point. 'What an odd question. Yes, I have several.'

'Which way do the stripes slope?'

The Commissioner's mind's eye got to work. Ringrose could see that he was picturing his image in the mirror and laboriously working out the reverse. Finally, he concluded, 'Downward from left to right. Why?'

'It's a question that Victor Massillon asked me. I gave him the same answer.'

The Commissioner's eyes narrowed. 'What's that crafty old devil up to?'

'I don't know,' said Ringrose, 'but my answer seemed to make him happy. He went off the line chuckling.'

Chapter Twenty-Four

From his eighteenth-floor office suite, Sidney Zuckerman could look down upon the concrete, steel and glass development that had once been the rural back lot of the 20th Century-Fox film studio where, in more innocent days, Tom Mix rode the range.

Sidney watched the hectic traffic on the Avenue of the Stars while he waited for Special Agent Emily Curtis of the Federal Bureau of Investigation to ascend from street level.

He savoured the name: Emily. Nah, all wrong, he decided. Too soft. Too poetic, like that Amherst dame . . . what was her name? If he were casting the role, he'd go for something a lot stronger, like . . . Casey. Yeah, Casey Curtis. A woman's name with balls.

Agent Curtis was ushered in by his very plain secretary – don't dip your pen in the company inkwell, was Sidney's motto – unaware that her name had been screen-tested and found wanting.

Sidney congratulated himself. This dame was no Emily; she was a real businesslike babe with a lean, mean body that shouted daily workout. He liked her cropped fair hair, too. It quivered when she moved in a way that suggested orgasmic passion. Definitely a Casey.

Introductions over, Agent Emily cut straight to the chase. She handed Sidney two fax sheets. Each showed one side of the visiting card that Commissaire Massillon had fished out of the seventh-floor garbage.

'What's the beef?' asked Sidney. 'I handed out scores of these during the Festival.'

'But they didn't all have "Golf?" and your room number scribbled on the back, did they, sir?'

'Correct,' said Sidney. 'This industry is tennis-mad, not golf-mad. This is the only golf invitation I handed out – to an English guy in the hotel elevator. I did it because he was carrying a golfing bag. I don't have his name but I do know he was in room 720. He gave me a wrong room number but the porter corrected him. Do I take it this guy was deliberately giving me a bum steer?'

Agent Emily did not answer. She asked, 'Did you get to play golf with him?'

Sidney looked disgusted. 'No. The one time I saw the jerk again, he gave me a cold shoulder.' Sidney described in detail the scene of the snubbing on the terrace.

Emily diligently wrote in her notebook a complete description of the jerk. 'Oh, yes,' Sidney added. 'I never saw him without a Panama hat on his head. I always thought a gentleman was supposed to remove his hat in an elevator.'

'Perhaps he was hiding a bald spot?' Emily suggested.

'I hope so,' said Sidney viciously.

The FBI woman had a thick wad of photographs in a folder. They were copies of the enlarged video pictures enhanced in the Sûreté laboratories.

Sidney took his time. Poring over the black-and-whites, he pointed out fellow producers, directors, film fanciers, showbiz journalists. 'Look, there's Marcello Mastroianni. What a great actor! If he'd been American, he'd have been another Brando.'

Emily patiently inked a number against each identified body and recorded the name in her notebook. Excitedly, Sidney twice jabbed a finger at the image of a man with a Panama hat shielding his face. 'That's the creep.'

Emily dutifully appended a number and wrote 'Suspect'.

When Sidney came to the first sighting of Betty Bentinck, he said neutrally, 'That's Betty Bentinck, the actress. She's one of us – an all-American girl.'

In as non-judgemental a voice as she could manage, Agent Emily said, 'Wasn't Miss Bentinck your companion on this trip, sir?'

'Yeah,' said Sidney reluctantly.

'Did she meet the man in the Panama?'

'Not to speak to. But she was with me on the terrace when he refused to let us join his table.'

Emily continued to feed photographs across Sidney's wide black marble desk. He whooped when she handed over a shot of the man in the Panama standing by the cashier's desk.

'It's him again!' he exclaimed. His gaze shifted and Emily saw him change colour rapidly despite the Riviera tan.

'What *is* this?' he said. He sat back in his leather chair, defensive as if she had tried to trick him.

'Excuse me?'

'Has this photo been doctored? What's going on?'

Emily stared at him. 'Nothing's going on. Why are you upset?'

Sidney could hardly utter the words. 'This – this dame with the arm in a sling, standing next to the jerk. It's Betty.'

Agent Emily was nonplussed. 'Your Betty?' She leaned across the desk to see where Sidney was pointing. Her breasts dropped heavily against her blouse. Despite his shock, Sidney still had room to wonder if he should try to date her. He'd never had an FBI agent.

The object of his sudden lust said, 'Are you saying this is Miss Bentinck?'

For answer, Sidney pressed the intercom and bawled, 'Donna, drop everything and bring in all Betty Bentinck's glossies.'

He sat fidgeting under Emily's cool gaze until the plain secretary came in with Betty's publicity photographs.

'Here,' said Sidney. 'Look for yourself.' He slid across a big, brassbound magnifying glass. 'Careful with that. It's part of Hollywood's history. That's the spyglass used by Basil Rathbone in those old Sherlock Holmes movies. Another bloody Englishman,' Sidney added bitterly, as an afterthought.

Emily studied Betty's posed portraits, her gaze going back and forth to the woman with the sling. 'Are you sure of this? Certainly the woman bears a resemblance but she's older and her hairstyle is much more severe than anything in these studio portraits.'

'Sure I'm sure,' snapped Sidney. 'Don't you think I'd know the piece of ass I lived with for two years?'

He saw Emily's lips tighten. Uh-oh. 'Piece of ass' was a no-no. He saw his chances of a date evaporating. Goddamn feminists!

He added aloud, 'I don't understand how this could be. Betty didn't even exchange word one with the guy.'

'Well, not in your hearing,' Emily remarked.

Her interjection stopped Sidney in his tracks. 'Wait a minute, I've just remembered something. On the day Conrad Niven got hit, I was crossing the Croisette from the beach side. I saw Betty sitting alone on the hotel terrace and the English jerk disappearing into the building. They could have been talking – I just don't know.'

Emily said, 'You referred to your relationship in the past tense. Aren't you and Miss Bentinck still together?'

Sidney wriggled uncomfortably. 'It's a mystery to me. We hadn't fallen out and I'd spent a great deal of money taking her to Cannes. But the moment we got back to California, she took a walk. Gratitude didn't come into it.'

'Does she have money?'

'That's another thing,' said Sidney. 'She had a TV series, but that was two seasons ago.'

'Yes, I remember it,' said Emily drily. 'About women agents of the FBI.'

'Yes, that's the one,' said Sidney unabashed. 'I subsequently gave her a break by putting her into my last movie. But the budget was tight so she agreed to take SAG – Screen Actors' Guild – scale against points in the producer's net.'

'Meaning?'

'Meaning that I didn't think she had a dime of her own,' said Sidney. 'Then she upped and rented a cabin in Laurel Canyon. I asked her what she was going to use for the green stuff and she, well, she waved some C-notes at me and said something very unladylike.'

'And what was that?' asked Emily sweetly.

'Fuck you,' said Sidney.

Chapter Twenty-Five

They pulled in Betty Bentinck at six in the morning. In the light of Sidney's revelations, Emily Curtis's superiors considered a home interview would not exert enough psychological pressure on her.

At the FBI's downtown LA office, Betty was placed in a windowless room and allowed to sweat for two hours. They made it obvious that a guard was stationed on the door. They brought her coffee and a Danish but otherwise she might just as well have been incarcerated in a prison cell.

Betty considered screaming and shouting for a lawyer but she had already let the opportunity pass her by. She had known the FBI would come for her: Sidney had telephoned and shouted, 'You bitch! You were making out with that English jerk behind my back. I've had the FBI all over me.'

At 8 a.m. Special Agent Emily Curtis introduced herself, together with a male agent who would take a deposition. Betty eyed them with something akin to despair. 'I'm in deepest doo-doo, right?' she said.

Agent Curtis shrugged. 'Ach, it doesn't have to be like that, Betty.

We're simply making some inquiries on behalf of the French government. You've come into the picture because you, well, literally came into the picture.'

Betty began to babble. 'Look, I had no part in his insurance scam. I was just helping him to get clear of a complication in his life. That shooting business – he didn't want to get his lines crossed with that. He had no part of that stuff. I was just the hired hand. He paid me to act the part of his wife for a couple of hours. Whatever Sidney Zuckerman has told you, I did not sleep with him.'

'Whoa!' said Emily Curtis. 'You're going too fast for us. Why don't we take it from the beginning? Then I'll put some questions to you that the French have sent us during the night. For a start: who is the man we're talking about?'

Fuelled with coffee but bereft of her usual bounce, Betty started at her first meeting with James Canning on the terrace and worked through to her goodbye warning at the door of suite 720.

'Very good,' said Agent Emily. 'Now let me ask you this: you confirm that you wore the sling but were in no way injured. You did not shed blood.'

'Correct.'

'Was James Canning injured? Did he shed blood?'

'No. No one was injured. I thought I made that clear. It was just a harmless deception.'

'Did you see any blood in 720?'

'I don't get it. Why this obsession with blood?'

'Is that a no?'

'Yes – it's a no.'

'Did you use, or have cause to go into, Canning's bathroom?'

'Yes, when I made myself up as his wife.'

'Did you see any blood in the bathroom?'

'Jesus.'

'Is that another no?'

'Yes – it's another no.'

'Did you observe in suite 720 a large metal case of the type that movie cameras are stored in?'

'No.'

'If one were there, could you have missed it?'

'If, as you say, it was large, I don't see how.'

'Did you catch sight of any firearms?'

Betty blanched and suddenly felt sick. She sat silent for a minute, her hands twisting nervously between her knees. She looked from the male agent, with his pen poised, to Emily. Betty said, 'This isn't about an insurance scam, is it? It's about the killing, isn't it? Oh, Jesus, he seemed such a charming, sexy guy. When I first set eyes on him I thought he must be a stuntman or a cowboy actor with that gorgeous bushy moustache. Rugged like Sean Connery, and a gentleman like Robert Redford.'

She began to cry and the male agent handed her his handkerchief. 'I've been such a dope. I was so anxious to get out from under Sidney Zuckerman that I left my brains at home. I was desperate for some money of my own. I had points in Sidney's last movie but did you ever know a producer who admitted to making a profit?'

They watched her snivel. Then Emily said, 'Cheer up. We've all been overboard for the wrong man.' The agent taking the deposition gave her an appraising glance as if he were surprised that she could own up to such a banal female weakness.

Emily said, 'I'm going to put you together with a Bureau artist. The French want the best portrait you can provide of Canning.'

'What happens then?'

'We ask you to keep a lid on what's gone down and we send you back home in a limo.'

'I'm not to be charged?'

'With what? You've co-operated with the Bureau, you've committed no crime on American soil – and I can't see, at this stage, that you've committed much of one in France. Stay loose and, as they used to say in that television series of yours, don't leave town. The French may have more questions.'

Betty felt slightly better when the male agent asked for her autograph.

Chapter Twenty-Six

Jack telephoned Southwold from a callbox. Ben answered and wailed, 'Dad, when can we come home? I'll lose my place in the soccer team.'

'I never thought I'd hear a son of mine plead to go back to school,' he countered with fake jocularity. A lump came to his throat. This was what he was missing – the daily cut-and-thrust with his boys. The comforting mundanity of domestic life – and wrap-round love from the three people he held more precious than his own life.

Grace took the telephone. 'Are you all right?' He felt a stab of guilt that she should sound so worried.

'Everything's normal,' he said. He had been about to tell her of the devices he had cleared from the house, but changed his mind. He'd upset her enough. He'd found bugs in the bedroom. She'd be embarrassed. Instead he said, 'I've made some interesting progress. I've already got the answers to some questions but let's not go into it on the phone.'

Like Ben, Grace asked, 'When can we come home? Up here's like being in exile. It's very quiet – the holiday season hasn't got going yet and it's making me jumpy with no one around out here on these dunes.'

'Be patient a little longer,' Jack pleaded. 'I want you to stay up there for a few more days – just to be sure there's not going to be any trouble.'

Grace didn't like the sound of that. 'You be very, very careful. They know who they're dealing with. You don't know who you're dealing with.'

When they hung up, Jack walked the streets, brooding. The last thing Grace had said was no longer entirely true. He had been to the public library to consult the electoral rolls for Holland Park and had established that the householder at the address in St James's Gardens to which he had tailed the Bentley was a certain Bulwer Tancred. It had been Tancred's entry in *Who's Who* that had thrown Jack into confusion.

Tancred – Marlborough and Peterhouse – was an under-secretary in the Cabinet Office, a Whitehall warrior.

Jack had been stunned. He'd been snared for the plot because he had allowed himself to be convinced that he was on a quasi-official mission, one that gave whichever government department that had recruited him the privilege of disowning him should the operation go belly-up. Jack understood that; he knew ex-SAS and ex-SBS guys were hired on this basis for undercover work that would not bear dispassionate examination by a parliamentary select committee. It was only when he had discovered the identity of his target that he had had to face a more feasible possibility: that he had been either the tool of private enterprise bounty hunters or the point-man for an Iranian murder squad. Now he was flung back to his original belief. Suddenly Jack felt tiny, a figure in a vast, tangled landscape.

That evening he had the only stroke of luck to come his way so far in the whole horrific mess. Each day he'd bought all the newspapers to keep abreast of the efforts to identify and capture him. It was a nerve-racking business, yet there was no indication that they might be on his heels. But did the newspapers know everything that was going on? Jack thought not.

One by one, he tossed the papers onto the carpet. He had little concern for what else was happening in the world. And then his eye caught her photograph on an inside page of the *Daily Telegraph*.

'Yes!' he yelled aloud to the empty room. Jane Canning's face – younger, hair fluffier, no heavy spectacles – gazed soulfully out at him. It was the kind of pearls-and-Peter-Pan-collar picture beloved of debutantes' mothers. The caption read simply: The Hon. Nancy Tintagel.

'Yes!' he shouted again in delight. Back to him came the sound of a voice in the dark shouting, 'Tinny!' when he and Mrs Canning had gone to have dinner in La Napoule. He remembered her sudden urgency to get away from the marina. Tinny for Tintagel. Yes!

Jack read on greedily:

A verdict of accidental death was recorded yesterday on Miss Nancy Tintagel, 35, elder daughter of Viscount Tintagel, who fell while out hacking on May 6.

Her riding companion, Mr Rupert Strang, a colleague in the Foreign Office, told the West Sussex coroner that Miss Tintagel was a skilled horsewoman. However, she had been unable to control her mount when it took flight at a sudden flurry of birds from a hedgerow and reared, throwing Miss Tintagel onto hard ground.

'Despite the hard hat she was wearing, she was knocked unconscious and I was unable to revive her,' said Mr Strang.

Professor Roland Askew, pathologist, said Miss Tintagel had died almost instantly from a broken neck.

The coroner, Dr C. C. Webber, said it was a tragic end to a high-flying career in the diplomatic service. Miss Tintagel had served in the Middle East and Bonn, and was already a counsellor. Great things had been expected of her.

The coroner offered his deepest sympathy to Viscount Tintagel who was too stricken to attend court.

Jack felt numb. He pored over the report once more and marvelled. These people were so powerful that they could conjure death scenes out of the air and present them to one of Her Majesty's coroners as fact. They could command the services of public figures and a pathologist and require them to perjure themselves. Apparently they could do anything they wanted, including have people murdered.

Even the date given as that of her death was wrong. On 6 May, Mrs Canning/Tintagel had been alive and well with him in France, plotting the death of Conrad Niven.

Jack gathered up the other papers and went through them again with more care. None carried the inquest report. Only the man from the *Telegraph*, the armed services' bulletin board, had been present in court with his shorthand notebook to inform the viscount's daughter's social equals of her untimely end. But at least Jack had one consolation: he now had three names, Tancred, Strang and Askew, plus two addresses to toy with. He had swiftly drawn a bead on Rupert Strang: his home address, in Markham Square, off the King's Road, Chelsea, came courtesy of the London telephone directory.

Jack bought a pint at the Markham Arms on the corner of the square. The evening was light and pleasant. He had only thirty minutes to wait before a taxi drew up and a slim, loose-limbed man mounted the half-dozen steps and let himself into the neat mid-Victoria house where pansy-crowded boxes perched on the window sills.

Once more, Jack breathed, 'Yessss!' Rupert Strang was one of the two suits who had supervised the collection of Mrs Canning's – Miss Tintagel's – coffin from Gatti's Repository. He drained his glass and went home to have an early night. He slept soundly without the dream, the Glock on the bedside cabinet and the Cobray M-11 in chamber-pot position under the bed. Unlike Pock Mark, Jack had a mighty thirty-two-round clip in place.

If they came for him, he'd make them pay a heavy price.

Chapter Twenty-Seven

Commander Ringrose's veneer mahogany desk was stacked high with the material still arriving in a torrent from Victor Massillon. The nobs and politicos of Whitehall were not going to like it, but the chance of producing a psychopathic Iranian to take the rap now appeared negligible.

A study of the French forensic reports and Betty Bentinck's plaintive statement left little doubt that they were looking for two people, one of whom had given every evidence of being British.

Massillon had finally explained the mystery of the striped ties.

Ringrose had examined his own collection that morning and, sure enough, the diagonals all sloped left to right. Then he'd flicked channels on the early-morning TV programmes until he found a noisy American game-show: the stripes on the host's tie went right to left.

Ringrose gloomily contemplated Massillon's plentiful offering. He could hear the French happily shovelling the shit to his side of the Channel. He called in Lionel Firth. 'I know nothing about sharp-shooting,' said Ringrose, 'but everyone seems to agree that, even with the finest weapon, it was a remarkable accomplishment. So we're looking for a trained marksman whose appearance approximates to this.' He tossed over Betty Bentinck's attempt at a likeness.

'Looks like Wyatt Earp in a stetson,' said Firth.

'It's meant to be a Panama,' said Ringrose.

He pushed back his white forelock and sat in thought. Firth waited. 'Our man can't have sprung from nowhere as a fully fledged marksman. He must have had some training, perhaps even won prizes. His prowess must be known to someone. Let's check out the rifle clubs and ask the Army for help in cobbling together a list of ex-service likely lads.'

Ringrose had an afterthought. 'Better include the lasses. The French may be assuming that it was the man with his finger on the trigger. But why not the elusive Mrs Canning? Perhaps she did it, with Mr Canning as the toerag left behind to clean up the room.'

He perused the FBI drawing again. 'This dizzy American girl put the suspect's age at around thirty-five. But let's leave ourselves a wide margin. Hollywood people are known to be rather careless about ages. Let's say Wyatt Earp here could be anything from twenty-five to forty-five.'

'You're right about Hollywood ages,' said Firth. 'She says our man is as sexy as Sean Connery, who's in his sixties, and as gentlemanly as Robert Redford, who's heading that way. There's hope for us yet, guv'nor.'

They were still grinning when Ringrose took a call from Paul Kaiser, who said simply, 'Can you make the Grenadier at six thirty?' Ringrose knew better than to say anything except yes on an unsecured line.

As an agent of the Central Intelligence Agency, Kaiser had one serious disadvantage should he ever be assigned to covert action: he could never disappear in a crowd. He was 6 feet 7 inches tall in his Sulka socks. He reduced the bar of the tiny Grenadier pub, tucked away in a Belgravia mews, to doll's-house proportions.

Kaiser was on a Grosvenor Square tour of duty from Langley and enjoying a notable success with London's society hostesses. Aside from his charm and bachelor status, his family ownership of a Wall Street finance house may have had something to do with this.

He and Ringrose carried their drinks out into the cobbled lane. The American was already consulting his watch. 'Sorry,' he said, 'this'll have to be quick. I have a theatre tonight.'

'*The Importance of Being Earnest?*' asked Ringrose innocently.

The sally was wasted. 'No, I think it's by that fellow who's always angry about something or other.'

Kaiser drew near, bending both knees to position his lips nearer to Ringrose's left ear. 'Mr Bishop – the chief – sends you his best regards and apologizes that he couldn't come himself. He wanted you to have the latest word from our assets in Tehran.'

'Fine. Shoot,' said Ringrose, matching whisper for whisper.

'The chief says the peculiar news is that there is no peculiar news. No one has come forward to claim the bounty on Conrad Niven's head – none of the terror groups, no headhunters, no amateurs.

'The chief says there have been the usual phoney claimants trying their luck. The Iranians have a jail full of them. Curiously, the ayatollahs seem relaxed – as if they're not expecting anyone to collect. All the phoney claimants went straight to jail without passing Go. There was no investigation into any of their stories. It was as if none of them had the right password.'

Ringrose sipped his ale. 'Maybe the million was just another desert mirage, something that never existed.'

'No,' said Kaiser emphatically. 'Our evidence is that the *fatwah* million was a genuine offer. Our assets say the cash was put aside, waiting for the team that could prove it had pulled off the job. But, two weeks after the event, there are still no takers.' He had recited the message as if he had learned it parrot-fashion at the knee of Jake Bishop, CIA head of London station and a close friend of Ringrose.

'Well, thank the chief for letting me know,' said Ringrose. 'I'd be glad to hear more, if your sources come up with anything.'

'The chief says you may depend on it. You're top name on his dance card. He likes you,' added the young agent, almost enviously.

'That's nice to know,' said Ringrose, glancing at his own watch. 'Don't forget you have a date with John Osborne.'

'I have?' said Kaiser, looking baffled.

Chapter Twenty-Eight

Jack sat in his window seat, watching the street for unusual activity and sipping his coffee. He listened to the messages on the answering machine: disgruntled friends with whom he had not touched base in weeks, two messages from the boys' school, both demanding news of their whereabouts – and numerous clicks where callers had rung off.

It was something of a relief to be back in the familiar surroundings of work. His deputy, Joe Carsby, had tolerated his extended holiday with his customary cheeriness. Joe was also ex-Army, a former staff sergeant in the Paymaster-General's office.

They made an effective team: Jack was expert with the guns and tuition and Joe was a wizard with the books and pretended to be good with the guns when dealing with the punters. Fortunately, he never essayed target practice when a club member was watching.

Now Jack did some catching up. 'Any troubles? Any visits from the VAT man or other pests?'

'Nothing heavy,' reported Joe. 'A guy poked his head round the door looking for you a week or so ago. Said he was an old chum. Didn't leave his card.'

Jack said, 'Tall? Slim? Terrific suiting? Tight-waisted – Savile Row?'

'Yeah. Spot on.'

'That's okay. He found me at home.'

Strang must have called, mused Jack, at around the time they were becoming anxious at Mrs Canning's failure to report in.

Before he went home that evening, Jack signed himself out a box of ammunition that he did not expend on the range.

He was a man with a mission. It suddenly came to him that, since he had decided he would not sit passively and accept his fate, he had had the dream only once – and Grace had promptly chased it away.

He fished around the kitchen cupboard for some food and liberated a tin of mackerel. Later, he found Viscount Tintagel's number in the book and telephoned.

His Lordship had been a junior minister in the dying days of the Macmillan government, held numerous directorships and dutifully did his four days a week in the House, accepting the government whip.

The voice sounded elderly. No, he could not see the reporter from the *East Sussex Courier* at home, but if he cared to present himself at three-thirty the next afternoon at the St Stephen's entrance to the Houses of Parliament, the security people would be expecting him.

This alerted Jack – or John Jones as he now styled himself – to leave behind the Glock, which was establishing an imprint above his buttocks.

Jack slipped away after a sandwich lunch at the club. The old boy, not as old as he sounded, guided Jack to a stone seat in a wide lobby lined with murals celebrating England's past glories. His hard-brushed hair was steel-grey and he wore the uniform of a politician for whom gravitas was a professional tool – dark, striped suit, black lace-up shoes, waistcoat with watchchain looped across an ample stomach. His one touch of colour was in the Oxford blue of his polka-dot bow-tie.

Jack took out pen and notebook which surprised His Lordship. 'I thought all you chaps used those miniature tape recorders these days.'

'Mine's on the blink,' said Jack, hardly missing a beat. He leaned forward and added earnestly, 'First of all, sir, I'd like to express my sympathy for your loss.'

Mrs Canning's father weakly raised a liver-spotted hand and let it fall back into his lap in a gesture of hopelessness. 'A terrible, terrible business. Her mother is taking it very badly – which is why I couldn't have you round at the house, my boy.'

Somehow, Jack had never thought of Mrs Canning as having been exposed to maternal love.

His Lordship regarded him quizzically. 'How many words will this obituary run to, Mr Jones? Left it a bit late in the day, haven't you?'

Jack said carefully, 'I thought about a thousand words, sir. We missed the inquest, you know.'

'So did I, dammit.'

'Yes, it would have been very upsetting for you. I saw the report in the *Telegraph*.'

'Lot of bollocks,' snorted Lord Tintagel. 'Too stricken to attend indeed! I went through the war, you know. Saw good men I regarded as brothers cut down. I wasn't "too stricken" then. One simply had to press on. Death is so random one should never be surprised.'

'Then what kept you away from the inquest, sir?'

'Those bloody spooks!' Lord Tintagel said it so loudly that a frock-coated attendant took several steps in their direction.

'Spooks, sir? I don't understand.'

'Look, you mustn't write this down.' He looked at Jack shrewdly. 'Are you an Englishman? Both sides of the family?'

Jack nodded.

'Thought so,' said Tintagel. 'Military family, perhaps?'

'I was a regular,' said Jack.

His Lordship patted his knee. 'Good! You've got the look. Signed the Official Secrets Act and all that?'

'Certainly.'

His Lordship patted his knee again and continued, 'Then you must know what spooks are.'

'Ghosts or spies?' offered Jack.

'Exactly. My girl had a brain. She was a marvel at languages. French, German, Italian. They put her through that Beirut school and she could even cope with Arabic. Her mother and I were delighted when she passed the Civil Service exams and went into the Foreign Office. She had all the intellectual equipment to carry her upwards to an ambassadorship.'

His pink, lined face darkened. 'Then those bloody spooks got hold of her, offered her a life of excitement and intrigue, I daresay. Not that she ever told us. It was a long time before her mother and I cottoned on that she was no longer what she seemed – an up-and-coming member of the Diplomatic Corps. We only started to suspect something rum was going on when she stopped telling us about her work.'

The old boy took out a red handkerchief and noisily blasted into it. Jack stayed silent and Lord Tintagel said, 'Where was I?'

'You suspected she was a spy,' prompted Jack.

'Ah, yes. Nancy was a game girl, you know. She had a marvellous seat, good at all the country pursuits – fine fencer, too.'

Jack saw again in his mind's eye that fine-toned, voluptuous body rising and falling above him in the half-light.

His Lordship was still talking. 'You can have that bit for your obituary. I think the reason she never married was because she would have been too much of a handful for most men. Too clever, too accomplished. I'm sure she put the fear of God into any chap who might have had designs on her. I always told her mother she'd have to wait for a chap who'd made his millions and was shopping around for one of those trophy wives I read about in the tabloid press.'

The old lad was right about the fear of God, thought Jack, remembering her Browning automatic, the cyanide pill and the cheesecutter. He said, 'You were going to tell me about the inquest.'

'Ah, yes. We're off the record again, my boy. The spooks brought the news of her death to us. They said Nancy had come off her horse while taking part in a surveillance operation. It was like something from the eighteenth century. What kind of surveillance was that – from a damn' horse? They said it was all very hush-hush. They couldn't say more.' The old man's indignation subsided into a resigned sorrow. 'Anyway, they said she had died in the service of her country which, I suppose, was their misguided idea of an expression of sympathy. They said they'd arrange a special sitting of the coroner's court and bring their man, Professor Whatsisname, down from London to perform the post-mortem. They asked my wife and me to stay away and they'd provide someone to give evidence of identification. They didn't want us to see her in her coffin. And no wonder. The effrontery! They'd got some ghastly undertaker to put a little bonnet around her face – like the frill on a pie crust. Not Nancy's style at all. She'd have thrown a fit.' Lord Tintagel stopped abruptly. 'Well, that's enough of that. I've probably said more than I should so I'm relying on your discretion, Mr Jones.' Despite his claim to take death as it came, he suddenly looked desolate. 'You know, young man, you're very easy to talk to. I can see why you're a journalist. I needed to get it off my chest. You turned up at the right time.'

Jack felt like dirt. This was a shabby deception of a heart-broken old man. There was no putting a gloss on what he was doing. Only a primeval instinct for survival was driving him onward and downward into a world of cancerous deceit.

Lord Tintagel, recovering, said, 'Open that notebook and we'll take all Nancy's life that's fit to print in chronological order from womb to tomb.'

Jack sat with him for another hour and pretended to make notes as the parental version of his intended executioner's life unfolded in all its surface detail.

Chapter Twenty-Nine

Bulwer Tancred tapped his pencil on the table and the other three gave him their attention. Present was the senior man (operations), Rafe Cummings, who with his long wandering nose looked like a ruddy-faced farmer, Rupert Strang, and Peter Hope-Casson, the youngest of the team who had been Strang's companion on the Gatti's pickup and who had been humiliated and immobilized by Jack Boulder in the Kent pub lavatory.

Tancred said with a crisp lack of concern, 'I trust the head's a little better, Peter.'

Hope-Casson touched his plaster and looked round the table to see if he could catch anyone smirking. 'Boulder got lucky,' he muttered.

'Doubtless,' said Tancred.

The trio at his table shared an unspoken low opinion of Tancred's taste in pictorial art. Above their master's head a framed poster hung from the panelling. It was a blown-up photograph of a short, nondescript man in a cheap double-breasted suit. His hair was plastered to his skull with some kind of hair oil. Brilliantine, they'd agreed, looking down their noses. The fellow looked decidedly as if he hailed from the great unwashed.

Tancred began rather portentously, 'The subject for discussion is Captain Jack Boulder and damage limitation. Firstly, it has to be said that, in so far as the objective was achieved, Nancy had a brilliant success. The planning for the removal of Niven was impeccable – a fitting memorial to a colleague of great talent.' He paused and his wintry face darkened. He stared downward pensively at his manicured hands. 'However, we are left with the problem of Boulder, a danger to us all. Last time, we voted four to one in favour of his elimination once the attempt on Niven, successful or unsuccessful, was completed. Ironically, it was Nancy who cast the minority vote. Unfortunately we proposed but Captain Boulder disposed, it was she who became the casualty,' he added bleakly.

'In Boulder's favour, it has to be said that Professor Askew and our ballistics people agree with the note he placed on her body. Nancy really did do it to herself, doubtless while she was attempting to kill him. Boulder, it would seem, had discovered Nancy's pistol and somehow spiked the sound suppressor – not difficult for a man of his expertise. He fought his corner and we can't – *pace* young Peter, here – criticize him for that. Also in his favour is the fact that he has not lost his head and gone running around crying *mea culpa*. So far so good.

'However, he is currently causing some concern. He has become very devious. He has discovered every listening device in his house and removed them. He has also learned the art of shaking off a tail. This would present difficulties enough for a full team following an unsuspecting target, but it's impossible for our tiny group, dealing with a man who now assumes he has company every time he goes out for a newspaper – which, I might say, he is understandably buying in large quantities. He seems as anxious as we are that he should remain out of the hands of the police. I think you will agree the tails are now a waste of our energies and so is the bugging. He'll not say anything significant where there's any possibility that he's within radius of a listening device. We are obviously not going to profit further from any of it.' Tancred nodded down the table at Cummings. 'Rafe, is there any news of his family since he evacuated them from the home?'

Cummings's ruddy face shone triumphantly. 'Boulder's last telephone message before the shutters went up instructed her to take the kids to wherever it was they spent their holiday last August. A check on his credit-card statement reveals that he used his card only in the Southwold area of Suffolk during the middle two weeks of that particular month. It's a small place. I'll soon have the holiday address.'

'That's good to know,' said Tancred. 'But for the moment there'll be no action against the family.' He pursed his lips. 'Boulder himself is another matter. I've almost convinced myself he's going to play the game. He took his money – our paymaster is being admirably philosophical about that – and has acted with a guile I would not have suspected he possessed. His utilization of the American woman was masterly. She helped him out of a tight corner and to get his hands on our money. Unfortunately, she has been traced and interviewed by the FBI. At the moment, the consequences of that development remain unknown.'

He hesitated, pondering what else he should reveal, then added, 'The Yard's reports are going up daily to the Home Office and thence to the Cabinet Office. So far, I've been able to glimpse two. Ringrose is supposed to exert every effort to repulse the French attempt to pin the entire cock-up on the British. Unfortunately he's an awkward devil and is turning a blind eye to the hint. Massillon has now fed him enough evidence to make it clear that an Englishman and a woman of uncertain nationality are the culprits. It's a matter of regret that Ringrose is difficult to control. He's been the Prime Minister's favourite copper ever since that beauty queens business.'

Hope-Casson was bouncing in his chair. He butted in: 'I say we don't take a chance, sir. Ringrose is hot stuff. We should have another go – dispose of Boulder before Ringrose gets to him.'

'If only it were as simple as that, Peter,' murmured Tancred. 'Suppose Boulder has already lodged a complete account of his little adventure with his solicitor? Told his wife? His mother? His best friend? Your little contretemps with him will have made him extremely nervous. He'll be trying to arrange some insurance.'

Hope-Casson subsided, chastened. Then he brightened. 'We could tip off the Provos about his role in the McGurk shooting, give them his home address and sit back to watch the fun.'

'It's an amusing thought,' said Tancred, 'but his death wouldn't prevent the leak of any written account Boulder has made, would it?'

'If it exists,' said Rupert Strang, soberly.

The quartet sat in silence, staring at the fine grain of the yew-topped table.

Finally, Tancred said, 'I think we have to leave our Jack to his own devices for the present – at least until we can be sure he's made no record of his little jaunt to foreign parts. Then we eliminate him. I'll do my best to keep tabs on Ringrose's progress. If I think he's getting warm, we may have to take drastic action sooner. If any whispers come your way from your various departments, I shall want to be informed *tout de suite*.'

Tancred sighed and swivelled in his chair. Gazing fondly up at the poster-sized image of the nondescript little man, he said, 'Albert never had to tolerate any of this confusion. In his day, everything was ordered, measured, timed. You affronted the State and Albert was always there to put an end to your perfidy.'

The other three rose, exchanged glances and made softly for the door. Outside, Hope-Casson whispered to Strang, 'I say, Rupert, do you get the feeling from time to time that our intrepid leader is just the teeniest bit off his rocker?'

Inside, Bulwer Tancred remained seated for a full minute, staring up at the photograph. Albert Pierrepoint, once upon a time Britain's official hangman, stared right back at him.

Chapter Thirty

A fine, dreamless night. The alarm clock went off at six thirty and Jack was instantly out of bed. He showered, rustled up some eggs, toast and coffee, and dressed, thrusting the Glock so far down into his back belt that the muzzle was touching his coccyx. He had a plan.

He slipped silently out of the rear door of the house and padded to the end of his small garden, ignoring the late spring growth now shouting for his attention.

He hauled himself up the side of his garden shed and dropped down into the better cultivated plot that was end-on to his own. Thank goodness he'd established excellent relations with his Welsh neighbours, the Rhys family. They'd even had the occasional drink together. Yesterday he'd spun them a yarn that the gun club was in financial trouble . . . the bailiffs were trying to serve him with a writ . . . he needed to leave the house without being ambushed . . .

Kevin Rhys had given him two keys, to the back and front doors of his house. And now Jack Boulder was making use of them, tiptoeing through without waking the family and out into the street that ran parallel to his own.

He strolled away, happy in the certain knowledge that he was without a shadow. He took the tube from Shepherd's Bush — always an uneasy journey since the dream had begun — changed at Notting Hill Gate and travelled round to Sloane Square on the Circle Line. The previous evening he had parked the Saab in Markham Square, in a space that gave him an oblique view of Rupert Strang's yellow-painted front door.

Sitting in the driver's seat, sipping coffee from a flask, and nipping out at eight thirty to feed the meter, Jack waited two hours before the door opened. A computer cab had drawn up. A jacketless Strang took in his milk and re-emerged fully dressed, as immaculate as ever.

The cab took off towards Sloane Square, turned into Lower Sloane Street and headed for the river. It turned left onto the Embankment and crossed the Thames at Vauxhall Bridge.

The journey was brief. On the south side, at Vauxhall Cross, Strang was deposited outside a fantasy building of green glass and cream stone that appeared to have been inspired by the Egyptian and Babylonian splendours of the film sets of the late Cecil B. DeMille. In the early nineties, Londoners had watched bemused as this edifice, with an overview of the nearby Southern Region railway line, climbed towards the sky on the riverbank. It had not long remained secret that this weird structure was to be the new headquarters of MI6 – Britain's Secret Intelligence Service. Jack watched Strang enter.

Driving away down the Albert Embankment, he tried to sort out the implications. He had veered from believing that he had been working as a freelance for just such an organization to the probability that he was merely the dupe of bounty-hunters. But, with Tancred, Strang and the Honourable Nancy Tintagel, he was back with the Establishment, the kind of people who, or so he had read, comprised an autocracy that really ruled Britain through old money, the network of old families and the accumulated wisdom of two hundred years of ruling an empire that had once covered the globe in a disarming pink.

Up to now he'd always taken this as left-wing bullshit. But why should the Secret Service kill Conrad Niven, a British citizen of impeccable character who was under the protection of the Special Branch of the Metropolitan Police?

The conundrum still turning in his head, Jack drove on to the City and his much-neglected job.

Joe Carsby was standing by his office cubicle with two men in civvies, the taller fortyish and well padded, the younger trim and alert. He heard Joe, smiling, say, 'Talk of the devil. Here's the man himself.'

The two strangers could not have advertised themselves more clearly as policemen if they had been carrying billboards. Jack did not like the way they glanced significantly at each other as he made his entrance.

Joe said, 'This is Detective Sergeant er . . .'

The older one stepped forward and introduced himself affably, '. . . Cyril Munday. And this is Detective Constable Bellew.'

They're always pleasant enough at first, thought Jack.

The Glock had suddenly turned into a branding-iron and was searing his back.

Joe said, 'These chaps are doing a firearms survey.'

'Yes,' said Munday. 'We're trying to compile a list of men and women handy with rifles. It's a routine inquiry.'

They always say it's routine, thought Jack. He looked dubious. 'I don't know that any of our members have any proficiency in that direction. There's no call for it. We train people only in the use and care of sidearms here.'

Munday gave Jack an encouraging smile. 'Don't you have members who were previously in the forces? Former mercenaries? That type?'

Jack put on a show of pondering. 'We'll have to go through the membership list to jog my memory.'

He said to Joe, 'Take them into the office, get the book out and I'll be right with you. Must have a slash.'

The younger detective started to say something but Jack was already heading for the locker room. He stowed the Glock and his jacket, and splashed his face with cold water to clear his head. He took his time returning.

The policemen looked up expectantly as he strode, businesslike, through the office door. 'Okay, Joe. I'll look after them,' he said.

Joe flicked him a salute and went off to take care of business.

The two visitors shifted their chairs apart to make room for Jack to sit between them. The invitation was unspoken but unmistakable and Jack started to sweat a little.

He pulled the ledger onto his lap and began to go down the list, using a pen as a pointer. Every now and then he picked out the name of an ex-serviceman and those of a handful of women.

'I can only tell you that they were in the services. I can't remember any of them telling me that they were any good with a rifle.' The younger detective dutifully noted their names and home addresses.

The exercise took nearly an hour, then Jack snapped the ledger shut and said, 'That's the lot.'

Detective Sergeant Munday looked at him slyly. 'You're pretty handy with a rifle yourself, aren't you, sir? Or, at least, that's what your colleague tells us.'

Jack could have throttled Joe. How long had they been chatting with him, wheedling information out of him, before he walked in?

'Oh, sure I was, very handy.' Jack shrugged, as off-hand as he could manage. 'But that was during my Army service. As you can see, the ranges here are totally inadequate for that type of shooting.'

He was addressing Munday, but from the corner of his eye he could see Bellew conscientiously scribbling.

'When was that, sir?'

'When was what?' Jack resolved he was not going to make it easy for the buggers.

'Your Army service, sir.'

'Oh, I resigned my commission eighteen months ago.'

'May I ask why that was, sir?'

'I was fed up. More importantly, my wife was fed up with being an Army wife, bounced from pillar to post.'

Munday gazed around the cramped office. He asked, innocently, 'Did you have this job to come to, sir?'

Jack looked at him steadily. In the silence they could all hear the sharp crack of pistol-shooting from the range. Jack knew that the time had come when a man with nothing to hide would be counter-attacking.

'Look,' he said. 'I thought you told me this was a routine inquiry. Why are you asking me for my life story? This club is properly run and regularly inspected. There's never been a word of complaint from the City of London police.'

Munday made a soothing sound as if calming a fractious child. 'I'm sure there hasn't, sir. Please forgive me. We're merely asking the kind of questions we'll be asking all those members whose names you've kindly supplied.'

'I don't get it,' said Jack. 'I doubt if any of these people even owns a rifle.'

Munday smiled tolerantly. 'It's not ownership we're registering. It's proficiency.'

'Why?' Jack decided that a show of aggression wouldn't go amiss.

Munday looked helpless. 'No one tells us. It's probably one of the Commissioner's initiatives in aid of something or other to do with extremist groups. Or the aftermath of Dunblane, perhaps.'

Bellew wrote down Jack's home address. Then Munday rose heavily to his feet and said, 'Thank you for your co-operation, sir.'

Jack gave them a curt nod and ushered them upstairs to street level. Munday was pushing on the door when he stopped, turned and said, 'Oh, there was one other thing, sir.'

Jack could not believe the transparency of the tactic. He felt a chill. Was there anyone owning a television set who had not, at one time or another, heard that little American detective in the shabby raincoat saying exactly this – and then asking a devastating question that led inexorably to the exposure and arrest of the hitherto oh-so-inventive criminal?

'What is it?' asked Jack, bracing himself.

'Would you mind telling me where you were during the first three weeks in May?'

Jack's brain went into overdrive. Christ, what did they already know from Joe. He said calmly, 'I was here, at home, and round and about.'

Munday gave him the smile that he was growing to fear. 'Any of it holiday?'

So this was the moment of truth. 'Part of it, yes – two weeks.'

'Spent abroad?'

'No, I was in London.' Jack thought of his unkempt garden. He added, 'Holidays at home – getting the garden up to snuff for the spring.'

'A bit late in the day, weren't you?' Munday was still smiling that bloody smile. 'I leave it to the missus. She's got more time.'

To Jack's relief, he appeared satisfied. Munday held the door while his partner stepped out onto the pavement, then followed. The door whispered shut behind them.

Jack ran the back of his hand over his upper lip. Not one of the lies he'd told them could trip him up unless they took a close look at his flower beds. He relived the encounter. No, he hadn't said anything that could come back to damage him.

The two detectives sat in their stationary car, gazing through the windscreen at the crawling traffic. Bellew, at the wheel, said, 'What do you think?'

Munday sucked on yellowing teeth. 'We should be so lucky. He's within the age range, though that likeness the American bint gave the Feds isn't much of a match.'

Bellew said, 'His number two, Joe Whatsit, was a bit awe-struck. Thought Boulder was a cross between Dirty Harry and Dead-Eye Dick.'

'Yes,' agreed Munday. 'He was very modest about his talents, wasn't he? Although that could be him following the code of an officer and a gentleman. What were his exact words?'

Bellew flipped through his notes. 'He said, "I was very handy."'

'Do you think that was the natural modesty of the true English gentleman? I have to admit, it does exist in certain quarters although I've not found much of it in the police service.'

'A gentleman – like Robert Redford,' cackled Bellew. 'Jesus. If we go by that silly American tart we'd be nicking every male wearing a bowler and carrying a rolled umbrella in Jermyn Street.'

'Get going,' Munday ordered. 'We'll shove it all into the computer and leave it to Ringrose's golden boys to fuck up without any hindrance from us. You watch, this investigation is going to turn up a hundred crack shots like Boulder.'

Chapter Thirty-One

Jack drove through the soft evening and made Southwold soon after nine thirty. He was gratified that Grace and the boys were excited to see him. He realized how lonely he had been, nursing his great secret and tussling single-handed with an unknown enemy. He hugged the boys to his windcheater and kissed Grace long and hard. They were usually circumspect about overt love-making in front of the boys, but Jack could now feel Grace's heat. Her tongue went into his mouth.

When Ben and Mal, protesting vociferously, had been shunted off to bed, he and Grace stood outside, sipping hot chocolate and watching the moon cast silver shards into the North Sea.

Grace said, 'How's it going?'

Jack waggled his hand, palm down, in a gesture of uncertainty. 'I'm not sure. There's been some police activity around the club, which may or may not be just a wide-net check on people who are useful with a rifle.' He described the visit of Munday and Bellew. 'Some of the pieces are beginning to fit together, but the less you know the better. What is still a mystery to me is why anyone, aside from the Iranians, that is, would want to harm a hair of Conrad Niven's head. But the further I dig, the more convinced I'm becoming that the ayatollahs had nothing to do with it. It's very frustrating to have the feeling that the answer should be obvious and that everyone knows it except me.'

Grace stroked his arm. 'Can you stay the night?'

'God, Grace, how I wish I could!' He groaned. 'But I have an instinct that I need to give every appearance of living a normal life. I've only come to collect the gun and get it back to the club where it belongs. I would have been up the creek today if those two coppers had asked to check the inventory and found the Super Magnum missing. What could I have said?'

Although it was a mild evening, Grace shivered and wrapped her arms around her shoulders. She said, 'I don't like keeping all that money here. It makes me frightened.'

'Where is it?'

'Where you left it.'

'Okay. I'll take it with me.'

They went back into the house.

From their shared bedroom, Ben and Mal listened to the downstairs floorboards creaking and the murmur of their parents' voices. Ben said, 'Have you ever known Mum cry so much? There's big trouble. Do you think they're getting a divorce?' Malcolm began to snivel. 'Oh, shut up!' said his brother. 'It was only an idea. But there's definitely something up.' He jerked his head in the direction of the door. 'Come on. Let's see if we can find out what's going on. But *keep quiet!*'

In their pyjamas, feet bare, the two boys eased the drop-latch upward and crept out onto the landing. Holding their breath, they kept to the sides of the stair treads and tiptoed down until they could peer through the banisters into the living room.

Their father had just taken a shiny object from his pocket. They watched their mother recoil. 'I don't even want to touch the beastly thing,' she said. He was offering her an automatic pistol, and saying, 'Grace, you simply have to take it, not only for your own sake but for the sake of the boys. I'm not saying you can expect trouble, but if it does arrive this will stop them dead.'

Like a salesman, he held up the weapon for her inspection. 'See? It's a dinky little thing. Easy to handle. Only seven inches long. It's a short version Walther PPK 9mm. There are seven rounds in the magazine. At short range, you'd just point it and pull the trigger. You couldn't miss.'

Their mother was shaking her head. Dad said, 'Grace, you've got to be strong. Just suppose men came bursting in here with the intention of doing you or the boys harm? What are you going to defend yourselves with? A broomstick?'

Ben heard Malcolm begin to whimper and clapped a hand over his mouth.

Downstairs, Grace froze and said, 'Did you hear something?' The boys took two steps back up into the shadows.

Their parents listened to the silence of the house for a moment and resumed their desperate dialogue. Dad pleaded, 'Just hold the gun in your hand for a moment. See how comfortable the grip is?'

'Comfortable!' she exclaimed in a disbelieving voice. But then they heard her ask, 'Is it ready to fire? Isn't there a safety catch or something?' She was coming round.

'It's ready to go just as it is – so don't touch the trigger. And remember the old saying, "Don't point it at anything you don't intend to shoot."'

Their mother's voice betrayed an unaccustomed quaver. 'I'll leave it in the bedside drawer.'

'Good girl,' their father said. 'And here's a little box of ammo to go with it.' They heard a series of metallic clicks as he demonstrated the loading of the magazine and how to lock it into the butt.

The old floor boards creaked again as their parents moved towards the hall. Ben pushed Malcolm back upstairs and they noiselessly returned to their bedroom.

Grace began to cry when Jack got ready to drive away. She was holding the Walther gingerly in one hand and the ammo box in the other. She held her arms wide, pistol pointing at the ground, as Jack embraced her and promised, 'Not for much longer. I know more about them than they could possibly suspect.'

But her tears and the break in her voice made Jack realize, with a sinking heart, that an essential ingredient of her sunny personality had gone. And it was all of his doing.

He arrived back in Shepherd's Bush at three a.m. and fell into bed, rifle and money alongside the Cobray and the bedroom door wide open onto the first-floor landing. He had rigged trip wires across all the windows and doors. The slightest sound would wake him.

Back in Southwold, Malcolm had crept into his mother's bed for comfort but Ben stayed in their room, hands behind his head, staring at the low ceiling and thinking.

By ten the next morning the rifle had been returned to the club's gun rack, safely chained. It suddenly struck Jack that he hadn't read whether or not the French police had recovered the two rounds that had put paid to Conrad Niven. If they had been salvaged, it would take a ballistics expert less than five minutes to match the striations to his Super Magnum. He shrugged mentally. It was a chance he had to take. He couldn't see any option short of destroying the weapon, which itself would bring further questioning from the authorities and would be tantamount to a confession of guilt. The life of a renegade in a society as regulated as Great Britain's was extremely complicated.

He'd put a brass padlock on the money holdall and handed the bag over the fence to Kevin Rhys. 'Look after this for me, Kev. It's the company books. I daren't let them get into the hands of the broker's men.'

'I'll stow it under the stairs,' said his neighbour. 'It'll be safe there.'

Jack watched the better part of eighty thousand pounds go swinging nonchalantly down the path.

During the day, while watching his punters pepper their cardboard targets when they should have been grouping their shots, Jack reviewed his options. From the moment he had learned the identity of the man he had shot, Jack's first option had always been to surrender to the police and tell all he knew. By turning the French equivalent of Queen's Evidence, he might at least ameliorate his own punishment.

Grace had fiercely opposed this. 'You'd be a bloody fool. There's no way of getting past the fact that you pulled the trigger. They couldn't just round up the others, even if they could find them, pat you on the back for doing your civic duty and let you go. You might not get a life sentence, but you'd go inside for a very long time.'

Since then Jack had more to trade in exchange for his own liberty. But the names he had come up with were of people who could wrap themselves protectively in the Official Secrets Act. If his shadowy puppetmaster really was the Secret Service, he didn't stand a chance. How could he carry the fight to such a juggernaut?

His mind kept turning to Rupert Strang. When Strang had left his house in Markham Square, Jack had seen him double-lock his front door. He would not have done that if there had still been someone inside. So Strang lived alone.

He was either a bachelor or had a wife in the country, with Markham Square used as a weekday *pied-à-terre*.

Jack chose his option.

He was nursing a drink outside the Markham Arms by six p.m. Strang returned home in a taxi shortly after seven. There were too many people about to accost him on the pavement so Jack bided his time. He'd have to knock at the door once pedestrian activity in the streets had died down for the evening.

'Damn!' he muttered under his breath. Another taxi had drawn up and Strang came out in white tie and tails as pristine as his suits. Jack caught a glimpse of his miniature dress medals – at least two – as he clambered into the cab and took off. He noted with satisfaction that Strang had again double-locked the front door. No one was in the house.

Strang, he reasoned, had not got himself up in that gear for a snack at a local pizza parlour. He'd be away for some hours. At an official dinner? Perhaps with the Queen at Buckingham Palace, Jack thought bitterly.

He sloped off for dinner at a King's Road bistro and was back on observation at ten. At least conditions were more agreeable than those he had endured on border ops in Northern Ireland.

He was slumped in the Saab when a familiar Bentley turned into the square from the King's Road and swept to an abrupt halt outside Strang's house. Judging by the kangaroo braking, the two occupants had dined well.

Strang eased himself out of the front passenger seat after a tussle with the belt. He bent to say something to the driver – Bulwer Tancred – which gave Jack time to slip out of the Saab, close the door quietly and edge down the street.

He did a quick survey of the square. The only movement came from cars passing at the King's Road end. Strang stood at the edge of the kerb and waved at Tancred's disappearing tail-lights. Jack pressed himself against a doorway.

His target stood for a few moments, sucking the last enjoyment from the end of a wet cigar. Then he dropped the remnant at his feet and ground it to a brown mess with his patent leather shoe, sniffed the night air appreciatively, turned and took the steps slowly up to his front door. He fished in his pocket for his keys as Jack moved closer.

Jack waited for the sound of the first key turning in the dead lock and braced himself for the second.

The double-click came, sharp and certain, in the silent square. Jack hurled himself up the stone steps as the door was opening. Strang turned and, had the evening's alcoholic intake not slowed his reactions, would have lashed back with his cigar-grinding foot and toppled Jack onto the pavement. But Jack was too swift for him. His body crashed into Strang and sent him tumbling into his hallway.

Jack took two steps inside and slammed the door closed behind him. By the dim streetlight filtering through the fanlight he could see Strang, dazed, on his hands and knees.

'Make one sound,' said Jack, 'and I'll blow your fucking head off.' His left hand groped for the light switch to the hall lantern. Strang crawled about-face, blinking as the light flooded the passageway. He saw the Glock in Jack's fist and his aquiline face tightened. White tension lines appeared around his nostrils and at the sides of his compressed mouth. He said nothing.

Jack rapidly took in his surroundings. He spotted a burglar alarm control box, red light blinking, in the corridor leading to the rear kitchen. It was the type that allowed the person entering via the front door a minute's grace before sounding off.

Jack moved forward, took Strang by his modish winged collar and pressed the gun into his temple. 'If that alarm goes off, you're dead and I'm out of here before anyone has time to respond.'

Strang spoke for the first time. 'The key is on my chain.'

'Use it,' said Jack, prodding him with the barrel.

Strang scrambled to his feet and de-activated the system. Jack pushed him through a door into a sitting room. The curtains for the window overlooking the square were open. 'Draw them and put on the lights,' said Jack. The gun's muzzle followed Strang around the room as he complied.

The room, with its carved marble fireplace, two facing couches, a Pembroke table for drinks, was a model of discreet good taste. 'Sit,' said Jack, waving the Glock at one of the silk-covered couches. Jack sat opposite on its twin.

A low, marble-topped table stood between them on which lay magazines, a model of an Egyptian obelisk and an exquisite miniature frigate carved in what looked like ivory, but which the small plaque at the base of the covering glass dome revealed to be animal bone, carved by bored Napoleonic prisoners on Dartmoor, whittling and whiling away the days until their repatriation to their beloved France.

Up close to Strang for the first time, Jack realized he was not as young – not by ten years at least – as he seemed from the distances at which Jack had been observing him. His long face betrayed lines and strain, and his dark hair was thinning. It was his trim figure, the artful tailoring and his easy movement that gave the appearance of youth. He was a man who kept himself in shape but he was more than forty-five.

Strang was recovering from his shock. He straightened himself and his clothes and said suddenly, 'I suppose there's no use my pretending you're just a burglar wanting cash, jewels and the family silver?'

'No,' said Jack. 'I'm sure you know who I am.'

'Yes,' said Strang, a note of regret in his voice. 'I know who you are, all right. How did you find me?'

'I just followed the smell of sewers,' said Jack.

'Oh dear,' said Strang. 'Is the conversation to be on that level?' He was definitely recovering his poise.

'This is not a conversation,' said Jack menacingly. 'This is me asking questions and you, under threat of extinction, answering them.'

Strang sighed and pinched the tired flesh on either side of his nose. His cold eyes looked heavy. 'You're not going to shoot me, Captain Boulder. It's not in your nature.'

'I thought you hired me because it *was* my nature.'

Strang shook his head in a world-weary manner. 'Setting aside for the moment the question of who did or did not hire you, you simply do not have sufficient cause to add me to your bag. I'm of no importance.'

Jack squinted at his captive's lapel ribbons. 'Do they usually award OBEs to men of no importance?' Jack then saw, with erupting anger, that the other decoration was a Military Cross.

On the mantelpiece was a silver-framed photograph of a younger Strang in a major's uniform. He was standing in the forecourt of Buckingham Palace, displaying the MC for the camera. Flanking him were a smiling middle-aged couple, presumably his parents. The father had a bristling white military moustache and the commanding air of a man who had once held senior rank.

'Christ!' said Jack in disgust. 'How could a man of your achievements get mixed up with these dirty bastards?'

'Captain Boulder,' said Strang, still in world-weary mode, 'we serve in our various humble ways. You simply do not understand what is going on. There are issues involved that, of necessity, have to be left to our masters. People like me and you are merely the foot soldiers.'

'I didn't know I was at war,' said Jack.

Strang loosened his white tie and undid his collar stud. 'The war is never-ending. Britain has passing concerns but permanent interests that remain unchanged, no matter what the complexion of the government of the day.'

'What has that to do with me or, for that matter, that blameless sod Conrad Niven? He only made movies, for God's sake!'

Strang shook his head. 'I can't talk to you about Niven. And you won't be able to make me.' Jack glanced again at that proud photograph and knew he was telling the truth.

Strang went on, 'As for you, I concede you have cause for complaint. We had a work-up done of your life – your biography, if you like – and while we could see you had a superhuman talent as a sniper, the McGurk business indicated to us that you could not always be relied upon not to go off the rails. We had devised several crude ways of disposing of Niven but they all involved the Special Branch minders or civilians being in the line of fire. Any harm to them would have brought down unacceptable repercussions. But there you were, capable of doing a clean, surgical job for us. As you so ably proved. Our error was not to trust you in the aftermath to take the money and keep your conscience to yourself. Anyway, you paid us back in spades for that lack of confidence. The woman you sent home in a case was a much-admired colleague. She's a great loss.'

Jack bit back his knowledge of her real name. Why should he show his hand? He said, 'I didn't kill her, you know.'

Strang nodded. 'Yes, we accept that. No blame attaches. Fortunes of war.' He leaned forward, resting his forearms on his bony knees, and adopted an earnest expression. 'Captain Boulder – Jack – why don't you let it rest at that, put your earnings into that overseas account we set up for you, and go away like a good chap?'

'Because,' said Jack levelly, 'I know too much and I've been taken for a fool. I want to know why Conrad Niven had to be killed. I'll decide then what has to be done.' He stood up. 'You go back to your people, whoever they are, and tell them that. Come back to me with their answer. You know where I live. God knows, you had enough listening devices planted around the place.'

Strang shook his head. 'I've tried to be helpful. You've been very foolish tracking me here. So far, you've behaved in a sensible – even reassuring – manner. But jumping me can only cause alarm in certain circles. Why the hell did you have to do it?'

Jack watched him shake his head like a parent disapproving of excessive behaviour in a teenager. He said, 'If what you say is a hint that you'll now have to come after me yet again, you'd better think very carefully. You know what I can do.'

'Yes, Jack. We know what you can do.'

Jack waved the Glock in the direction of the passage. 'Step through and take off all your clothes.'

Strang said, 'For Pete's sake!' then caught Jack's expression. He stripped to his underpants, then hesitated.

'Everything,' said Jack, 'and throw them over here.'

Like Mrs Canning, Strang had a well-muscled and defined body. He would not be a pushover in hand-to-hand combat.

Jack scooped up his clothes and backed towards the front door. Strang stood silently in the hallway making no attempt to shield his dangling genitals.

'I guess you won't be chasing me down the street like that,' said Jack, and backed out into the fresh air. He deposited Strang's clothes five yards from his yellow door and jogged away into the Chelsea night.

Chapter Thirty-Two

The two Surrey detectives reeled off the formula being repeated by policemen at gun clubs and firing ranges throughout the British Isles. 'Firearms survey ... compiling list of expert rifle users ... some sort of list for wartime emergencies ... routine inquiry ...'

'That's a tall order,' said Greg Rankin, who was wearing blue overalls with RANGEMASTER sewn in white letters across his left breast. He handed them ear protectors and said, 'Here, you'll need these while this bloke's banging away. He's calibrating one of his weapons and I have to supervise until he's finished.'

Five yards ahead, a man in khaki dungarees was sprawled in the dirt, left leg braced out to the side. He was swearing volubly at the long-barrelled rifle propped up by his left forearm.

The range ran the length of an exhausted gravel pit. To the detectives the butts in use seemed awesomely distant. A black-and-white concentric circle was up. The marksman took aim and measured off five shots. He raised his head a fraction and watched as a small red disc on a stick, held by invisible hands below ground level, rose in the air.

The disc briefly touched three separate spots on the target and was withdrawn. The gesture sent the marksman into a paroxysm of cursing.

Rankin turned to the policemen and grinned. They both lifted an earpiece to hear what he had to say. 'Either of you two men ever take a firearms course?' They both shook their heads. Rankin nodded at the man on the ground, who was now bad-temperedly fiddling with a small screwdriver and adjusting something on his weapon. 'He's got a rogue shooter. Happens sometimes. No matter what you do, it sprays rounds every which-way. He's trying to coax the bloody thing to place the shots in one place. But he won't get it until he calms down. When his body's shaking, how does he think he's going to get the rifle to stay still?' He raised a cautionary hand. 'Don't move. Wait here while I have a word with him.'

They watched as Rankin walked forward, knelt alongside the marksman and began sweet-talking him out of his rage.

One detective raised his partner's earpiece and whispered, 'Reminds me of what the Guards officer had to say about the beaches of Dunkirk: "My dear, the noise! The people!"'

Half an hour later the detectives had finally managed to get Rankin's attention. They sat inside the brick clubhouse, with its steel doors and shutters and silent intruder alarms.

Rankin said, 'We have members and we have day bookings from visiting members of other clubs. The problem is that the majority could be said to be rifle-proficient. We're talking a couple of hundred names.'

Detective Constable Fred Hall asked, 'Would it be possible to fine-sift that number? Just give us the outstanding names?'

Rankin shifted his legs off his desk and reached behind him for the membership book. 'We can but try.' He sighed.

After a laborious session that left the detectives as bored as Rankin, they had a dozen possibles, all male. 'These are the real gravel-bellies,' said Rankin.

'Gravel-bellies?'

'Gravel's what you get in your belly button when you've been lying out there in the dirt too long.' He laughed.

Hall tapped his notebook. 'Of these men, are there any whose skill makes them stand out even from the others?'

'That's easy,' said Rankin. 'Captain Jack Boulder is the star of stars. Queen's Prize competitor and all that. He occupies a class of his own.'

'He's in the Army?' Hall and his colleague both seemed disappointed.

'Correction,' said Rankin. 'He was. Took his bowler hat a year or so ago.'

The detectives brightened. 'Tell us more,' encouraged Hall.

'Jack has an extraordinary eye. Always did have. He once let on that he had a shotgun licence at the age of twelve. Mind you, proficiency with a shotgun doesn't always translate into proficiency with a rifle, but Jack was born to be a shooter. He used to go in for all that mystical Zen Buddhist stuff – learning to breathe and achieving self-forgetfulness.'

'How does that help?'

'Beats me. He used to carry around this little book that said too much thought interfered with the aim at the target. Calculation created miscalculation and so on. I think he was trying to achieve some kind of advanced mental discipline – a oneness with his weapon. You'll have to excuse the psychobabble. I don't understand it myself but you can't argue with the results.'

'Do you see him often?'

'He was a regular at one time, but tours of duty abroad kept taking him away from us. A shame. Watching him at his best was one of life's greatest pleasures. It was sheer artistry.'

Rankin, with his bristle head, did not have the appearance of a man given to lyricism. They were impressed.

'Ever see him these days?'

'As a matter of fact, his head appeared above the parapet last winter. He was out there on the long range, even in the snow. Sharpening up for the summer competition round.'

'Is that what he told you?'

Rankin frowned at them. He caught their look of scepticism. A touch bellicose, he said, 'Is there a reason you shouldn't believe me?'

'Of course not,' said Fred Hall hurriedly. With his long experience of interrogations, he knew it was time to make a show of returning notebooks to pockets, as if the interview was over. 'It's just that we have to make a special list of the best shots. We have to be sure their motives for using rifles are . . .' he searched for an inoffensive word '. . . are pure. I think there's some kind of recruiting campaign going on.'

'Oh, I see,' said Rankin, relaxing. 'Well you could try me. I didn't get this job because I only handle pea-shooters, you know.'

'About Boulder . . . ?' said Hall, delicately returning to the subject.

'Super chap. Good-natured. A bit crazy like most of us.'

'A bit crazy how?' said Hall, folding his arms comfortably across his middle to remind Rankin that he was taking no notes.

'Well, you know, Jack's a good man's man. Usually up for a lark. I hear that's what got him into trouble with the brass.'

'Oh?'

'Yes. A bloody shame. I don't know the exact details but rumour has it he went AWOL and put the fear of God into a bunch of Micks on the wrong side of the border.'

'The Irish border?'

'Yeah, where else but in bloody Ireland? I heard it was just a prank but Jack had to resign. When he reappeared in civvies this year, I offered him commiserations. He didn't say too much, just that it could have been worse.'

'What do you think he meant by that?'

Rankin made a sour face. 'I suppose he meant they could have court-martialled him. Court-martial for a bloody prank! I think the British Army has had an operation to remove its sense of humour.'

'What's Jack like – physically, I mean?'

'Big lug. In good shape. Women fancy him – lucky sod – but I've never heard that he plays away from home.'

'He's married, then?'

'Yeah, with a couple of kids. Gorgeous wife.'

'What sort of age would he be now?'

Rankin reached for a box file. 'I can tell you that precisely. Like everyone else, he had to fill in a membership form, giving his date of birth.' He went straight to the Bs and said, after a moment of mental arithmetic, 'He's thirty-four.'

The two detectives drove until they were out of sight of the clubhouse. 'Stop the car,' said Fred Hall. 'I want to get down all that stuff about the Army before I forget it. Our profile of the shooter might have been tailor-made for this guy Boulder. He definitely has to go into the pot.'

Grace argued with the boys. Fearful of leaving them alone, she wanted them to get into the now-clean Volvo and accompany her on a shopping trip. 'Shopping's boring,' said Ben. 'We're going out on the beach.'

'I don't mind going shopping,' whispered Malcolm, still upset at what he had heard on the stairs the previous evening. He wanted to be near his mother. 'We could get some ice-cream.'

'Shut up!' hissed Ben. 'We've got our own plans.'

'Have we?'

Ben draped a friendly arm round his young brother's neck, holding him back.

'We'll be all right,' promised Ben. 'We won't go near the water.'

Grace hesitated, not knowing how to deliver another kind of warning. 'Ben, look after your brother. If strange people come to the house you're not to let them in or go near them. Do you understand? They may be perfectly harmless, but Daddy has had a quarrel with some people in London and they may come here to make a nuisance of themselves. It's not likely, but they may.'

Ben nodded. Some quarrel that needed his mum to have a handgun, he thought. 'We'll stay away from the house – stay out on the sands,' he said out loud.

They watched their mother drive away. 'We haven't got any plans,' complained Malcolm. 'And we could have played computer games in the mall.'

'Oh, yes, we do have plans,' said his brother, grimly. 'C'mon.' Ben, suddenly purposeful, ran back into the house and up the stairs. Malcolm dragged after him. He watched Ben lift their parents' bedroom door latch.

Malcolm said, shocked, 'We can't go in here! We're not allowed!'

'Don't be so lame,' said Ben. 'We've got work to do.' He strode boldly across the rugs on Grace's side of the bed and opened her cabinet drawer.

As a result of their father's occupation and their own introduction to the firing range, neither boy was inhibited by firearms. Ben picked up the glistening Walther and said, like a professional, 'Nice piece.'

Malcolm said, 'Mum'll kill us.'

'No, she won't,' said Ben. 'Weren't you listening last night? It's other people who want to do the killing.'

Ben looked at his brother's frightened face. 'Don't be such a miserable little turd. It's really good news for us. They've been doing so much whispering, and Dad's been away so much, I thought they were getting divorced. I got that all wrong. The family's okay.'

'So what are you doing with the gun?'

'We're going to get in some target practice. Mum's useless. Until last night I don't suppose she'd ever touched a gun in her life. If there's going to be any trouble, we'll protect her.'

Ben withdrew the box magazine competently and inspected the rounds, the chamber and the barrel. He slapped the magazine back home and handed his brother the box of ammunition. 'Let's go.'

'She'll come back and catch us,' said Malcolm, uncertainly.

'No, she won't,' said Ben, looking back to check that their trainers had not left incriminating prints on the floorboards. 'Shopping always takes her about two hours, specially if she stops for a coffee. You should know. You've been with her often enough.'

Ben led his brother back into their own bedroom. 'Put your rucksack on,' he ordered. 'We'll carry the gear in that.'

'Why me?' wailed Malcolm.

'Because who would suspect that a little kid like you is going around with a 9mm handgun mixed up with his school stuff?'

The two boys trudged along the sands until no one else was in sight. 'What are we going to shoot at?' asked Malcolm.

'This,' said Ben, draining the last drops from his Coke can. He placed it on a groyne and retreated eight paces. He took the Walther from Malcolm's backpack, adopted a wide-legged stance and a two-handed grip as he had been shown by his father, and took aim. The pistol jerked upwards, left, but Ben corrected his aim and on the third shot he sent the can flying. The sharp reports were lost in the roaring sound of the sea.

'Wicked. Just like that man on *Baywatch* last week!' said Malcolm. 'Can I have a go?'

The grip was too big for Malcolm's hands but Ben said kindly, 'Just one. You won't hit anything but it won't matter. Just as long as one of us can...'

Malcolm emulated his brother's stance, took aim with an exaggerated closing of one eye, which he should have kept open, and shot wide of the can. Just as his brother had predicted.

'Bet I'll be able to hit it every time when I'm your age,' said Malcolm.

Ben finished off the magazine and hit the target once more to prove that the first time had not been a fluke.

'Let's get back. I've got to clean this up.'

When they got home Ben refilled the magazine from the box of rounds while Malcolm boiled water to scald the barrel. Ben took some dressing from the first-aid box, impregnated it lightly with sewing-machine oil and found a piece of twine to make a pull-through.

The weapon, clean, bright and slightly oiled, was back in the bedside cabinet twenty minutes before their mother returned. 'You're both looking suspiciously angelic,' she said. 'What have you been up to?'

'Did you bring any ice-cream?' said Malcolm.

Chapter Thirty-Three

The meeting of the group at the home of Bulwer Tancred and beneath the pebble-eyed gaze of Albert Pierrepoint was not a happy one.

Tancred's customary air of cool cleverness had been dented by his obvious perturbation. The team had listened with disbelief to Rupert Strang's account of Jack's visit.

Tancred's fists were clenched. 'This is appalling. The wheels are coming off in this operation. We have seriously underestimated Boulder,' he snapped. He looked down the table at the subdued Strang. 'Did he give any indication as to how he got on to you?'

Strang shook his head. 'None at all. And with that pistol pointed at me I was in no position to insist on an explanation. I did my best to keep him sweet. I told him the heat was off him. I said we believed his version of how Nancy died. I admitted frankly we'd made a blunder trying to bump him off after he'd done such a splendid job for us. I told him the money was his and he should go off quietly and enjoy it.'

'And?'

'And it didn't wash. He appears to be more pissed off at being taken for a patsy than he does at Nancy and Peter's bungled attempts to kill him. I suppose it's because, as a soldier, he was used to people trying to do him in and not succeeding. He appears to have taken that in his stride. What he really wants to know is why we wanted Niven dead.'

Tancred snorted. 'It's none of his damn' business.'

'Try telling him that,' said Strang. 'And there's no knowing what he'll do next.'

'First things first,' said Tancred. 'There's been a serious breach of security. How else could Boulder have got to you?'

Rafe Cummings said, 'It was that blasted report of Nancy's death in the *Telegraph*. There was nothing wrong with it in itself – it was immaculate of its kind, and the right people were told without compromising security. The culprit was the accompanying photograph. Boulder must have spotted it. As you say, sir, he's much smarter than we've allowed. He must have zeroed in on it, recognized Nancy and put her together with Rupert.'

'Yes, it's the logical explanation,' conceded Tancred. 'But how did the *Telegraph* get that photo? I assume that when Nancy joined the service she did the usual thing – weeded her school and college pictures, filleted the family album?'

Cummings, as usual, had the answer. 'I rang the *Telegraph*'s picture desk this morning, sir. I said I was related and asked if I could purchase a copy. They bounced me over to their picture library who said no can do. The picture was a *Country Life* magazine copyright. They had paid *Country Life* a fee for a single publication. It's a portrait they took of Nancy when she was a deb. She must have overlooked it.'

'Thus we get mighty consequences from minor circumstances,' mourned Tancred. 'The question now is: what next?'

'We kill him,' said Peter Hope-Casson.

'Yes. I believe that's becoming inevitable,' said Tancred slowly. He turned to Strang. 'Did Boulder give any indication that he might be a whistle-blower?'

'As I recall, he reserved his position. He seems to have only the haziest conception of where we, his erstwhile employers, are from.'

'He said nothing about putting pen to paper?'.

'Nothing.'

Tancred came to a decision. He slapped his pencil down on the table, which bore no paper, no doodle-pads. He said, 'We can't take a chance on this. If there's a written history of the killing of Conrad Niven we have to find it and destroy it. I'll draw up the operational plan. The only thing we must not do at this stage is touch his house. We leave Captain Boulder until last.'

Tancred's team began to vacate their seats. The meeting was breaking up with a renewed sense of purpose. But Tancred's voice stayed their departure for a moment.

'Rupert,' he said, looking expressionlessly down the length of the table, 'so that we may sleep peacefully in our beds tonight, I have to ask you formally. Did you – under duress, of course – tell Boulder why we needed Conrad Niven dead?'

Strang froze. His lean face turned into a stone mask. 'I'm sorry you felt you had to ask me that question, Bulwer. I told him in plain English that he would not get it from me. Without actually inviting him to shoot me, I made it abundantly clear that this would be his sole option if he insisted on knowing.'

He swept icily from the room.

Chapter Thirty-Four

Commander Tom Ringrose and his French counterpart were swapping titbits on the telephone. Victor Massillon said, 'The investigation is staggering to an ignominious halt at this end. We have been demoted to the inside pages of *Nice-Matin*. Nothing could be more telling. Cannes is losing interest and reverting to what it does best – stealing money from the pockets of the innocent tourist. Thirty-five francs for a coffee! I'm thinking of heading back to Paris. This place is too rich for my blood.'

'Any luck with the bullets?' asked the Englishman.

'It's not luck we need,' said Massillon. 'It's a vacuum cleaner capable of sucking up half a square-kilometre of seabed. No, my friend, they are now the property of the fishes. And you?' he continued. 'What news from 221B, Baker Street?' It was Massillon's conceit that this was the address from which Ringrose did his work.

'I'm down to the last two hundred and fifty suspects,' said Ringrose drily.

'Is that all?' Massillon laughed.

'And that's just the men,' Ringrose added. 'We're proceeding on the assumption that the sniper might as easily have been the woman.'

'Would it not be wonderful,' said the Commissaire dreamily, 'if you and I could prove that this was an all-American bounty-hunting exercise? Perhaps the Mafia. We could dump the whole mess on the White House lawn, sing "God Bless America", go home, watch television and make love to our wives.'

They were speaking on a secure line. Ringrose said quietly, 'There is one oddity that has come to my notice, Victor. No one has yet come forward to claim the money. Have you heard anything about that from your people in Tehran?'

'I've heard fuck all from either the Quai d'Orsay or the Deuxième Bureau. Even the FBI have been of more help.'

Ringrose said hastily, 'You didn't hear this from me, OK? I'm getting briefed via a back door. But why don't you go to your intelligence people and ask the question as if it had just occurred to you?'

'My friend, it *did* occur to me. How could you doubt it?' Massillon adopted a tone of mock reproach. 'But the answer is still the same. I got nothing. Which doesn't mean I won't be giving those oily bastards at the Quai another prod up the *cul*. Give my regards to Dr Watson,' he said. He meant Lionel Firth.

Ringrose replaced the receiver. He should have known better than to think Victor Massillon would have overlooked the Tehran connection. He was a fox of the old school.

Ringrose strolled into his incident room. He had recruited a uniformed inspector to act as maestro of his computer-search programme. Police forces all over Britain were still feeding into their terminals the results of their laborious local inquiries. No definitive analysis of this material was yet possible.

Adrian Dawson was an information-technology freak. Behind his back he was known, even by Ringrose who had a healthy respect for his brainpower, as Dawson the Dalek. He was young for an inspector, the holder of an impressive maths degree from Cambridge, and on the fast-track that had him earmarked for high rank in the high-tech police service of the early twenty-first century.

Now he rushed forward to greet his boss, for whose own computer – the one between his ears – Dawson also had a healthy respect. Although whey-faced from too much computer-time, he had the attractive, bouncy personality of the dedicated enthusiast and was in his true element when attempting to convert the technologically challenged to the marvels of which his expensive toys were capable.

Ringrose looking quizzically at a screen was enough encouragement. Dawson moved in. 'Let me explain my approach, sir,' he said, taking a swivel seat in front of a screen. His fingers danced with butterfly pressure over the keyboard, sending the monitor into a frenzy of geometric patterns.

'It's as if you take each known fact about the suspect and place it in a separate box – let's call it a red box. Then you make a different type of box – call it blue – and feed in the details of each interview that has been conducted either with or concerning a rifle-proficient person.'

Dawson rubbed his hands as if anticipating a juicy reward for this revelation. 'Now you're ready to ask the computer any number of questions. The aim is to tease from the blue boxes all the facts that match the facts in the red box. The more you can match the facts in the red box to a blue box, the more promising the blue box becomes.'

A glazed Ringrose looked around desperately for rescue and Lionel Firth rushed to his side. He gripped Ringrose's arm melodramatically and hissed just loud enough for Dawson to hear, 'Guv'nor, I must speak to you urgently.' He had already experienced the coloured-box lecture.

Ringrose said, 'Sorry, Adrian. Just let me know when the blue boxes have got the red box surrounded.'

'Oh, yes, sir. Of course. The moment it happens.' The Dalek looked wistful, then bounced back momentarily. 'When you have time, sir, there's another stage . . . green boxes . . .'

Ringrose waved a warmly insincere acknowledgement of the offer as he retreated to the door.

'Lionel, lead me to a pint,' he said.

Chapter Thirty-Five

Jack had played his first card, his opening shot – no, he retracted hurriedly, not his opening shot. He had long since passed that catastrophic point of no return. Strang had been satisfactorily rattled and would have gone scuttling back to Them with his message.

It crossed Jack's mind that he was duelling with two pronouns: Them and They. In that amorphous condition They were an unsatisfactory, vaporous, shifting target.

Alone in his house, lying in the dark, listening in his imagination to the echoes of his faraway family, he'd had much time for self-scourging and self-examination. He knew now why he had to blunder on into the maze, striving to penetrate the enigma, until he had put flesh and substance on They and Them.

For his normal routines, Jack had reverted to using his front door. If they wanted to shadow him to the shops and to his workplace, let them waste their time. He wondered what form their response would take.

It came three days later from an unexpected quarter. He was shaving when his mother rang from Sidmouth. She was sobbing, which was more than she had done when his father had died. However, it was only after she had been so uninterested in and unwelcoming to Grace that he had admitted to himself that he did not love, or even like, his own mother.

Looking back, he had come to realize how little time she had devoted to him as a child. For a while there had been a nanny and babysitters, followed by boarding school, college and, of course, the Army. His prowess as a marksman had meant little to her. She called it 'an overgrown schoolboy's hobby'. On one of his rare off-days, when she had witnessed him achieve only runner-up for the Queen's Prize, she had not shared his bitter disappointment. Instead, she'd had difficulty in preventing her forced smile from degenerating into a contemptuous sneer.

Jack wiped the soap from his chin and listened with no great sympathy. Was her latest lover – an apologetic dentist who had steered clear of Jack on his last visit to Sidmouth a year ago – dead?

'Oh, Jack, you never saw such a mess. The place is contaminated. I'll never be able to sleep in this house again.'

Well, there's always the dentist's house. You've slept there often enough, he thought callously.

He realized he had missed the beginning of her tale of woe. 'What did you say has happened?'

'Burgled, Jack. I've been burgled. The swine have torn the house apart. The damage is appalling. They've smashed all the inside locks and ripped open the sofas, cushions and mattresses. Jack, what on earth did they expect to find here? They've made piles of my clothes and things in the middle of the rooms. They've even been up in the attic. One of them put his stupid foot through my bedroom ceiling.'

Jack caught background voices. His mother turned away from the phone and he could hear a distant babble interrupted by her shrill sounds of outrage.

She returned to him, crying again. 'The evil bastards, Jack! They've chiselled out the little safe that Daddy had cemented into the wall at the back of our wardrobe. Oh, Jack, they've got my jewellery.'

'Where were you?' said Jack. 'Are you hurt?'

'That's the peculiar thing,' she sobbed. 'The police – they're still here – say they went to lengths unheard of around here to get us out of the house.'

Jack went cold. 'How do you mean?'

'We had a telephone call from a hospital in Bristol to say Howard's mother – you met Howard, Jack – had been taken in with a suspected stroke. They thought he should be at her bedside. Well, you can imagine, he was in a state.' His mother had abandoned all attempts to conceal Howard's cohabitation. 'I said I'd drive. As we were going out of the door he remembered he ought to ring his sister. But our phone had gone dead.'

Her voice adopted a note of wonder. 'Jack, they actually went to the trouble of cutting our phone line after the call from the hospital. Well, as you must have guessed, the whole thing was a cruel hoax to get us out of the house. When we got to the hospital, they knew nothing about any stroke. We rang Howard's mother at home. She actually answered the telephone. She's fine. The nice policeman here is flummoxed. He says big-time thieves only employ those tactics when they're plundering manor houses and places stuffed with valuable antiques. They don't know what to make of it. They've no idea what the thieves were after. The so-and-sos have been through all of Daddy's papers and my letters. They're scattered everywhere. What on *earth* did they expect to find? Only the house deeds are of any real value and they're still here.'

Jack raged silently. So that was the bastards' response to his threat. They thought he might have left some written account of the killing with his mother that would blow their conspiracy sky-high.

They were also letting him know how far their tentacles reached.

Jack suddenly had a shocking thought. Cutting across his mother's keening voice, he said, 'I'm very sorry at your news, Mother, but I'll have to get back to you later.'

'Jaaaack!' she wailed, but he was gone.

He rushed to the kitchen dresser where Grace kept their address book and flipped through the pages. Her parents lived in Wilmslow, near

Manchester. He rapidly punched in their number, mis-hit a button, cursed, and punched again. Number unobtainable.

'Shit!' he said, and tapped 100 for the operator.

She came back to him after two intolerably stretched minutes. 'I'm sorry, there's a fault on the line. I'll put you through to the fault-reporting department.'

'Don't bother.'

He dropped the receiver back on the wall mount and returned to the address book. Grace's parents were elderly and she kept their neighbours' number in case of an emergency. This was an emergency, all right, he thought grimly, as he heard the ringing tone. Almost instantly, thank God, the phone was picked up at the other end.

A comforting, deep, no-nonsense Northern voice answered. 'Swinton here.'

'Mr Swinton, this is Jack Boulder. You know, the Jack married to Grace – Grace Turnbull as was.'

Horace Swinton took a moment to digest this information. Then his cheery voice came down the line: 'Aye, lad. This is a surprise. How is little Gra—'

Jack cut in desperately, 'Mr Swinton – Horace – please don't think me rude, but would you go to your front window right away and tell me if you can see any sign of Grace's parents?'

There was a puzzled silence, then Horace Swinton said, 'Half a tick, lad.'

Jack danced from foot to foot, breathing heavily as if he'd run a mile. Then he heard Horace fumbling for the handset. 'They're just getting into their car. You're going to need to be a bit sharpish if you want a word.'

Jack had to stop himself yelling, 'Horace, go back to the window and shout to them. Whatever you do, don't let them leave!'

Horace Swinton started to say something at this extraordinary breakfast-time outburst, but registered the urgency in Jack's voice and thought better of it. 'Hang on,' he said briefly, and went away.

After an agonizing few seconds, Jack heard him bellowing. For a man of his age he still had impressive lung power.

'Come on! Come on!' Jack urged silently.

After a pause, Horace Swinton's stertorous breathing grew louder and louder and then he was puffing directly into the mouthpiece. 'Don't go away, lad,' he said unnecessarily. 'I'm just going downstairs to let Grace's folks in. They seem to be in a bit of a lather.'

There was another long pause and then Grace's mother's voice. She was crying, 'Jack! Jack! Please, dear God, don't tell me my Gracie's dead.'

'Milly!' shouted Jack. 'Calm down. Listen to me! Listen to me. No one is dead. There's nothing wrong with Grace. She's not ill. She's not been in an accident. No matter what you've been told, she's one hundred per cent okay.'

Milly Turnbull abruptly ceased weeping. She was bewildered. 'But the call from the hospital . . .'

Jack said firmly, 'You've been the victim of a vicious hoax. You know where she is in the country. Give her a ring yourself but please don't worry her by mentioning this little incident.'

'*Little?*' Milly said, on a rising note of indignation. 'This is the nastiest thing I ever heard. Who would do such a wicked thing?'

Then, suspiciously, she lowered her voice and said, 'Are you and Grace speaking to each other? You seem to be spending an awful lot of time apart.'

'Milly, I swear to you that Grace and I and the boys all love each other very much – and we love you and Arthur. This hoax was none of my doing, but I got to know about it in time to prevent it going any further.'

Milly was only half listening to him. She had turned away to reassure her agitated husband standing at her side.

Jack said, 'Put Arthur on the line.'

Grace's father said, 'Is this true, Jack – Grace is all right? There's been no accident?'

'Perfectly all right, Arthur. Now, listen to me very carefully. The people who made that call to you this morning are the same people who played a similar trick on my mother down in Devon yesterday. Only she wasn't so lucky. She fell for it, and while she was driving to and from the hospital during the night, they ransacked her house. They intended giving you the same treatment.'

'I don't follow,' said Arthur Turnbull. 'What the hell can they be after? If a pawnbroker came to look round our house, he'd just laugh.'

'They're after a secret paper to do with my Army service that they think I've written and maybe left for safe-keeping with my nearest and dearest.'

Jack could almost see his father-in-law scratching the bristle of his steel-grey head. 'What's in this paper?'

'There is no paper,' said Jack. 'They just *think* there's a paper. Although I'm beginning to think there ought to be a paper.'

This convolution was too much for Arthur Turnbull to absorb. He was now deeply perplexed. 'About what?'

'Something I can't talk about.'

'Oh, it's like that, is it? Hush-hush? I hope you're not getting our Gracie into bother, Jack. I'd never forgive you—'

'Arthur, I give you my solemn oath, I'd never let anyone harm a hair of her head.'

'Or the little lads?' The old man sounded as if he were getting ready to march south at the head of a company of the Lancashire Fusiliers.

'Or the lads,' swore Jack.

His father-in-law was mollified. 'Now, Jack, do you want me to contact the police? This is a bad business. If what you tell me is true, these characters can't be far away.'

Jack pondered. Could Milly and Arthur be in any physical danger? He dare not rule it out. The bastards could be sitting just round the corner, waiting for them to leave the house.

He said slowly, 'Let's do it like this. Tell the police you had a hoax call. Tell it just the way it happened. You'll find that your phone line has been cut, but let the police find that out for themselves. Tell them you rang me from an outside phonebox before you set out for the hospital in case I'd left a message for you on the answering machine. That's important: I didn't ring you. Even more important, you must insist on police protection while there's a chance the burglars are still in the vicinity.'

The silence on the line was deafening. His father-in-law was a canny man. He sensed the subtext of Jack's speech, which spelt danger. He said, 'I don't know, Jack. You folks down in London get up to some funny capers. How did these buggers get on to us, of all people?'

Jack recalled Rupert Strang's world-weary words: 'We had a work-up done of your life – your profile, if you like.' He wondered how many generations back into his past they had delved, rooting out a history of which he himself was only dimly aware.

He said, 'I don't know. But it isn't difficult to guess. They get marriage certificates, that sort of thing...'

Grace's father said shrewdly, 'That place you've sent the family to – is that to keep them out of harm's way?'

'Yes,' said Jack bluntly, and without elaboration.

'You'd better be sure you're doing the right thing, lad. And you'd better get yourself dug out of whatever shithole you're up to your neck in. No names on the phone, but are they the same fellows you upset the year before last?'

'Yes,' said Jack. It was as good a lie as any.

There was no satisfactory way of ending the conversation. 'Keep your head down,' said Arthur gruffly.

'You too,' said Jack.

It was another two days before Jack spotted a report in his local weekly newspaper that his solicitors at Shepherd's Bush Green had been burgled. The office safe had been expertly opened by a genuine cracksman and ransacked.

'You don't see work like that any more,' a police inspector had said, almost with regret. 'Safe-crackers today have no time for finesse. They either blow the back off or take a pickaxe to them. This bloke was a real craftsman.'

'We bugged and burgled our way across London.' The words were unforgettable. And Jack remembered that they had been said by an old MI5 man about a time when he and his will-o'-the-wisp co-conspirators, all servants of the State, had attempted in the sixties to destabilize the elected government of the United Kingdom. On that scale, Jack knew he was merely an irritant blip on the screen.

He gritted his teeth. At least he was still holding off the phantoms.

Chapter Thirty-Six

It is not true that criminals return to the scene of the crime. However, like pyromaniacs craving the heat of flames, they become drawn to less hazardous manifestations of their exploits: the activity outside the police station, the throng of neighbours and ghouls jamming the street outside the victim's home, the comings and goings of the television crews with their space-age equipment, promising exciting glimpses of the star reporters they see on the news bulletins every evening.

The compulsion was about to entrap Betty Bentinck.

Although a British passport holder, Conrad Niven had been compelled, by virtue of the parlous state of the home film industry, to work in Los Angeles, which is where his body had been flown after the French authorities had completed their post-mortem examinations and released it. The mortuary staff returned his organs to approximately their original sites, tugged the detached skin and hair back over the bare dome of his skull and crudely stitched up the savage Y-shaped incision where the police pathologist had fruitlessly rooted around for bullet fragments.

The sensitive Beverly Hills mortician who, with practised reverence, received the coffin off a Boeing 747 at LAX had shuddered delicately at the sight of the brutally invaded corpse. It had taken the highest cosmetic skills to restore poor Niven to a semblance of his living self.

Hollywood was determined to give their murdered son the send-off of a prince. Gregory Peck read the lesson, Sir Anthony Hopkins recited Dylan Thomas, and Lord Attenborough gave an address. Jack Nicholson, Keanu Reeves, Brad Pitt and the three Baldwin brothers were among the honorary pall-bearers.

Interment followed at a cathedral-sized mausoleum in the heart of old Hollywood, where the elaborate casket was slid into a concrete pigeonhole and a marble slab, suitably inscribed, cemented over the opening.

That should have been that, but Los Angeles is infested by some of the sharpest and most inventive British and Australian reporters on earth. And one had a stunt in mind. He waited for two days after the funeral and went into action. He hired a young actress for a day's work, and sent her to a theatrical costumier to be fitted with a black lace dress and matching veiled hat. Then he drove her to the cemetery. His proposed stunt was inspired by the legend of the Lady in Black, who for many years had placed each week a red rose in the little metal flower-holder fixed to the nearby tomb of Rudolph Valentino, the silent screen's Latin lover.

The reporter was about to give birth to a new legend, with accompanying photographs, at the tomb of the young British director who had been both handsome and a lover of many women.

On entering the echoing mausoleum he discovered an obstacle to the successful execution of his plans. A Lady in Black was already *in situ*. She was weeping, with one slender hand pressed passionately against Niven's marble plaque. The reporter could not believe his ears or his good fortune. She was crying, 'Forgive me! Forgive me!'

The reporter looked around wildly. Had some other fucking journo scooped him? But no one else was there. He stared wide-eyed at the genuine article.

True, her clothes were subdued rather than black and there was no veil but – God was smiling on him – she was actually holding a dozen red roses.

Heartlessly abandoning his counterfeit Lady, he crept forward and took aim. The searing white-out of the camera flash in the churchlike gloom made her jump and scream. She wheeled round, instantly took in her predicament and ran. Unfortunately, she had to pass the reporter on the way out and was wearing high-heeled shoes. He had exposed almost a roll of 35mm colour film of her before she reached her car. As she slammed the door, she made the reporter even happier. She shouted at him, 'No comment! No comment! I've already told the FBI all I know.'

He watched her skid out of the gates. He knew the face. It was that actress from *Girl Agents of the FBI*. What was her name?

He checked the cast list and developed his pictures. Then he presented himself at the Beverly Glen offices of Betty Bentinck's agent, ready to twist arms. The agent said he'd get back to him. The reporter said it had better be before the end of business today.

The agent, a realist, listened to Betty's story on the phone. He was angry with her for having kept him in the dark but hid it. Don't get mad, he told himself, get cash. He said, 'He's got you by the beaver. If he has to do it the hard way, you'll get smeared. Co-operate and he promises a sympathetic story.'

'God! What shall I do? The FBI told me to keep my mouth shut.'

'Fuck the FBI. Don't ask what you can do for the FBI; ask what the FBI can do for you. The publicity could be mega. There could even be an HBO docudrama in it – with you playing yourself.'

'You honestly think so?'

The agent sat back in his chair, talking into the headset that left his hands free to write, drink coffee, punch his laptop and throw heavy objects at his male secretary. 'I honestly think so. I'll fix for you two to meet – under my supervision in this office, of course – at ten in the a.m. tomorrow. He's pond scum but I'll make sure I have on tape his assurances of a fair shake.'

Jack Boulder jogged round to the newsagent's to pick up the Sunday papers. Betty's winsome face stared out of the rack. STAR ADMITS: I HELPED KILLERS/ NIVEN MURDER – FILM STAR SHOCK/ KILLER IS BRITISH, REVEALS STAR.

Jack gathered up everything Sunday journalism had to offer and hurried home. Under the shrieking headlines, Betty's account was much as it had happened, although Jack flushed to find himself described in fulsome terms that left little doubt that she had seen him as a sex object. She had used the word 'stud' several times, which Grace was definitely not going to like.

He noted that she had discreetly left her liaison with Sidney Zuckerman out of the narrative and that Jack had paid her ten thousand pounds for her impersonation of Jane Canning. In Betty's version, she had done it 'for kicks'.

The hunt was on, the newspapers informed their reading millions, for a husband-and-wife assassination team – and had switched to Britain. She was quoted as saying, 'I think I was falling in love with him. That's why I behaved without thought of the consequences.'

Jack assumed at first that this was a reporter inventing a purple passage for her. Then he changed his mind. He could still hear her claiming, 'I'm not from Oshkosh.'

Well, if she could wriggle out of trouble by telling a few lies, good luck to her – even though it did mean further stormy weather for him with Grace.

But Betty's début as a media star did not please Ringrose. Until now, the focus of the investigation had been on the South of France and Ringrose's people had been working quietly, away from the glare of media attention.

The newspapers were still energetically sniffing out Iranians and trying for interviews with Conrad Niven's Special Branch minders, who were awaiting disciplinary hearings.

Now Ringrose was centre-stage and everyone would be on his neck for instant solutions – the press, TV, MPs, Conrad Niven's high-profile relatives.

The phone rang just as Helen was clearing the breakfast plates. The family always had the full, sit-down breakfast on Sundays to compensate for the pell-mell chaos during the week. Helen came back into the room. 'It's Peter Lancing of the *Daily Mail*.'

The circus was starting already, Ringrose threw down his napkin. How was it that every time he ordered a new ex-directory number Lancing found it? 'Tell him I can't talk to him now,' said Ringrose.

Helen came back again. 'He says he has something important to tell you.'

An old reporter's trick. 'Oh yeah? Tell him to tell it to the Press Bureau. I'm having my breakfast.'

He heard Helen deliver the brush-off and hang up. She came back and said, 'He says he'll catch you some other time.' She turned to their two daughters. 'Daddy's got his grumpy boots on this morning. So don't go near his cage.'

Chapter Thirty-Seven

Ringrose was still grumpy when he reached his office on Monday morning. Dawson the Dalek's electronic blue boxes were now bloated with information concerning citizens of the United Kingdom who had at any time in their lives displayed noteworthy skill with a rifle.

His computers whirred into action, eliminating old soldiers, the infirm, a couple of circus performers who had been compelled to confess that their uncanny skills with single shots owed more to hollowed bullet cases packed with tiny lead shot than to a deadly eye for hitting tossed coins with a single undoctored bullet.

The computers churned on, inexorably rejecting men and women outside the target age group, shooters whose physical attributes clashed markedly with the video images of Mr and Mrs Canning, those who could prove beyond a doubt that they had been anywhere but at the Cannes Film Festival between the relevant dates.

With the aid of opticians' information fed to his boxes, Inspector Dawson was also able to eliminate a further group whose eyesight was no longer up to the job.

One by one, his blue boxes began to surround his 'control' red box. The names emerging then underwent a further, even more vigorous, scrutiny by the computer.

And eventually, inevitably, out spewed the name of John a.k.a. Jack Gordon Boulder, aged thirty-four. Dawson took over a monitor, furiously tapped in repeated challenges to the outcome, and was finally satisfied with what the screen was telling him. He green-boxed John Gordon Boulder and ordered a printout.

Ringrose sat in his office, moodily working through a stack of please-call messages. The one from the *Daily Mail* went straight into the bin. He looked up to find Inspector Dawson tapping discreetly on his open door. He was carrying a concertina of paper with perforated edges. He looked inordinately pleased with himself.

'Got something for me?'

Dawson crossed the regulation carpet to Ringrose's desk almost at a trot. 'I truly believe I have, sir. Take a look at this.' He placed the print-out on Ringrose's blotter. 'This is the only green-boxed name to emerge so far.'

'Green-boxed?'

'Green for Go, sir. As I was trying to explain a few days ago. It's the last stage of the computer search.'

'This is a body we can put in the frame? A front runner?'

'Yes, sir. Way out in front.'

Using his fingers as a comb, Ringrose brushed back his forelock and stared dubiously at the wad of computer paper. Like most traditional thief-takers, he had come reluctantly to the electronic age. The computer could not look into a man's face and notice the twitching cheek muscle, the avoided gaze and the sweat beginning to form on the upper lip. It could not hear his voice tremble or see the nervous glance at the friend – the glance betraying that they shared a guilty secret.

Yet Ringrose was no foolish technophobe. Computerized information had lifted a massive burden of dogged routine searching and comparison of crime patterns from the shoulders of his detectives.

He said to Dawson, 'Come round to this side of the desk, Inspector. Pull up a chair and run me through this stuff.'

Dawson rushed to obey. He pointed at the first fold of the concertina. 'Here we have a man who meets all criteria. He's the right age, right physique and, by widespread consent, an outstanding shot – a Bisley competitor who was once runner-up for the Queen's Prize.'

'Any alibi?' Ringrose was becoming interested.

'Only a very loose one. During the control period, he says he was either at work – he manages a gun club – or taking a holiday at home. No attempt has been made as yet to confirm this with his wife. She'll almost certainly support her husband, regardless of the truth.'

'Yes,' agreed Ringrose. 'Wives' testimony isn't worth a damn.'

Dawson's excitement was building. He refolded the concertina to a fresh section. 'Now here's an interesting incident. When he was interviewed at his place of work, he willingly supplied the investigating officers with club members' names but was extremely shy about revealing his own prowess. In fact, he failed to mention it at all until he was reminded by a Detective Sergeant Munday.'

'Innate modesty?'

'Perhaps, sir. But only perhaps.'

Dawson flipped over a few more folds. Ringrose said, 'Wait one moment, Dawson. I want Lionel Firth in on this.' They waited while Ringrose's number two was found. Crisply Ringrose brought him up to date.

The computer expert, now seated between the two detectives, continued. 'There are further encouraging factors. Remember the American actress's obvious sexual attraction for the male suspect? Now look at this.'

His finger ran along a line of Greg Rankin's statement. '"Women fancy him,"' he read out.

'So?' said Ringrose. 'I'm sure women fancy Lionel here. But that doesn't make him a killer.'

'Ah!' said Dawson, raising a pedagogic finger. 'But what about this?' The finger found another line in Detective Constable Fred Hall's report. Dawson read, '"Question: Ever see him these days? Answer: Last winter he was even out there in the snow. Sharpening up for the competition round."'

'So?' said Ringrose, once more the devil's advocate. 'If he's Bisley class he'll naturally be keeping in practice.'

Dawson's supreme moment had arrived. He paused for maximum effect. 'I can find no evidence, sir, that he is entered for a single rifle-shooting competition in the United Kingdom this year. Not one. And we have checked with all major sporting organizations in that field.'

'Well,' conceded Ringrose, glancing thoughtfully to catch Firth's reaction, 'that is interesting. Do you have any other titbits for us?'

Dawson said quietly, 'Boulder did not use his credit card from the second of May until the twenty-fourth. Yet he is a consistent regular user of his card – a Visa – for small purchases. Since he began using it eight years ago, there has never been a blank period of anything approaching three weeks in his monthly account.'

Firth broke in. 'What about the purchases on either side of the gap? Did he buy anything abroad?'

Dawson shook his head. 'No. All his buying has been of a domestic nature – petrol, food and so on – in England. In fact, his credit-card record shows he hasn't been off this island for more than eighteen months.'

'Where was he before that?' asked Ringrose.

'Northern Ireland. Which brings me to the next point. Boulder was a serving Army officer there but abruptly resigned his commission. He was a substantive captain but, if Rankin, the rangemaster, is to be believed, he left under a cloud, due to what he describes as "a lark" that misfired.'

'Do we have Boulder's records from the Ministry of Defence?'

The computer wizard coughed. 'Far be it for me to think unworthy thoughts, sir, but I suspect our khaki friends are being less than candid.'

'How so?'

'This record' – he flicked the print-out contemptuously – 'is only remarkable for what it omits. They have sent us the completely pedestrian account of recruitment, training, qualifications, progress through the ranks, commanding officers' comments and so forth. His resignation is noted with regret, but without any further comment. There is no mention of larks or misbehaviour. This record has been through the laundry. His various commanding officers' reports lift the curtain a little. Boulder was very popular with both fellow officers and his men. He did his stuff to everyone's satisfaction during the Gulf War, was admired for his marksmanship because it brought prestige to the regiment. One CO notes that he has a tendency towards a certain recklessness and impetuosity, but does not provide any evidence for this – which may, of course, have been removed from the papers sent to us. What there is only goes part of the way towards confirming Rankin's summing up of Boulder as "a bit crazy".'

Dawson had finished. The three men sat still, eyes focused on the white concertina. Finally, Ringrose suggested, 'Perhaps there's no mystery at all about his resignation. He might have done it out of disappointment with his chances of ever sewing those red tabs onto his uniform.' He turned to Firth. 'Have another go at the MOD. Tell them we want everything they've got on Captain Boulder – and tell them we want it on the double. That's the language they understand.' He fell silent again. Then he said, 'When does the City of London firearms control officer next make his routine inspection of that gun club?'

Dawson said tentatively, 'If you care to log-on to your terminal, sir, perhaps I can help . . .'

Ringrose tapped in his password to gain entry and Dawson leaned over him to punch up the City of London police records. He accessed the firearms files and began scrolling a list up the screen. Finally, he said, 'It's not due until next November, sir.'

'Damn,' said Ringrose. 'If we go in prematurely, he'll know something's up – if, indeed, he's our man.' He thought for a moment. 'Do we have his picture yet? No? Then put someone discreet with a long lens onto him,' he instructed Firth. 'You can tell our snapper that if Boulder spots him he'll have a job for life photographing the bodies the river police fish out of the Thames. And another thing. Lionel, I want you to find me a firearms officer with a bit of nous and place him undercover as a member of that club. He might just get lucky.'

The three men went back to the beginning of the material that Dawson had gathered and, line by line, began to examine once again the known facts concerning the life of John Gordon Boulder.

Ringrose carefully dissected the report compiled by Munday and Bellew, the only two policemen who'd had face-to-face contact with the man.

After several minutes of silent study, he said, 'You'll notice an apparent attempt by Boulder to mislead Munday and Bellew. He never placed his own skill at anything beyond "handy". He gave the distinct impression to them that he had not touched a rifle since his Army service. He made no mention of refreshing his marksmanship last winter. Instead, he quite cleverly switched the conversation to the inadequacy of the range he manages.'

Firth said, 'Would it help if we took his deputy manager, Joseph Carsby, aside for a quiet chat?'

'No. Hands off him,' replied Ringrose immediately. 'He's also a former Army man. His loyalty will be to Boulder. He'll be about as reliable as a wife. If we front him up at this stage, he'll go running straight to Boulder. But one thing's for sure. Thanks to the Inspector here we have a name at last. I think we're on to something.'

The two detectives both shook Dawson's hand warmly, sending the Dalek downloading into electronic heaven.

An hour later Firth poked his head round Ringrose's door. He made a sour face. 'The MOD say we have all there is on Jack Boulder. I mentioned the larks and the "leaving under a cloud" stuff and they said they didn't know what I was talking about. They said it must be idle barrack-room gossip and we should ignore it.'

'Really,' said Ringrose, tightening his lips. He'd had experience of Whitehall obduracy and various government ministries' jealous guarding of their own turf. 'Get me the name of the officer who signed Boulder's discharge papers.'

General Sir Francis Cashin settled Ringrose into an armchair of ancient cracked leather and signalled to the bar steward for two snifters of brandy. He was a small, wiry man with a penetrating gaze that must, in its time, have intimidated whole cadres of junior officers.

The steward placed the snifters on the table between them, together with some bottled soda water. The General unscrewed the cap and said, 'Splash?' Ringrose nodded. 'Damn bottles,' grumbled the General. 'Do you remember when we had proper soda siphons – lovely glass bottles with silver tops that made a most satisfying hiss when you pressed the lever? Somehow, that sound was a vital ingredient of a correctly poured brandy-and-soda.'

Ringrose, who did not remember any such thing, offered a placatory, 'I know just what you mean, General.'

General Cashin lifted his glass. 'It's a pleasure to meet you, Commander. I remember well your handling of that beauty queens business. A first-class piece of work. It was a great sadness to the Army, you know, the involvement of those three misguided officers.'

Ringrose made an apologetic face. 'Yes, General. I was sorry it had to be them. Which, unfortunately, leads me to another matter involving an Army officer, this time one who was under your command.'

General Cashin shot him a keen look from under bushy eyebrows. 'I see from the papers that you're in charge of the UK end of the hunt for the killer of that film chap.'

'Yes, sir, and our inquiries have raised questions concerning a former captain named John Gordon Boulder.'

'Ho-ho!' said the General like a pantomime villain. 'Is that boy in trouble?' and, without waiting for an answer, added, 'I'm not surprised.'

Ringrose said, 'The MOD have let us see his records, which are not particularly revealing. They insist they've shown us everything but my officers have found witnesses who suggest he left the Army under a cloud. If that's so, I don't understand why none of it's written into the record.'

'Ah, I see,' said General Cashin, gently replacing his glass on the table.

Ringrose watched the sharp face close down and turn wary.

After a moment, the General asked, 'Is this inquiry absolutely essential to your investigation?'

'The only honest answer is that I don't know. But I suspect that it is.'

The General leaned forward and looked around to confirm that nobody but Ringrose was within earshot. 'I want your word, Commander, that what I tell you will not later be attributed to me in any way, shape or form.'

'You have it, sir,' said Ringrose instantly.

'Good. Because if what I tell you ever becomes public knowledge, there would be an unholy row. The Government would be seriously compromised by what was the cover-up of a scandal engineered by a great many people from me downwards – and from the Northern Ireland minister upwards to who-knows-who. Our justification was that we desperately needed to maintain good relations with the Dublin government. It was a case of turning Nelson's blind eye to a lesser evil to serve the greater good.'

The General finished his brandy with one deep swig and laid out for Ringrose the full story of Jack Boulder's unauthorized one-man mission across the border into the Irish Republic to avenge fallen comrades.

'If we'd court-martialled him or – horror of horrors – handed him over to Dublin to stand trial in a civilian court, just think of the propaganda victory for the IRA – the millions of dollars that would have flowed into their funds from those fools who live in America and call themselves Irish even though they've never been near the benighted place. In wartime I'd have been pinning a medal on Captain Boulder's chest. But, as it was, I was obliged to hand him his bowler hat.'

Ringrose could feel the goose pimples rising on his arms and neck. Boulder's profile was perfect.

The General was still standing. 'I liked Boulder – what little I knew of him personally. But he was a bloody fool to take out McGurk. We'd have got that gentleman sooner or later by more orthodox means. But Boulder's blood was up and he just couldn't stop himself. Kicking him out was the least we could do in the circumstances.'

Ringrose said. 'You say his blood was up. But, in your opinion, would he also be capable of killing in cold blood?'

The General snorted. 'He's a trained soldier. The temperature of his blood is an irrelevance. Captain Boulder is capable of killing full stop. Amongst combat soldiers, the sniper enjoys a unique privilege. He sees a head pop up, he fires, the head disappears. He rarely has to view at close range the results of his handiwork. He doesn't have to have his mind disturbed by the sight of blood and gore.

'There's something extremely clinical about successful snipers. They keep their hands clean. They send death by long-distance mail, as it were. During the Winter War that the Russians ill-advisedly conducted against the Finns before the Second World War, there was one chap – a farmer turned sniper – who was credited with having left dead in the snow an incredible five hundred or more Red Army troops. I'd wager that the fellow never lost a night's sleep over it. If he had, he'd never have scored that many not out. He'd have been retired, unfit for duty, long before.'

General Cashin leaned forward and said deliberately, 'I believe Captain Boulder is just such a man.'

Chapter Thirty-Eight

'Boulder's profile fits so snugly that it's almost too perfect,' said Ringrose. He and Firth were seated in Ringrose's room, studying the wet prints of the photographs taken earlier in the day of Jack Boulder emerging from a lunchtime sandwich bar in the City. It was late and few of Ringrose's team were still toiling in the outer office. Even Dawson had gone for the night.

Firth held the print alongside the best of the bunch taken from the Hotel Berthier's security cameras. Their eyes went back and forth from Boulder to 'Mr Canning'.

'Body size and shape look right,' said Firth. 'Pity about that blasted Panama.'

'Deliberate,' grunted Ringrose. 'He knew what he was doing. The American producer said he didn't take it off ever, not even in the lift or elevator as he called it.'

Firth said, 'Do we give him a tug?'

'There's nothing at this moment I'd like to do more,' said Ringrose. 'Roar up to his drum, break down the door and grab him while he's eating his supper. The problem is, what happens then? He's had more than enough time to clear his house of anything incriminating – assuming anything was there in the first place. Then he'll shout for his lawyer and give us his impersonation of the three wise monkeys. We can't nick a man because he didn't use his credit card for a few weeks.' He went on, 'Lionel, I want you to arrange round-the-clock surveillance. I want to know about his financial position – the usual checks for unexplained sums of money – and I want to know about his family and friends, especially any who claim to have seen him in May.'

The Commander held out his hands and began to make squeezing motions, the fingers slowly closing into the palms. 'I'm still trying to get a feel for this chap. Let's you and me take a little drive down to Shepherd's Bush and have a run by his house.'

Firth was surprised at the suggestion but resisted glancing at his watch. They took a nondescript car from the pool. It was a fine early June evening but the sun was already down and the light was starting to go by the time they found Jack Boulder's street.

They stopped at the corner of Hellespont Road. Ringrose's eye roved over an urban landscape of little distinction. The houses were late-Victorian, most semi-detached with small front gardens, some of which had been converted into parking spaces. The larger houses, he judged from the plethora of door intercoms and bell pushes, were in multiple occupation.

Boulder's was not one of them. His was a storey shorter. A downstairs light would seem to indicate that the object of their interest was at home. The front garden had not been obliterated like so many of the others along the street, but it was showing signs of neglect. It was not the habitation of a man who had just earned himself a million pounds in bounty money.

Firth drove slowly to the end of Hellespont Road and Ringrose said, 'Let's go round again.' Firth turned left and left again. He said, 'These streets all look alike. You couldn't tell the difference if it weren't for the name plaques.'

They halted once more at the corner. Despite the fading light, a handful of householders was still enjoying the mild evening and pottering in their garden patches. A youth tinkered with his motorcycle, and half-way down the three-hundred-yard stretch of the street a mixed group of teenagers eddied and flirted.

On the way back to Victoria to pick up their own cars, Ringrose was thoughtful and made little conversation with his second-in-command. Something was nagging at him. He arrived home still mildly disturbed, a mood that persisted through supper with Helen and the girls. They recognized the all-too-familiar signs: Daddy has a problem. They knew better than to distract him.

Ringrose fell asleep, leaving his subconscious to grapple with a shapeless worry. The answer came at four in the morning. He woke with a start and sat up. 'It's the trees! The bloody trees!' he said into the darkness of the bedroom.

Helen rolled away from him and groaned into her pillow. 'Bugger the trees. You're having a nightmare, Tom. Go back to sleep.'

Ringrose did as he was told – happily.

'It's the trees,' repeated Ringrose next morning to Firth, who waited patiently for the explanation of his guv'nor's animation.

'The trees along both sides of Boulder's street have been pollarded – cut back to reduce the new foliage,' said Ringrose.

'Yes, they're London planes,' said Firth helpfully, casting his mind back to his view of Hellespont Road on the previous evening. 'Did I miss something?'

'We both missed it,' said Ringrose. 'We drove in a box shape, taking in three other streets. You said yourself you couldn't tell one from the other, apart from the names. The houses were identical. The pavement trees were all the same type – London planes, as you say.'

'Right,' said Firth, still puzzled.

'But there was a difference. The planes in the other three streets were in full summer growth with masses of leaf. They had not been pollarded. Why?'

'Perhaps they didn't need it,' said Firth.

'Exactly,' said Ringrose, leaving him none the wiser.

He shifted to a new tack. 'You're busy setting up the surveillance on Boulder. Right?'

'The team is almost complete.'

'They'll find it helpful that Jack Boulder doesn't have a huge leafy mass in front of his house to obscure their view.'

'Yes, sir. That's a piece of good luck.' Ringrose seemed to be making a meal out of a minor example of happenstance.

'Is it luck?'

'I don't follow.'

Ringrose asked pedantically, 'Why should Boulder's street get a special tree-trimming treatment? I want you to go personally to the borough council, sort out the officer responsible for the trees on the highways and ask that very question.'

Firth's face registered the uncertainty of a man given an incomplete briefing.

'Lionel, trust me on this. I have an awful suspicion, growing bigger by the hour, that you and I are not going to like the answer one little bit.'

Ringrose's aide was too wise in the ways of his master to challenge the instincts that had proved so uncanny in past cases. He located Fred Manners, the borough arboricultural officer, a Wiltshire man transposed uncomfortably to the cement fields of the big city, supervising remedial treatment for an ailing elm in a tiny park off the Goldhawk Road. The ruby face that topped a portly body was alive with suspicion. He studied Firth's warrant card closely, walked to the car and checked that the uniformed driver seemed to be a genuine copper, asked for *his* card and requested that an increasingly exasperated Firth hold a two-way conversation over the Metropolitan Police Radio with a dispatcher to prove conclusively who he was.

'Even now I'm not sure I ought to be having a conversation with you,' said Manners, as he tapped his boot against the kerb to shed clay.

'Why not, Mr Manners?' Firth did not think the man's name entirely appropriate.

'Official Secrets Act,' said Manners gravely.

'Look,' said Firth, beginning to lose patience, 'I've proved to you beyond all reasonable doubt that I'm a senior officer of the Metropolitan Police. I signed the Official Secrets Act many years ago. My rank should tell you that I have encountered and preserved many secret matters in the course of my duties. Please tell me what the problem is.'

'I was instructed that this was a top secret matter, that I wasn't even to tell the council's ways and means committee chairperson.'

'I am,' said Firth heavily, 'engaged in a most serious investigation. The business of the plane trees may have no connection with it but I need to know in order that it may be eliminated. Now, please put me in the picture or we shall all have to go along to the town hall and afterwards you may have to accompany me to New Scotland Yard.'

He tried not to make it sound like a threat.

'It's something to do with the IRA,' said Fred Manners reluctantly. 'Two Secret Service officers came to see me at the end of February. They said they were keeping an eye on someone living in Hellespont Road – a surveillance operation, they called it. They wanted to get the trees cut back before the sap began to rise. Otherwise, they said, the leaf growth in the coming spring would block the sightlines for them and their long lenses. I said if they told me which house they were watching and which house they were using to spy from I'd cut back the trees in their way.'

'And what did they say?'

'They wouldn't tell me the address. They said if I had my blokes pollard only a handful of trees it would give the game away to the bloke they were watching. They insisted on the whole street, both sides, being done in the usual way.' He shrugged. 'I argued the toss for a while. The planes in that street weren't scheduled for a short-back-and-sides for another year.'

'So what did you do?'

'They were a couple of real old-school-tie types, very snotty, the sort of people who always get their way in the end. People who've got connections, if you know what I mean.'

'I know exactly what you mean.' Firth nodded, trying to get him to the point faster.

'Anyway, to save further aggravation, I whistled up the gang and the cherry-pickers and we went through the street next day like ferrets through a burrow. I never saw the toffee-nosed buggers again. There was no thanks, no nothing.'

'You say they were watching one man. Are you sure they didn't mention a group of men or say "them" or "they", indicating that they were interested in more than one person?'

Fred rubbed his chin, transferring to it a few grains of earth from his grubby hands. 'No, I'm pretty sure it was just one bloke they were after. I looked at the newspapers for a few weeks after we did the job to see if anything exciting had happened — a shoot-out with the SAS, something like that. But there was nothing.' He looked crestfallen. 'So I kept my mouth shut and got on with the job. I didn't even tell my missus. You're the first one—'

'What were the two men's names?' Firth interrupted.

'I only had one. It was an odd name, like one of those old music-hall comedians. He had a very official-looking identity card.' He pondered for a moment, head cocked, visualizing the little oblong of cardboard in its plastic holder. Finally, he said with assurance, 'It said it belonged to Eustace Murgatroyd. I thought at the time it didn't sound very glamorous for a spy. I mean, it's not in the same class as James Bond, is it?' His eyes narrowed. 'Have I been taken for a ride? Were those blokes genuine?'

'Relax,' said Firth. 'I think they were. What we have here, I guess, is two official organizations getting their wires crossed. You're still obliged to keep shtum about it.'

Manners visibly relaxed. 'Bit of a cock-up, is it?'

'You could say that,' said Firth, wearily.

He had himself driven to the corner of Hellespont Road. Boulder's house was on the west side of the street; therefore the surveillance must have been done from a house on the east side. He knew MI5 preferred to use vacant property rather than risk a security breach by asking householders if they could commandeer their upstairs front rooms.

Firth said to his driver, 'You wait here. I'm going for a stroll.'

169

There was one house for sale on the east side, offering an oblique view of Boulder's frontage.

The estate agent, a smooth youth in a tennis-club blazer, did not even have to refer to his books to remember arranging the minimum six-month letting from February. 'The market's dead so the owner was quite happy to accept a short let. They're a couple of businessmen on a temporary assignment in London. They've paid the full amount in advance plus a deposit against the wear and tear.'

Firth stirred. 'Are you telling me they're still there?'

'They've not been in touch but, yes, I suppose they are.' The agent looked anxious. 'I hope there isn't going to be any trouble.'

'I wouldn't count on it,' said Firth. 'Did they provide a reference?'

Now the agent needed his file. He returned to his desk with a manila folder. Sorting through the paperwork, he said, 'They're in the film business.'

Firth heard the bells sound in his head. 'Camera-equipment suppliers?'

'Yes, how did you know that?' The agent was impressed.

'I just had a funny feeling,' said Lionel. 'And I bet the address given by the referee on that headed notepaper you're holding in your hand is in Tilney Street, Mayfair.'

'Spot on.'

'Jesus!' said Firth.

Chapter Thirty-Nine

Tom Ringrose returned in a hurry from his interview with the Commissioner. 'This investigation is going in so many directions it's beginning to look like Spaghetti Junction,' he complained to Firth. 'Once again, we have the repeated assurances of both the Secret Intelligence Service and the Security Service that they have no operation in progress either involving anyone named Boulder or Hellespont Road, Shepherd's Bush. Neither does either service admit to employing any officer whose real or trade name is Murgatroyd. And that being the case,' said Ringrose grimly, 'they won't be able to squawk that our activities are compromising theirs. The one positive thing that's come out of this development is that we've established a definite link between Boulder and the shadowy

Cannings. Although if Boulder really is the shooter, why would the others in the conspiracy be mounting a surveillance operation on one of their own?

'Lionel, I want you to obtain the spare key from the agent and make a discreet entry to the house. It has to be done on tiptoe because it's essential, while we're still floundering in the dark, that we don't alarm Boulder across the road. Take a full forensic team and give the place a thorough going over.' Almost as an afterthought, he added, 'Oh, and if you should be so lucky as to find warm bodies on the premises, nick 'em. We'll think of a charge – Peeping Tommery, if necessary.'

Firth was still in the outer office organizing the raid when Ringrose's intercom buzzed and, unusually, he was summoned to return to the Commissioner's office.

The Commissioner's bluff and blokish manner was camouflage for ravenous ambition. He was not held in high regard by those beneath him on the pole. He had never displayed any outstanding flair for battling crime on the streets but this had proved no hindrance at all during his climb to his exalted rank. Despite the blue and silver uniform, he was a politician, skilled in the art of pleasing his masters as he rose unimpeded through the ranks. He was adept at passing examinations, convincingly glib in oral interviews by promotion boards, a good committee man and paper shuffler, a great slogan coiner, a man who knew how to please. These were the well-greased paths to power.

He looked, for once, a little hesitant, embarrassed, even – the look of a man preparing to sugar a pill. Ringrose was immediately on his guard but accepted the invitation to sit down.

The Commissioner studied his own fingernails as if he had discovered an offending cuticle. 'Tom,' he said, with synthetic warmth, 'a word to the wise. There's something I should warn you about. Whitehall is getting the jitters regarding this Niven affair. Your latest moves involving the cloak-and-dagger brigade aren't helping.'

'If they aren't doing anything they shouldn't be doing, why should they worry?' said Ringrose.

The Commissioner's face twisted into a pained smile. 'It's not so much a problem with them. Our problem is with the Government. The Home Secretary has just spoken to me and as good as told me he's speaking on behalf of the Prime Minister. He's reluctant to grant us a phone-tapping warrant until we can produce more convincing evidence that Boulder is involved.' He decided to take the plunge. 'The upshot is, they simply don't want us to take the can from the French. After all, it did happen on their turf. To put it bluntly, they don't want to prove it was a UK citizen who pulled the trigger. God knows, we've suffered enough mockery in the press because Conrad Niven was nominally in the charge of Special Branch. We don't want any more dumped on us. The row would be as politically unacceptable and embarrassing for us and the Government as we experienced when we were lumbered with that investigation into British soldiers' conduct during the Falklands War.'

'I thought we were supposed to be immune from government interference.'

'Come on, Tom. Put away your rattle. Who do you think holds the purse-strings and is quite capable of wrapping them round our necks and pulling hard?'

Ringrose held down his anger. He'd never been so blatantly got at in his entire career. 'Look, sir, I'm just a serving officer. I can't guarantee where this investigation is headed. What am I to do if I turn up an Englishman? Make sure I get him a foreign passport before I haul him in?'

The Commissioner made a placatory gesture. 'Tom, I know better than to interfere with an officer of your calibre. You go ahead with your inquiries, but I want you to proceed with the utmost discretion. That means absolutely no information for the press – and absolutely no arrests until you and I have sat down and discussed the implications. Until now, I've been forwarding your reports to the Home Office with just my initials added. But your results so far are starting to get circulated around Whitehall – and especially to those cobras in the Cabinet Office. All we've succeeded in doing is getting them stirred up about the Government's image. So, in future, I'm going to reword the reports somewhat – make them anodyne, throw something of a smokescreen over your more interesting activities. I just don't want to give them any more ammunition than I have to.'

'That's your privilege, sir,' said Ringrose, glinting. 'But I'd hate to feel I was being badmouthed or sabotaged in some subtle way by my own service. That would constitute a resigning matter on my part.'

'There's no question of it,' said the Commissioner hurriedly. 'Nothing shall interfere with your handling of the case. And I will jump on anyone who slanders you in my presence with both feet. All I ask is that you make no precipitate move, such as an arrest, that will force the issue into court and into the public domain before I have had an opportunity to lay out the results of your investigation for our political masters to chew over.'

'Chew over or suppress?'

The pained smile returned. 'Tom, let us please leave a delicate subject right there for the present. I am as unhappy as you are but in the real world we have to live with these people. They have many ways of damaging us if we earn their enmity. I'm just anxious to make sure you don't unwittingly stir the cobras into using their fangs. Rest assured, I have your best interests at heart.'

And you have your own best interests even closer to heart, thought Ringrose, disgusted, as he stood up to go.

He was still brooding in his office when a disappointed Firth returned from Hellespont Road. 'The birds have flown. They wiped the place clean. No garbage. No prints. Nothing. The neighbours on either side hadn't even been aware anyone had moved in. It was a classic spook job.'

'Then we might as well take over the place ourselves.'

'Just what I was thinking, guv'nor. It's certainly ideal as an OP for Boulder. Do we also get a phone-tap clearance?'

'We do not,' said Ringrose. Firth stared, surprised. 'The Home Secretary, in his vast wisdom, does not consider that we have produced sufficient cause.'

'Look, sir, we now have positive proof that we've not blundered into an IRA unit stalking Boulder for revenge. The Tilney Street camera company provides the link between what's been going on in Hellespont Road and the collection of the camera case from Gatti's. The descriptions of the two men involved in each incident match. We're definitely on the right track. Why are those Whitehall bastards fucking us about?'

'I think they're afraid of what we might find.'

'Come again, sir?'

'Remember, I still only know unofficially why Boulder left the Army. Government ministers were undoubtedly implicated in getting him off the hook. I think they're worried because we're drawing close enough to Boulder to spring the whole sordid story. If we nick him for involvement in the Conrad Niven conspiracy, how long do you think it would be before you read about his little Irish adventure in the Sunday papers? Someone in the know, but personally in the clear, would sell him out for sure.'

'So how do we proceed?'

'Softly, softly,' said Ringrose. 'But proceed we will. And let the chips fall where they may.'

'Yeah. Anywhere but on our heads,' prayed his deputy.

Ringrose slid a sheet of notepaper across his desk. 'What do you think of this?'

Firth leaned over to look. 'It's okay,' said Ringrose. 'You can pick it up. Forensics have had their go at it. It arrived here in this morning's post.'

The anonymous message, pasted to the notepaper in various typefaces, had been crudely cut from newspapers. It read: MR RUSHDIE IS IN NO DANGER FROM ME. I WAS TRICKED BY BRITISH, NOT IRANIANS. THE SNIPER.

Ringrose tossed across the envelope. 'City of London postmark. Cheap paper. Modelling glue. No prints. No saliva for DNA purposes. The writer wetted the stamp; he did not lick it.'

'Smart-arse crank making mischief?' suggested Firth. He dropped the sheet onto the desk. 'If we take this as genuine, we're dealing with a hired gun who was deployed by non-Iranian bounty-hunters possessing organizational skills and excellent intelligence.'

'There's nothing to exclude Captain Jack Boulder, is there?'

'He's a perfect fit,' said Firth. 'I wonder if he makes models?'

Chapter Forty

The police surveillance team moved in a day too late to observe Jack Boulder's singular activities.

Jack, still smarting at the operations conducted against his blameless relatives, sat over breakfast enumerating his successes so far in his counter-campaign. He knew that one of the conspirators, Rupert Strang, was – ostensibly – a member of one of the Security Services, as indeed, definitely, had been Nancy Tintagel. He also knew that Strang was linked to a Whitehall mandarin, Bulwer Tancred. They were connected to the guarded estate outside Frant in East Sussex.

Conclusion: it was time to find out more about Frant.

This time, Jack drove down in daylight. There were two pubs in the village and Jack tried them both. The locals were not inclined to chat freely to a stranger and Jack felt inhibited at asking outright about ownership of the high-walled property with its razor-wire and armed gateman.

He discovered the answer to his question pinned on the parish noticeboard. The most prominent name on the handwritten poster arrested him in his tracks as he wandered around the village green. It was that of Sir Gilbert Metzhagen of Fern Hall, Wadhurst Road, sponsor of the summer cricket tournament. The same Metzhagen of MetzCorp, aboard whose yacht Conrad Niven had spent his last hours.

This was too much of a coincidence. Jack stood stock-still, head buzzing. How much wider did this conspiracy spread? The implications were dizzying. Fern Hall simply had to be the place where Strang had taken Nancy Tintagel's corpse.

Jack buttonholed a passing villager, described the place he knew and asked the question. 'That's the place. Fern Hall,' confirmed an elderly man, pushing an old-fashioned iron-frame bike. 'It's been Sir Gilbert's British home for years. He's got houses all over the shop. Bought it off one of those families from the landed gentry that had gone broke. They tried to stay on in one wing by selling the place to the National Trust but the Trust wouldn't take it on. Too much upkeep and no income. Sir Gilbert came to the rescue. He gave the family more than it was worth. They asked if they could rent a wing, but he wasn't having any of that. He wanted to do the place up and have it for himself. They had to move out. Sir Gilbert does a lot for the village but he likes his privacy.'

There was no sign of the guard as Jack drove past the locked gate. But now he could see what he had missed in the dark. Chiselled into the mellow stonework of the gatepost were the words FERN HALL.

Jack parked where he had left the Saab before, changed into rubber boots, slipped into the field alongside the Hall and followed the wall round. He could find no gap in the razor-wire and there was only one rear gate that had not been bricked in. It was set into the wall and was made of unbudgeable sheet metal. A hop garden abutted the rear where the young vines were already curling up the rough strings.

At the edge of the field he made an interesting discovery. He walked up to a mounting platform, alongside which, in a cradle, were three pairs of the stilts that hop workers wear, strapped to their legs, so that they can attach the climbing strings to the overhead wires and train the vines upwards.

Jack looked round. The field was not being worked. He could hear distant tractors but no one was in sight. He took two stilts up to the platform, sat down strapped them on. He wriggled forward on his buttocks to the edge, lowered the poles to the ground and pulled himself upright. Steadying himself by clinging to the overhead wires, he took a practice walk along a hop row. He was twelve feet tall and a kid once more. He was a giant in seven-league boots. He was performing in the big top, his head up aloft with the sequined girl on the flying trapeze.

His strides became more daring as his thigh muscles grew accustomed to the strain. After much wobbling and near-disaster, he let go of the wire and managed four steps before he began to topple. He grabbed hold and tried again. In an hour his thighs were throbbing but he had mastered the trick of short steps to maintain a centre of balance.

Jack strode boldly back to the platform and unstrapped himself. Metzhagen's wall was high but even he could not prevent trees obeying the laws of nature by seeking the light. In several places they bent towards the wall and poked branches over the top. A number cleared the razorwire quite comfortably. Jack now knew how he could get in.

He felt that he had neared the centre of the web, had touched the black spider. But what would he find? What would a wealthy man like Metzhagen have gained from the death of the yacht guest he had so cunningly manoeuvred within sight of Jack's lethal eye? He had cold-bloodedly cast poor Conrad Niven in the role of clay pigeon, flung aloft to be shot out of the sky. And, equally cold-bloodedly, cast Jack as his killer. Even to ask himself the questions made Jack's fury return in a molten rush.

All the same, he drove home happier for the knowledge he had gained. What was next? Should he threaten Strang again? Or descend like an avenging Fury on Bulwer Tancred?

Chapter Forty-One

Bulwer Tancred saw Peter Hope-Casson alone. They stood on the curving path, admiring the sixteen-inch guns in their battleship grey aimed over the heads of visitors to the Imperial War Museum. They were on the unfashionable south side of the river where there was much less likelihood of their being seen together.

Tancred was not happy. 'The raids were only partially successful. At any rate, we turned up nothing to indicate that Boulder has committed anything to paper. But, of course, we don't have proof positive.' He sighed. 'It's most irritating, but the damned man is becoming increasingly sharp. He reacted like lightning when he learned that his mother's place had been turned over. Our Jack is beginning to know us rather too well for my own peace of mind.'

'So why don't we give the IRA the bugger's home address and tell them he did for McGurk.'

Tancred shook his head. 'It's too messy, Peter. We have to bear in mind the bigger picture. They'd probably have to activate a sleeper unit, they'd take ages doing a reconnoitre, and then they'd more likely than not make a hash of it and the peace process would really go up the spout. Our nincompoop political masters who covered up in the first place would be gravely embarrassed. All kinds of inconvenient facts might start to leak. We can't risk that.' He eyed the big guns with distaste. 'Even more to the point, if the IRA tried and missed, Captain Boulder with his trusty rifle is going to come looking for those who betrayed him – those who have already betrayed him once and tried to kill him twice. I wouldn't want to be in their Guccis, would you, Peter?' He smiled bleakly at the younger man. 'However, he has to go. We can't continue like this. The Scotland Yard reports are becoming increasingly opaque. God knows what Ringrose is really up to. He's almost as big a menace as Boulder.'

Hope-Casson's eyes shone with pleasurable anticipation. 'You want me to get him, then?'

Tancred sighed again. 'I fear so. Just remember what I've said and don't get caught, there's a good fellow.'

The upstairs front room in Hellespont Road from which Rafe Cummings and Peter Hope-Casson had maintained their observation on Jack Boulder's domestic activities was now occupied by two detective constables, Owen Sullivan and Adrian Glaister, from the surveillance team set up by Lionel Firth. They were somewhat less fastidious than the previous occupants had been: chewing-gum and chocolate-bar wrappers littered the floor.

They had the usual equipment for their task: network radio to maintain contact with every other officer in the team, binoculars, night glasses mounted on a tripod, and a zoom-lens camera. As the house was furnished, they also had a refrigerator, tea-making facilities and beds where they could take turns at napping.

At 9.30 p.m. they had logged Jack Boulder parking his Saab in the street and entering his house. He had not come out again and he had no callers. All his lights were out, as was every alternate street lamp, by midnight. This economy by the borough council had the effect of creating alternate pools of jaundice-yellow light and darkness from end to end of the slumbering street. Hellespont Road was a place for families and ordered lives.

Sullivan, who was keeping a desultory watch at 1.30 a.m., assumed correctly that Boulder had gone to bed. He glanced across the room at Glaister, who was snoring gently on his back with his mouth open. Apart from his loosened bootlaces, he was fully dressed and ready to go. The two officers were working a four-hours-on/four-hours- off watch. Sullivan would wake Glaister at two.

Sullivan was turning back to the window when he saw a movement, more a shifting of the darkness. A black car with no lights was moving slowly down the street, achieving invisibility and then visibility again as it progressed from light pool to light pool. A medium-sized saloon of no distinction, the vehicle passed Boulder's house, slid once again from light to sheltering dark, then stopped alongside Boulder's blue Saab.

Sullivan could only glimpse the subsequent action because it was taking place on the far side of the road. Through his light-intensifying night glasses, he saw the top of an opening door and a head emerge. The door was shut quietly and the car waited a few seconds before moving off as sedately as it had arrived.

Hellespont Road now appeared clear again but Sullivan knew that someone was now under Boulder's car attaching a tracker device that would send its signal up to a satellite then down to the policemen following Boulder from a safe distance.

Sullivan wrote in his log: 1.33 a.m. Technicals arrive.

The black car returned fifteen minutes later. Sullivan caught a fleeting glimpse of fair hair reflecting street light, the nearside passenger door opened briefly to readmit the electronics specialist, and the car glided silently away.

Sullivan conscientiously logged: 1.48 a.m. Technicals depart.

At 2 a.m., as scheduled, Sullivan shook awake a groaning Glaister and settled him in the window with a cup of tea. Before hitting the mattress himself, he made a routine radio check with the nearby control wagon. 'All quiet. Technicals have been and gone.'

There was a silence that remained unbroken for ten seconds. Over the hissing, crackling air, his sergeant's voice abruptly cut in, 'Say again?'

'All quiet. Technicals have been and gone,' repeated Sullivan.

Another silence followed. Once again his sergeant came on. 'Use the landline.' The voice was peremptory.

Sullivan looked at Glaister and gave a what's-up shrug. He picked up the bedside phone and dialled. His sergeant answered on the first ring. 'Sullivan, are you pissed? Did you say Technicals have been and gone?'

'They went fifteen minutes ago, Sarge.'

'Then how come they're still sitting here in the prairie schooner, fiddling with their little box of tricks?'

Sullivan digested this information and said, 'You mean, it didn't work? They've got to come round for a second try?'

'No, you dickhead. They haven't been round at all yet.'

'Then who was it who did a drop-off and pick-up at the target car within the last half-hour?'

The Sergeant's sarcasm disappeared. Sullivan was not really a dickhead. He said calmly, 'Sullivan, just tell me what went down.'

At the end of the brief recital, the Sergeant said, 'Oh, shit!' Then, rapidly, 'Sullivan, take a torch, go over to the car and see if there is any sign of tampering. Whatever you do, do not touch the vehicle. Do you understand that? Do *not* touch the vehicle. Make a visual check. Through the windows and underneath. BUT DO NOT TOUCH THE VEHICLE.'

Glaister was bewildered. 'What the fuck's going on?'

Sullivan said, 'Something's wrong but I don't know what.'

'Is the Sarge jerking your chain for a bit of fun? Does he think we're both asleep here?'

'Nah, he wouldn't do that and risk jeopardizing an operation like this. I've got an awful feeling I've dropped a bollock. Where's the torch?'

Sullivan let himself out of the house and padded across the road. He felt exposed. Any householder who happened to glance out of his window right now would immediately dial 999 and report a car thief at work.

He arched his body to avoid making contact with the Saab's metal sides and shone the torch through the rear window. A couple of magazines were scattered on the rear seat. There was nothing untoward in the footwell, as far as he could see. He worked his way from window to window, careful to follow his sergeant's edict. He could see nothing that ought not to be there.

There were no scuff marks on paintwork around the handles, or on the window rims where thieves usually inserted their long, thin, hooked blades.

There was nothing for it. He had to get down in the gutter. He was wearing a new pair of jeans.

First, Sullivan examined the dirt-encrusted underside from the front. This car needed a good hosing down. Still, dirt had its uses. It showed up where there had been tampering, if any.

He crawled along the nearside. Nothing.

He found what he had prayed he would not find when his torch beam swept the rear underside. A small square area had been swept clean of filth. It was such an efficient job that the droppings had not been left on the tarmac. In the square, scraped clean to expose the bare metal, hung a tin box that had once contained Oxo cubes. Two strips of insulating tape sealed the lid and the contraption had been attached to the car's underside by a round magnet.

'Christ Almighty!' said Sullivan, and rolled away.

Tom Ringrose had moved to the downstairs telephone to avoid disturbing his wife's sleep. George Medlicott, the anti-terrorist squad commander, called back after 4 a.m. 'I'm sorry, Tom. We couldn't do it without evacuating the street. There was no way of knowing in advance how much explosive the bastards had packed into the tin. I just couldn't risk blowing people out of their beds.'

'What was it?'

'Enough Semtex to send your Mr Boulder speeding on his way to a better life. Usual mercury tilt switch. I reckon that if he'd taken the car into town, the slope of Notting Hill Gate would have done the trick.'

'Your chaps okay?'

'Yeah, it took them forty minutes playing Bill and Ben, the Removal Men, but they did just fine.'

'Thank God. If they'd bought it, I think my guys on the spot would have cut their own throats without waiting for an order from me.'

Medlicott said quietly, 'Tom, if I have your solemn assurance that this is not Provo handiwork but is strictly confined to your investigation, I'm going to leave it to you. As you asked, I evacuated Boulder with all his neighbours and made sure they were so far back they couldn't see what was going on. Officially, it'll be a false alarm – suspicious parcel dropped under a car.'

'I owe you one, George. This Niven shooting is turning into a Chinese puzzle. I know Boulder's implicated – and it's not just Dawson's computers saying so – but who is trying to kill him, or why, has got me disappearing up my own fundament. Perhaps the Iranians hired him to do the job but he backed away.'

'Took the hit money without doing the business?'

'Could be, George. But they certainly found someone who could be Boulder's clone, although his bank account, as yet, doesn't show any sudden windfall from a dead aunt. Anyway, this little drama gives me a legitimate opportunity to meet him face to face. So far, I've kept my distance for the very good reason that he has ostensibly done nothing that would warrant a copper of my rank inviting him to tango.'

'I've eased your path, Tom. I interviewed him only briefly on the pavement. He's still under the impression it was just a frightener, nothing lethal. I told him to expect a senior officer to come calling later today.'

'How did he take that?'

George Medlicott paused before he answered. Eventually, he said, 'The word is "thoughtful". But, then, you and I both seem to have that effect on people, don't we?'

They were both too tired to raise much of a laugh. Tom Ringrose crawled blearily back into bed for another two hours' sleep. The muffled voice of Helen rose from the depths. 'A policeman's wife's lot is not a happy one.'

'You'll get no argument from me there,' said Tom, cuddling her warm back. He slid instantly into the welcoming land of counterpane.

'Marvellous!' said Helen, now wide awake.

Chapter Forty-Two

Ringrose and Firth had their heads together planning their tactics. 'Where do you want him braced, guv'nor?'

'At his home,' said Ringrose instantly. 'I want to get the feel of him at close range. You'd better ring him before he leaves for work.'

Jack Boulder was sitting cross-legged, breathing slowly and steadily with enormous control, when he heard their car draw up outside.

Jack opened his front door, affecting a casual pose, leaning against the jamb. He wore black chinos and a Canadian lumberjack shirt.

Ringrose and Firth introduced themselves, Firth even flashing his warrant card which Jack ignored. He was looking at Ringrose, who was lean, with his distinguishing lock of silver hair, and properly hawklike as every schoolboy imagined a famous detective to be. His photographs in the newspapers had been good likenesses.

Jack went ahead down the corridor, leaving Firth to close the door. Ringrose stopped to study the contents of a glass cabinet, on three shelves of which Jack's shooting trophies were arrayed. Some were so tall that they'd been placed on their sides. Above the cabinet hung a framed poster from an old movie. It showed the Hollywood actor Gary Cooper dressed as a First World War doughboy. The film title was *Sergeant York*.

Jack came back and stood beside Ringrose. 'My wife gave it to me to celebrate our tenth wedding anniversary. Sergeant York really existed, you know. He was just a hillbilly but he was a phenomenal self-taught marksman. I was hoping to see the movie sometime on television but I've never yet caught it.'

'It's an impressive poster,' said Ringrose. 'Was he better than you?'

'Who knows? You'd have to put us side by side in a trench and persuade a lot of Germans to volunteer as moving targets to get the answer to that.' Jack managed a grin. He added, 'Why don't you go into the sitting room? I've a pot of coffee on the hob.'

'That would be nice,' said Firth. 'We both take milk and sugar.'

While he was gone, the two detectives let their eyes rove the room. There were family photographs, but one, in a Victorian silver frame stood out: it was of Grace at a military race meeting, wearing a floaty apple-green organza dress with ribboned cartwheel hat. Young officers, in and out of uniform, formed an admiring half-circle around her. The picture said that Jack Boulder had captured the trophy, as he had so often on the shooting range.

The furniture was John Lewis traditional repro, nothing tatty but nothing valuable either. A needlepoint kit lay on the floor next to a rocker with a partly completed canvas draped over one arm. A self-assembly kit for a model of a Stealth bomber, in similar unfinished state, was scattered in a far corner. Firth strolled across. The glue was missing.

These humdrum artefacts, thought Ringrose, gave the impression that the Boulder family had fled the house in the face of some cataclysmic event.

Jack returned, with three china mugs, sugar bowl and milk jug on a tray. 'Help yourselves.' Ringrose and Firth, sitting shoulder to shoulder on a couch, made no move. They watched Jack drop into the rocker. The unfinished needlework fell to the carpet.

Jack had placed himself inadvertently in an adversarial position directly facing them. Still, the strong-boned face with the broken nose betrayed nothing except amiability.

The two detectives stared at him. The room faded; the face and body language were everything in an interrogation of this sort.

'Well, Jack,' Ringrose said quietly, 'what on earth made you think you could get away with it?'

They watched the brow rise and crease, the tiny tic appear at the right corner of his mouth, the athletic body stiffen. Amiability gave way to wariness. For a moment it seemed that he was about to speak, but instead he sipped his coffee.

'Get away with what?' He had to clear his throat to get the words out.

'Come on, Jack. Don't play innocent with us.'

'I'm not playing anything.'

Firth leaned forward, an encouraging expression on his sharp, ferret face. 'We thought you'd be proud of your achievement – happy to boast about it.'

Jack leapt up, leaving the chair rocking violently. He moved to the fireplace and rested an elbow on the mantelpiece. Four eyes lancing through him were more than he could endure face-on. 'I'm sorry. I don't understand. What have I got to boast about?'

'The fantastic marksmanship,' said Ringrose. 'I'm told that only three or four men in this country – perhaps in the world – would stand a chance of pulling off such a coup.'

'Coup?' Despite his obvious efforts at self-control, they could see that his upper lip was beginning to shine.

Firth leaned forward again. 'Jack, there's no need to be defensive. It happened in another country.'

They watched him take a long swig from his mug. His face was a study in concentration. The two detectives left the air dead between them and him. They waited for him to fill the void.

Finally, he said, 'Don't you think you ought to be more specific? What happened in another country? What are you talking about?'

'Don't you remember, Jack? You took your sniper rifle and you killed a man,' said Ringrose. 'No doubt you had your reasons and we'd like to hear them.'

Jack Boulder desperately wished they'd give him respite by drinking their coffee. But the gently steaming mugs stayed on the tray, unmilked, unsugared, growing colder. 'You're not drinking your coffee,' he blurted out, immediately wishing he hadn't.

'The coffee can wait,' said Firth. 'Tom here is right. We'd like to hear your side of the story. No one does what you did without some justification. Just tell us how it began. Look. See.' Firth held out his hands, palms up. 'We're not taking notes and we're not tape-recording you.'

Jack put down his mug on the mantelpiece. 'All right,' he fenced. 'Cards on the table. You tell me what I'm supposed to have done and, if I can, I'll give you a briefing.'

'A briefing, Jack?' Ringrose raised an eyebrow. 'That sounds very pukka. We're just having a friendly chat about the man you shot.'

'This doesn't sound like a friendly chat to me. Anyway, I don't know how many men I've shot. I was on active service in the Gulf and in Northern Ireland, you know.'

'Ah,' said Firth, winking slyly. 'But you were also in another country, weren't you? That wasn't active service, was it?'

Jack was now agitated, shifting from foot to foot. 'I'm beginning to think I need a lawyer,' he said flatly.

Both detectives went through the pantomime of turning to each other and evincing surprise. 'What have we said?' asked Firth.

They knew now that he wasn't going to crack. He was on his feet, a powerful presence still holding himself in check.

Ringrose bent forward and poured milk into his lukewarm coffee. 'Jack, we do know about Sean McGurk,' he said mildly.

They watched the tension flow out of him like an evaporating miasma. He said, 'Would you excuse me for a moment? I need a pee.'

He left the room, closing the door behind him. Ringrose nodded at his aide, who moved silently to the door and opened it an inch to listen.

'Well, he's the man,' said Ringrose with certitude. 'That, at least, is a relief to know. I hope he hasn't trotted off to put a bullet through his brain.'

'No, he's in the bog,' said Lionel Firth, his ear cocked. 'If I crept nearer, I bet I'd hear him having a second breakfast.'

Chapter Forty-Three

Lionel Firth was wrong about that. Jack Boulder was still holding on to his breakfast – just. He ran cold water in the basin and repeatedly scooped it up in his cupped hands and dashed it against his face. The serenity of Zen wasn't proving much help in confrontation with these two.

They knew! THEY KNEW! They had been teasing, playing with him like cats with a ball of wool. Grace's agonized pleas for him not to destroy his family rang in his ears. He had to fight himself, get a grip. He was appalled at how overwhelming the compulsion had been to tell them everything and purge himself of the corroding guilt.

Jack slowly dried his face as he struggled to control his breathing. In the mirror his face still looked flushed and his eyes over-bright – the eyes of a man against a wall with a mind working furiously, seeking a line of escape.

He flushed the lavatory and, heavy-hearted, went back.

Ringrose was seated as before but Firth was by the fireplace, which forced Jack to return to the rocker.

Firth loomed over him and said, 'Tell us about McGurk, Jack.'

He shrugged. 'Irish terrorist. He's dead now.'

'Yes, and you shot him.'

Jack felt on safer ground. 'If you know all about Sean McGurk then you know I'm not permitted to speak about this – not even to Scotland Yard detectives. If you want more information, you'll have to apply to the Ministry of Defence.'

'Yes, but it's not the Ministry of Defence that has to look after you now, is it, Jack? Your troubles have become our concern.'

They were still saying one thing and meaning another. Jack said, 'What troubles do I have?'

'Your casual attitude surprises us,' said Ringrose. 'If it were me that the IRA was trying to bump off, I think I'd be a little more concerned than you appear to be. I mean, look at you. Making coffee and not spilling it. Dressed as if you're off for a good day's fishing.'

'Who says the IRA's trying to get me?'

'Well, aren't they? That wasn't just a parcel of dog shit placed under your car last night. That was just a fib for Joe Public. Your little present was Semtex, enough to blow you to Kingdom Come the moment you drove that car up a hill. If a passer-by hadn't spotted someone tampering with your car, by tonight little pieces of you would be hanging from the roadside trees.'

They both watched his head sag. They knew exactly what he was thinking. 'Just suppose your beautiful wife and your sons had been in the back,' said Ringrose, snatching the silver-framed photograph and thrusting it at him. 'You wouldn't want us to apply to the Ministry of Defence for permission to go after the bastards who did it, would you?'

Jack rocked like a man only half-conscious. They stopped questioning and waited. Finally, Jack said, 'The IRA don't know about me — not unless there's been a leak.'

Ringrose was on the attack immediately. 'And that's another puzzling thing about you, Jack. We're not so sure the IRA's responsible, either. In the bad old days, after an incident like last night's little drama, their routine was to telephone a newspaper or news agency, use an agreed code word to establish authenticity and claim credit. This time there's been no sign of them putting their hand up for the job. Neither did they give the usual advance warning of a random act of terrorism.'

Jack was still staring at the carpet, locked in his own thoughts.

Ringrose said, 'Look at me, Jack. Tell us who's trying to kill you — and isn't too bothered about you taking your wife and kids with you.'

'Is that what you want, Jack? One big family-sized grave? Four names on the headstone?' added Firth.

Jack came to his feet, shouting, 'For Chrissake, isn't this bad enough without you two rubbing it in? My family's in no danger.'

Ringrose said levelly, 'That brings us to another interesting point, Jack. Where are they?'

'They're on holiday at the seaside.' He was now sullen and the answer came grudgingly.

'During term-time? Isn't that hurting your boys' education?'

'My wife's a supply teacher. She keeps them up to date.'

Firth said, 'You're lying, Jack. We think you sent your family away because you anticipated something like last night's parcel delivery. We think there are people out to get you in the worst possible way. We're only baffled that you didn't come to us sooner and ask us to protect you and yours while we hunted the bastards down.'

Jack tried weakly to return the interrogation to the IRA. 'Once you've served in Northern Ireland, you have to spend the rest of your life being careful. That's all. You can't keep running to the police every time you hear someone sing "When Irish Eyes Are Smiling".'

Firth said, looking up at Jack who was half a head taller, 'If you want to go with a load of old bollocks like that, it's your funeral. But we don't think the people who are after your guts have Irish accents at all.'

'How the hell can you know that?'

Ringrose moved in for the kill. 'Because the people who pulled that very old trick on your mother and your in-laws spoke very good English as they impersonated hospital doctors and traffic policemen.'

'Yes,' said Firth. 'Slipped your mind, did it, Jack? Thought we wouldn't get to hear about it in London?'

'Well, it *did* slip my mind,' said Jack, still sullen. 'What has any of that got to do with me?'

'I thought you were an intelligent man,' said Ringrose bitterly. 'We came here to help you. But all you've served up is coffee and hogwash. I ask you again: who is trying to kill you? And why?'

'It has to be the IRA,' muttered Jack doggedly. 'And you know why. It's because of McGurk.'

Ringrose sprang up angrily from the couch. 'Come on, Lionel. Let's get out of here. This man isn't worth the saving.'

He strode to the door, wheeled round to face Jack and flung his card on the floor. 'The number of my direct line is on that. I believe you'll need it quite soon.'

Firth, too, fired a parting shot. 'When we're gone, just spare a thought for this: suppose, by chance, they get your wife and children but they don't get you. Suppose you stay alive and healthy and there are only three names on that headstone. Have a nice day!'

They slammed out of the house and Jack slumped with his head in his hands.

Outside, Ringrose instantly dropped the angry pose. 'That's rattled his cage well and truly. Despite my mug having been all over the papers for weeks, he didn't once ask why a job for the anti-terrorist squad was being conducted by a policeman known from Land's End to John O'Groats to be in charge of the Conrad Niven shooting.'

'The giveaway. The clincher,' said Firth with great satisfaction. 'We're on the way. Victor Massillon should send us a crate of champagne.'

Chapter Forty-Four

Paul Kaiser of the CIA had his Morgan with the strapped-down bonnet parked ready for the off. 'Weekending in Wiltshire,' he explained to Ringrose, who could only boggle at the mental picture of this elongated American inserting himself into the nippy little sports car.

Once again they were outside the Grenadier, sipping drinks on a perfect summer's evening.

'The boss sends you his best,' said Kaiser, 'and wants you to know that the Tehran situation is unchanged. No one has come forward with a legitimate claim on the bounty.' He contrived to look sly, a considerable feat for someone so open-faced. 'But he thinks you should know that there has been another fascinating development down among the ayatollahs.'

'Oh?'

'Are you aware that your government, despite all its professed policy of keeping the Iranian regime at arm's length, has an unofficial delegation in Tehran at this very moment?'

'For what purpose?'

'Well, their cover, if blown, will be that the purpose of the visit is purely cultural. In fact, they're a hard-nosed bunch of businessmen being shepherded around by a Foreign Office team, not one of whom admits to being anything other than an interpreter.'

Ringrose was genuinely puzzled. 'Why should this be of any interest to me?'

'Because,' said Kaiser, sighing at his obtuseness, 'the offing of Conrad Niven has put the Iranians in a very sunny frame of mind. If there are British businessmen who want to drive the proverbial coach and horses through the trade embargoes, our excitable friends are ready to co-operate.'

'With the connivance of the British government?'

'Don't be naïve, Commander. You won't find a ministerial fingerprint anywhere – certainly not since the Matrix Churchill fiasco when even Pie Eyes couldn't save 'em.'

'Pie Eyes?' Ringrose was out of his depth.

'Public Interest Immunity Certificates,' explained Kaiser, who now did not seem so corn-fed and innocent. 'When you British can't wrap something in the Official Secrets Act, your political masters clamp down on potential trouble by issuing those extremely useful pieces of paper. They prevent official documents being seen by the lower orders. That's how they save their asses – they make sure the skeletons remain in the family vault by claiming an overriding national interest.'

Kaiser looked with some concern at Ringrose. 'Forgive me, but a man in your position should know about gems like Pie Eyes. How do you survive in the thickets of the forest?'

'I still don't see how any of this touches my investigation. I steer well clear of Whitehall politics.'

The CIA operative placed his glass on a window-sill and looked earnestly into Ringrose's troubled face. 'Commander – may I call you Tom? – my boss is very fond of you and doesn't want to see you shafted. He senses that things unethical are going on behind your back.'

'Like what?'

'Like that Bentinck dame. Are we correct in thinking you asked the FBI if they could persuade her to come to England to talk to you, and to stand by to put the finger on the man you know as James Canning?'

'Is the Agency spying on the FBI now?' Tom Ringrose marvelled at the secret complexities of American life.

'What do you think, Tom? Would you trust those arseholes since J. Edgar Hoover proved to be the biggest blackmailer of the American ruling class that the world has ever seen?'

'All right. So I asked for Betty Bentinck to be sent over.'

'Well, don't hold your breath.'

'Oh?' said Ringrose, for a second time. 'Why's that?'

Kaiser was enjoying himself. 'Because she's been signed to a fat movie contract and rushed off to the Sawtooth Mountains of Idaho where filming has begun.'

'Yes, that's bad luck,' said Ringrose.

'Correction,' said Kaiser. 'Not bad luck, Tom. We think it was malice aforethought.'

'Oh?' He had to stop saying 'Oh' like an idiot.

'We can confirm that your embassy people in Washington have been nosing around, asking about her "availability". Was she certain she could identify the guy, et cetera. They were told she was available and, yes sir, she'd be able to nail him. We thought this curious. After all, we were well aware you were already liaising with the Bureau and asking similar questions. Why the fuck did the British Embassy need to poke their long noses in?'

'I see what you mean,' said Ringrose thoughtfully.

'There's more, Tom.'

Ringrose just managed to stop himself saying 'Oh' yet again.

'Who do you think personally flew to Hollywood a short while after your embassy learned dear Betty was rarin' to go? And who do you think personally signed her up and had his Gulfstream IV shag-in-the-sky jet fly her to the Idaho location and out of the clutches of those nasty Limey policemen? Who do you think paid off the second female lead – to the tune of two hundred thousand dollars – so that Betty could move in and have gainful employment?'

'Go on,' said Ringrose, 'I'm all ears.'

'It was none other than that Metzhagen guy, Tom. The same Metzhagen who was Conrad Niven's host on the boat on the fateful day. He's the principal shareholder in the company making the picture. Doesn't it all strike you as more than a coincidence?'

Ringrose sipped his drink and mulled over the revelation. 'It could be a publicity stunt,' he offered. 'After all, Betty Bentinck is currently in the headlines. Perhaps Sir Gilbert just saw the opportunity to capitalize on her notoriety.'

'It's OK by us if you want to believe that, Tom. And Jack Kennedy was really a virgin. The actress who got the shove had been filming for ten days. They had to scrap every scene in which she figured. The cost was enormous but Metzhagen is personally footing the bill. As costly publicity stunts go, it's up there with the hunt for the actress to play Scarlett O'Hara.'

Tom Ringrose did not know what to make of any of it. It was too easy to fall into paranoia during this type of investigation. But he had to admit, reluctantly, that there were too many coincidences flying around for comfort. Was he really being shafted from above? And if so, why?

They drained their glasses and Ringrose watched fascinated as Kaiser, immaculate in a crisp linen suit, fitted himself into the Morgan. His knees were almost level with the dashboard, even with the bucket seat right back. Two tennis racquets and an overnight bag were visible in the rear, together with a bunch of flowers and a shiny package tied with a gold ribbon. Presents, no doubt, to facilitate the charm offensive on his hostess-to-be. Tom felt a twinge of envy. Youth really was wasted on the young.

'Thanks for taking the time,' he said. 'And please convey my gratitude to Mr Bishop. If anything else comes your way, I'd like to know.'

'Depend on it,' said his new-found CIA friend. 'I'm getting quite intrigued myself. I'd love to know where it's all headed. You're on my dance card now, Tom, and I'm saving the last waltz for you. Don't let the ayatollahs grind you down!'

With that and a cheery wave, Paul Kaiser vroomed out into Wilton Crescent and headed for his weekend pleasures, leaving Tom Ringrose to return their empty glasses to the bar.

Chapter Forty-Five

Jack Boulder was not deceived. If the watchers had ever gone, they had now returned. He did not believe for a second that a passer-by had stumbled upon the bomb being planted. The watchers, he felt sure, had inadvertently saved his life.

Then he had another, more creative, thought. Perhaps there had been no bomb at all. Perhaps the alarming events of the night had been an elaborate charade, staged to rattle him and trigger a panicked confession.

How could he know? But he dare not take the chance.

He strolled to a public callbox to telephone Grace, his neck prickling at the thought of the eyes, real or imagined, trained upon him. He made no attempt either to look for or shake off a tail.

Grace was breathless. 'The little monsters are wearing me out,' she puffed. 'I bought them a baseball set because they've been getting bored hanging around the house. When they're not having lessons, it's a job to keep them amused. I don't like them straying too far.'

'I miss you,' said Jack miserably. 'Do you still love me – just a little?'

'I've never stopped loving *you*, you big wally. It's some of the crazy things you do that I don't love.' Her tone softened. 'Jack, we all love you and we all miss you. How much longer is this terrible business going on?'

He decided not to mention the bomb or Ringrose's visit. 'There's something I have to do overnight but I thought I might drive up later in the day.'

Grace sounded delighted. He could hear off-stage noises. 'The boys want to talk to you. I can't hold them off. See you around tea-time, then?'

Jack had five minutes of inane conversation with his boisterous sons before his phonecard ran out of units. 'It's swimming in the sea for everyone when I get there! No excuses accepted for absence on parade!' he yelled as the connection broke. The last thing he heard was Mal wailing in mock horror at the prospect of plunging into the icy North Sea.

Jack stood under the phone canopy laughing. With a sudden heart-stab, he realized he had not laughed wholeheartedly in many weeks. That was what They had done for him.

He spent the day in devious pursuits. He went to the club as usual, sent Joe Carsby out to a City hardware shop on his behalf, and openly returned home at six p.m.

The watchers – if there were any – saw him drag out a hose and water his tiny front garden. Then he went inside and locked his front door, ostensibly home for the night. He did not go near his parked Saab.

After a quick meal, Jack took his holdall, went over the back wall, waved to the Rhys family, and headed for the local car-hire depot he had telephoned earlier to reserve a Range Rover.

By seven thirty he was on the way to Frant, leaving Ringrose's men patiently watching his empty home and his nobbled car.

He did not get the first inkling that his plan was destined to take an unconsidered twist until he had passed through the village and turned into the Wadhurst road. He found himself in a slow-moving column of traffic that seemed to consist largely of shiny limousines. Some were self-importantly flying pennants. Jack overtook the first three. All the occupants were in evening dress. Sir Gilbert Metzhagen was having a party.

'Damn!' said Jack, driving past slowly and observing the cars being checked through the gate of Fern Hall.

This time, he did not leave his vehicle in sight of the road. He drove the Range Rover round the estate's perimeter and parked alongside the hop stringers' platform. He sat pondering his options as the last of the daylight faded into purple. At least he could recce the grounds.

He pulled on his black overalls and blacked his cheeks and forehead with commando cream. He left the Cobray but took the Glock and a scope in a small backpack. With the rope that Joe Carsby had bought for him that day looped around his neck, Jack strapped himself to the stilts and did a tentative practice walk, making his way along the hop field but staying within grabbing reach of the wire until he was opposite a section of the Fern Hall wall where an oak had pushed a sturdy branch out of the gloom of a coppice and over the boundary into the open.

To reach it, Jack would have to cross, unsupported, an open space of some fifteen yards. He calculated that would mean thirty short steps, any one of which could topple him onto his arse in the dirt.

He shuffled round until he was facing the wall, drew a deep breath and set out. The first five steps went well. He wavered on the sixth when the left stilt sank a fraction lower than its twin into the earth, and eased it upward, swayed, and regained control. He counted twenty-eight more gut-churning steps before he was under the tip of the branch and could raise his arm over his head to steady himself. His thighs throbbed and he was sweating inside the thick overall.

He moved in closer to the wall and to the thicker end of the branch, pulling it downward to test its strength. Could it take his weight plus that of the stilts as he hauled himself upward? At best, it would be a clumsy manoeuvre. He took a firm grip, chinned the branch and swung his hugely extended left leg up and over until it was lodged on the tree. The other stilt dangled as he heaved himself up into a sitting position. The branch creaked but held. He leaned forward to peer beneath. Good. He was still eighteen inches clear of the razorwire.

Jack unbuckled the stilts and let them drop to the ground. He sat still for a minute – he had not come this far without making a certain amount of noise – and listened for evidence of an alarm having been raised but all he could hear was distant music.

He shuffled himself sideways and vanished into the density of the tree on the far side of the wall. He listened again. Nothing. He looped the rope round a branch, let it dangle alongside the trunk, then lowered himself into Sir Gilbert Metzhagen's lair.

He flitted from cover to cover, edging nearer to the music, but discovered that the woodland and undergrowth petered out three hundred yards from the house, which was a finely restored Georgian mansion. Here, the well-tended landscaping began.

At any other time it would have been a sight to enchant him. Every window glowed with golden light against the darkening mauves, purples and oranges of the night sky. Thick candles in glass bowls lit the terraces and lawns, which were thronged with Metzhagen's elegant guests. The drive was lined with flambeaux, lighting the way to the parking area. Servants bearing silver trays of drinks and platters of food made constant traffic from the two marquees pitched on the far side of the house. A string orchestra, at the shallow end of the vast swimming pool, was playing under the stars. Jack spotted peacocks wandering the immaculate parterre garden. Some of the guests were trying to tempt them with morsels of food.

He wriggled his way as near to the action as he dared and settled down with his 'scope. Within the hour, he had spotted at least a score of famous faces – actors, two cabinet ministers, various television personalities – and Rupert Strang, who was accompanied by a typical upper-class dreadnought, a woman with a spare body, iron jawline and thrusting nose. Jack assumed she was his wife. The pair of them, he saw, were on chummy terms with one of the ministers, which reinforced his fears as to the power of the people he was up against.

He wormed his way into the rhododendrons for a better view of the terrace. He had not yet seen Metzhagen. Dislodged petals fell onto him, improving his camouflage, he thought, which comforted him – he had identified a number of security men prowling the party's edges, whispering into handheld radios.

Suddenly Jack heard voices drawing near. He took a deep breath and froze.

There was a pleading, urgent note in the man's voice. The woman was giggling. Jack turned his head slowly. They were only six feet away from him.

She was a blonde of pallid prettiness, dressed in a pastel cream minidress and black Lycra tights that shimmered in the gloaming. Jack shivered. Those legs reminded him of his dream, the mysterious woman crossing and uncrossing her legs.

Her escort was a well-built jock, fair hair falling over his forehead. He had one arm round her bare shoulder and was attempting to turn her towards him.

She was saying, 'Peter, we can't do it here. If we get caught, he'll chuck me out. And he'll devise something quite horrible for you. You know what a bastard he can be.'

But Peter was beyond caution. 'Fuck him. We're safe here.' He pushed her further into the shadows cast by the bushes. She wailed, 'Stay on the grass!' But he swept the bootlace straps off her shoulders and tugged the dress down to her waist. She was not wearing a brassière and his mouth immediately zeroed in on her right nipple.

Her head tilted back and she gasped, 'I thought I said no.' But the man wasn't listening. Jack watched him pull off her dress and lay her on her back. Her tights and pants were soon a crumpled heap four feet from Jack's nose. The man's clothes followed.

Jack was beginning to feel he should be arrested as a Peeping Tom yet he dared not turn away his gaze in case he was heard. Also, he was fascinated. He had never in his life witnessed a couple copulate. Now they had surrendered to sheer animal lust.

When she came, her partner had to clap a hand over her mouth to muffle her scream and they rolled over, nearer to Jack but oblivious of anything but themselves. Until Jack risked an almost imperceptible change of position to counter the onset of cramp.

Instantly, Peter's head turned. He said, 'What was that noise?' He seemed to be staring directly at Jack. And, for the first time, Jack had a full view of his face. Peter was the suit he had assaulted, the man who had accompanied Rupert Strang to Gatti's Repository to recover Nancy Tintagel's body.

Without waiting for his companion's reply, Peter pushed her away and leapt, naked, to his feet. He looked dangerous.

'It's all right, old boy,' whispered Jack. 'We're only doing what you're doing. Mum's the word, hey?'

'Oh, my God!' said the blonde.

'Shit!' said Peter.

They brushed themselves down hurriedly and scrambled into their clothes. They obviously had no intention of confronting him in the bushes and Jack returned the Glock to his backpack. He last saw them sauntering casually towards the pool, chatting politely like people who had only recently met.

'Phew!' Jack fell back and studied the underside of the rhododendrons. He decided to change his observation point, in case friend Peter decided to tell the security men that something funny was going on in the bushes. He backed away into the darkness and continued to pace round the periphery of the parkland.

At last Jack pinpointed Metzhagen, recognizing him immediately from photographs published in the press. His original intention had been to get into the house and confront the magnate, let him know that his involvement in the death of Conrad Niven had leaked from the circle of secrecy. Frighten him. Find out why Niven had had to die. But with all these people thronging the grounds and house, that wasn't possible.

Through his 'scope, Jack watched Metzhagen holding court on a balustraded stone stairway leading up to the terrace. He was a forceful-looking man of late middle years and middle height, with dark brows, an almost swarthy pampered face, a shock of iron-grey hair and expressive continental manners. He had been born in Hungary but was a naturalized British subject. As if to offer grateful thanks for his citizenship, this owner of film studios and heavy-engineering companies was renowned for his support of charities close to the hearts of members of the Royal Family. He owned his own polo team, had twice been an overnight guest at Windsor Castle and had accompanied the Duke of Edinburgh on a voyage of the royal yacht *Britannia*, the purpose of which had been to stimulate trade in the Middle East.

Jack studied this paragon closely. He wore a white tuxedo, with a burgundy red cummerbund that matched the rose in his lapel. His audience was attentive. He was making them laugh.

Frustrated, Jack knew that he could achieve nothing more by hiding in the bushes. But at least he had succeeded in pressing one more piece into the jigsaw. He had a man named Peter to add to the list of conspirators.

Jack withdrew silently to the oak tree and climbed up the rope.

As his plan to jump Metzhagen had aborted, he'd be able to get to Southwold earlier. He'd ring in the morning to alert Grace.

They leaped on him as he opened the driver's door of the Range Rover. A single blow behind the left ear and he remembered no more.

Chapter Forty-Six

Ringrose and Firth had both forsaken Saturday at home, the garden and the cricket – and, with deplorable lack of remorse, the obligatory carrying of the week's family shopping.

Their hangout, away from the usual Yard pubs, was the bar of the nearby St James's Hotel. They supped their pints and brooded.

'I just know we're being stitched up,' said Ringrose. 'At every turn this investigation has run into the footprints of the Security Services. I get intimations of a parallel world, where our mirror images are busy diving and ducking and making identical inquiries.'

'Matter and anti-matter,' offered Firth. 'If the stuff collides, there's an almighty explosion.'

'Exactly,' said Ringrose. 'We never quite touch them and they never quite touch us. I've made repeated applications to the Co-ordinating Committee, stressing the evidence of Security Service interference. Each time the Co-ordinator comes back with smarmy assurances of complete co-operation from Five and Six but always coupled with complete denial of any involvement.'

'Lying bastards,' said Firth, wiping foam from his upper lip.

Ringrose had never imparted to a soul, not even to his loyal deputy, details of his long-standing friendship with Jake Bishop of the CIA. He was not about to start now but he said, 'I can't put a finger on Five or Six. Can't prove they've told me a single porky. But I do know that Six and the Foreign Office are withholding information from us.'

'Oh?' said Firth, looking up. He'd thought he knew every detail of their investigation.

'Don't ask,' said Ringrose, signalling the barman for two more pints. 'It's information from Tehran. The killers still haven't come forward to claim the money on Conrad Niven's head. What's more, the Iranians don't seem thrown by this. It's as if they're not expecting a claimant. Remember those television pictures of the money in US dollars being displayed in a glass box as the ultimate temptation? Well, I'm told the box is now empty. The money has gone back into their government's foreign currency reserves.'

'Does the FO know about this?'

'That's the point. They almost certainly do, yet this interesting piece of intelligence has never been passed down the Whitehall line to us. A serious omission, wouldn't you say? One that might be germane to our work?'

'What does the Co-ordinator say about it?'

Ringrose let his arm rise and fall in a gesture of frustration. 'If I ask, all sorts of interested parties will want to know how I got this information in the first place. And I'm unable to tell them. So if I'm keeping secrets from them, they'll feel justified in keeping secrets from me.'

'It's a bitch,' agreed Firth. 'I wish we knew who's on whose side.'

'It was made clear to me early on from upstairs that the Government would not welcome us producing a UK citizen as the guilty party. I think the cold shoulder we're getting is a sign that our political masters have put on their Teflon suits.'

'They're going to be awfully pissed off if we feel Jack Boulder's collar.'

'*When* we feel Jack Boulder's collar,' said Ringrose grimly. 'There's no doubt in my mind.'

They remained silent while the barman placed their beers on the mats, took their empties and went away.

Lionel said, 'Have you brought Victor Massillon up to date yet?'

Ringrose heaved a deep sigh. 'No. I'm already doing to him what Whitehall is doing to us. If I tell him our suspicions, the French will be dancing in the street and leaking to their newspapers before I've put down the phone. I can just see the headline: "Perfidious Albion. Niven Suspect is an Englishman. France Exonerated".'

Once again they fell silent, both men deep in thought. There they would have remained, glumly sipping beer except that, simultaneously, they felt a presence at their backs.

Both policemen turned and groaned in unison. Beaming at them were the chubby, irrepressible features of Peter Lancing, the *Daily Mail*'s ever-diligent crime reporter.

'Tom, Lionel,' said Lancing, blithely ignoring the less than cordial acknowledgement of his presence.

'Peter, isn't Saturday normally a day off for a daily-paper man? Shouldn't you be doing your expenses or something?'

Lancing chuckled, signalling the barman to fetch sustenance. 'There's no day off, Tom, when the big one's running. Even my swindle sheet has to take second place.'

In the past week, Tom had binned twice-daily requests for an interview from Peter Lancing. Their relationship was actually a friendly one – Ringrose and Lancing had known each other since Ringrose had been a detective sergeant at Savile Row. But there were times when it was wiser for senior officers not to be seen consorting with the press.

Contrary to screen depiction of crime reporters as loutish hacks, Ringrose knew that the best, and in this he included Lancing, were people of acute intelligence and perception. He was also wryly aware that operators of Lancing's standing were paid as much as an assistant commissioner and seemed to have inexhaustible expenses with which to seduce meagrely paid innocent policemen.

Lancing proceeded now to deploy his financial strength. He clicked his fingers. 'Let me buy us something a little more stimulating on the auspicious occasion of this chance meeting. Barman, a bottle of Pol Roger, if you please.'

Firth scoffed, 'Chance meeting, my arse. Have you been following us Peter?'

Lancing placed a meaty hand over his heart and raised his eyes to heaven in the manner of a Victorian tragedian. One of the secrets of his success was that no one could be angry with him for long. 'I never cease to be amazed at the wickedness of some people's thoughts,' he said to God.

The barman popped the cork and the champagne bubbled into the flutes. 'Don't think this is going to get you anywhere,' said Ringrose. 'There's bugger-all we can tell you about anything at this stage.'

Lancing was not dismayed. 'I know that, Tom,' he said gently, as if he were rebuking a geriatric for wetting the bed. 'For more than a week now, I've been trying to tell *you* something. But all I've seen of you has been a very cold shoulder. My feelings are hurt.'

'Just a minute. I must find my handkerchief,' said Firth.

'All right, Peter,' said Ringrose. 'We're listening. But if this is a con in the hope that we'll accidentally drop you a morsel, we won't be best pleased.'

They watched him expectantly as he took a deep swig of champagne. 'It has come to my knowledge,' he began carefully, 'that your prime suspect is a man, the evidence pointing to British nationality, who goes nowhere without his Panama hat jammed down over his eyes.'

Firth could not quite disguise his look of concern, which Lancing caught. 'Don't worry. I wouldn't print anything to foul your pitch. I'd always come to you first.'

Tom nodded. He knew that was true enough. In the past, Lancing had sacrificed exclusive stories rather than prejudice an investigation. His reward came later when no harm would come of the news being broken. Then Lancing justifiably called in his markers.

He went on, 'I had a couple of weeks off in May. Took the wife and little princess down to the South of France for a breather. The film festival was taking place along the coast in Cannes and the *Mail*'s show-business man fixed us up with invitations to an all-night festival party at that chateau with all the peculiar statuary in La Napoule. The little princess wanted to see some movie stars in the flesh. It was an eleven o'clock start and we'd just parked the car near the marina when I spotted a woman I know very well.'

'How well is "very well"?' asked Firth. 'Was she a once-a-week Legover Lulu, or what?'

Lancing was not offended. 'Nothing like that, worse luck. She's a woman I sometimes go hunting with.'

'Another reporter?' asked Ringrose.

'Sorry, I'm not putting this as well as I might. Perhaps because I'm still puzzled. Her name is – was – Nancy Tintagel. She's Lord Tintagel's daughter – you know, the old politician. She and I sometimes went out with the Eridge.'

The two detectives looked blank.

'The Southdown and Eridge Hunt down on the Kent–East Sussex border. Fox-hunting.'

The two policemen looked incredulously at Peter Lancing's portly frame. 'You? Fox-hunting?' said Ringrose.

'Now I've heard everything,' said Firth.

Lancing grinned self-consciously. 'It takes a bloody big horse, I can tell you! The local fox population voted me Horseman of the Year for my kindness and consideration in not following too closely.'

Ringrose and Firth shook their heads in disbelief. Ringrose said, 'Give us time to adjust, Peter. But do carry on.'

'Anyway, Nancy was about a hundred yards away and I shouted, "Tinny," her nickname. It was as if I'd kicked her in the back. She stiffened, so I knew she'd heard me. But she didn't turn round. Instead, she grabbed the arm of her male companion and hurried him away. Almost dragged him, actually. It couldn't have had anything to do with me personally. I was a voice in the dark – could have been any of her chums. So I assumed she wasn't at home to anybody – thought she was on holiday with someone else's husband. I chuckled to myself and thought no more about it.'

Ringrose said, 'Peter, is this getting us anything other than a glass of champagne?'

'I'm coming to that. In the next three weeks, two things happened that started to ring funny-business bells in my head. First, via Paris, I learned of police interest in the man who pulls his straw hat down to his ears. Nancy's fancy piece had a Panama pulled hard down to the point where he looked like a comedian. And it was eleven at night, for chrissake.'

'Describe him,' said Firth.

'As I said, I only glommed a back view. But he was tall, well-built, wearing a light-coloured suit. A bit crumpled so it was probably linen.'

'Age?'

'Difficult at that distance. But from the easy way he moved I'd certainly put him at under forty.'

Ringrose and Firth stared at him. Lancing now had their full attention. He was, they knew, an observant man. If he hadn't turned delinquent and gone into popular journalism in his youth, he'd have made a successful detective.

'What was the other thing? You mentioned two,' Ringrose reminded him.

'This happened,' said Lancing. From his inside pocket he produced a clear plastic wallet containing the *Daily Telegraph*'s account of the inquest on Nancy Tintagel. He pushed aside a dish of nuts and laid the wallet on the bar. The two detectives craned forward and read the neswsprint through the plastic.

'So?' prompted Ringrose.

'So the report says Nancy was killed on the sixth of May.'

'So?' said Ringrose again.

'So how come I saw her alive on the ninth in the South of France?'

'The *Telegraph* must have made a mistake. It's a misprint.'

Lancing pursed his lips and shook his large, round head.

'No, Tom. I checked with the coroner's officer. The *Telegraph* report is an accurate account of the proceedings. And another thing: how come the *Daily Mail*, or for that matter any other national newspaper apart from the *Telegraph*, failed to carry this report? I asked our news editor. The answer is: the newspapers never learned of her riding accident nor were given the date of the inquest. In that neck of the woods, the coroner sits on Wednesdays at ten in the morning. It's his unvarying routine. Local press men are always in attendance. Nancy's inquest took place at eight thirty on a Tuesday morning, with only the *Telegraph* man in the press box.

'The coroner's officer agreed with me that the speed was unheard of. He said it must have been done out of consideration for the family. Old Tintagel yanking a few strings. But I know different. I think there's another reason and that the inquest was a sham.'

Lancing saw, with enormous satisfaction, that neither detective was joshing him now. They'd replaced their drinks on the bar and were listening intently.

'Keep going,' said Ringrose.

'What it says there about Nancy being a Foreign Office high-flyer is all balls. The Secret Intelligence Service snapped her up years ago. She's been passport officer, counsellor, first secretary, commercial attaché, press attaché – you name it – in all sorts of hot spots to cover her real job, which was to spy on Johnny Foreigner. I'm told that she was much admired, with a DBE and principalship of an Oxbridge college doubtless in her glittering future.'

'Why haven't you printed your suspicions?' said Ringrose sharply.

Lancing beamed. 'That's where you and Lionel come in, Tom.

Believe me, I was tempted – but I thought, If I rush into print I'll run headlong into the Official Secrets Act. And so far I have smoke but no fire. Then I thought, Wouldn't it be grand if I were the first crime reporter to identify Conrad Niven's assassin? Wouldn't it be grand if my two dear friends, Tom and Lionel, took me into a cosy corner and whispered world scoops into my ever-receptive shell-like? Can you imagine the size of my byline and the tears of gratitude in my editor's rheumy old eyes?'

'We get the picture,' said Ringrose. 'You made the wise choice. If you'd gone ahead, that edition of the *Daily Mail* would never have left the building.'

'So am I seeing dirty work at the crossroads where there is no crossroads or am I on to something?'

Ringrose said, 'Stay put. Lionel and I are going to the other end of the bar for a chinwag.'

Lancing watched them go, sighed happily and signalled the barman to recharge his flute.

'What do you think?' said Ringrose softly. The bar had been empty but two couples had just entered and taken a table.

Firth said, 'I think he's hit the jackpot. I really do think we're going to end up whispering into his shell-like.'

'He's the first person in this entire worldwide investigation who has come up with anything like a convincing identification of Mrs Canning. We have to take him along for the ride. I don't see any other way.'

'Agreed, guv'nor. But you'll have to caution him. If he goes for premature publication, you and I can kiss goodbye to our pensions.'

'Peter has always played the game before. But I'll read him the Riot Act, all the same.'

By noon, Lancing had been shown all the relevant tape from the Berthier's video cameras and had positively identified the man known as Mr Canning. 'Same hat, same linen suit, right build,' said the reporter crisply.

His identification of Mrs Canning was more tentative. 'The body looks right. You should have seen her in jodhpurs. Fantastic bum. But I've never seen her wearing glasses and the hair is all wrong. Much too schoolmarmish.' He fretted over the poor quality of the material. 'Why don't these bloody hotels invest in cameras with decent lenses? The depth of focus is atrocious.'

'On Monday,' said Ringrose, 'we'll put you into a makeshift identification parade. Our suspect will be on the Up escalator at St Paul's tube station, one of the work-bound crowd. You'll be on the Down side. When you get to the bottom you'll tell us whether or not you spotted him. The courts have previously accepted this type of identification as a proper procedure.'

'Lead me to it,' said Lancing.

After he had departed, Ringrose spoke on the telephone to both Lord Tintagel and to Professor Roland Askew, who had carried out the postmortem on Tintagel's daughter.

Tintagel retreated into vagueness and redirected Ringrose to the Foreign Office. Askew was a more sensitive proposition. Ringrose was well aware that, on the list of Home Office pathologists, the eminent Askew was the expert most frequently called upon by the security services and by Special Branch. He was their creature.

Ringrose harboured no illusions about the probity of great men. The most famous of British pathologists, Sir Bernard Spilsbury, had committed suicide by stuffing a gas hose up his nose. Colleagues had rigged his death to look like an accident.

Askew was immediately on his guard. 'I don't see what interest the case could possibly be to you, Ringrose. The poor girl fell off her horse and broke her neck. Perfectly straightforward business.'

'Why was the inquest held in virtual secrecy on a day when the coroner does not normally sit?'

'Was it? I merely acted on instructions from the appropriate authorities. In any case, there was nothing secret about it. I remember reading a report in the *Telegraph*.'

Ringrose let it pass. 'Who were the appropriate authorities?'

'Ringrose, you are well aware of certain duties I occasionally perform. I'd leave well alone, if I were you. You're not doing youself any favours.'

Firth was listening on the extension and he made a triumphant thumbs-up sign to Ringrose. The time had come to hit hard. This man was rattled.

'Professor, what would you say if I applied for an exhumation order and brought in my own pathologist for a second opinion?'

Ringrose heard a roaring noise in his ear. Askew was breathing heavily into the mouthpiece. 'I'd say it was a confounded impertinence,' he shouted, and slammed down the receiver.

Ringrose listened to the dialling tone for a moment and said, 'Well, well. I think matter and anti-matter just touched each other.'

Through the open door, they watched Inspector Adrian Dawson advancing towards them like a supplicant for an audience. Ringrose waved him on. 'Problem?'

'A small puzzle, sir. All the surveillance team's situation reports since Friday evening place Boulder at home. He has not ventured out since. However, he made a credit-card transaction at six forty-five last evening that the team have failed to record.'

'What did he buy?'

'He didn't buy anything, sir. He hired a Range Rover. Car hire companies won't take cash. That's how we know. His own Saab is still in the street where he parked it – still being kept under observation.'

'Christ!' said Firth. 'He's done a runner.'

Their clash with Professor Askew went into the pending tray.

Cursing, Ringrose turned to his operational radio and summoned up the surveillance team leader. 'Where's Boulder?'

'At home, sir. He hasn't stirred since last night.'

'Do you know anything about him hiring a Range Rover?'

The officer's puzzlement was palpable. 'Not to our knowledge, sir.'

Ringrose said, dismay showing, 'Send a couple of woman officers over to the house. Any pretext. They can be Jehovah's Witnesses – anything. I want to know immediately what response they get.'

The three senior officers lingered anxiously in Ringrose's room for twenty minutes. 'I hope he's not sent them to buy Bibles before they go calling,' muttered Ringrose crossly.

There was panic in the team leader's voice when he reported back. 'The girls can't get any reply, sir. What do you want us to do? Do you think he's topped himself?'

Ringrose fought to keep his voice steady. 'Have you got anyone there who can do the locks without kicking in the door and drawing a crowd?'

'I can do that myself, sir.'

'Well, get over there. Get in – alone – and report back.'

The second vigil seemed interminable. When the return call finally came, the three men converged in a rush on Ringrose's radio.

It was a subdued team leader who came back. 'He's flown, sir. He must have gone over the garden fences. He's known all along we were watching.'

Ringrose snapped, 'I'm on my way with Detective Chief Inspector Firth.'

The journey, with the siren howling until they reached the Shepherd's

Bush roundabout, took thirty minutes in the Saturday afternoon traffic. An unhappy team leader met them at the corner of Hellespont Road.

Ringrose and Firth entered the silent house and closed the front door behind them. They moved slowly through the ground floor and found it unchanged since their previous visit.

The upstairs search gave them their first opportunity to sort through Jack Boulder's wardrobe. There was no Panama hat but there was an off-white linen suit. In a kitchen drawer they found a part-used tube of modelling glue. But Boulder had got rid of the cut newspapers. As useful evidence it was as lightweight as the linen suit.

Otherwise, the two men drew a complete blank.

In the living room, Ringrose seated himself in Boulder's rocker as if it would help him to burrow into the marksman's head and excavate answers to his questions.

Eventually he said, 'What do you make of it, Lionel?'

Firth shrugged. 'I don't think we'll be riding the tube escalators on Monday. He could be half-way to Iran by now to ask the ayatollahs to refill that glass box and hand it over.'

Ringrose shook his head. His silver forelock fell over his tired eyes. 'I know that's the logical conclusion. But somehow I just don't see it. I rather liked him. Didn't you? There was nothing of the cold killer about him as General Cashin described.'

'It didn't prevent him offing Sean McGurk.'

'He had a pretty powerful justification. If someone killed you, I think any number of your fellow officers wouldn't think twice about plugging the bastard who did it.'

'That's comforting to know,' said Firth drily.

Ringrose stood up and wandered round the room. His eyes came to rest on the answer machine. The digital display revealed that there were no messages.

He said thoughtfully, 'Lionel, do you have your mobile telephone with you?'

His aide fished the instrument from his pocket and held it up.

'Good. Dial Boulder's number. Let's hear what callers get when he doesn't pick up.'

Firth looked down at Boulder's machine and tapped the digits into his own phone. The detectives listened to their suspect's phone ring six times before his answer machine whirred and the pre-recorded tape came into play.

Jack Boulder's disembodied voice sounded strained and, on the first run-through, they were not sure they'd heard him correctly. He stumbled several times.

Jack Boulder said, 'This is a message for my RAF friends. The friends who called earlier this week. You'll need to go to York for what you want to know.'

That was it. The rest was silence, and the two detectives rewound and played it yet again.

'I've got it,' said Ringrose suddenly. 'He's not talking about the Royal Air Force. RAF is us – Ringrose and Firth. Very ingenious.'

'But what the hell's in York?'

Ringrose snapped his fingers and strode into the corridor. 'That's York.' He was pointing to the framed poster at the foot of the stairs of Gary Cooper playing Sergeant York. 'Remember – I thought it very striking.'

Firth had the poster off the wall before Ringrose had finished uttering the words. He turned it face down. A folded sheet of notepaper was taped to the hardboard backing.

'Don't breathe,' said Firth, carefully peeling it loose. 'I think the sun is coming out.'

Chapter Forty-Seven

Jack Boulder's skull inflated to the size of a beach ball and then subsided until it was no bigger than an apple. Again, he could feel his head expanding into an echoing immensity and then imploding until the skull bones were grinding together, crushing his brain into a pain-filled sac.

Sound, throbbing and hurtful, came and went. He felt nauseous. Somewhere he could hear a male voice bellowing. Jack kept his eyes tightly closed because he knew that if he opened them the light would burn out his irises.

After a while his head began to lessen its rhythmic expansion and contraction. He began to separate one word from another. The voice was guttural but cultured and very close.

'Is he in a coma? Have you killed him?'

A lighter voice said, 'I sapped him behind the ear. He'll come round.'

'Was this the weapon he had on him?'

'That's the one. Please, Sir Gilbert, either point it at the ceiling or the floor, but not at us. It's carrying a full magazine.'

'Do you think he'd come to kill me?' The guttural voice struck a note of wonder as if this possibility was beyond all belief.

'Well, I don't think he came to admire your orchid collection.'

'He's a madman.'

'No, sir. Not a madman. In his way, he's a great artist. That shot of his should be in the record books. I hate to admit it, but he's a great pro. I wish he were working for us.'

'He *was* working for us. He's a menace. He's jeopardizing everything.'

'I understand your anger, sir. If I'd not heard a sound in those bushes, right now you might well be asking St Peter if your suite is ready.'

'It is intolerable.' Some unintelligible mouthings followed. And then: 'I'm profoundly grateful to you, my boy. God! To think he got so close! How could he have done such a thing?'

The voices hovered above his face. The one the blonde girl in the garden had called Peter said, 'His eyeballs are twitching. He'll rejoin the land of the living quite soon.'

'That's one of the matters we have to discuss.' Metzhagen sounded grim.

'The contractors are still in the grounds dismantling the marquees,' Peter said. 'But the house is clear. They've all gone except our little group. They're waiting in the library.'

Jack could feel hot, dry dragon's breath on his face, a hint of sulphur. Someone was nose to nose with him. 'Is he really unconscious or is he pretending?'

Peter drawled, 'It doesn't matter either way. Clever Jack has been a very bad boy and he isn't going anywhere. He'll be quite safe here while we try to sort out this mess. Just leave one of your security chaps here – but outside the door, if you please. On no account must Boulder get a chance to talk to him. The leaking has gone far enough.'

Jack heard feet shuffling. A door closed and the space around him went quiet. He tentatively opened an eye and peered around.

They had imprisoned him in Sir Gilbert Metzhagen's gymnasium. The equipment was state-of-the-art for body-building and stretching. In one corner was a sauna cabin and, to one side, a plunge pool – empty.

Jack moved his head and pain sliced it in two. He closed his eyes again and began slowly rotating his neck until the agony subsided. Peter was diabolically efficient with a sap. Jack's left arm was awkwardly placed above his head. He attempted to bring it down to massage his sore nape but found himself tugging at a heavy object.

He twisted his body and looked up. They had handcuffed him to a Nautilus body-builder.

The room was windowless. He judged that it must be in the cellars of Fern Hall. He rolled onto his back and stared up at the white acoustic tiling of the ceiling.

Jack Boulder shook his head painfully to clear it for thinking and gave a futile pull on his bonds.

What to do?

The entire core group was assembled. Peter Hope-Casson, Rupert Strang and Rafe Cummings, as the field men, sat virtually shoulder to shoulder under a large Fragonard, whose fragile figures in an Arcadian landscape provided a sharp contrast to their own forceful masculinity.

At a distance, Bulwer Tancred was hunched over a telephone, murmuring and listening. Then Metzhagen came in, anxiety written across his face. Tancred softly dropped the receiver into its cradle and watched their paymaster throw himself violently into a winged armchair.

Sir Gilbert was fuming. 'How could you have let this happen to me? On my own doorstep!' His clenched fist pounded the leather. 'I thought this man Boulder was just a hired gun? He'd do the job, and then be paid off or disposed of. No fuss. No consequences.'

He pointed a trembling finger at Hope-Casson. 'It was you, Peter, who first proposed having Nancy kill him. If you hadn't almost certainly saved my life last night, I'd be inclined now to take the bloody man's pistol and kill you instead. We should have trusted him, let him take the money and run. If later he had become a threat to our security, *then* we could have killed him. Now we have this vengeful idiot knowing who we are – God knows how – and haunting us.'

Hope-Casson made to speak, but Tancred stopped him with a raised hand as peremptory as a traffic cop. His usually pallid features had deepened to ashen. 'Hold on, Peter. Something very grave has happened.'

'Aren't things grave enough?' shouted Metzhagen. He had removed his white jacket. His cummerbund had slipped, along with his *sangfroid*.

'Gilbert,' said Tancred, 'you'd better listen to what I've got to say. Roland Askew has just reached me. He's in a terrible state. Ringrose is asking questions about Nancy's death. He wouldn't be doing so unless he'd made the connection between her and the Niven operation.'

His words fell like a stun grenade into the centre of the room. Metzhagen's chin dropped.

Rupert Strang said firmly, 'It's obvious the group is dead. Somewhere along the line, there's been a monstrous betrayal. Is it conceivable that Boulder forced Nancy to talk before she died?'

Tancred said coldly, 'It was either Nancy – or it's one of us?' His glinting eyes swept the room.

Rafe Cummings, their senior operational man, faced him and said sharply, 'Let's have none of that, Tancred. We've all been in these operations from the beginning. We all know everything there is to know about each other. Enough, anyway, to create havoc. Nothing went wrong until we recruited Boulder and mistook him for just another Neanderthal mercenary.'

He surveyed his colleagues. 'What we have to do now is make sure we have destroyed all physical evidence that links us either to Nancy or Boulder.'

Tancred said, 'There won't be much time. Ringrose is threatening to exhume Nancy's body for a second autopsy.'

Metzhagen appeared to be coming out of a daze. He focused with difficulty on Tancred. 'His wife and children. That's the answer.'

The others stared at him.

'We have to show Boulder that it won't just be him killed. We have to show him how vulnerable his family is. Rafe, you and Peter will have to fetch them here.'

'I don't like it,' said Strang.

'Sir Gilbert is right,' said Hope-Casson. 'We can't begin to limit the damage until he tells us what he's told and to whom he's told it. The only way to be sure of getting that is to seize his family again.'

'Get ourselves some leverage,' added Cummings.

'All right,' said the tycoon slowly. 'But this is going to be man to man. Boulder can't do me any harm. You go and fetch his family. Let me have the pistol.'

Hope-Casson was dubious. 'Do you know how to use this thing?'

Metzhagen beckoned irritably. 'Don't be impertinent. What's there to know? You point it and pull the trigger.'

He took the Glock from Hope-Casson's reluctant hand and marched out of the room.

He left behind a worried silence. Each man was running his past activities through his own mind, identifying what might yet loom up to ruin him.

Chapter Forty-Eight

They were taking advantage of the balmy afternoon and having tea on the lawn in the traditional way. Grace had dragged a table from the living room, covered it with a white cloth and proudly set down her centrepiece – a pink blancmange that she had allowed to set overnight in a genuine old copper mould rescued from the back of a kitchen cupboard.

She had been unable to find a cakestand so the shop-bought rock buns and the slices of Tottenham cake were arrayed on coloured napkins. 'Yummy, yummy!' said Malcolm. 'It must be Christmas.'

Normally Grace rationed cakes strictly. She wanted the boys to grow up lithe and muscular like Jack, not pot-bellied porkers like so many of the fathers who had come to the schools where she had taught.

She glanced at the wristwatch Jack had bought her for their tenth wedding anniversary. He should have arrived by now. She'd been horrified at the cost of that watch – it was a genuine Piaget – and had started to remonstrate. 'Eeeh. She's got a bit of a tongue on her,' Jack had said, turning to the boys.

They'd all collapsed laughing before Ben had reminded her, 'Mum, aren't you going to kiss Dad? It's a smashing watch.'

The boys had witnessed, with approval, Grace melt into Jack's arms.

'Yuk!' said Mal, pretending to throw up.

The brothers carried their own chairs from the house and Grace finished laying the table before emerging from the kitchen with the teapot. She wore a plain blue shift over her bikini. She'd been sunbathing, lying quietly on the grass, tussling with herself over whether or not to remove her top for a strap-free tan and what to do if the boys reappeared suddenly from the beach. She knew what her mother would say: 'Don't take the top off in the first place, lass.' Grace decided that Ben and Malcolm had never done anything silently in their lives. She'd hear them coming. She took off the top.

The boys had been topless, too, romping barefoot in their khaki shorts, but she made them put on their T-shirts to sit at the table. Grace poured and Ben passed the cakes. 'You can have a rock bun or a piece of the pink one, but you can't have both at once,' he said, lecturing his brother.

'For goodness' sake, don't be so bossy. We're on holiday and you're beginning to sound like me,' said Grace, who knew her faults.

Again she consulted her watch. 'Can't think what's happened to your father.'

The last of the blancmange disappeared down appreciative throats and they were on their second cup of tea when Ben said, 'Listen. I can hear Dad's car.'

It took Grace and Mal several seconds to confirm Ben's acute hearing. A vehicle was, indeed, coming down the lane. Mal knocked over his chair in his hurry to get away from the tea table and ran down to the gate, climbed a bar and leaned out for a better view.

The engine sound grew louder, mingling with the hoarse cries of the gulls. Mal was leaning so far forward that Grace opened her mouth to shout a warning. But just then, her son turned to look back at them. Disappointment was written across his face. He climbed down and trotted back to the table. 'It's not, Dad,' he said, in disgust. 'It's a big car with black windows.'

Ben said, 'How can it have black windows? The driver wouldn't be able to see out.'

'Be quiet a moment,' said their mother. Ben studied her face from across the table. The expression that had reflected the carefree afternoon had been replaced by lines of concern.

The car was travelling slowly, as if the driver was a stranger to the area.

Malcolm began chattering again but Grace laid a hand on his arm. 'Not now, Mal. Let Mummy listen.' Through the bars of the gate, she watched the shining black bonnet of a long limousine slide into view and then the glossy body of a Daimler. As Mal had said, the side windows were made of smoked glass just like a pop star's fan-proof conveyance.

There was a cluster of cottages further down the lane, but the Daimler eased to a stop. The driver's door remained closed but two men emerged from the back. Both were tall and wearing country suits. The fair-haired one sported a brown trilby, perched forward over his brow, and the other a checked cap. They looked as if they were off to the races or perhaps to a point-to-point.

Ben watched his mother's left hand tighten on Malcolm's arm. When she let go to stand up, he saw the white mark where her fingers had been before Mal's skin resumed its usual appearance.

Ben said quietly, 'Is something wrong, Mum?'

'I don't know. Just sit still.'

The two men were smiling unctuously, like cold-calling insurance salesmen. They lifted the latch and entered the garden, advancing towards them across the grass.

They both touched their headgear in polite greeting and the older man, who had a long, wandering nose and penetrating hard eyes that no amount of charm could disguise, said, 'Mrs Boulder?'

Grace nodded. 'How did you find us here?'

'Oh, it wasn't easy. This place is quite remote, isn't it?' His chuckle was as counterfeit as a three-pound banknote.

'I meant,' said Grace, slowly and deliberately, 'how did you know we were living here?'

'Ah,' said the Nose, 'Jack told us where to find you.'

'That's odd. It was a secret between us.'

'A secret no longer, dear lady. Your husband has charged us with the duty of safeguarding you and the children.'

'This is not the first time I've been told that. Safeguarding us from what?'

'Well, I'm sure you know the answer to that better than we do.' The Nose scrutinized Grace's face keenly.

She betrayed no emotion. 'I'm afraid I haven't the faintest idea what you're talking about.'

'Come, now,' said the Nose, smiling indulgently. 'You must have asked Jack why it was necessary to exile yourself to this part of the world when your sons should be at school?'

'There are times when it's best for a wife not to ask too many questions. My husband served in Northern Ireland and I assumed we were here as a result of some difficulty that has arisen in connection with that.'

There was a silence while the Nose and his companion simply stared, as if waiting for her to elaborate. Instead, Grace said, 'You haven't yet given me your names or told me where you're from.' She had not encountered either of these two on their previous 'safe-keeping' absence from home.

Peter Hope-Casson exchanged glances with Rafe Cummings and said, 'Mrs Boulder, our names are unimportant. I'm sure that when you were an Army wife certain subjects were only circulated on a need-to-know basis. Well, that's the situation we have here. Suffice it to say, we're here on government business. You may call us any names you like.' Another fake chuckle.

'What are you proposing to do – set up machine guns at each corner of the property to repel attackers?' Grace made no effort to moderate the sarcasm.

Cummings shook his head. 'This place is hopeless from that point of view. We want you to come with us. Jack is waiting.'

'Waiting? I don't think so. He's due here at any moment.'

'I'm afraid not, my dear,' said the Nose. 'There's been a change of plan. You really must come with us. We simply cannot accept any arguments. Think of the well-being of your sons.'

Malcolm had moved close to his mother and was clutching the folds of her dress. He stared wide-eyed at Cummings. He could sense his mother's alarm.

She said, 'I'd like to hear about the change of plans from Jack.' She took a step towards the house, with Malcolm still holding on.

As if on cue, she heard the muffled click of door locks and, over her visitors' shoulders, saw two heavily built men in jeans and sweatshirts step from the front seats of the Daimler. One had a bandage round his thick neck.

Grace's lips tightened. 'Please wait here. I'm going to telephone.'

Cummings was shaking his head again. 'I don't think you'll find Jack at any of the numbers you have.'

Grace ignored him. She prised Malcolm's fingers from her clothes and strode briskly towards the house. Despite her instructions, Cummings and Hope-Casson followed.

They blocked the doorway, watching her pick up the phone and jiggle the cradle. She listened and tried again. She met their gaze square on. 'The line is dead. Have you had it cut?'

Hope-Casson was the picture of wounded feelings. 'Why should we cut it? But if the line is cut, it could be a danger sign – a sign that Jack's enemies are closing in. We should leave here as fast as possible.'

Grace's mouth was dry. She was fit and she could probably outrun them if she made a dash through the kitchen and down to the beach where the Daimler couldn't follow. But what about Ben and Mal? She couldn't abandon them.

She said, 'I must go upstairs to pack a few things.' She had suddenly remembered the pistol in her bedside drawer.

She struggled to keep her voice steady. 'How long do you think we'll be away? Or does Jack want us to close up the house completely and return to London? That'll take an hour or so.'

Hope-Casson gave a quick, impatient shake of his blond head. He turned his left wrist upward to consult his watch. 'That won't be necessary. An overnight bag will—' He stopped abruptly, dropped his trilby, and said, 'What...?' His long legs bent and he looked down to find Ben's tousled head thrust through the narrow gap between him and Cummings.

Ben was looking apologetic and desperate. 'I'm sorry, Mum. It's all that tea. I must go to the lavatory right away.'

The two surprised men stepped aside and Ben entered the cottage in a stilted walk, his knees seemingly glued together. Malcolm followed. 'Me, too,' he said.

Grace inclined her head towards the stairs. 'Well, hurry up. We're going on a trip. While you're up there, put your pyjamas and some clean pairs of pants in a bag.'

Cummings and Hope-Casson relaxed a little. Hope-Casson said, 'I'll have our chaps bring in the tea things while you pack.' Grace moved toward the stairs but Cummings stepped in front of her. 'Which is your room?'

'The one facing as you reach the top.'

'Just a precaution,' he said, and was already taking the stairs two at a time before she could object.

She could hear the boys moving around and the lavatory cistern being flushed. The creaking of the timbered ceiling told her that Cummings had invaded her bedroom and was nosing around. Would he think to look in her bedside drawer?

The pistol was now looming in her mind as a last-chance symbol of hope. She had never used a gun and even hated touching those that Jack brought home. But these men were not to be trusted and they were involving her children in whatever they were up to. Grace's palms were clammy. She wiped them down the sides of her shift, summoning the resolve that she would need if she were to use that obscene thing in her drawer.

Cummings reappeared at the top of the stairs. 'Everything's OK. You can come up now.'

Thank God. He hadn't discovered the Walther. He gazed steadily down at her as she took each step. Grace was suddenly aware of the brevity of her shift. She glanced up into his face. She knew that look well enough – that combination of speculation, appreciation and lust.

At the bedroom door she snapped, 'I hope you don't think you're coming in here while I change.'

The corner of his mouth twitched. He said coolly, 'That won't be necessary. But please hurry. We have a long journey to make.'

Grace angrily slammed the door behind her. She stood for a moment scanning the room. Nothing appeared to have been disturbed. She moved to the window and peered out. One of the two henchmen stood strategically back from the cottage at a point where he could monitor two frontages.

Grace stepped back softly and went directly to the drawer. She slid it open and only just managed to suppress a loud scream. Both the pistol and the ammunition were gone. The only trace that they had ever been there, to confirm that she had not dreamed the episode of Jack handing them to her, was a smear of machine oil.

She made a sharp, unconsidered gesture, pushing the drawer closed with a loud clatter, and stood wild-eyed, thinking. The bastard had found the contents, after all. He'd slipped them into his jacket. He was just toying with her.

She felt dizzy. She tried to persuade herself that the men really were helping Jack, that she was letting her imagination run away with her. But it was no good. In her bones, Grace knew that they were a threat to Jack – and perhaps to her and the children too.

On automatic pilot, she dropped some clothes into a tote bag and changed into slacks, blouse and trainers.

She came to a decision. Now was not the moment to resist. There were too many of them. She would comply with their wishes – for now.

She threw open the door. Cummings was leaning against the wall. 'I'm ready,' she snapped. 'Where are the kids?'

'Making a lot of noise,' said Cummings snottily. Grace clenched a fist and itched to smash it into his nose.

Mal shuffled out of his room, a picture of misery. 'Mum, Ben's pinched my Indiana Jones backpack. I want it for myself.'

His brother was right behind him. They'd both put on trousers and their lumberjack shirts and Ben wore the backpack with the red straps clipped securely across his chest.

He said, 'I don't know what Mal's complaining about. I'm carrying his stuff as well as my own in this thing.'

Grace stroked her younger son's head. 'It's all right, Mal. Ben's only trying to help. He'll give it back later.'

Cummings levered himself from the wall. 'Let's go!' he barked, and shepherded them down the stairs.

Grace's hands were trembling as she locked the front door. Her keys rattled and she silently cursed herself for revealing her panic.

The interior of the Daimler was huge compared with the interior of the cars to which she was accustomed. She and the boys sat in a row, the Nose and his younger companion sitting impassively opposite. The Nose had fastidiously unbuttoned his jacket. She could not see the Walther.

Ben looked uncomfortable. He was perched forward on the leather seat. 'Why don't you take off the backpack? Put it on your lap,' suggested Grace.

'I'm all right, Mum,' he said shortly, and his face shut down.

Up front there was now only one of the two thuggish men, who had remained silent throughout.

Grace peered through the tinted window. The other was driving the Volvo with the false number-plate out of the garage.

The Nose followed her gaze. 'The car has to be returned, you know.'

He tapped on the dividing glass and the Daimler began to move. Grace put an arm round each of her sons and clasped them tightly to her sides.

Chapter Forty-Nine

The pyjamas stayed packed. Grace Boulder and her sons remained resolutely fully dressed in their suite.

'Suite' had been the word used by the men who called themselves the family's escort but were, as far as Grace was concerned, their captors.

During the road journey south, a surface air of courtesy and consideration had prevailed inside the Daimler. According to the Nose, they were on the way to be joyously reunited with Jack at a 'safe house'. Grace held her tongue, which was furnace-hot and more than ready to shout 'Liars!'

The younger of their 'escorts' was even a little skittish with her. 'I'm sure Jack can't wait to see his cracking wife.'

He was chucklesome and his lively blue eyes wandered appreciatively up and down her body. She could have biffed him. To show her feelings, she ostentatiously did up her collar button. Thank goodness she'd put on her trousers. Otherwise, seated face to face as they were, he'd have been leering at her knickers all the way to – where?

Malcolm, wide-eyed and puzzled, passively submitted to heavy-handed adult questioning. Where do you go to school, young feller-me-lad? What do you want to be when you grow up? Do you play rugby or football?

Mal mumbled polite replies but Ben refused to be drawn. He shrank back as best he could with the pack on his back, surly and uncooperative. 'I want my dad,' he said.

'Soon, Ben, soon,' said the Nose. He beamed synthetic encouragement.

But it had not been soon. They were on the road for almost four hours before they turned into a driveway and Grace looked back to see a heavy metal gate closing behind them. They were back at the place she and the boys had been taken while Jack was in France.

The Nose said, 'They won't be able to get at you here. We'll see to that.' It was exactly what she had been told before.

'Who are "they"?' Grace wanted to know once again.

The Nose smiled indulgently 'Jack's the chap for all the info. Be patient a little longer.'

This time they were ushered through a rear door of the main house into a narrow hallway littered with gumboots, a stand of walking sticks, and waterproofs hanging from pegs. This was not the red-carpet entrance of their previous arrival.

A tall, lean man, incongruous in a crumpled evening suit, came down the cream-painted corridor and spoke briefly to the Nose. The party followed him through sharp-turning corridors. When they clattered down an unpainted wooden staircase, Grace's unease gripped her. They were beneath ground level.

As they were hurried along, they passed several open doors. Grace glimpsed a deserted kitchen, a larder with tins and packages filling the deep shelves, and a carpenter's workshop. Twice they passed doors displaying male and female silhouette signs.

Their 'suite' was apparently situated in the working quarter of this massive edifice.

It turned out to be a medium-sized bunker, which, judging from the sealed-off Victorian iron piping, had once been a boiler room, since renovated and its stone walls whitewashed. The windowless space contained three camp beds, blankets, a plastic-topped table and four wooden folding chairs.

Their guide, the lean man, had slipped silently away, but Grace rounded furiously on the Nose. 'Is this your idea of a hotel suite? This is a prison.'

The Nose was pained. 'Please, Mrs Boulder. Have a little understanding. We're dealing with an emergency. We had to make arrangements in a rush. Bear with us for now. Show a little fortitude.'

'Fuck fortitude,' spat Grace, who never swore in front of her children. 'Where's my husband?'

He wagged his head, silently chiding her as he backed out of the door. Before he closed it, he said, 'Get some sleep. Tomorrow will be an important day.' She did not hear a key turn.

Angrily, Grace paced their prison. The boys' eyes followed her. She stopped to inspect a bricked-in chute where coke and coal must once have cascaded down through an outside delivery grating. No escape route there.

She crossed her arms over her breasts and wheeled around the room, barely able to contain herself.

Mal said suddenly, reproachfully, 'Mum, you said a naughty word.'

Grace swept him up in her arms and kissed him. She could feel tears welling up. 'I'm sorry, Mal. You know Mummy doesn't usually swear. But these men have upset me very much.'

'I don't like them,' said Mal. 'They're creepy.'

'The one with the fair hair fancies you,' interjected Ben, matter-of-factly.

'Well, he can fancy on,' said Grace.

'I hope Dad gives him a black eye,' said Mal, who was looking sleepy.

'Would you like to go to bed?' Grace set him on his feet and checked the time. It had just turned eleven p.m.

Mal was rubbing his eyes. He said, 'Yes, please, Mum. But I want to go to the bathroom.'

'Oh dear.' Grace glanced around. The 'suite' contained no such facilities. She twisted the door knob and, to her surprise, the door immediately opened inward. Grace almost fell over. It had never been locked.

Staring directly at her, from his chair against the wall opposite, was a big-chested man she had not seen before. He came instantly to his feet, a guarded expression on his face.

'My son wants a pee,' said Grace. 'I saw a loo along the corridor...'

The big lummox was thrown by this simple request. He shot a look down the deserted corridor. 'I'm not supposed to talk to you,' he said, in a South London accent. 'Strict orders from the boss.'

'I'm not looking for conversation,' said Grace, with a cutting edge that the boys rather relished. 'I'm looking for the lavatory. Or are you providing a bucket?'

A moment later she wished she hadn't said that. He looked the sort of moron who would blindly take up her suggestion.

The fat on his neck bulged and quaked as he turned his head this way and that. Finally, he grunted, 'I can't take 'im and leave you two alone.'

'Well, just lock us in while you show him where to go.'

'Can't,' said the guard. 'There's no bolt or anyfink.'

For the first time, Grace had the opportunity to examine the outside of the door. Sure enough, there were no bolts – and no keyhole. The door was held shut only by a simple spring-loaded tongue of brass in an old-fashioned black japanned housing. There had never been any call to lock up the boiler while stokers moved in and out. So, as the Nose had told her, they really were in an emergency. At short notice, they'd found a suitable cell for her and the children but the door furniture had failed to meet penal requirements.

'I tell you what,' said Grace. 'We're all about to go to bed. We'll go together.'

She watched his synapses grind rustily into action. He mulled over the proposition for at least half a minute, chewing his lip. 'No funny business?' he said.

'What funny business could there be?' shouted Grace. 'Do you think my kids are going to wrestle you to the ground and tie you up?'

He grinned unpleasantly, 'I don't fink so. But *you* can try any time you like.'

Ben said, 'Another one, Mum.'

With great effort, Grace relaxed her clenched fists. She summoned up a bright smile. 'Now, now!' she said, the instant coquette.

The fat hunk was still grinning. 'The boss said no talking. He didn't say no wrestling.'

Mal was tugging at her slacks. 'Mum, I'm bursting.'

This seemed to decide their jailer. He said, 'OK. I'll take you all along together. But don't do anyfink to get me mad. Right?'

'Right!' agreed Grace.

For the sixty-foot walk, Fatty held his great hams of arms wide, his dirty fingertips practically scraping the walls. He was nervous and he herded them so closely that they stumbled into each other.

219

The male and female loos were mirror images of each other – washbasins, cisterns, lavatory bowls. Their utility suggested they were for the use of below-stairs staff. Fatty poked his head suspiciously into each, head turning like a bull walrus.

Satisfied, he nodded. Grace stepped into one, slamming the door in case Fatty had other ideas, and Mal scampered into the other.

Ben, the Indiana Jones pack still on his back, faced Fatty alone in the corridor. 'Wot you starin' at?' said Fatty.

'Something beginning with P,' said Ben.

Fatty's brow contorted for the five seconds it required for the insult to register. He took a menacing step forward. 'You little prick. I'd tan your arse if I was your dad.'

'Well, he can't because he's not here,' retorted Ben, deliberately provocative.

'No,' said Fatty, a grin suddenly emerging from the blubber. 'He's busy getting plenty of exercise of 'is own.' Then he laughed in a meaningful way that chilled Ben. The big oaf was hinting at something. The flabby mouth clamped shut. 'That's enough talk. You get in there and 'ave your piddle.'

Afterwards, he herded them back down the corridor. Another man had appeared from the far end. As they approached, he waved a friendly greeting at Fatty, deposited a vacuum flask and a plastic sandwich box alongside his chair and retreated the way he had come. So Fatty was their guardian for the night.

Inside their room, Grace said, 'Let me have Mal's pyjamas.'

Ben took a sharp step back before his mother could touch the backpack. 'I didn't pack 'em.'

She sighed. 'Oh, Ben!'

Mal was already half asleep so Grace helped him undress down to his underpants and he lay down on a musty-smelling camp bed.

Ben waited until he was sure his mother and Mal were asleep before he made his move. He'd reasoned that, if they'd needed the lavatory, so would their guard some time during the night.

In the darkness, Ben slid from his camp bed and pressed his face to the tiled floor. Under the door, he could see Fatty's boot tips.

As the night dragged on, Ben fought his tiredness with a grim determination. Several times he nodded and his head tilted sharply against the hard floor. He was nervous that the minute sound might alert Fatty. He wished he'd snoozed in the Daimler when he'd had the chance. But then he might have lost his grip on his backpack. And that would have been disastrous.

Fatty's chair was old and creaked every time the man shifted his bulk. Whenever he heard this noise, Ben eagerly pressed his cheek to the ground. Fatty stood up several times and Ben heard him drinking from the cup-lid of the flask and taking food out of the box.

Ben's moment came some time after three a.m. The chair creaked and he saw that their guard's right foot was sideways on to his sightline. Fatty was facing down the corridor towards the lavatories.

Some seconds of indecision followed, and then the boot moved forward, revealing the other. That, too, now moved. Ben wanted to yell in triumph like a goal-scoring footballer.

He counted to twenty. He could see the chair legs but no sign of Fatty's boots. They did not reappear. Ben said a prayer and inched the door open. If Fatty was merely stretching his legs ... well, Ben did not relish a pounding from those weighty fists.

He stayed kneeling and poked his head out just six inches from the ground. Fatty was already two-thirds of the way to his destination. Ben withdrew his head and counted another ten before venturing a second look. Fatty had made it. He was nowhere to be seen in the receding pools of light created by the overhead bulbs.

Ben scrambled to his feet, hitched up his backpack, stepped into the corridor and gently pulled the door closed behind him. It shut with a tiny click.

'Yesss!' he murmured and, heading in the opposite direction to the lavatories, melted into the shadows of the great sleeping house. He felt no fear.

Chapter Fifty

Having captured and corralled him, they had a problem: what to do with him. Jack Boulder could imagine the agitated discussions going on elsewhere in Fern Hall.

They had abandoned him for the night, during which he had slept fitfully and had woken once with a tremendous thumping of his heart. He had had the dream again. The shadow-wreathed woman ... the horror and the screaming ... the final realization that oblivion waited. He was sweating like a pig, and reluctant to close his eyes again. But exhaustion overcame him and some time later he woke with a start at the sound of the door opening.

How long had he been asleep? Jack looked along his body and between his splayed feet saw Sir Gilbert Metzhagen, carrying a brandy bottle and a glass. He was alone, and he kicked the door closed behind him.

He walked round Jack's prone figure at a distance and then closed in. His teeth flashed white in his dark, Slavic face. He studied Jack thoughtfully through grey eyes, the unusual colour acting as a veil drawn over whatever he was thinking.

His masculinity was cast in an exotic mould and Jack could see at this close range what the newspaper pictures failed to capture: his charisma. He could have been a forceful leading man in one of the movies he financed. Now he used his fine teeth to tug the cork from the bottle and half filled the tumbler. 'Here, drink this.'

Jack turned his head away.

'It's not spiked. You've been unconscious long enough. Here. Look.' Metzhagen took a generous swig himself and topped up the glass.

Jack accepted it with his free hand and swallowed gratefully. Metzhagen nodded his approval.

The industrialist presented an odd, hastily clothed figure in open-necked, lace-fronted shirt, and white cricket trousers held up by a knotted old school tie. He had the appearance of a swashbuckler more at home climbing the rigging of a pirate ship than presiding in a boardroom. The effect was enhanced by Jack's Glock tucked into the waistband.

Metzhagen leaned against a rack that contained rows of weights in varying sizes. 'Captain Boulder, you have invaded my property, armed and intent on killing me. Why?' He shot the words at Jack like bullets.

Jack took a second slug of the brandy and felt himself beginning to revive. He set down the glass deliberately and said, 'First of all, I did not come to kill you. Yes, I did invade your property but your men have, no doubt, told you I was in the act of withdrawing when they pounced on me.'

'Then why did you come?'

'I wanted to confront you. I didn't know you were having a party.'

Metzhagen took the tumbler and drank some of Jack's brandy, as if trying to establish a form of comradeship. 'And if I had not had a house full of people?'

'I would have hunted you down, put the muzzle of that pistol to your mouth and forced you to tell me what I needed to know. The moment was delayed, that's all.'

'But if you had no intention of killing me, why should I tell you anything?'

'You're well aware that I've killed at least two people. Why would you believe I'd extend any mercy to you?'

'Ah, yes. I see your point. A case of your reputation preceding you.'

'That's why I'm here. I never wanted that reputation. The first man I killed deserved his death sentence. The second man died because I was tricked, lied to, given to understand I was on an undercover operation for my country. My reward has been to have three attempts made on my own life.'

Jack observed that his words were having a depressing effect on Metzhagen. He was staring at the floor, lost in thought. Then he said almost sadly, 'Captain Boulder, in that much I owe you an apology. I realize now we should never have dealt with you at arm's length. Given your praiseworthy disposal of that Irish scum, we should have welcomed you openly as a brother-in-arms. We needlessly offended you. Is it too late to appeal to you to take the hundred thousand pounds we provided and hold your peace?'

'Far too late,' said Jack bluntly, gazing at Metzhagen, hard and uncompromising. 'You'd simply continue trying to kill me. You only have to succeed once.'

Metzhagen made a motion with his hand as if this was a minor irritant in their new relationship. 'I might even be able to arrange for the million-pound bounty to be paid by the Iranians into a bank account of your choosing. I believe we've already opened for your benefit one of those handy little Austrian accounts that defy all probing.' Metzhagen essayed a twinkle.

'It's also far too late for bribery,' said Jack. 'What you don't know is that Scotland Yard is closing in. That copper, Ringrose, has already visited me. He knows I did it. He knows there's a link between me and you.'

'*Merde!*' said Metzhagen. He began to pace between the machines. He looked back at Jack over his shoulder. 'What did you say to him?'

'I said nothing that he didn't know already. It can only be a matter of time before he acquires enough hard evidence and takes me in. Before

I ruin my family's happiness, I want to know why it was so vital to go to such elaborate lengths to assassinate Conrad Niven.'

Metzhagen said nothing. He stopped his pacing and took a slug of brandy directly from the bottle.

Jack prompted him: 'You're at the heart of this – this conspiracy, or whatever you call it. Only you could have provided the considerable funds needed to organize the operation. I know for a fact Mrs Canning's – Miss Tintagel's – body was brought directly to your house by members of the British Secret Service.'

'Yes, you have been extremely clever,' murmured Metzhagen. He was deep in thought. He looked up abruptly as if an important decision had been made.

'Captain Boulder, you must not doubt your patriotism for one moment. You performed a fine service for your country by disposing of the Irishman, and you were right again to kill Conrad Niven. Like you, everyone in my unofficial little group – from government departments and from the Security Services – is a patriot, deeply committed to furthering the cause of the United Kingdom and its ancient institutions. If anything, my patriotism runs deeper than yours. I *chose* to be an Englishman. My father was a victim of Admiral Horthy's torturers. I could take you to the very room in the Gellert Hotel in Budapest where they removed his ten toenails and branded him on his buttocks with a red-hot wire.

'Noble British friends of my father took me in, a lost and bewildered child refugee, just another piece of flotsam thrown up by Continental Europe's violent upheavals. They could have given me a bun and a cup of tea and handed me on to an orphanage or the Sisters of Mercy. Speedily washed their hands of this little nuisance. Instead, they welcomed me into their homes, put me into fine schools, raised me alongside their own children. Made me an English gentleman.

'The philosopher George Santayana said that in the days of their mighty empire, the British were the sweetest masters. I experienced the full force of that pronouncement. I love Britain with a passion that you, native-born, taking your immense good fortune for granted, cannot begin to understand. I have poured many millions of my personal fortune into this dear country's institutions – libraries, colleges, art galleries, hospitals, medical-research establishments. I have also poured much money into a secret endeavour to save those institutions from the barbarians.'

Metzhagen, Jack realized, was not making this speech for the first time. The words were spilling out of him in a torrent. There was no challenging his fervour.

He was still speaking. 'I should correct one thing: my group cannot actually *save* any of those institutions any more. At best, we shall succeed only in prolonging their existence. I'm a realist. You don't know it yet, Captain Boulder, but our country is doomed.'

For the first time, it crossed Jack's mind that Metzhagen was mad. Jack equated doom-sayers with wild-eyed men on boxes at Speaker's Corner and those ragged visionaries patrolling Oxford Street with their sandwich boards and their predictions of God's wrath to come.

Metzhagen had the weary look of a man who'd spent a troubled night. But the fatigue was not diminishing his passion.

'Little by little, this sweet and heroic island is slipping into history. We are becoming an irrelevance. The rot cannot be stopped. We have sucked up the wealth from beneath the North Sea and thrown it into the bottomless pit of our debts. Desperate governments have raised cash by selling everything from the water you drink to the Queen's right to be portrayed exclusively on our postage stamps. And still it has not been enough. Our proud, unconquered island has become an outer province of Europe. There is no money for true universal education and the cretinization of a brave and steadfast people proceeds at a reckless speed. Their minds are assaulted by imbecilic television spewing from a hundred poisoned channels, by music fit only to be heard by animals of the farmyard, by newspapers produced for idiots and movies that glamorize a primitive appetite for violent behaviour.

'The people have lost their nobility. They've become cynical, debased. They feel betrayed. They have no gods any more. Their cathedral is the shopping mall.'

Metzhagen wiped his mouth on his white cuff. Jack stayed silent in the face of the rant. Where was it leading?

In his rage, Metzhagen had drawn incautiously near to Jack's feet. For a moment, he contemplated lashing out and kicking the tycoon in the shins. But the satisfaction would have been short-lived. Jack could not have got his hand on the gun as he reeled away.

Metzhagen said mournfully, 'Our governments give the impression of robust activity to counter these ills but, in actuality, all they do is construct illusions to ensure their own survival. Lesser breeds will build their monuments on our rubble. It is the ultimate fate of all empires. We may only hold back the day.'

Jack watched him take yet another swig at the bottle. A drunk with a handgun was a dangerous combination. He said in a placatory tone, 'This is all very interesting, Sir Gilbert, but I don't see where Conrad Niven fits into your alarming picture.'

Jack waited for him to elaborate but Metzhagen resumed his pacing, deep in his tortured thoughts.

Jack tried again. 'Sir Gilbert, a man should know the reason why he has killed another man.'

The tycoon wheeled round and came up close – so close that Jack's free hand was just within grabbing distance of the Glock. But Metzhagen, despite the amount he had drunk, must have detected the calculation in Jack's eyes. He moved smartly back two paces.

'Captain Boulder, the man you so brilliantly shot was a reckless and worthless individual. A vain man and an adulterer. Islam is a great religion but it is a vengeful one. By deliberately taking a distinguished author's unhappy experience and using it as a basis for his movie, despite the unfortunate man's pleas and protests, he slapped all of Islam in the face. A deadly business. I warned him not to do it. I even offered him a contract to direct a Hollywood feature on another more elevated subject that would have enhanced his career. But he was arrogant and stupid. He craved notoriety and, perhaps, martyrdom. Well, thanks to you, he got it.'

'Why did you send me after Niven and not Rushdie?'

Metzhagen gave a snort. 'I think the ayatollahs have come to realize that, alive and existing in a twilight world, Rushdie remains a warning to all non-believers that you cannot insult the Prophet with impunity. It suits their purpose that he continues to live.'

'Did you collect the Niven bounty?'

'Do not insult me. No one collected the bounty. The money was never the object.'

'Then what was?'

'Niven was the human sacrifice. Niven's corpse was evidence of our sincere wish to restore good relations with the world of Islam. I promised Iran I would deliver him up.'

Jack swore. 'You had a man killed so that a bunch of fucking diplomats and deal-hungry businessmen could be pals again? You're so fucking sick, you should be in a padded cell.' He struggled angrily, tugging at his manacle and widening the red weal around his wrist.

Metzhagen reacted furiously. He made a claw of his right hand. 'I would have plucked out his heart with my own hands and carried it to Tehran myself if I could have got away with it.'

Jack watched the Glock weaving backwards and forwards as Metzhagen's features became wilder. He'd put the brandy bottle on the floor. It was now two-thirds empty.

The magnate fell silent, brooding. He gazed at Jack speculatively and came to a decision. 'Captain Boulder, I will now reveal for you the heart of the matter. Then you must judge for yourself whether or not your own role was justified. Thanks to my initiative, there is now a small unofficial British mission in Tehran. Its members have been received most cordially. The ostensible purpose is to restore the trade between our two countries, the loss of which caused grievous economic problems on both sides. But the underlying and more urgent purpose is to establish a sting operation.'

'A sting operation?' echoed Jack. 'To catch whom?'

'To catch the thieves who would destroy the planet with their greed. The smuggling of fissionable materials has become a nightmare. The breakdown of the Soviet Union has created a deadly black market. Plutonium, some of it in the weapons-grade 235 and 239 isotope, is leaking out of Russia as fast as fake icons. It is being plundered from warheads, submarines, research laboratories and nuclear storage bunkers. Underpaid workers in the nuclear industry are selling uranium pellets in exchange for bottles of vodka. Old East German Stasi and Russian KGB officers have set up smuggling networks. Poles, Czechs, Germans, Hungarians are all endangering future life on Earth. The International Atomic Energy Agency is floundering under the onslaught. For every so-called 'mule' caught with a lead-lined suitcase in his possession, a score may be getting through to hawk their deadly cargoes to Islamic fundamentalists who dream of a twenty-first-century reconquest of Europe.

'It was the Germans who first had the idea of setting up a nuclear sting operation – which they did with some success in Bremen. But it has made the smugglers wary. They're suspicious now of doing business with agents in Europe. Instead, they head for the Iran border and what they think will be a safe trade.'

Jack was gripped. 'Why should the Iranians allow us to set up a sting to trap plutonium smugglers?'

'Ah, Captain Boulder, I see I have at last wiped the look of resentment from your face. Good! You will, perhaps, learn something about the difficulty of clinging to moral absolutes.'

Metzhagen rubbed his hands together vigorously in a gesture of great satisfaction, like a schoolmaster who had at last penetrated the skull of an obtuse pupil.

'For a long time working with the Iranians has been unthinkable and, officially, still is. They are international pariahs. They've secretly pursued their nuclear bomb programme for which they recruited a number of renegade scientists from Russia and we have maintained our trade embargoes. But it is beginning to get through to them that co-operation with the West will make them stronger – not in nuclear weaponry but in the peaceful uses of nuclear energy. They have watched the North Koreans abandon their illicit gathering of nuclear materials in favour of American economic aid and help in developing their legitimate energy sources.

'All this has begun to have a telling effect on the Iranians. But when I went to Tehran, put this to them and handed them a blueprint of the proposed sting, they still looked for the catch. They wanted evidence of good faith.'

Metzhagen drew breath. 'I told them getting rid of Rushdie was out of the question. Even though the British Government would dearly love to see the back of him, they have invested too much prestige in keeping him alive and his death could bring them down. That was a price no British politician would risk paying.

'It took all the power of my tongue to keep the talks going. Then they said, "Conrad Niven. You either deal with Rushdie or that piece of camel dung Niven. It's your choice".

'Once again, I pleaded for a more civilized approach to our differences. But they were adamant. So, finally, I thought, why not? It would mean one worthless human being exchanged for the lives of countless millions in the next century – millions who would not die because the threat of nuclear war between the West and the forces of fundamentalist Islam would have been removed.

'They sent me away to think it over. I asked Professor Askew about the possibility of infecting Niven with a fatal disease. He said such an attempt would be hit and miss and could possibly kill others.

'We considered an engineered accident but that, too, might have killed his innocent bodyguards. In any case, an accident would have to take place anywhere but on British territory. I believe that no matter how efficiently it was executed, the deed would still have raised grave suspicions of a conspiracy that had been permitted to go ahead by a government known to be less than enamoured of Conrad Niven.

'After we had considered and dismissed all other approaches to this problem, we arrived at you, Captain Boulder.

'You might be heartened to learn that, three days after you had done your job with such clinical skill, the Iranians sent me a message. Our mission to Tehran is even now setting up the sting. The bargain is being sealed.

'Yes, Captain Boulder, the human sacrifice that you presented to the Iranians is about to be rewarded. So let us hear no more of your contempt. Rather, start to feel some pride in the service you have rendered.'

Jack asked quietly, 'Who else have your little band of renegades killed as the final solution to the world's ills?'

Metzhagen scoffed, 'We're not an assassination bureau. Conrad Niven was at an extremity of our operations. Our methods of ridding Britain of those who could undermine it – the drug barons, the disloyal politicians, the financiers who would wreck the currency – are usually much more subtle. These are people who buy juries and lawyers, people who mock all legitimate attempts to bring them to book for their treachery.' He waved a hand airily. 'There are car accidents, suicides to be encouraged, public careers wrecked by exposed sex scandals, incriminating documents filched and placed into the hands of those who will exact justice ... We are able to call on the good offices of some of the most upright people in the country.'

He looked sadly at Jack. 'With your extraordinary skill with firearms, you could have joined the élite, Captain Boulder. Once in a while, you would have received a phone call from a new-found colleague, a sum of money would have been placed in that Austrian bank account, and you would have gone off to rid the world of some swine who was using our country as a public lavatory.'

'What about the rule of law?' said Jack. 'You and your grand friends are above it, are you?'

'Go ahead, indulge your ruptured sense of morality, Captain Boulder. Your own government is not so fastidious, I assure you. At this very moment, Israel has its agents from Mossad roaming Britain and winkling out its Arab enemies. Those Israelis illegally carry arms but the British government looks the other way.

'You see, Captain Boulder, the truth is our government loathes trapping foreign terrorists. To capture one alive means a messy public trial, retaliation, perhaps the shedding of yet more innocent blood and certainly it means serious harm to trade, our lifeline. Far better to let Mossad drug, kidnap and shoot, and in other ways clean up any mess that is too embarrassing for us to clean up for ourselves. My little group can do only so much. You could have taken a crucial role in that work.'

Jack did not like Metzhagen's mournful use of the past tense. 'It's too late for me, is it?'

'Far too late, Captain. The play, as far as you are concerned, is ending. In your mindless pursuit of explanations you have undone the work of a decade. That is how long it has taken me to evolve our band of helpers. Now you know everything and now you must pay for your knowledge.

'I had intended confronting you with your family – letting your lovely wife persuade you to cease your activities. But since, as you say, Ringrose has already pinpointed you, you cannot now save yourself by a sudden change of heart. He must never be allowed to squeeze from you the secrets of our higher purpose.'

'My death won't help you,' said Jack. 'I've told others.'

Metzhagen gave a thin smile that Jack did not like. 'Told others? I don't think so, Captain Boulder. Perhaps only your wife...'

Jack felt the chill from Metzhagen's accurate insight. He said, as casually as he could, 'She'd be the last person I'd tell. Have you ever known a woman able to keep a secret?'

'Well,' said Metzhagen, once again with that unsettling smile, 'we shall soon have the opportunity of finding out.'

'How's that?' Something icy clutched at Jack's chest.

'For convenience, I've had her and your two sons brought here to the house.'

'You don't even know where they've been staying.' Jack heard his voice rise in incipient panic.

'Captain Boulder, we made one blunder with you. We would not make another. Does Southwold in Suffolk hold any meaning for you?'

Chapter Fifty-One

Tom Ringrose had three pieces of paper on his desk. One alarmed him, one impressed him and one made him extremely angry.

The first was the note that Jack Boulder had taped to the back of his movie poster. It read simply, 'I've gone to see Sir Gilbert Metzhagen.

He has the answers. If I disappear, go to Frant.' Boulder had headed this: 'Friday, 7 p.m.'

The second piece of paper, at substantial length, was a computer print-out prepared by Inspector Colin Dawson detailing Sir Gilbert Metzhagen's many financial and industrial interests, his known charitable bequests – and, ominously, his close friendships with many powerful figures in political life. The biography said to the wise that he was not a man to cross lightly.

The third was a single sheet, a message from the Assistant Commissioner (Crime) that he tossed across for Lionel Firth to read. The Home Secretary, weekending with friends in the Cotswolds, had urged caution in the matter of Miss Nancy Tintagel's exhumation. He wasn't refusing the order but he wasn't approving it, either. It was an extraordinary business and he'd like more time to consider aspects of the case of which Commander Ringrose was perhaps not cognizant. When he was back in Whitehall on Tuesday and a fuller report available to him, the Minister would take the matter under review once again, etc. etc. . . .

'We've touched the parallel universe again, guv'nor,' said Firth. 'What now? Do we obtain warrants and turn over Metzhagen's country drum?'

'No,' said Ringrose, shaking his head. 'What have we got to justify a raid? That Niven was a guest aboard his yacht? That he gave a part in a film to one of the female witnesses? A cryptic note from our chief suspect? There isn't enough there for us to nick Metzhagen for causing an obstruction on the pavement. Besides, the magistrate would take one look at the name on the search warrant and become as coy as the Home Secretary. He'd need a fuller report, need to take the matter under advisement, and so on . . . However,' Firth saw his chief turn cunning, 'we do have reason to believe that a deranged gunman is on the loose and that Sir Gilbert is in personal danger. The least we can do is follow the trail which – surprise! – leads directly to Sir Gilbert's country seat at,' Ringrose consulted the print-out, 'Fern Hall, near the village of Frant in East Sussex. We can offer him night and day protection until the miscreant is caught – the very same miscreant who is nursing a bizarre notion that Sir Gilbert, perish the thought, had a hand in the conspiracy to assassinate Conrad Niven. Now what could have occurred to make this insane individual think such a terrible thing? Can Sir Gilbert throw any light on this?'

Firth laughed at the slyness of Ringrose's scenario. 'Do we go mob-handed and tooled up?'

Ringrose shook his head. 'No. You may draw a sidearm, Lionel. Though I wouldn't fancy your chances against Jack Boulder. Otherwise, it's just you and me taking a pleasant Sunday drive in the country to make a helpful call on a distinguished public figure.'

Ringrose had an afterthought. 'To cover our asses, you'd better let the East Sussex constabulary know we'll be on the patch.'

Chapter Fifty-Two

Ben Boulder guessed he was having the same astral experience that a ghost would have, flitting and gliding through the silent corridors and panelled rooms of a great castle, except that he couldn't pass through brickwork. He wished he could. The sensation of haunting was eerie but it was also exciting enough to make him forget his fatigue.

On the ground floor, there was plenty of light slanting in through the tall windows to cast his moving shadow onto carpets and walls, because the terraces surrounding the house were floodlit. Through the panes, he occasionally glimpsed a patrolling security man and hurriedly drew back, but the interior of the house was quiet. He found the vast drawing room, the library, a long dining gallery lined with oil paintings, which Ben was careful not to touch – he knew about art galleries where each painting was wired to an alarm system.

Up the broad white marble staircase, he put his ear to carved doors and sometimes heard snoring and nocturnal murmurings. Up a further flight of less impressive stairs, he pushed through a padded, soundproof door into a realm lacking fine panelling or pictures. He heard someone moving about and hastily withdrew.

His dilemma was that he had no idea of what sort of situation his father was in. Could he really be working with the men Ben had met so far? Ben agreed with Mal: they were a bunch of creeps. He hated the one who looked at his mother like *that*.

Ben finally decided that his dad, like Mum, Mal and himself, was under guard. He remembered the warning about strangers that Dad had given Mum when he handed over the pistol. But where in this rambling hulk of a building would he be?

All the upstairs doors opened when he silently turned the knobs so Ben eliminated those as prisons. The top-floor accommodation seemed to be for the servants and he returned to the basement baffled. Perhaps daylight would bring enlightenment. He peered down the corridor to where his exploration had begun. Fatty was on his chair, chin slumped on his mighty chest, apparently asleep.

Ben retreated. In one storage room he discovered a stack of delicate gilt chairs. He wriggled between the rows and found himself a shielded space against the wall. He unhooked his backpack and slipped it under his head as a makeshift pillow. They'd have to move chairs to find him here. Ben decided he'd snooze till dawn and then eavesdrop on the wakening house in the quest for his father. The backpack felt a bit lumpy against his cheek – but also reassuring – and Ben fell instantly into a deep, dreamless sleep.

When he woke he had no idea of the time because it was dark. Then he remembered: the sound that had roused him had been someone passing the store-room door.

Ben wriggled frantically out from under the chair stacks, pushing his backpack before him, and peered into the corridor. A man in cricket whites was walking away from him, carrying a bottle and a tumbler in one hand. In the other – Ben barely suppressed the gasp – was his father's Glock, or its twin. He had helped clean it several times.

Ben opened the backpack, took out the object that he had guarded so zealously since yesterday teatime, and went in pursuit.

His quarry had vanished, but Ben spotted him again from the next corner in the maze. The man was making heavy-footed, determined progress. 'Marching as to war' came to Ben's mind from a rousing hymn he sang at school assemblies.

He repeated his tactic of waiting for the man to disappear before speeding on his trainers to the next corner. This time when Ben peered round he pulled his head back sharply. The man in white had stopped to speak to the underling who, the previous evening, had brought Fatty his supper. He, too, had a chair outside a closed door. He was now opening that door with a key.

Ben, at last, understood Fatty's cryptic remark that his father was getting his exercise. At the corner junction was a small arrowed plaque with GYMNASIUM/SAUNA etched into the metal.

He watched the door open and the guard stand aside deferentially. White Trousers was framed in profile by the brilliant strip lighting inside the gymnasium. The man turned to the right and was speaking to someone out of sight. Ben was too far away to catch the words. The door slammed shut, leaving White Trousers inside with . . . his father?

He glanced back along the corridor down which he had tracked White Trousers. He could hear voices. He felt no fear.

The guard still faced the entrance to the gym. Ben took the opportunity to nip across the mouth of the corridor and, on the far side, find a door that yielded. The room was in darkness. Ben squatted down and peered out once again, at ground level. The two men who had escorted them from Southwold wheeled into view and approached the gym. He could hear them murmuring with the guard.

For the first time, he experienced real apprehension. He was intensely aware that a man armed with a deadly weapon had gone into a room where he now believed his father was being held. Furthermore, that man had done the unthinkable, taken that gun from his father. He would never have surrendered the Glock without a struggle.

Ben rocked on his haunches. Three men outside and at least one in the gym: too many for him to tackle. The minutes dragged by. He made one resolve: if he heard a shot, he would go for it, regardless of the consequences.

He ceased rocking and came alert like a gundog. The voices were getting louder. He peered out as the two he knew from Southwold emerged from the gymnasium corridor and went back the way they had come. They were arguing. The fair-haired one who had eyed his mother was saying, 'There's no alternative. We just have to let him do it.'

Ben watched them disappear. Now was his moment. He stepped boldly into the gymnasium approach and began walking forward. The guard saw him immediately. They faced each other, like gunslingers of the Old West.

'Who let you out?' the guard said, truly surprised. 'You're not supposed to be wandering about like this, you little bugger.'

'I let myself out,' said Ben.

'Oh, yes? And what was Harry doing all this time?'

'If you mean Fatty, he was sleeping his stupid head off.' Ben was amazed at how calm he felt.

The guard's eyes narrowed angrily. 'You cheeky little sod.'

He took a step forward.

Ben took the object he had nursed so long from behind his back. The guard took one look and laughed.

Ben assumed a firing position with the Walther and said, 'Mister, you will turn round and open that door.'

The guard was still laughing. 'I'm sorry. I didn't realize it was you,

Clint.' He took another step forward and now loomed only six paces from Ben. The boy could not miss.

'I'm warning you. This is a real gun. Open the door.'

'Where d'you buy it? Hamley's?' The guard made his lunge and Ben fired.

The round nicked the guard's thigh, ricocheted along the cement floor with a fearful whine and embedded itself in the door's architrave.

The effect on the man was paralysing. He froze and grasped his stinging leg through the torn jeans. 'You little bastard, you've shot me.'

'The next one,' said Ben, composed, 'goes straight through your face. Now open the door.'

'It's not locked.'

'*Open it, you bastard!*' Ben thrust the Walther forward and aimed directly at the guard's face.

He flinched and shuffled about painfully, trying to stem the trickle of blood with his hand. 'All right. All right. Take it easy. Don't be a silly boy.'

'I'll show you just how silly I can be if you don't get that door open by the time I count three. One...' The guard put blood on the handle as he pushed the door inward and shuffled into the room. In his shadow, Ben heard White Trousers ask anxiously, 'Who's shooting? What's happening?'

Ben stepped into view and said, 'This is happening. Drop your weapon and raise your hands in the air.'

Gilbert Metzhagen's gaze, levelled at the Walther in a small boy's hands, was one of incredulity. The single syllable, 'Who...?' hung in the air. But the look of amazement switched instantly to one of fury. The man who gave orders and never took them snarled, 'Like hell, I will,' and began to raise his firing arm.

Ben hesitated. Did he really have the nerve to shoot a man down?

He was concentrating so hard on White Trousers that he was only dimly aware of a figure in the corner of his eye. But that figure – his father – was suddenly moving.

Jack Boulder drew his legs up to his chest and kicked out with all his strength at Metzhagen's knees. The tycoon screamed in agony. The Glock waved wildly and sent a round into the ceiling. The guard cried, 'Jesus!' and threw himself to the ground.

Metzhagen was tottering backward. He tried desperately to save himself from falling and would have succeeded if he had not backed himself up to the rim of the empty plunge pool. He fell backwards and they all heard his head crack on the tiles. The Glock fell from his grasp as Ben rushed forward and looked down. Metzhagen was out cold.

Jack Boulder was as thunderstruck as his captors at the sight of his son wielding a handgun like a veteran. But he was still self-possessed enough to shout, 'Ben, the man on the door has the key to these 'cuffs in his right-hand jacket pocket.'

The boy walked over to the guard, who was still stretched out alongside a rowing machine. He pointed the Walther at his head and said, 'Come on, mister, hand it over.'

'You wouldn't shoot an unarmed man, would you, son?' The guard had lost all his bounce.

'They're the best ones,' said Ben coldly. 'They can't shoot back.'

'Jesus,' said the guard again. He groped in the pocket and produced the key.

Keeping the gun trained on him, Ben backed towards his father and handed it over. 'Can you manage, Dad?'

'Perfectly, Ben,' said Jack, bounding to his feet and massaging his sore wrist. 'Keep an eye on him and on the corridor while I have a look at Mr Big.'

In passing his son, Jack ruffled the boy's hair. 'You little demon, you. Well done.' The tears in his eyes signified part-gratitude for his deliverance and part-sadness for his son's premature introduction into the world of violence.

Metzhagen was stirring and groaning. Jack seized the Glock and briefly inspected it for damage. It seemed in working order and there was plenty of persuasion left in the magazine.

Ben said, 'Mum and Mal are here, Dad. We've got to rescue them.'

Jack cursed under his breath. He looked around at the section of the gym he hadn't been able to see from his position on the workbench. In a rack hung a number of skipping ropes attached to ballbearing handles, the kind used by boxers in training.

He heaved Metzhagen from the pool and hogtied him back to back with the guard who was whingeing. 'I'll bleed to death.' Jack inspected the livid furrow in his flesh and said, 'I'm sorry to say we won't have that pleasure yet.'

Now that their immediate danger had passed, father and son lowered their weapons and hugged each other fiercely. 'Ben, I think I owe you my life,' said Jack, kissing the top of his head.

'Any time,' said Ben awkwardly.

'Now tell me about Mal and your mother. And for God's sake be careful with that gun.'

Ben led the way through the maze of corridors back to the boiler room. The chair still stood opposite the door, which was now open, but it was empty. As they came nearer they could hear Fatty bellowing, Grace crying and Mal screaming. Father and son broke into a gallop.

They could hear Fatty shouting, 'Where is the little prick? How did he get out,' accompanied by the sound of flesh being slapped.

'Here I am,' said Ben, appearing as if by magic in the doorway.

'Why, you little . . .' Fatty's eyes bulged and he lunged forward. As he came through the doorway, Jack stepped into view and punched him hard on the side of the jaw. He did not go down so Jack hit him again. The man was like an ox who had just survived a stun gun but this time he collapsed groggily onto one wide knee. Then he prised himself back to his feet, still bellowing like a bull after the picadors had begun to work him over.

He lashed out at Jack and caught him on the shoulder. With awe, Ben watched his father react. A flurry of punches and kung-fu blows rained on Fatty's neck, chest and head. Slowly, he sank to both knees, his piggy eyes losing focus and his ham-like arms drooping as if the weight of his own great fists had proved too heavy a burden. Jack finished him with two merciless blows behind the ear. Over he went, sideways like a reclining Buddha.

They found Mal backed tearfully into a corner and Grace picking herself up off the floor. Her face was already beginning to show the bruises where Fatty had slapped her.

Jack scooped up Mal and embraced his wife fiercely. As they hugged, he said, 'Ben, do you know the way out of here?'

'Follow me,' said his son who was feeling marvellous and leaped happily over Fatty's prone form.

Then Grace noticed what he was carrying in his right hand. 'Where did you get that gun?' she gasped.

Jack said, 'Grace, there's no time for questions now. Let's go.'

Ben led them through the corridors and up the flight of stairs that he knew came out into the grand entrance hall. They had not quite reached the top when Rupert Strang's face appeared over the rail. Jack placed a round in the wall over his head.

The sound was deafening. Strang's head disappeared and they heard him say, 'God Almighty, Boulder's out and armed. Everybody get back!'

Jack said to Ben, 'If you see anyone, aim a single shot to strike the floor at their feet. I don't want you killing them.' He heard Grace give a small shriek at this but she did not argue.

At a rush, the Boulder family came out into the hall. Immediately they saw heads bobbing in the shelter of the marble balustrading. Jack fired over their heads, sending splinters of wood panelling showering down on them.

They could hear Strang shouting, 'Jack, Jack. There's no need for this. Let's talk.'

Jack's response was to send another round overhead. 'Talk about what? Murdering my family?' he roared.

'Jack, I swear, that was never our intention.'

'In that case, you won't mind if we leave now.'

Father and son, back to back with Mal in the crook of Jack's left arm and Grace following in a crouch, edged towards the main double doors.

Ben saw a man in a dark suit appear in a doorway and obeyed his father's instructions to the letter, sending a round skittering along the marble floor. The man jumped quickly out of sight.

Jack said to Grace, 'Open the front door, then stand back.'

She did so and Jack handed Mal to her. He sidled out cautiously and surveyed the terrace and gardens. Two security men were standing uncertainly in the mid-distance. Jack made up their minds for them. He fired over their heads and they dived for cover.

His hired Range Rover was standing on the gravel. He shouted back into the hall, 'Quick, follow me!'

The family came out into the sunlight and raced after him. Ben, bringing up the rear, was suddenly tempted. For fun he placed a round in the closed half of the great oak door. 'Stop that!' said his father sharply. 'Never waste ammunition.'

Jack opened the rear passenger door and rummaged under the seat. His captors had been lazy. They had discovered neither the Cobray nor the spare ignition key.

'Everybody get in. Ben, you sit in front,' said Jack. He took out the Cobray and said, 'I'm going to discourage anyone from following us.'

He stood four-square to the great house, shimmering in its summer glory, with its floor-to-ceiling windows and its blazing Virginia creeper. Then he raised his daunting weapon and deliberately enfiladed the ground floor from corner to corner, sending glass shards exploding into the elegant rooms and pock-marking the grey stone facings of Sir Gilbert Metzhagen's home.

Satisfied, he climbed into the driving seat, placed the Cobray on Ben's lap for safe-keeping, and said, 'We're going on holiday.'

His hand gripped the wheel. His sleeve fell back revealing that Metzhagen's heavies had stolen his wristwatch. 'What's the time?' he asked Grace. He was surprised when she told him it was still not eight a.m.

Chapter Fifty-Three

Tom Ringrose wished he had not allowed Lionel Firth to utter the words 'deranged gunman' to the East Sussex Constabulary. This, plus his own nationwide reputation coupled with the name of Sir Gilbert Metzhagen, had achieved the same effect as poking the Chief Constable's finger into an electrical socket.

At dawn, with only the newspaper boy and the anxious-to-please village bobby as witnesses, an operational control van and two battle-wagons packed with East Sussex's best uniformed and body-armoured officers rolled to a halt on Frant Green.

Instead of a tactical team leader of middling rank, Ringrose and Firth were confronted by the Deputy Chief Constable, no less. They were being deliberately outranked.

Inside the van, the reason was made instantly clear. The DCC said anxiously, 'The Chief is extremely concerned, Ringrose. Sir Gilbert Metzhagen is a highly regarded figure, leader of the community and all that. And, *entre nous*, a personal friend of his.'

The DCC was actually wringing his hands, another jobsworth who no doubt applied to every selection board for a county of his own.

Ringrose said mildly, 'We merely wish to make a courtesy call on the man. For reasons connected with my investigation, it has to be a surprise and I have, perhaps, overstressed the danger from our quarry. He does not use firearms haphazardly. Our understanding is that he wants to talk to Sir Gilbert rather than shoot him.'

'Well, if he tries anything in East Sussex, he'll rue the day,' said the DCC vigorously.

'Oh,' said Ringrose innocently, 'I'd have your chaps keep their heads down, if I were you. The chap we're interested in could shoot the buttons off your uniform one by one and not leave a mark on you. He's probably the world's greatest living sharp-shooter. A quite uncanny talent.'

The DCC's handwringing went into overdrive.

A sergeant had rigged an Ordnance Survey map on the van wall and used a pointer to outline for Ringrose and Firth the extent of the Fern Hall estate.

Tom turned back to the DCC. 'Perhaps, sir, as a precautionary measure, the deployment of men along the boundary walls might be in order... When DCI Firth and I go up to the house, there may be persons other than our sharp-shooter who may not wish to see us. I don't want anybody to be permitted to leave the premises until we have checked them out.'

Before the tactical team leader, who so far had stood by deferring to the DCC and saying nothing, could make his move, a flurry of radio traffic from the set at the far end of the van halted them in their tracks.

The radio man swivelled in his seat, pressing his earpiece to his skull, listening. 'We have a mobile unit reporting gunfire from the direction of the Wadhurst Road.'

Ringrose and Firth exchanged baffled glances. 'Early huntsmen?' suggested Lionel Firth tentatively.

The DCC gave him that look, a mixture of pity and contempt, that country people reserve for ignorant townsfolk. 'Huntsmen don't shoot.'

The radio man said, 'It's automatic fire, sir.'

The senior officers raced to their cars with the battle-wagons following in pursuit.

The gate of Fern Hall was jammed two-thirds open. The leading edge was buckled where a vehicle had ploughed through and the metalwork had been punctured by three rounds of ammunition. The gateman was sitting on the gravel holding his head, gibbering.

Ringrose raced to his side and forcibly pulled his hands from his face. 'Stop that! Tell me what happened.'

The man looked up with wild eyes. 'The crazy bastard shot my hat off my head.' Sure enough, over by the gatehouse, a sunhat was lying in a flowerbed showing signs of ill-treatment. 'He said the next one was for me if I didn't get the gate open double-quick.'

'Who was he?'

'I dunno. Big bloke, youngish. I was having my breakfast. I came out when I heard a vehicle coming. He just leaned out the window and let fly.'

Firth joined Ringrose as the tactical boys in their bulletproofs began to spread out through the grounds. 'A bit late for that,' said the gateman, nodding at the frantic activity. 'They're well gone.'

Ringrose and Firth said simultaneously: 'They?'

'Yes.' The gateman squinted up into their faces. 'Fancy spraying bullets around like a lunatic when you've got your wife and kids with you.'

Again the two officers spoke simultaneously: 'Wife and kids?'

The gateman was recovering his equilibrium. 'Are you two Siamese twins or something? It was his wife and kids. She was in the back with a young 'un and he was driving with an older boy by his side.'

He stopped speaking abruptly and swore. 'You know something? It's coming back now. I think that little bugger had a gun of his own. What was it? Bonnie and Clyde on a family outing?'

'Describe Bonnie,' said Ringrose quickly. He could see the DCC stalking self-importantly across the drive.

'Oh, a real looker. Sort of silver blonde. She had a kid pressed into her shoulder and was covering his ears. I should bloody well think so. What sort of a parent exposes a child to that kind of thing?'

The two detectives lifted the gateman and led him to his own front door. 'Don't go away. We'll need you later. By the way, was the car a Range Rover?' asked Ringrose.

'Yeah. How did you know that?'

'It's Clyde's favourite marque,' said Ringrose solemnly.

The DCC caught up with them. 'Do we have a line on the car and number?'

'No need to bother, sir.'

'No need to bother, Commander?' The DCC's blood pressure rose visibly under the film of sweat caused by these unaccustomed early-morning exertions. 'This man has committed serious firearms offences.'

Ringrose said quietly, 'You do understand, sir, that I am engaged in an investigation of the utmost delicacy – a task for which I was personally chosen by the Home Secretary?'

Looking into the DCC's doubtful face, Ringrose decided to elaborate: 'And with the full approval of the Prime Minister.'

That did the trick. 'Ah, yes, of course. I understand perfectly,' jabbered the DCC, not understanding at all but not prepared to make an enemy so close to the seat of power.

Ringrose lowered his voice to a conspiratorial whisper and Firth, hands behind his back, stood innocently by, watching the blue uniforms advancing on Fern Hall.

'There is no need for pursuit because I know where I'll find the man,' said Ringrose. 'By all means, prepare firearms charges, but other matters may yet have to take precedence.'

Ringrose raised his eyebrows, which were showing the first tendrils of grey. They signalled that he had imparted vital information to the DCC. 'Utmost discretion is crucial.'

'Am I permitted to know his name?'

Ringrose was soothing. 'Later, sir, everything will fall into place. Meanwhile, if you could have your men assemble everyone on the premises, DCI Firth and I would like to ask a few questions.'

They watched the DCC march away, scattering orders to his blue army. Firth said, 'Is it possible? Could Metzhagen have been holding Jack Boulder's family here all this time to guarantee his silence?'

They surveyed the shot-up frontage of Fern House and Ringrose whistled. 'Well, something just as upsetting sure got our Jack good and mad.'

For the remainder of the day, Ringrose and Firth listened to lies. No one knew the identity of the hooligan – perhaps a business rival? – who had rampaged through the house. Sir Gilbert himself had nothing to say about anything. He was taken to hospital suffering from concussion. His lawyer was soon by his bedside.

A member of the household security staff, one Kenneth Cross, was taken in the same ambulance suffering from an obvious flesh wound caused by a passing bullet but which he insisted had been the result of his own clumsiness when handling equipment in Sir Gilbert's personal gymnasium.

Another, Harry Dixon from Bermondsey, refused medical aid for facial bruising – the result, so he said, of walking into a glass door although the police could find no glass door on the premises.

But by late afternoon, Ringrose and Firth had sifted out the staff, and the hired thugs and were left with a quartet of 'house guests' who, naturally, hadn't the faintest idea of what was going on.

Rafe Cummings, Rupert Strang and Peter Hope-Casson presented bewildered faces to the world and identified themselves as friends of Sir Gilbert, and civil servants in the Foreign and Commonwealth Service.

Ringrose couldn't be bothered with any more Whitehall bullshit. He knew where he'd find out what he wanted to know.

He stepped out to the Constabulary control van, now parked in front of the house, and placed a secure call. It was patched through to a private house in Hampstead and Ringrose read over the three names. 'They're at MI6,' said Jake Bishop promptly. 'Cummings is a senior officer, Hope-Casson is an awful shit. Likes pulling the wings off flies. Strang is a straight arrow.'

Ringrose said, 'Jake, I have another name here. Bulwer Tancred. Says he's an under-secretary in the Cabinet Office.'

'Hold the Don Ameche. I have to go to another extension.'

Ringrose could hear Jake Bishop opening and shutting filing cabinets. He returned to the phone. 'Yeah. That's kosher. He's a low-profile kind of guy. There's not much else I can tell you about him except, with a name like that, his father must have had one hell of a sense of humour.'

Ringrose thanked the CIA chief and was about to ring off when Bishop said, 'Hey, Tom. I hope I'm going to get the full works over a five-course dinner at Rules. That's a colourful cast of characters you have there.'

'I'm booking the table where Mark Twain sat. It'll be real soon,' Ringrose promised.

Chapter Fifty-Four

On the race back to the East Anglian coast, the Boulder family stopped off at a Little Chef. They were all famished and tucked into eggs and bacon. They were in such high spirits that people began to stare. Grace had to hush Ben and warn him to keep his voice down as he related his night's adventures.

He acted out his part, excitedly jumping up and crouching alongside the table leg to demonstrate his tracking skills.

Jack's knuckles were raw from the beating he had administered to Fatty. 'Kiss them better,' piped up Mal. And Grace, swollen face notwithstanding, obliged. She even held her tongue over Ben's suddenly revealed knowledge of handguns. Her one-woman board of inquiry would come later.

Jack shot fitful glances out of the window to where the Range Rover was parked. Would Metzhagen's people come after him? He now knew everything and the sooner he placed on record every last detail – his confession, in fact – the sooner he would have insurance against further attempts to kill him.

Would they really have slaughtered his family? He looked with anguish at Grace, Ben and Mal, the morning sunlight slanting through the plate-glass windows and wreathing their heads in gold. He couldn't bear to think of life without them. The Glock was back in his belt. Just in case.

Metzhagen had made him his unwitting instrument so that businessmen could snare fat contracts and wrap their greed in perverted patriotism. Bile welled in Jack's mouth. He was trapped between Metzhagen's murderous intentions and Ringrose's duty to call him to account.

Grace was forced to pay the breakfast bill because Metzhagen's lackeys had emptied his pockets. This prompted Mal to inquire as to the whereabouts of his Indiana Jones backpack. Ben clapped a hand to his mouth and said, 'Oh! It's still in the storeroom.' His brother wailed but Grace cuddled him and said, 'Daddy'll buy you another.'

Back on the road, they stopped briefly for Jack to buy a large notepad. He would write a true account of the past weeks the instant they reached Southwold. Would he then simply hand it over to Ringrose with all that that meant for his own future? Unnoticed by a still euphoric Grace, his eyes turned bleak as the road unreeled beneath his wheels.

That night, with the first words on paper, Jack slept downstairs with the Glock, the Walther and the Cobray all at hand. At two a.m. the phone rang. An upper-class voice said, 'Jack, this is Rupert Strang. Please don't hang up.'

Jack moved swiftly across the darkened room to the window. There was no suspicious movement outside.

'Well?' he said.

'Jack, some of us have been having a very serious meeting and we have spent the day having further consultations with . . . well . . . let's say with associated parties. We have devised a plan of damage limitation that requires only one thing from you.'

'And that is?'

'Your confirmation that our version of events is the only true one.'

'And what does that mean for me and my wife and kids?' Jack glanced up. Grace was tiptoeing downstairs in her cotton nightie.

'It means you may have to stand in the corner for a bit. Plead guilty to a certain naïvety. But there should be no question of prison.'

'And you and your Secret Service friends – how do you come out of it?'

'Smelling of ordure, I'm afraid. We, too, have explaining to do. I gather Metzhagen told you why we've been doing these things as a breakaway group. He didn't lie to you, Jack. We're still proud of what we've done for our country. We weren't misguided then and we don't accept we're misguided now that we're in this quandary and – let's be honest – this fight for survival.'

'Don't you have any doubts at all about the morality of what you and your friends have been doing?'

'No,' said Strang. 'Just as you had no doubt when you went after Sean McGurk. You cannot escape it, Jack. We're all of a kind. We've lost faith in the democratic process to save us from the barbarians. The only difference between us is one of degree. You see the individual outrage. We see the big picture and what's happening to this country.'

'I don't like the idea of vigilantes,' said Jack. 'If I had my time again, and knowing what I know now, I'd leave McGurk strictly alone. He was the sort of rat who would eventually have walked into a bullet without any intervention on my part. I was idiotic not to see that at the time. Instead, I've come near to disgracing my regiment and destroying my family. My own son, at the age of twelve, already knows what it's like to fire a lethal weapon at a fellow human being. It's not the upbringing I planned for him.'

Strang remained silent. Jack beckoned Grace over to share the earpiece. 'You spoke of a plan. What is it?'

Rupert Strang talked for nearly an hour, carefully refracting the events of the past month through the prism of his own Machiavellian mind. By the end of this exposition, nothing was as it had seemed.

Jack and Grace listened without interruption. Finally, Strang said enticingly, 'That's it, Jack. One bound and you're free.'

Jack looked inquiringly at Grace. She said slowly, 'It's ingenious. Will Commander Ringrose go for it?'

Rupert Strang heard the question. 'Mrs Boulder, fear not. No matter how distinguished, Ringrose is a serving police officer. Even he has his superiors. Each of us who serves has to yield occasionally to others. My colleague and I are working on this aspect.'

Grace shrugged and put a bare arm round Jack's shoulders. 'Tell him we'll co-operate, but there are conditions.' She laid them out and Strang listened.

Before he rang off, he said, 'Gilbert has a nasty headache but I'll be able to talk to him at length first thing in the morning. I'm sure Mrs Boulder's suggestions will find favour.'

He paused, and then added, 'I'm relieved at your attitude, Jack. You and your family sleep easy.'

Chapter Fifty-Five

Ringrose and Firth called on Inspector Colin Dawson at 7 a.m. on Monday morning. With Dawson at the word processor, they sealed themselves in Ringrose's office and began to compile their report on the assassination of Conrad Niven.

They carefully picked through the evidence and in four hours had constructed a picture of the truth that was admittedly part-deduction but in most respects was accurate. They named Jack Boulder as the suspected sniper, with four members of the Secret Intelligence Service (one female deceased), as co-conspirators, along with a senior civil servant currently working in the Cabinet Office.

Ringrose pointed to Sir Gilbert Metzhagen as financier of the complex and expensive operation, with the strong likelihood that the aforesaid renegade members of the SIS had made unauthorized use of their service's facilities for covert operations.

Ringrose requested that the Foreign Office be asked to confirm an unofficial report (source not stated) that the bounty money had not been claimed.

Ringrose and Firth said frankly that they could furnish no other motive for the killing but pointed out that, in English law, none was necessary to obtain a conviction.

However, as the major crime in their catalogue of offences had been committed on French territory, Ringrose recommended that he be allowed to fly to Paris to present the complete dossier to Commissaire Victor Massillon and invite the French government to apply for the arrest and extradition of the named persons to stand trial in France.

He applied again for an exhumation order on the grave of Nancy Tintagel.

Dawson made a single printed copy and Ringrose sent it upstairs in a locked file. Dawson made a further copy on a floppy disc which he handed to Ringrose. He then wiped clean the computer's memory of this item.

The three men sat looking quietly satisfied. A long, intricate investigation had been brought finally into focus on eight foolscap sheets of paper.

'I give it thirty minutes until we hear the first cries of a body in pain in the Assistant Commissioner (Crime)'s office. We should be able to hear it from right here. Then another half-hour until the sound of sobbing from the Commissioner himself.'

Ringrose checked the time. 'Let's go and eat.'

They were summoned back from the canteen in exactly fifty minutes.

The Commissioner looked as if a brilliantined gigolo had run off with his wife. He was ashen. 'Tom, in my entire police service I've never come across a hotter potato.' He was balancing the report gingerly on his fingertips demonstrating the point.

Ringrose could see him struggling to hold back what he really wanted to say, which was: 'Ringrose, this is a heap of shit. I don't believe a word of it.'

Instead, the Commissioner managed: 'It's shocking. The SIS involvement ... after all the reassurances ... hard to credit ... the fallout will be cataclysmic ... God, the French will gloat!'

He had a sudden alarming thought: 'How many people in the building know about this?'

'Five. You, me, the AC (Crime), Firth and Dawson.'

'Is there anything in the computer system that can be accessed by unauthorized personnel?'

'No, and there's nothing to be accessed by authorized personnel, either. Dawson has cleaned house.'

The Commissioner jumped up and paced his carpet. He was beginning to regroup. 'Right. Let's keep it that way. Where's Boulder now?'

'He hasn't returned home yet, but he won't be far away. He has his family with him – and a traceable hired Range Rover. If you give the word, I'll pull him in.'

'No, no!' The Commissioner was horrified – as Ringrose had expected he would be. 'For the moment, don't let's launch any course of action that we can't stop. Anyway, the man hasn't actually confessed, has he?'

'No, but Jack Boulder is as ready to unburden himself as he'll ever be. I take him for a basically decent man who has been led with a ring in his nose by the people who concocted this business. The caper has come apart at the seams because they made the mistake of threatening his family.'

Ringrose was not going to give the Commissioner any straw to clutch that might allow him to bypass the incendiary file burning a hole in his mahogany desk top. Ringrose said bluntly, 'If I bring him in, he'll tell me everything.'

The Commissioner's hands were fluttering at his frizzy ginger hair. 'I don't doubt it, Tom. Don't doubt it at all. There's enough here,' he pushed the report across the desk as if he desired to return it permanently to its author, 'for you to nail him to the floor.'

'So what's our next move, sir?' Ringrose asked, as if he did not already know the answer.

'Well, of course,' said the Commissioner, starting to bluster, 'there are extensive political ramifications here. This is going to tear Whitehall apart. From the start, they've been sour on the prospect of your discovering that the assassin was British. I just don't care to predict what the reaction will be when they learn that not only is their worst fear confirmed but that he's part of a conspiracy involving our own Security Services. It's altogether too shocking.'

Ringrose decided to have mercy on him. 'You'd like me to shut down while you finesse this through the Whitehall jungle?'

The Commissioner looked grateful for not having to utter the words himself. 'It's going to be a delicate business, Tom. They have long memories for bad-news bearers.'

Chapter Fifty-Six

Tuesday. After twenty-four hours of pandemonium in Whitehall and at Vauxhall Cross, garish headquarters of MI6, the ranks had been steadied.

The Commissioner wore his civilian clothes, which was his own way of signalling that a matter for discretion was in progress. He and Tom Ringrose made the short journey to the Cabinet Office in Whitehall in the Commissioner's official limousine.

The assembly awaiting them was as august as it gets: the Secretary of the Cabinet and Head of the Home Civil Service, the Director-General of MI6, and the elderly knight who was Co-ordinator of all the secret branches of British Intelligence.

The policemen were seated facing them.

The Cabinet Secretary was in snappish mood. 'There will be no notes taken. This is a meeting that never took place.' He shifted his cold gaze from face to face looking for dissent. He detected none.

Tom Ringrose was interested in the single sheet of paper in front of the Co-ordinator. It was the only item on the highly polished round table. He could not quite read the upside-down typescript.

'I need hardly tell you that the Prime Minister and the Home Secretary were horrified to learn the contents of Commander Ringrose's report,' said the Cabinet Secretary. Tom noted wryly that it was still *his* report and not the report of the Metropolitan Police. He glanced sideways at the Commissioner, who kept his gaze steadfastly to the front.

'The potential scandal is on the Burgess–Maclean scale. However, in the past twenty-four hours the Director-General has conducted intensive inquiries in which he has had the fullest co-operation from those members of his service identified in Commander Ringrose's report. He has also been assisted by Sir Gilbert Metzhagen, who is still recovering from an accident.'

The Cabinet Secretary paused to take a delicate dab at his nostrils with a cambric handkerchief produced from his sleeve. 'The Co-ordinator has subsequently interviewed the Director-General and is satisfied that we now have the true account of what transpired. This differs markedly from Commander Ringrose's version but, given the various handicaps under which he carried out his investigation, his interpretation of events is entirely understandable. Therefore, no blame attaches.'

That's big of you, thought Ringrose savagely. The oily bastards were all looking at him, smiling at the invalid, and murmuring, 'Hear! Hear!'

'Of course,' said the Director-General, bluffly butting in. 'Commander Ringrose did absolutely the right thing hauling in my chaps. They've been bloody fools. Went way in over their heads. They're going to get some stick, I promise you.'

Get some stick? Was that all? Ringrose registered the first intimation of what was to come.

The Cabinet Secretary came in again. 'I think we had better let the Co-ordinator take things from here. He has the briefing paper.'

The old boy, an admiral without a fleet, harrumphed noisily and grasped his document in both liver-spotted hands. 'I am satisfied,' he began reading, 'that the MI6 officers referred to by the DG, with the aid of a senior civil servant from this office and financed by Sir Gilbert Metzhagen, a noted patriot, were engaged in a foolhardy and entirely unauthorized attempt to save their service from a public humiliation. They were trying to cover up the misdeeds of a colleague who, acting alone, plotted the death of Conrad Niven for the squalid purpose of collecting the million-pound bounty on his unfortunate head. When they discovered what the colleague had done, this group of close friends held what we might call a council of war. Stupidly, instead of confiding in their Director-General, they chose to go it alone.'

Tom Ringrose interjected, 'I take it that the renegade colleague is, in fact, the MI6 officer Nancy Tintagel who went under the name of Jane Canning?'

The admiral glared. 'Quite so. Quite so.'

Ringrose continued, 'My information, admittedly from unofficial sources because our people in Tehran appear to have gone to sleep, is that Miss Tintagel made no attempt to collect her reward.' He wasn't going to let them off the hook that easily.

The Cabinet Secretary at his most mandarin murmured, 'Perhaps we could have questions later . . .'

The Co-ordinator rumbled on. 'Miss Tintagel, quite unaccountably, took leave of her senses. Her father, a personal friend of mine, I might say, is devastated. The reason she failed to claim her blood money is quite clear. When she returned from what her superiors had taken to be a holiday in France, she was immediately placed on an official surveillance operation that necessitated a cross-country journey on horseback. Tragically, she was thrown and killed before she could make her claim on the Iranians. To disguise the nature of her work, the service sought the co-operation of their consultant pathologist, Professor Askew. A verdict of accidental death was arranged.'

Ringrose was not having it. 'May I now have the exhumation order to confirm this?'

'No, you may not!' The retort rang across the table from the Cabinet Secretary. He was no longer indulging Commander Ringrose. 'The Home Secretary says, and I agree, that no one is best served by turning over more stones. Let the wretched woman lie in peace.'

The admiral asked, 'Shall I finish this?' To give the old boy some credit, he now appeared to be executing a most distasteful act.

But before he could carry on, Ringrose – his Commissioner looking agonizedly at him – interjected, 'How do you propose to deal with the actual sniper, Jack Boulder? He isn't answerable to any government agency.'

The admiral, looking increasingly unhappy, said, 'Ah. Here we come to the nub of the matter.' He peered over his half-glasses at Ringrose in a quite kindly way. 'I'm sorry to say, Commander, that the central premise of your report has gone entirely off the rails. The sniper was actually Miss Tintagel.'

'What?' Despite the hushed and gentlemanly nature of the proceedings, Ringrose could not contain himself. He leapt to his feet, sending his chair toppling backwards. 'That's absolute bollocks.'

The blunt expletive, far removed from the silky language of diplomacy, hit them like a flicked wet towel in a locker room. He could hear the Commissioner at his side imploring him to resume his seat.

The Cabinet Secretary recovered first. He turned steely. 'Bollocks or not, Commander Ringrose, that is the gospel we shall all carry from this room. We will not have SIS disgraced because of the mad doings of one greedy operative. Please pick up your chair and hear out the Co-ordinator.'

'Ah, yes. Thank you,' said the old boy, going back to his sheet of fabrications. 'Somehow, Miss Tintagel obtained the Army record of Boulder, noted his skill with a rifle and recruited him to give her an intensive course on the shooting range. We believe they secretly travelled to Scotland for this purpose and, at some stage, became lovers. She had discovered that her friend Metzhagen would have Niven aboard his yacht at that film festival in the South of France. Everything fell neatly into place. Thanks to Boulder's training, she was ready in May to make the attempt.'

The admiral rattled on, anxious to get the beastly business over with. 'Boulder appears to have been excessively trusting. She took him to Cannes as her lover not as her accomplice. Only after the event, after she had sent him off on some errand while she dispatched Conrad Niven, did he discover the appalling truth and realize that no one would ever believe he had not been party to the crime. That's when he enlisted the American girl to try to cover both his own and Miss Tintagel's tracks.'

Ringrose said evenly, 'The two shots that killed Niven, at the distance required, were possibly within the competence of no more than ten sharp-shooters in the entire world. Nancy Tintagel could have trained in the Highlands for half her lifetime and still not achieve such expertise.'

'Let's just say she was a very gifted learner,' said the Cabinet Secretary irritably.

Ringrose waited for the Commissioner to speak, but as his boss was taking a sudden interest in his lace-up black shoes he asked what the Commissioner should have asked: 'What do we do about all the cover-up artists?' He did not bother to disguise the sarcasm.

'As the DG has indicated, those in his employ will feel the full force of his disapproval, as will Bulwer Tancred in my bailiwick,' said the

Cabinet Secretary, impervious to Ringrose's hostility. 'Gilbert Metzhagen, apart from being warned by me personally, will not be charged. Neither will Boulder. He'll be left strictly alone. He could bring the temple tumbling down. At best, you could only hand him over to the French on minor charges from which he would certainly walk away once SIS officers had given evidence confirming his unsuspecting role in the crime.'

'You've forgotten one thing,' said Ringrose.

'What?'

'Not only do I have a witness who happens to be a *Daily Mail* reporter, but, out of necessity, he has seen the videotapes of Nancy Tintagel at the Berthier Hotel. He's keeping quiet because I asked him to. He won't hold off for ever.'

They looked stumped. Then the Cabinet Secretary said, 'If you can't shut him up with the Official Secrets Act, you'll just have to brazen it out and confess that your investigation took the wrong turning. Nancy Tintagel was in the clear. Just wild coincidence that she happened to be in Cannes with a lover answering the wanted man's description.'

'He's no fool. He won't buy it,' predicted Ringrose heavily. He got up and turned away. He found himself facing a superb oil painting of one of Villeneuve's warships taking a Nelsonian broadside. He immediately thought of Victor Massillon. Christ, what would he tell him? Victor wouldn't buy it, either.

On the return journey to the Yard, Ringrose and the Commissioner were silent until the limousine was rounding Parliament Square. Then Ringrose said, 'You hold the Queen's Commission. They can't sack you. You can tell them all to go fuck themselves and let me go ahead with the charges.'

The Commissioner actually squirmed in his seat. He said tiredly, 'Life isn't that simple, Tom. They have all the witnesses by the goolies. It'll be a concert party. They'll sing what they've been ordered to sing. The only consoling factor is that Nancy Tintagel paid the penalty just as if she'd had a breakfast appointment at Wandsworth Prison with Albert Pierrepoint. Justice was done, even if not seen to be done.'

'Jack Boulder and his family will be dancing in the streets,' said Ringrose.

'Put it behind you, Tom. He's the one that got away,' said the Commissioner, gazing morosely out of his window at Churchill, in a foul mood on his stone plinth.

And they left it at that.

Epilogue

Within one year, this is what happened to those who had been caught up in the plot to assassinate Conrad Niven.

- *Sir Gilbert Metzhagen* was created a life peer in the New Year Honours List for his services to charity. He made headlines for his generosity in setting up a million-pound trust fund to benefit the two divorced wives and three children of the late Conrad Niven. The gesture had been recommended to him by a Shepherd's Bush housewife.
- *Mrs Jessie Pocock*, a Battersea widow, was surprised to receive an annual pension of £4,000 from an ex-servicemen's charity that had received a donation of £86,500, which happened to be the exact sum that the Boulder family had in their savings account.
- *Inspector Colin Dawson* was promoted to the rank of Superintendent. Underlings ceased calling him the Dalek.
- *Miss Betty Bentinck* suffered a career setback when her feature movie failed to recover its negative cost. She returned to daytime television hell.
- *Ben Boulder* disobeyed his parents' orders and told his schoolmates of his extraordinary adventures. No one believed him.
- *Malcolm Boulder* never did get a substitute Indiana Jones backpack. He settled for a Fred Flintstone wristwatch.
- *Commissaire Victor Massillon* accepted with cynical amusement the Whitehall account of the assassination. He was told this on the day preceding publication of a London *Daily Mail* exclusive story in which a British peer's daughter was sensationally fingered as the executioner. In the House of Commons, the Prime Minister confirmed that this possibility had been investigated but that he had been advised that the allegation was untrue. He refused an independent inquiry.

- *Peter Lancing* was nominated for the title of Reporter of the Year but, in view of the Prime Minister's denial, didn't get it.

- *Lionel Firth* and *Tom Ringrose* remained in their ranks and at their posts. It was implied to Ringrose that if he cared to petition the Selection Board, who were sitting to fill a vacancy at Deputy Commissioner level, he would be warmly received. Recognizing the bribe, he declined.

- *Jake Bishop* and *Paul Kaiser* got dinner at Rules – and the truth from Ringrose, who withheld only Jack Boulder's identity. At his regular weekly meeting with the President, the CIA Director relayed Bishop's information. The President was alleged to have said, in an admiring tone, 'Those fucking Brits! They'd have taken the Nixon tapes and sworn they were really spaghetti.'

- *Sidney Zuckerman* still has not had a female FBI agent.

- *Bulwer Tancred* was transferred to the European Commission in Brussels at a vastly increased tax-free salary. He took his Albert Pierrepoint poster with him. He developed an interest in the life of Dr Guillotine.

- *Rafe Cummings* and *Peter Hope-Casson* were posted abroad. Hope-Casson had an unfortunate experience in Mexico City where he received a severe knife wound in the chest. There appeared to have been a dispute over someone's wife.

- *Rupert Strang* continued his career at Vauxhall Cross. He subsequently attempted a friendship with Jack Boulder, with future utilisation of Jack's special skills in mind. It was bad luck that Mrs Boulder picked up one of his calls and sent him packing.

- *Mrs Grace Boulder* banned all firearms from the family home and the boys were forbidden to touch them ever again.

- *Jack Boulder* never again had that dream of descending into the underground and following the dark lady into unspeakable horror. In high places, it was decided that Captain Boulder – in Lyndon Baines Johnson's heartfelt words – was safer inside the tent pissing out, rather than outside pissing in. Following Strang's failure to net him, Jack Boulder's army record was discreetly laundered and he was returned to duty, promoted to major and posted to the Special Air Service where his talents would be of some future use to the State.